GAD FACTORY

Dereck J. Cram

Slug's Bottom Press

Inscribed to the memory of my grandmothers,
Clare Jean Kingscott Cram
& Marvel Magdalena Weatherholt Sarasin

With special thanks to William D. Edwardson III
For getting me to work on time

CONTENTS

Appendix:
The Birds Over Wall Street

"…The full stomach of the rich denies them sleep."
—Ecclesiastes 5, 11

SINGLE

I

The Voyage to the Factory

Bumbling up and down elongated asphalt warts, curves, and fifth trimester pregnancies of the road in a leaping and sputtering insect-like vehicle was one Edgar E. Weatherholt, a thirty-three-year-old male Caucasian appearing just beyond the abyss of youth (as seen by your run-of-the-mill quantum observer) while a pair of roseate oak-rimmed glasses slid up and down his slightly curving nose. His eyes and facial hair were earth-brown, with elements of sangria, copper, and Persian Plum staining deeply in the background of less primitive forms. The left palm outstretched before him presented a long and battered lifeline. Edgar observed this lacerated landscape suspiciously. It seemed to be changing. The pigment was dark salmon above a faint violet aura seeking sanctuary beneath a blue long-sleeved cotton shirt—otherwise, a wild Hyperborean hide moderately tanned from the summer sun, denoting a mysterious Indo-European genetic link, which was rather carelessly, but with a gasping degree of American probability, assumed to be Sarmatian through a possible Romano-British bloodline.

Edgar removed the rose-colored glasses cynically; they did not seem to be working. He was becoming increasingly more irrelevant. And, despite the UV protection sticker[1], the summer sun

---

[1] An advertisement pertaining to the ultraviolet range of radiation wavelengths, in that the transparent materials are said to be able to block such wavelengths far better than the 26 miles of stratospheric ozone occurring naturally in the atmosphere between 4 and 30 miles above the surface of the Earth, but which have been decreased in column density by pollutants (such as supersonic jet fuel,

was evermore fond of zapping his pupils from every direction. He was glad that Edina's car had been designed by people who understood these sensitivities and that it was still morning. Hopefully he would not get despondent and sink through the floorboards. He tried thinking of kittens.

"You're dying inside, Uncle Edgar, and the rot has come out your eyeballs—even momma says so!"

"What? I'm perfectly fine..."

Edgar was annoyed that his blond little niece was the one disclosing these simple truths.

"Then why do you squint so much? Are you crying?"

"I'm not crying—it's from the War; too much sun in your eyes scathes your irises and screws up your tear glands, makes you squint."

"Crybaby!"

"I'm not-"

"Cry crybaby cry, tee he he!"

"Jeezzusssers...I should have just taken a cab."

"Cabs don't go here anymore—only me he he he!"

As he sat comfortably, yet with a degree of anxiety, Edgar did not appear to be the kind of person who was dying inside, as quietly claimed of late, and in fact his brain cells had recently replaced themselves—right on schedule, according to a team of leading neurologists from Great Britain; He had read all about the process over the internet. Furthermore, his view of America had changed—not just visually transformed, but seemed to have been physically and mentally replaced somehow—during the War of Buktu's Well. The war was just a conflict of the times, both internally and externally, and was the dropping of a gigantic aircraft carrier into an unstable pool of "international friendship", to quote a former diplomat. The strategy of the war was a swirling eye of enfranchisement that had changed Edgar's view of the world forever. And at home everything seemed different; America had

---

chemical compounds used in firefighting, various chlorofluorocarbon applications, and solar electromagnetic radiation with wavelengths below 300 nanometers), and without which would expose the surface of the Earth to lethal ultraviolet radiation; In the event of severe ozone depletion, the wearer's eyes will remain victorious due to the protection provided.

been taken and altered as if by some unfathomably Brobdingnagian[2] hand and then set back down again during his year-long absence. The awareness of this impossible feat and the logical conclusion that it must be false made him angry. But he grew out from under the discrepancy and continued to grow, despite having fallen on hard times. Indeed, this feat was made easier by the sheer number of human beings who were finding it equally difficult to live in a world dominated by the ignorant and unfeeling, in which 70% of residential suburban reclaimed H_2O was used to water lawns thick with Devil's Grass. Edgar lived on the advice given to him by an eccentric street musician, which was never to remain comfortable in your illusion:

> ("Music becomes discordant
> When body and soul are acolytes in greed—
> A banal world makes beauty irrelevant;
> The magical harmony
>
> Sounds just like a felony:
> When the instrument plays that familiar tune
> Falling into those same chords and melodies
> It's time to find something new...").

"You are what you eat! You are what you eat! You're a vegetable! Tee he he!" The little girl squirmed in her seat and nearly lost control of the automobile.

"That's what I wish *you* were..." Edgar said, matter-of-factly, "You should eat things that are green."

Edina reached into the candy compartment and displayed a handful of unearned treats. "Some of my candy *is* green, see?"

"Try it on vegetables."

"Bowwwwwrrrring! Bow-ring bow-ring!"

The little girl was right about him, to a point: Edgar truly was vegetative in nature, but more in the category of aged and

---

[2] Adjective form of Brobdingnag, one of those awkward, yet beautiful, Scandinavian words often omitted from contemporary American English dictionaries; in reference to the land of giants in Jonathan Swift's *Gulliver's Travels*.

beaten Percival than regenerative Green Knight. He was recoverable in mind, yet not in body—at least, except for the hair; Even though he claimed to have been clean shaven as of early that morning, his facial foliage was already pushing its way out to dot his face in rough dark microscopic ivy (actually it was in no way visible to the oblivious observer, but Edgar himself was certain that he would be forced to wear a beard-net of some kind). He loathed the fact that he never appeared clean-shaven, which was always something of a point of honor and civility to the Lord and Lady ethos of such establishments as a business, company and corporation, but certainly not as such to the unemployed bachelor. And yet Edgar knew that he would never receive a reverential job if he did not appear chivalric and that he would be forced to spend his miserable existence shoving squeegees, mops, and brooms and performing general labor, as he had done during the arduous trial and error period of attending public university. Edgar had passed through the university with "flying colors" as it were over three years ago, but had found the enduring hope of gainful employment extremely difficult to obtain due, he claimed, to a cannibalistic economy, an illogical workforce, and the flatulent over-meddling of the government. He was therefore at that very moment on his way to the gad factory, or Gad Growers Incorporated, or GGI, as it appeared in financial sectors. The insect-like vehicle spit and sputtered toward it as the operationally exclusive driver put forth a grown-up effort to avoid heavy traffic, yes, but also the piracy of subsidized highwaymen (oil baron assassins, roadside merchants, and patrolling militia men/ women in supercharged automobiles who were out to criminalize citizen drivers in order to fund militia salaries and/ or just to flatten pedestrians).

The driver *actually was* Edgar's nine-year-old niece, who as it turned out was the only person he knew with legal driving privileges, and who had been kind enough to drive him to and from work under condition that he fund her daily sugar addiction of ice cream and hot cinnamon capsules.

"Eew! Stop picking your nose, Uncle Edgar!"

The vehicle swerved slightly with uncontrollable streamlined grace under distraction of blond little Edina. Her button nose wiggled as she sent him a blue-gray saucer-like look of disgust similar to that which her own mother would have made at that age.

Edgar was embarrassed to have been scrutinized under spotlight by a child, but managed to regain his adult-like continence. "I need to look presentable! Just keep your eyes on the road, please!"

"I don't want your boogers in my car! I just had this thing upholstered! Couldn't you just wait 'til we got there? You got the job, didn't you? So why worry about appearances?"

"It's important, that's why! Someday you'll understand..."

"Someday you'll get your own damn car!"

"Hey! Now, w-watch your words!"

"I'm sorry, you...you booger-snatcher! Anyway, Dad swears all the time. How can I watch my words when grownups use so much profanity around me? I should tell Mom what you said this morning when you cut yourself shaving."

"You little...damnwidget, you little eavesdropper is what I was thinking to say...why did I almost...Alright, you have a point. I'll tell you what: every time I say a swear you get another dollar toward that self-destructive little sugar fund you've got going, but, if *you* say a swear, I cook asparagus for dinner."

"Deal. You owe me a dollar."

"You can't enforce the deal before it's been made."

Edina puckered her lips and made a sour face at Uncle Edgar.

"W-watch the road!" Edgar sputtered nervously.

Edina giggled.

There was a wisp of divine intervention controlling the vehicle and keeping the passengers from certain death, which Edgar supposed was why Edina had been given a license at such a young age in the first place—things in modern society were, as they say, unhinged. And though it was true that only a madman would present a driver's license to a child, the world itself had gone mad. In adjustment to an almost constant mental state of civil war, most people were at odds about everything. While a battle of resources ripped the brittle domestic fabric of nationhood, so the concept of universal harmony was shattered by strife abroad. Havoc was wrought in both virtual and real, leading to a revolution of terror as new weapons were developed; for the first time in human history, genetically modified organisms, computer hacking, identity theft, social networking, Massively Multiplayer Online Role Playing Game bullying, robotic sewing machines, weather manipulation, abnormally large insects, environmental terrorism, the bitter truth, became effective components in the arsenal of warfare. Prosperity was absent of thought and the deserts were encroaching. The planet had become a mental wasteland.

And So the Profitless Voyage Continues

They had driven to the distant outskirts of a city where a fresh aquatic breeze blew from a pond over the road and into the chemically treated orchard hills of gads glistening tantalizingly from golden-white trees. This was Gil postal-wise, but cartographically just one of many country roads within Grand Traverse County. For some unexplained reason, the rural nature of their surroundings must have made Edina think of Home.

"Uncle Edgar? Who's gonna tend the algae while you're gone?"

"I thought *you* were going to take over for me," teased Edgar sleepily.

"What? I can't do it!" sputtered Edina. "I don't know anything about algae! They'll dry up like Mom's plants did that time she and dad were passed out drunk in New Orleans and missed their flight and then got hit by that hurricane. You couldn't watch me, remember, 'cause you were in Timbuktu fighting little Malian girls!"

"I was not."

"The coyotes howled and yipped every night, and in the day you could see huge footprints in the fields—the fields where the sunflowers used to grow...used to. The wells were all dried up. We had to order our water through the mail. But you chose to be adventurous and join the army, even though you hate taking orders, uniformity, and all that stuff...and you were caught in your own lie! And it was you who sent the hurricane—it was your own turbulent anger!"

"What's that supposed to mean?" Edgar shook his head languorously to be sure that he was hearing things right, and also to wake himself. "Anyway, relax. I was just kidding. The algae are in a remedial state. All they're good for right now are sea cookies and algae burger...algin maybe...and as an ingredient for Inisheer-based Elixir Végétal, but that's illegal. Especially without a monastery."

"They gotta be worth something! Your future depends on that stuff!"

"They're worth about zilch. And there are only five of them. And they're planted in pots on your mother's discolored old roofless porch with specialized dew-bags extended from the gutters to collect evaporating water. The idea is to hybridize them so that by the third generation they'll be good for oil. That's what's worth something."

"Even with only five of them?"

"With only five of them, they're still worth zilch. We need an army of them, a vast algae forest."

"How much is zilch, exactly?"

"Nothing. Zero."

"Oh. That's why my dad's a traveling sugar salesman? All he has is zilch."

"Yep. But don't worry, Lady E. It'll work out. Someday that stuff 'll be worth more than all the decomposed residue in the universe."

"How will that help *me*?" the little girl wondered.

"It just will."

Edina opened a compartment full of red and yellow suckers and stuck one in her mouth during a sudden, grinning compulsion.

"Seriously," he added, more for his own assurance, "alga is gold."

"Ik tu shay toe."

For Edgar, algae were THE BIG PROJECT, and not just microalgae, but surface-attainment seaweed, such as freshwater lake specimens floating in spherical goldfish tanks on a grandmother's hand-crafted wooden table of memory. Edgar was experimenting with the lesser-studied genus *Sargassum*, named after the Sargasso Sea, which was South Wales fertilizer, Chinese herbal medicine, and an ingredient for Inisheer-based Elixir Végétal. Sargassum, *the weed of deceit*, was the long-armed anti-Lugh of shorelines reaching for the heliosphere and the ambient flow of interstellar dark matter. A weed indeed, it grew abominably in numbers, each reaching around 10 m, appearing tea-brown or sea monster dark green, consisting of a holdfast, a stipe, and many fern-like fronds. They were soft, delicate ocean thorns of conscience, a vital food source for Lenten fish, protecting the titanic rabbits of the sea with the aid of elusive diffraction. They, too, could attract attention due to the mental wasteland, or logical cyclone, as an energy contender of miraculous what-ifs. Like microalgae, they could thrive under harsh conditions, using polluted water and dirty air to produce clean CO_2, or grown in irrigated deserts to create a highly enriched food source.

Large, intertwining kelp rising from the depths like Jack's beanstalk occasionally made way for mysterious bubbles—a sure sign of whales, sharks, sea dragons, mermaids, sunken ships, coral reefs, thermal vents, beginnings and endings. On land, there was a vast discrepancy between the human and natural understanding of beginnings and endings. Not so in the water. The undulating waves were an algorithm; mechanical, recursive, computational. But the natural waves did not act like the assimilated ones of dim algoristic light. The natural waves, when insubordinate, incredulous, chaotic, were thirty meter algid hammers.

"Uncle Edgar, you're drooling in your sleep again."

Thus the mind of Edgar, who thought about his Sargassum on a daily basis, was not completely in the sun—that is to say, he was as an enormously elevated and skyscraping George Orwell crawling deep within the narrow Wigan coalmine for a better perspective.

"Uncle Edgar..."

The probing eye of Balor Whale-Killer, the anti-heroic Off-Green Giant of the Battle of Magh Tuireadh Under the Sea, brought our soft-muscled warrior out of his early daydream depths.

An unlit sign appeared over a lone building in the middle of an industrialized field. This was a place he had experienced in name only (largely because he had a phobia of public nudity), a strip club called **Velvet Touch**, which was apparently not only sleazy, but surprisingly upscale—according to a friend of a friend. Edgar thought of poor little Edina, whose father had become a traveling sugar beet sugar salesman, and awkwardly positioned himself so that she could not see the scarlet letters through the lens of the eye. His actions needed no apology. The more iniquity kept out of sight, the better. Meanwhile, the self-propagating waves of ill health angled off from every direction. Everywhere was the malevolent glance of the stranger.

An Apparent Accident Involving a Green Bus

There appeared to be an accident up ahead at a blinking yellow-lighted intersection and Edgar advised Edina to slow down with hysterical howls. A black van with tinted windows had apparently collided with a green school bus and a mob of angry Latinos were holding their aching body parts and shouting at each other in Spanish while one pale-skinned mountain man-looking fellow in suspenders leaned over the crossroad ditch and loudly broke wind. It was all Edina could do to get around the sore thumb of a bus without getting hit head-on by a potentially opposing vehicle.

"Need someone to call the police?!" Edgar shouted at the wrangler-jean-wearing bus driver from the recently-opened compound eye lens projecting from the passenger-side door.

"Naw! We got fuzz comin' all the way from Mexico by now! Thanks anyway!" The exasperated bus driver waved them on along the angularly sunlit path of asphalt destinations.

"Peculiar place to have an accident," Edgar said once they had accelerated toward Gil again, "...but I guess the hour is right for that sort of occurrence. All nature of craziness happens early in the morning."

Main Supply Route 114 had replaced Highway 37 after the left turn and was taking them to the western reaches, but would reemerge into Highway 31 down the sand-blasted coast to connect with the rest of the country. For all practical purposes, however, 114 was a dead end.

"Wachya wanna bet that wasn't accidental?"

"Edina, what is it with you and betting on everything? That's trouble you don't need, kid. Take it from me, your vagabond uncle. Stay in school; do as you're told—at least in the presence of authority figures. Don't cheat. No cutting corners, no schemes. That doesn't get you very far, especially in your own eyes. There's a time to play and a time to get serious. Let's see that serious face."

Edina glanced disgustedly at her uncle, who continued,

"You can do anything you put your mind to if you just stay in the boat and row."

"But Uncle Edgar...you *did* stay in school and do as you're told. Look what happened to *you*."

"That's not the point. What happened to me was an unfortunate set of circumstances which, combined with my easy-going personality, left me destitute, downtrodden, haunted, and nearly drove me nuts. But that doesn't mean it'll happen to you or anything. Just...do what you do. You'll be alright."

"Uncle Edgar, you sure talk funny sometimes."

As they continued westward, the hypotenuse of light hit the car's mirrors from the trajectory of an illusionary right angle, causing Edgar to squint defensively, yield to the powers of the sun, and appear to cry; Edina only blinked rapidly her childlike eyes and was apparently low enough in the vehicle to be unaffected.

Those of slowly-flexing irises were instantly blinded. To Edgar, the momentary world was a wondrous, vast stage of penetrated warmth and goodness effectively washing away the negative aspects in his life. The whitened dew of golden wasteland prairie held the tumbleweeds in place.

They drove past the brave stand-bys; the survivors; these people on the outskirts who were complacent in their own tiny kingdoms of poop and dust. Theirs was a torch that had to be carried at all times, no matter how dim. Even now, the flames could be seen in their eyes. The soul was diminished, dehydrated, and feeding on the aura of the land where the battlements haunted the living. Their assiduousness was thought to have gone out with the lumber barons. Who knew how they got by, but they did. The right price could drive them out. A desirable aspect or two would have them enacting the tragic fate of the Nibelung in miniature or perhaps a cyclical Alamo of the mind whenever a prospective buyer came around. Ownership was a cruel fantasy: On one hand, there was death to contend with; on the other, a banker. The property-law-anchors which saved Europeans from drifting nationally in the storm of foreign wealth had never gone over well in the Land of the Free where patriotism had become their ocean. Mere shackles awaited the breadwinner as the Grecian warship swept towards nowhere. All was strange to the dust-eaters.

The wastewater-irrigated countryside around them reverberated with a silent recuperative beauty. The sun had risen only recently and the foliage was enveloped in mist. There were patches of untouched giant arborvitae white cedar past the assassin aphids of rogue crimson sunflower and even granules of sand spilling over onto the road in beautiful overlapping patterns. Quaking aspens overtook a hill in fragrant clusters and rattled their congregation into bliss. A rare breeze took refuge in gentle spades of green, defiantly caressing the landscape.

The change was a rude awakening, hitting the travelers without warning. Large obnoxious billboards advertised a demonic-looking divorce lawyer available 24/7 for free litigation council and the newly-constructed Spider Lake Battleground Memorial Gift Shop where senior citizens could get a discount. A draconic lake of fuel emissions glistened like Avalon in the godless air of a fortified RV park with a moat.

Edgar rested his eyes for a moment. They were losing function again.

"Some company you are," Edina protested. She hit a silver button and the chattering voices of strangers penetrated from the speakers. A nearby market was being robbed by television personalities—so said the human voice carried within sound waves. Jay Leno and David Letterman had tripped over Larry King getting to the cases of Klondike Bars at the back of the store and Larry's face had been temporarily kicked off, revealing a second face (that of a famished and despairing female college student with a caged grimace). As things became heated, Conan O'Brian had to be pulled out from under a high school wrestling champion who was then shot in the left gluteus with a paint pellet gun by Craig Ferguson's robot; Craig and his robot sidekick had finally made primetime, like they deserved. People were advised to avoid the intersection of Highway 37 and MSR 114 if possible and to resist any temptation to pick up hitchhikers.

The Approach to the Factory

There were rows of red pines growing near an abandoned train rail where sat a ghostly link of silver orphaned passenger cars. Just after these and set in along a vast parking lot of blackened million-year-old vegetable corpse residual tar was the white security checkpoint to Gad Growers Incorporated, and little Edina made a sudden screeching stop to allow herself the scientific probability of obeying universal law regarding a-change-in-direction-during-linear-velocity-while-steering-a-massive-object, which was to say, the moment of inertia, followed by the heavy application of friction upon the breaks, the wheels, the angular momentum in space, and the parking lot—not to mention an apparent impetus in human affairs.

"Orientation?" the guard said casually, leaning on the outer shelf of what appeared to be a ticket booth.

"Yes, please."

The security guard motioned them on tiredly and with a serious glance toward the quickly filling parking lot.

"See. He didn't even ask," teased scrawny little Edina. "That's an extra five boxes of gummy monsters!!"

"Tsssss," Edgar hissed and shook his head. Without a doubt, the little shit was right. He had expected a lot of questions. In the least he had expected a "Say, where are you from?" or, after a long period of watchful silence, an "I've been meaning to ask you..." at which he would usually reply, without much thought, "Oh, up by the canopy in the clouds, along the floating, mirrored lake, which we identify with a name you've never heard of, which is to say Nenaa'angebi, about fifteen miles north of Way-muk-kwana, where hailed the lovely Sky Woman, leather-clad warrior of otter skins, and the stubborn settlers who farmed the hamlets within once-remarkable bogs and forests, where once croaked the golden toad, where once whooped the silver crane, where once the tawny panther crept silently. That is where the makers of this fine automobile performed miracles." He always said "up" without thinking, because he in no way meant "up" as in "north", but "up" as in skyward, upward, cloud-ward, heavenward. In short, it was a place of dreams. The bizarre, insect-like vehicle should have given them away, but the guard had not cared to ask and was not the least bit surprised by the vehicle's hard, scaly exoskeleton and barbed feelers, nor the uncommon age of the driver. Yet the murky parking lot contained a menagerie of vehicles of various ages, rusty expositions, power output, shapes, colors, skins, shines, smudges, cracks, and dents.

"See you around four, unless I get carried away with my dolls," Edina said when Edgar exited stiffly between the sets of wings.

"Thanks Lady E. You're the best. Ask your mom if she wouldn't mind turning the pots for me."

Edina stuck out her little tongue at Uncle Edgar and buzzed out of the parking lot.

Edgar was alone and eating dust. He turned to face a sprawling grey building of strip-metal and concrete replication and a tingling sensation ran down his post-athletic body. The Herculean pillars resembling ugly steel sides of the doorframes were mere darkness to the light of his approaching moon. For Edgar E. Weatherholt, there was no turning back. His future existence weighed heavily upon GGI and the enigmatic, restorative, discursive, desiccative, delphinium tree yolk.

Definition of Gad

And just what was a gad? Was there ever really such thing as a gad?

Edgar would have been straight with anyone who asked and would admit that he, too, questioned this entire business of gads. 'Why have I never heard of a gad?' was asked time and again by his conscience, until it became necessary to check sources. He could have only assured the inquisitor tentatively that gads had bearing in the real world. What he could have said for certain was thus: All fruits are not equal.

The agricultural tree currently known as the gad is a genetically modified hybrid organism designed to provide a nutritious food source for arid climates and revitalize the

fruit market since the sterilization of the industry and mental drought of the nation. They are now roughly in their second season.

- An almost indistinguishable cultivar introduced illegally to gad orchards across the globe by a disgruntled employee is otherwise easily recognized by the ninth or tenth year of growth by its long, acacia-like thorns and has been known to spit acidic quills from hollowed switch-like branches. For these reasons, the gad harvester should always wear a suit of ballistic armor in proximity of fruit-bearing hostess.

- No one knows for certain how the host organism came to bear its name. Complicating the unraveling of what has recently become a successful product in marketing strategy for the term "superfruit" is that a single fragment constituting the whole sacramental element has yet to be scientifically identified. Although the resulting hybrid is technically interspecific between two or more interfamilial hybrids of previous crosses, the unidentifiable plant ancestor of the fragment in question has been shown through isolation to contain the dominant pair of all strands tested thus far. The current and resultant trademark has therefore risen to legendary status in the minds of those within the industry.

- Popular myth has it that they were the prize of a forgotten hero who had climbed halfway between heaven and earth and then fallen to his death over the skull of Adam; a forest balsam of the mountains blossoming in the signs of the messianic, saved from the Great Deluge by magic birds from a holy garden soon after submerged under salty sea; rediscovered by silversmiths near the source of three rivers; briefly, a muse of weavers of the plain until a thief robbed them of their bitter fruit; then purchased by shepherds along the Euphrates and cultivated in the Levant; snatched up on a pitchfork at Shiloh, even becoming a houseplant of the Witch of Endor; taken back across the Dead Sea to Gilead; but had since migrated vaporously North with a

small tribe of bladed warriors, fallen into the hands of
Scythians and Tocharians, presented to Scordiscian Druids
of the Danube, been lost for centuries somewhere in the
high Alps, discovered and cared for by rural Alsatian
farmers, then a series of adroit monks who used them as a
secret ingredient for Elixir Vegetal and Liqueur d'Elixir de
la Grande-Chartreuse—where they remained virtually
unknown until being stolen, dissected, hybridized and
genetically altered by the U.S.-based multinational
agricultural biotechnology corporation Monstrosso into
what we currently identify as gads.

- In Zoroastrianism, the drink of the sacred fire celebration,
  Yasna, which accompanies bread, milk, and meat,
  originated from the fruit of a shining white tree that grows
  on a paradisiacal mountain. According to scripture, divine
  birds brought sprigs of the plant down to earth. The name
  of the liquor, *haoma*, is the Avestan form of the Sanskrit
  soma. Although any honest association between the shining
  white tree and the gad is impossible to determine, the
  advertisements claim vague snake-oil authenticity.

- Ancient scrolls uncovered from cavernous temples in
  Cappadocia obscurely allude to the idea that an equally
  enigmatic fruit possessed hallucinogenic properties, even
  the capacity to induce transformations upon True Believers
  in conjunction with sun gazing rituals.

- According to Lydian historian Xanthus of the mid-fifth
  century BC, the fruit of a mysterious white tree gave them
  the idea to invent coinage.

- In the early 1970s an accomplished group of German
  scientists claimed that a rare dwarf fruit tree guarded by
  Carthusian monks had originated from the planet Jupiter,
  possibly even the far reaches of deep space.

- The strong, water-resistant bark takes on a Turkish rose to cinereous color and retains medicinal substances thought to alleviate pain in small doses, but which may cause irreversible nerve damage to chronic users over their duration. An older species of higher elevations was said to have smooth and shiny magnolia-white-colored bark, but was last seen by sixteenth-century Tibetans and is considered extinct.

- The fruit of the gad tree, which matures from small tear-drop buds into a perfectly-rounded heart-like shape, roughly half the size of a plum, is beautiful to look at, yet imparts a certain aura of fear (studies have shown that the leaves release mood-altering pheromones). The ripened ovary has a single central edible seed with nerve endings throughout the rich sweet-sour flesh of the berry, simultaneously appearing black, white, violet, brown, golden, blue, and red, depending on the mood the tree wishes to induce.

- Despite constant efforts by the Monstrosso Corporation to sweeten the fruit of the tree through genetic infusions with pomegranate, blueberry, wolfberry, and other plants heretofore kept secret, a slight bitterness can be detected from the palate of sensual consumers.

- Monstrosso Corporation guarantees a bright green future for their newest GMO. As with all current commercial applications of modern biotechnology, the gad tree has been engineered to express the genes for herbicide tolerance as well as insecticidal *Bacillus thuringiensis* bacterium to reduce dependence on pesticides and other agrochemicals manufactured by the company.

- The azure-green leaf is waxy and spade-shaped, and occasionally, in late maturity of the tree's development, with a dense circular edge capable of severing human limbs.

20

● **Blossoms are always bright pink and appear in late spring.**

How Edgar Came to Work at the Factory

And just what had led Edgar to enter the bland portal of Gil's most significant food industry for a very insignificant rate of hourly pay? The conflict had many sources. Perhaps the instigation of European settlement was to blame; or human footsteps across continents. During the boundless era of sawmills, Wild Western type saloons, brothels, and "S&W" lettered sidearm sic passim archetypes, the original settlement had taken on the mythical name of Gilgamesh[3], but had split in subsequent years to become two separate postal codes within Grand Traverse County.

Gamesh had expanded around a clear-water bay with imitable girth and snobbishness, paving roads for leisure automobile club affiliates, land-filling the twin of two small lakes, kicking the Ojibwa to the curb, cutting the massive oaks, maples, hemlocks, and white pines like the raising of curtains before the window of an eternal living room and erecting luxurious mansions, hotels and condominiums to block the view of passersby in their stead; yet Gil had remained a rural agricultural thoroughfare. Perhaps they were lucky, for all that remained of pre-Michigan native hunter/gatherer flourishing were misrepresented place-names and shadowy swales along forgotten trash-ridden back roads. Gamesh was not even a city-state in the ancient sense of armies and high walls, but through association in that the very pioneers who first cleared the land for a meager living had few descendants with enough girth to stay within a region of such outstandingly inflated value. Reluctant to stray very far from all they had ever known, the descendents of pioneers had at first elected to mingle at the outskirts (including the township of Gil, where the gad factory currently prospered), but most had, over the subsequent centuries and decades and years, scattered as wide as the earth allowed. Gamesh, therefore, was controlled by the

---

[3] Gilgamesh was the legendary fifth king of Uruk. A demigod of superhuman strength, he built an imposing wall to defend his people from threats against their city along the Euphrates trade route.

prosperous former dwellers of distant metropolises and retirees in search of its mysterious secrets—ironically, this latter group was the most insistent that the landscape be urbanized and that the mysteries be stripped. In Gil, where the miniscule mayoral legislature was petitioning to change the town's name to Gilead (which they said was what the founding fathers had intended in the first place), it was the prosperous landlords who had squeezed the meeker farmers out. However, few in the current era had much choice in the matter. America's young were exported along with the jobs, out of country, out of planet, into the dangerous unknown. Those who stayed faced few prospects, and those who were without connections were as good as dead.

These were troubled times for the region—no doubt, for the entire world—and the summer solstice had become the Season of Work for many people. The instance of trouble was not new to humanity, but more of a series of high financial waves battering a wall of congealed sand; nor was it completely without prediction, or cause, or hopelessness. The epidermal of fatty acid weighing buoyantly within this diseased skin had not even been affected (and was in fact prospering), whereas the middle and working bottom layers were a chaotic mass of vascular debt and disillusionment. Many pioneering young prospectors had traveled overseas for jobs and had disappeared between culture clashes and turf wars, unknown even to themselves. Perhaps they would emerge reborn, or float away on piles of junk.

And concerning Edgar E. Weatherholt? He had returned from a greatly insignificant war to find a wasteland of improbability and swirling, cyclonic verbal meltdowns. The scholasticism he had once endeared as the central core of purpose and self-loathing had since wavered away in irritation to leave him stifling in isolation beyond a vastly shrunken circle of globally scattered friends; he had finished his final and flatulently prolonged year of learning in a state of depression, graduating *cum disparage* from university without the expected, proper initiation into society. The act of playing little mouse in the labyrinth of traps and pitfalls, of finally pressing the correct button only to receive no reward had driven Edgar crazy. The Ministry of Love, Citizens' Affairs, if in fact such an organization existed, would have been right in singling him out as a problematic would-be assassin (in accordance with paranoid assumptions). But precautionary experts were career cutthroats and Edgar knew them for what they were: mere puppets upon the stage of disillusionment and false promises. They could have sent an army of therapists, and each one of these babbling psycho-doctors, no matter what school of thought they followed, would have to admit that he had completed the tasks set out before him. He had done everything he could on his end and now it was time for society to own up and let him get to work. Only it wasn't. His goals had been fulfilled, the victory cup found emptied. They had screwed him. But millions had suffered the same fate. The government had seen to it personally.

Edgar was determined. Every known corner was sifted for a sign of opportunity. He had journeyed extensively along the bovine hoof marks of migrating animals, the ruinous Illinois prairies, the haunted Mark Twain National Forest, the parched Oregon Trail, but could not keep himself from stumbling helplessly into debt. Edgar therefore did what most ruined people do: He looked to the trees; he followed the birds back home.

II

David Hernando

Either he was a young adult or an old adolescent (he could never decide), but the man who was barely eighteen hobbled down the aisle of the green bus holding his left foot and wincing. This was David Hernando, a migrant from El Paso, Texas who had journeyed far along the seasonal cornucopia to Hart, Michigan where he had worked the state's last patch of asparagus, and was now adventuring farther north to the gad factory of Gil. The asparagus typically came in early and was ready by Midsummer's Eve along with the calendula, which gave the migrant workers plenty of time to prepare for the cherries or gads, and then move on to the apples, sunflowers, grapes, and pumpkins of the autumn season. The asparagus had been late this year, but so had the gads. Between the two, it was a farmers' co-op, and this was the co-op's bus. But David Hernando was not surprised it had crashed because the driver was a lunatic. Most probably, the wrangler-wearing S.O.B. had run right through the stop sign at the crossroads. What reason would he have had to do otherwise, considering that he had not stopped at any of the others that morning? "Satan. Satan is my problem," he hissed. That S.O.B. had thought everyone was sleeping, but David had been awakened several times during those three hours, such as the time when someone sat on him. That time, the rude person had disappeared before David could get his revenge on anything but the seat cushion. Most of the time there was nothing to see but darkness. Once he had glimpsed a phantasmal glare from the reflectors of plastic construction barrels and then another time there was a deer running just off to the side of the road. When again he slept he had dreamed of a deer made of orange safety reflectors running along a liquid road through hillsides of newspaper-grass and yield-sign-trees, and when it had stopped to drink from the dark smelly road, along came headlights from a few rushing submarines. Committed to some determinate point, they had waded through the asphalt at torpedo-speed, appearing to the deer like deadly leviathans breathing fiery light as the dark toxic sludge bubbled at the surface above them; the deer did not wait, but sprang back amongst the grass. The plastic hindquarters had shined like the sun for mere seconds. The morning of the 15th of July had ceased to exist and David's spiritual attention fished down into the road, through the residual boiling crude which was unusually clear and fluid, becoming one with the bait, and was caught in the gills of the green submarine as it swam by. Suddenly, as the road had intersected a rushing river of crystal blue, he had seen a hunting band of half-naked Ottawa riding whirling white panthers in pursuit of a web-footed elk of the deep. In the dream, the bus driver had been a ghost captain of the green bus-like submarine and there had been a wrangler jean ghost family for the ghostly S.O.B.. The migrants had been chained to their seats through thick ivory bracelets and collars. Four spooky children had run up and down the aisle, laughing at them. David himself had been at first omniscient and then rider of the dunes as a sand-boarder on a sharp obsidian sports craft (decaled in his favorite design of a skeleton mechanic) and the dunes had risen up on the right side of the road and contained a border-crossing way station with empty water jugs and later an oasis occupied by bikini-clad female moon-bathers and the bones of dinosaurs. All of this sand-boarding had been done under light of a large yellow lunar sphere and the sand had been like grains of silk. That had been a pleasant dream.

But then the entire Universe had been shaken. He had received quite a jolt when the bus was suddenly pushed sideways several feet as it skidded to a stop. He had been sleeping with his feet dangling out into the aisle near the emergency exit and was awakened in mid air in time to see his foot come down on someone's head. It had not even been a small head but an abnormally large and thick one. The head had missed the cushiony sneaker and had taken the bare ankle instead. The owner of the head had been very upset despite a lack of visible damage—unlike David's ankle, which was red and painful—and vowed revenge; not just slanderous words in a fit of anger, mind you, but a promise of vengeance in the form of a peon's thick fist being waved in the air like a hammer. David had sleepily shrugged it off. It would not have been the first time he was bested by a woman. His luck had changed little, it seemed, for he could not find his electronic cigarette. The bus had been sideswiped in the rear and the entire load of passengers were left with the feeling of being violently displaced from the universe and then set back slightly off kilter. He waited for his brain to settle and hoped that by some miracle things had been altered so that, instead of an impoverished young migrant jolted from the smelly seat of a bus, he was the proud owner of an estate somewhere nearby; however, this new placement seemed not to have changed much in the world for there was still injustice.

The S.O.B. bus driver cursed his way down to the pavement and did not even bother to ask anyone if they were okay. For him, it seemed, the best way to assess a shipwreck was to wade into the water.

Turning to face the windows, it was possible to gain somewhat of a bearing on where they were in the world. To the left was a crossroad with a dangling stoplight. The other route was clear and recently dusted, but directly behind the bus and somewhat to the side was a smoking black van with tinted windows. He was unsure which of the roads was Highway 37 and which one was the path previously unknown to them, and just at that very moment he saw a cute and very pale young woman in a pair of pink running shoes exit the passenger side of the van and hightail what he thought was a respectable posterior maladroitly away and into a thicket of trees. At the same time an alarm was going off seemingly from inside his throbbing head and people were pulling themselves together and scrambling from the green bus in all possible directions.

At the Scene of the Accident

David winced as he was accidentally shoveled in the foot by a woman in black combat boots, baggy black-green-tan camouflage trousers, and a plain azurite-colored sweatshirt.

"Whoa..." she said. "Woe. Where you at, Noah?! Noah!"

"On the God-forsaken floor, Norma-Jean!" This had escaped from someone under the middle seats. It was the small, pastel-faced, bearded guy in overalls—David recognized the voice: This guy had accidentally sat on him early that morning in the dark after the bus stopped to pick up more passengers from some thickly wooded mobile town along the way. Now it all made sense; these

26

two blind acrobats were the American version of mountainside villagers. Hillbillies, he believed they were called: Pale, shadow-eyed things. There were versions of them in Mexico, where rugged individuals used their rotten teeth to crunch through fried beetles, worms, and grasshoppers (which he supposed, in this case, was in substitute of raccoons and opossums). Little wonder that they were born to the still of wild elixirs and to the alchemical masters of good poison because their poor bombarded stomachs were depending on it.

The sound of someone or something loudly breaking wind came from the direction of the fallen Noah. "Lord Almighty! Your grits ain't agreein', Norma dear…"

"Noah, I didn't make no grits! Now, when do I have time to cook?"

"Honey, then what was in the fryin' pan?"

"Oh, prolly somethin' the kids made."

"Well…your kin must have somethin' powerful 'gainst me, dear, 'cause the devils in Hell prolly hear the cryin' of my bowels!"

"Don't be crude, Noah. Yar in public! Now get up off the floor!!" Norma-Jean had growled this as quietly as she could, but to David she still sounded like a badger.

Norma-Jean helped Noah from the floor, at which point they both propped up their sliding pant-areas using an improvisational form of choreography, and together they skipped down the narrow aisle and vanished into a sea of migrants.

Likewise, David pried himself from the sticky vinyl backseat and observed his surroundings, which had become relatively subdued, despite the solitary flatulence from the middle aisles. Outside, though, the populous raged like cranky Athenians before a dissolute senate. Within, only a few simplistic middle-aged men remained.

Glancing back through the window again, he witnessed a further oddity: Two suspicious governmental-type men with metallic sunglasses shook themselves free of the smoking van and were impatiently looking for something they must have lost. They were wearing business suits that were too tight with tacky ties that were too short, and the pants of one man split at the seams when he took off down the adjoining crossroad and into the thicket of trees.

They had apparently pried their way out of the van's airbags. Strange, he thought. And yet a lifetime of annual cinema gathering at the rundown El Paso shopping mall had prepared him for these encounters. In some respects, America really was like a movie.

A beautiful cylinder of mixed and bastardized tobacco wrapped in sweetly perfumed paper dominated his tormented thoughts. David checked under the seats to no avail. His 'smokes' had vanished. Like tumbleweeds, they had been blown into the gigantic Midwestern ashtray of the unseen—the desert rationale known as *what-the-frick*. He had seen these uprooted things around El Paso, and even further down along the urinary Great Plains, in Sweetwater, Abilene and Mineral Wells. David felt like those same tumbleweeds as he was propelled helplessly along the desert of an hourglass, blowing from town to town, through the deserted streets of humanity and into a racist sandstorm.

"Where the Devil could they *be*?" he hissed in rage. The day promised to be a distressing one. The worst of it was that they were not cigarettes in the plural, but one semi-permanent electronic device with detachable parts that joined to form an inhaler. If the thing was not broken somehow, it had definitely become unsanitary because he had forgotten to seal the bag. It was also fairly expensive and would be difficult to replace. He could hardly imagine what dark dank dirty hole the thing had fallen into.

David hobbled his way down the aisle to the steps of the sliding door, resting on seat-backs to check the floor as he went. When he had made his way to the driver's seat, listening inattentively to the pair of elders' discussion of cockfighting, he turned at a slight movement from the horizon of his left eye and just noticed the cute Caucasian girl adeptly returning to the van and momentarily vanishing under the steering wheel. But, before he could hop his way firmly to the middle of the pavement and hobble over to offer assistance, the van quickly started up, backed out, and quietly drove off down the road. Everyone was so busy with their own aches and pains that they did not even notice the missing van, which had played an integral part in their calamities.

"Of all the incompetence!" people were saying in Spanish. "At this rate, we'll be lucky to get any hours at all this season!"

"My aching back!"

"My sore knees."

The plebeians complained to themselves.

"Dave, man, you alright?" This was from David's friend Carlos, who had grabbed his extending hand with a slow-motion cobra strike.

"No, man. *No bueno.*" David explained to Carlos how he had hurt his foot and regrettably misplaced his electronic cigarette.

Carlos said that he had banged up his knee, but was otherwise unhurt and had always retained his cigarette and the accompanying liquid by attaching them to his pocket with a chain.

"That's an excellent idea. Too bad I didn't think of it. Hey, man, did you see that *una chica guapa?*"

His friend Carlos had regrettably not noticed the girl.

"Why? Was she life-changing to look at or something?"

David explained her nerdy curves and contours with verbal bravado, carving her likeness in the air, and described how her knitted white winter hat sat thickly and fuzzily above a mass of short dark-chocolate hair. "...And there were these two gringos in suits looking for her, man!"

"That's crazy. Do you mean they were gringos to *us,* or just gringos?"

"I don't know. They were weird; Governmental. I think she's in some kind of trouble!"

"That's not saying much, considering where we are...*ironico unbuenlio*—a pretty mess..."

An odd looking sports car pulled up to the S.O.B. bus driver and then sped off again, leaving a sweet smell of lollipops. He could not place the make or model; perhaps it had been a custom build, like Uncle Ernesto's old gas-guzzling Pinto.

At Which Point the Authorities Arrived

The county police finally showed up sometime later with an ambulance in tow.

David went to sit down in the back of the ambulance.

"You injured?" the paramedic, who had stayed back with the vehicle, asked.

"I hurt my foot and my ankle is pretty sore."

"Is it life-threatening?" asked the paramedic.

"I don't think so…"

"If it isn't life threatening, they probably won't do anything for you. You're from a Right-to-work state[4], right? You probably have crap insurance[5]."

"Really? They won't help me? Last season I worked in the cherry orchards with a guy who drank twenty-seven beers. They helped him, but then he got fired. He moved on to another farm and the hospital became stuck with the bill. He thought it was pretty funny, but I didn't. That's prolly why they won't help me. Not much I can do about it now though. He died not long after—was stabbed to death."

"That's too bad. Who stabbed him?"

"It was on the job," David explained. "He got drunk mowing someone's lawn and ran over a pair of brush trimmers."

"Ouch. How did you find out?"

"I heard about it in Texas. That's where I live, when I'm not following the seasons. In Texas I get help—it's mostly illegal, unlicensed type stuff. But it's practically sorcery along the border, you know."

"I don't have very good insurance, either," admitted the paramedic. "I'm only part-time."

"What do you do?"

"Usually I just work it off." The paramedic shrugged. "So, you're harvesting the gads?"

---

[4] The right-to-work law was a misnomer government statute prohibiting labor unions from forcing non-union workers to pay union dues, thus giving employees the right to benefit from collective bargaining without paying for it and consequently weakening the power of the union.

[5] Health care coverage reform in Michigan was in gridlock since 2013 due to the efforts of powerful think tanks with completely opposing views: It was the Mackinac Center for Public Policy's policy that a high-deductible health savings account (HSA) should be implemented to ensure tax advantages and the highest quality of care possible for themselves and their rich fellows; The Obama administration's federal health care law, on the other hand, was aimed at "decreasing the number of uninsured Americans and reducing the overall costs of health care" simply by throwing money at it (mechanisms to include mandates, subsidies, tax credits, and brute force, with the desired result that all applicants were covered and all rates remained the same for everyone).

"Yeah, supposed to be," said David Hernando.

"Oh, wow. This your first time?" Something in the way the paramedic spoke made David feel uneasy.

"Yes, first time with gads," David said. "I did cherries once, before the Grand Convulsion, or Whopping Takeover, or whatever you call it..."

The paramedic looked around suspiciously and said carefully, "Don't even mention that around here. Look, friend. Anyone tell you about gads?"

"Whadya mean, like what they taste like?"

"Have you heard any...stories?"

"No. This is the first time since the...since the thing that they've called for any migrants. No one I know has ever worked them."

"Listen...Good luck out there," said the paramedic, who grabbed David's hand to produce some kind of urban American handshake.

"What? Please, amigo. Tell me what you were going to say—what stories should I have heard?"

"Well..." began the paramedic, "you working the orchards?"

"The factory," David answered. "That's where we should be right now, instead of at the crossroads."

"That's good. The factory's safer. Be sure to request lots of extra equipment, if they offer it. Stay alert in there."

"What do you mean by that?"

"You'll see," the paramedic said. "Here, show me that ankle. I should take a look."

David removed his left shoe and put his foot up into the back of the ambulance.

"Can you wiggle your toes?" the paramedic asked.

David wiggled his toes. There was noticeable redness at the ankle, which was slightly swollen and white at the bone.

"No, you didn't sprain it. The swelling is probably at the joint, but I'm no doctor; couldn't get the cash for medical school." The paramedic slid further into the ambulance and handed David an ice pack and a medium-sized bottle of aspirin from his medical kit. "These will help you pull yourself together."

David thanked the paramedic and hobbled back toward the bus. He was feeling better already.

The pandemonium seemed to have become worse now that the police were handling things. One female police officer was busy writing down about twelve statements at once in broken Spanish-English-Hillbilly while two others assessed the damage to the rear of the bus.

The Investigation into the Crash

Minutes later, the police were still buzzing from their efforts at crowd control. They waded through the confusion like professional athletes in a second grade read-a-thon.

"Did anyone get a description of the other vehicle?"

"Did we ever, Sir. We got enough eyewitness testimony to start a new genre in crime fighting."

The assisting officer produced the word-littered screen of a computerized tablet notebook[6]. So far, they had the bus driver's description of a black van with tinted windows, a hillbilly's conspiracy theory of how his live-in girlfriend's children were trying to kill him by flatulence, one description of the interior of a green bus, a second-hand account of a cockfight, and at least three eye-witnesses of whom were positive it had been a UFO."

"Good Lord...Sorry I asked...well, just call it in as a hit and run. Advise everyone to be on the lookout for traces of green paint on a black van. That's the best we can do this early in the morning. I'm practically sleepwalking through events."

---

[6] A fallacy concerning this product of the late Steve Jobs and his flagship company Apple, Inc. was that only government employees and Welfare recipients had them; yet, surprisingly, they were eventually made affordable to all by the Tri World Bank's Indentured Servitude™ program, which was heavily endorsed by billionaires and credit card companies both major and minor.

"Could these be the TV personalities who robbed the Chum's Desert Market?"

"Nothing would surprise me at this point. Let's get some coffee."

Late For Work

Once David had boarded the bus again he sat down with the ice pack and waited to be able to work off the injury. He was worried that someone would notice and that he would be turned away. He would have to be careful not to limp or to wince at the pain. The aspirin would do the trick, if only he could figure out what happened to his jug of water, which had vanished along with his lunch and his e-cig. He did not really have the heart to look for it.

Soon the bus was moving again—seemingly propelled by a series of Hail Maries. With the help of a just God, they would arrive in physicality (or so they hoped). The bus, reflected David Hernando, had become in some ways like a green submarine. It tilted and creaked in the long-armed depths of the sea-cows, leagues and leagues under Heaven. David himself was trapped within and feeling sick. A Swiss version of his soul howled into the ocean wake shimmering above like a competent German submarine captain of the *Siddhartha*. "Owoooo!" it cried. "Ooph, owooo!"

Something under him fell to the floor with a light clatter and when he looked he saw to his surprise that it was his electronic cigarette, which must have gotten stuck between the seat cushions. Now if only he could locate his lunch. He checked the seat. Nothing was there.

The northwestern Michigan scenery was much better in full morning daylight. There were rusted truck-skeletons hiding like deer ticks in the wild emaciated grains, a half-starved forest of leaves and needles appearing for mere seconds, and suddenly a clear sapphire lake of serpentine dimensions slithering along orchards and the occasional charred remnants of a summer home.

The green bus slowed with an unholy squeak.

He saw a row of pine trees, a high chain fence topped with three lines of barbed wire, and a silver passenger train minus the locomotive which appeared to be in permanent stagnation. Looking at them, with their little rectangular windows, they seemed quite tall and he imagined what it would be like to live in one.

"I bet I could fix that up real' nice," thought David. He had always wanted to ride in a train. Perhaps, he thought, there was a family of raccoons living in them. Maybe it was even a raccoon city.

The bus pulled in to the factory, seemingly ignoring a security booth just beyond the gate, and circled the parking lot nearest the main building where there was a place sectioned off in yellow paint. Before the driver could apply his foot to the brakes, a force of variously-aged workers pried open the sliding door with many anxious fingers, flew like lemmings through the remaining obstacles of the parking lot, and hustled centipede-like into the factory so as not to lose another second of their day. Those who had achingly risen in pursuit fell like dominos in their wake, but were not dismayed. It was not the first time their cage had been rattled, and it would not be the last. Soon enough, they were up and then down breathing pavement.

"Disrespectful sonsabitches..." mumbled the S.O.B. driver.

III

Concerning the Mystery Woman from the Accident

"I wasn't meant to live like this!" decreed Eddie in a disgruntled manner, checking his body for abnormalities.

A confused expression accompanied John's feeling of irritation over his partner's increasingly pessimistic behavior. "Whaddya mean? Like a private security guard?"

"I hate being on the road! I have fatty genes!"

"There, there, cupcake! You'll be ripping muscle again before you know it. Now, keep an eye out for a sandwich place so we can eat. "

"It's five in the gall-dang morning. We'll never find a good place to eat at this hour!"

"Never-mind that. We've been driving all night to make up for lost time and I need to make a stop, and it's gotta be quick."

"I can't just eat any old sandwich! I've gotta watch my weight!!"

"Jesus, Eddie. Why didn't you just pack a gigantic bag of oats and save me the hassle."

"Lay off, John! Do you want a fat, lazy partner who can't even keep up, who's a danger to himself and to everyone around him?! Well, do you?!"

"Alright, just relax. We'll get you some yogurt or something at the gas station."

"There's…there's a supermarket in the next town. Open twenty-four-hours." This had been the mystery woman, a curtained figure in her middle twenties who was seated behind and—from the point-of-view of the insects that were splattering the windshield with their internal organs and fluids—directly between two muscle-bound private security guards in a black van with tinted windows. Within a hooded poncho of purple and red checkered cotton patterns, she appeared smaller than she really was, at a shrunken 5 foot 4.17 inches tall, with intermediate, disheveled black hair cascading out from under a white knit winter cap and over a slightly hexagonal face as bright as a moonlight orchid, despite an absence of makeup. The eyes made the difference, even though she hid them from almost everyone. They were a captivating Avalon mist at contact, contained within squinting saucers of iris muscle; but askew they were a dark maelstrom of frustration hidden behind a dimension of glass.

Eddie turned his massive frame with great difficulty and a gentle smile illuminated his giant face. "Hey, she just said something."

"I believe she did, genius," held John.

"Wha'd you say, ma'am?" inquired Eddie tenderly.

"I'm starving," the woman said.

"We're all hungry, lady-" said John matter-o-fact-ly.

"For sushi," the woman added.

Eddie nodded: "Oh, I could go for that. Whadya think, John?"

"Shut up, stupid," said John in a very contemptible manner. "And you, whatever your name is…Epiphany…"

"It-it's Antiope," the woman said flutteringly.

John sighed weightily and continued: "I don't know how you even obtained this information, but…this supermarket, is it on the way, or what?"

"…It's a little out of the way, Agent John Mathews, *sir*," said the woman. "But you won't find anything else around here. We're in the Wexford-Missaukee Desert. Most places have rolled away with the tumbleweeds."

"Forget it," shot John with finality. "I've hauled your ass all the way from the middle of the goddamn Atlantic and I'm gonna get you back *right on time*! No more adventures for you, bucko. I'm not going to give you a chance to run off again. A little out of the way? No dice!"

"You said we were going to eat somewhere," interposed Eddie on the young woman's behalf. "A supermarket is somewhere."

"Just shut up!" John barked. "I meant something fast; something for breakfast; an egg mc muffin or pancakes; something that won't take forever to get out of."

36

Eddie folded his massive arms and a frown became etched on his lovable Mediterranean face. "Forget it, then, I'm not hungry."

"Jesus, Eddie, you're like a baby. We'll stop at a grocery store and get you some apple sauce. Will the baby stop whining if we go to the store?"

"Fuck you, John. But yeah, that would do it."

"You're somethin' else," chuckled John. "What about you, Epiphany?"

"Antiope..."

"Right...Untie-o-pee," John taunted. "Why is it you didn't speak before? Being uncooperative? I asked you all those questions, dragged you through two airports like dead weight. You just stared off into space with that blank look. We thought maybe you were retarded..."

"I'm not a retard...far from it..."

"I know I know...I didn't mean that you were...just that...you kinda made things difficult."

"Difficult? You don't know difficult."

"You had it rough at school. You were picked on. I read all about it."

"You don't know anything about me."

"What, the name calling? I was only joshing," John said matter-of-factly. "Your entire dossier is converted to memory: Untie-o-pee Penuel. Born on June Twenty-Four, Year of the Sheffield Winter Gardens. Abandoned; ward of the state. Mother, Henrietta Penuel, retired factory worker. Father unknown. Diagnosed with a rare mental disorder."

"Non-specific high-functioning autism," Antiope remonstrated: "A modified form of said disorder artificially created by your generous employers. They dispersed them in fertility drugs marketed through a front company, utilizing a growing trend in sterility to their advantage. They altered our DNA during prenatal development in an effort to win a secret government contract to make America competitive. It's all true."

"Shows signs of antisocial behavior. Highly creative. A compulsive liar. I know you like a book."

"You really think I'm only seventeen?"

John gave her the look he gave people to convince them that he was a human lie detector. "Why are you so gung ho on running away from the Academy? You'll graduate in less than a year. You were top of your class until you stopped doing your homework. Why can't you appreciate what the Monstrosso Corporation is doing for you?"

"I graduated ages ago. I'm not seventeen—wish I still was. I was born the Year of the Motorola StarTAC Wearable Cellular Telephone[7]."

"Sure you were," retorted John.

"I hate that place! I'm not going back there."

"Oh yes you are, young lady!" loudly interposed Eddie Monstrosso from the passenger's seat.

Antiope glared at both of them and began to sound morose. "It's terrible…You don't know what it's like…what they're doing to people…"

"Whatever," John said. "It's a school. A school for…special folks."

"It isn't really a school, you idiot. They enslave people; they experiment on little children there. Doesn't that bother you?"

John glared at her through the rearview mirror: "Wow, kid. You have a really warped outlook on life."

"Warped, huh?" she said, griping at the mirror. "Does an education typically consist of forcing students to behave like machines that are incapable of communicating with the outside world? Using them as slave labor in some stupid factory? Why do you think so many of us look alike? It's the fertility treatment! They won't stop there, you know; they're planning on going global. The entire lower income population will become drones for the elite establishment."

"Stop being so melodramatic," John bleated peevishly.

"They give us mind-altering drugs," Antiope murmured. "It's worse for those who rebel: exposed to dangerous prescription drugs and made to think it's the *in thing* to abuse them. They actually send in federal operatives disguised as troubled students— overly stereotypical, I might add, straight out of twenty-ten, as if we

---

[7] Motorola released this model in 1994.

38

wouldn't be able to tell. If we refuse, we're restrained and medicated through force-"

"-Yeah, whatever," John held coldly.

"Don't you rental cops have any feelings at all?!"

"Hey, watch it with that talk!!" scolded John with blundering, physical violence upon the wheel. The van swerved slightly along the sand-covered asphalt and he fought to regain control. The sleeplessness was getting to him. "We can give you warped, if that's what you're into," he said, regaining control. "Agent Monstrosso here's been pumping iron most of his life, held the Mister Milky Way title for six weeks running, and I'm a decorated military veteran, seven wars—was a Blue Beret in the Air Force, special operations, and I can snuff the glint of life right through your pretty little nostrils. We're no one to mess with."

"Impressive," the woman chimed in bitter satire. "You must have paved a hell of a lot of runways…"

"Excuse me?"

"All your efforts are in vain, you know. I'm leaving that place for good."

"We're bringing you back: accept it," John said.

"I accept nothing," Antiope affirmed, becoming Tiger Lilly of the Piccanniny Tribe with her arms crossed and her head held high.

A grumble reverberated from under John's dark dress uniform, which was for the most part a gentleman's business suit (minus the jacket, which had found a new home somewhere along the back seat). To his loyal mind, this act of defiance against his employer's wishes was a threat to world order. All wrongs would be righted, if the agency had any say in the matter. This troubled backlit machinery was on her way back to the Academy, whether she liked it or not.

Antiope ignited their costumes with lighthearted thought: Agents Eddie and John were both wearing white 100% polyester shirts made in Thailand with the tops unbuttoned. Both had their crinkled ties (a golden threaded weave over black with white tips and a red x✝ at the dividing line between the two contrasting colors) dangling loosely from thick, sweaty necks. Both were on the job. They had driven all the way from New Orleans, where they had followed a retired couple in an SUV hauling a large sailboat to Calypso Bay Resort. They had suspected that the cargo they were chasing, a young female student who had escaped from Duck Lake Academy, was stowed away inside the hull, but she turned out to be a small monkey-like robot (created and assembled in Japan by the robot experts) that was sending programmed text messages on the student's cellular telephone. When intelligence at headquarters—that is, the rented office of ExTemplar Security, located in Gamesh, Michigan—alerted them to the real whereabouts of the student, information they had obtained through spy drones and an online cruise ship log for recent excursions to Bermuda, they were able to apprehend their cargo on the King's Wharf in Bermuda's City of Hamilton and fly with said female back to New Orleans. At first, John had decided to fly their human cargo all the way back to Duck Lake Academy, leaving Eddie to drive the van back to headquarters by himself. But the cargo had escaped during a stopover in Saint Louis, had joined a tour group to Mammoth Cave in Kentucky, had then emerged from the miraculous bowels of the earth only to return to Saint Louis where a secret weather satellite posing as shiny space junk had captured her nestled happily at the top of the Gateway Arch as she looked out of the leaning window toward freedom. She had been 200 feet in the dirt and 600 feet in the air. R. Lewis Knight[8], owner and CEO of ExTemplar Security, was less than happy about the added expenses. After bouncing around on several false leads, John had rejoined Eddie in the black van with tinted windows and had decided that it was best to keep a contained watch on the young woman. So they had taken turns driving the rest of the way from downtown Saint Louis and were both hungry and exhausted.

---

[8] R. Lewis Knight, the only son of tulip bulb magnate Ralph Graef Knight, is a graduate of Hillshire College in Holland, Michigan, and owner and CEO of ExTemplar Security Services. The family Anglicized the Dutch surname Cnyt sometime during the early Colonial period of America, having confused Cnyt with Cniht. His employees refer to him as "Munchkin" behind his back because of his squeaky, high-pitched voice.

Shopping the APS-9

Out near the ruins of a shopping mall overlooking unlit, vacant signs and billboard platitudes of early daylight hours was a massive all-purpose store called APS-9. There were dead trees in the fields between dried grass and sandy parking lots.

A guard in an outdated military uniform strode around the outside perimeter with a laser-guided pea-shooter while a couple of high school kids in safety-yellow aprons chased the disheveled carts.

A small crowd of elderly people were swarming in and out of the store on motorized wheelchairs, reeking of oxygen, insulin, and battery acid. A sandstorm appeared on the horizon opposite the faint glow of the sun, from where the Great Michigan Basin encircled what was left of the Great Lakes.

The agents exited the van and motioned for their female captive.

"Don't try anything funny," warned John. He grabbed Antiope by the upper arm and pointed to a bulky stun gun attached to the wide calf of his leg.

The large all-purpose store appeared silly to their weary eyes. Due to the surrounding desolation, they found it difficult to imagine such a place at the capacity it was built for.

It was far too early for the errand boys and college students from the local oasis of learning, but a few housewives could be seen arriving for the daily specials.

As she was roughly escorted through the parking lot, Antiope noted with satisfaction that the integrity of her footgear was being compromised. She scraped along the coarse asphalt and would have tripped on her face if not for the two strong security agents who were absorbing the force of gravity upon her.

"Damn these shoes," Antiope uttered as she was dragged into the supermarket by the two goony overdressed security agents. The wooden heel of her left clog had finally come off and she just managed to bend down to retrieve it, but had to hobble on the good shoe to avoid being dragged along on one leg.

Eddie let go to accommodate, but John kept a firm grasp.

"Why do you even have shoes like that?" grumbled John sleepily. "It's nothing but a block of wood glued to a dead cow's ass."

"Have you ever sat on those uncomfortable metal stools with the water dripping everywhere and tried to sort fruit all damn day? It isn't just your feet you have to worry about. And tennis shoes will get soggy and give you a nasty foot disease. I need these shoes. They make my life bearable."

"Fine, fine! I don't have time for this!" John snapped, shoving the prisoner over to Eddie. "Meet me at the deli!"

They watched him perform a reconnaissance of the aisles and disappear near the bread and bagel section.

"Well, come on then," Eddie sighed with a shrug. He led the much tinier person on with uncharacteristic delicacy.

The APS reflected all the modern trends of shopping in that selection had diminished significantly since the heydays of the 1980s and "90s. As products saw most of their advertising dollars go overseas to China, India, and other highly rated locales, a lower quality resulted (yet typically failed to warrant a drop in price).

"Ooh!" exclaimed Antiope. "I could really use one of these!"

They had come upon chintzy metal baskets of Bogeyman Hair Gel and Wang Pow Super Crazy Glue that were situated mysteriously in the middle of the main walkway.

"For my shoes," she explained.

Eddie allowed her to grab a container of each. She tried slipping an extra tube of glue into her pants pocket, but the giant captor scolded her. "What you do will come back three-fold, young lady! Now, what do you want to eat?"

"Natural fruits, seeds and nuts, fish from happy waters, animals from happy pastures," she said.

"I don't think we'll find any of that here," said Eddie doubtfully.

Shelves full of fluffy pillows appeared to their right, where the bedroom supply section started, and Antiope began sobbing.

"What's wrong now?" asked Eddie, looking embarrassed. It stressed him out to see a woman cry.

"Nothing. It's just that…I've been sleeping on an armrest for days…they look so soft!"

"We don't have time for pillows. Come on. John will be pissed…"

"Can't I just browse really quick? I have money. You're partly responsible for this abuse, you know."

"Me? Abuse? Hold on, now. Jeez. I can't believe I let you bawl me into this…well, come on, then. Pick out your pillows…"

"You're sweet Eddie. Much sweeter than John…I mean Agent Mathews. How did you get this far down the totem pole? You're a Monstrosso, for pity's sake; a distant cousin to the owner of the company. Said so yourself. Not only that, but ExTemplar's biggest client is *your flesh and blood*. You should be the one in charge, not him."

"Don't say things like that—it's mutiny! You're not a comminist, are you? I'm not supposed to contrive with those pink bastards."

"What are you worried about? A big, strong guy like you… Afraid of little old me?"

Antiope pulled a second large fluffy white pillow from the middle shelf.

"Do you really think I should be the leader?"

"Oh, absolutely!" she chimed.

Eddie beamed for a few seconds and was subsequently overtaken with fear.

They arrived at the deli with a shopping cart full of pillows and a few smaller items that Antiope had picked up along the way: tiny plastic water pistols, an old fashioned analog alarm clock, a utility knife, an emergency first aid kit, sleeping pills to replace the ones she had slipped into John's coffee during the night, a small bag of big rubber bands, a medium-sized bag of trail mix with white chocolates, a bottle of cranberry-pomegranate juice, and plastic zip ties.

John was furious once he woke up from his nap against a wire basket full of boxes of donuts. "I won't even ask!" he growled sleepily, the smell of powdered sugar rising into the air. "You better be right behind me! I'm gonna go put these ham sandwiches on the expense card, which is what you'll eat, like it or not! Don't…say…a word!!" He pointed menacingly at the both of them in turn and grumpily motioned for them to follow the gravity of his anger. "Be out in five minutes or I'm pulling you out, with or without that goddamn cart!"

Antiope grinned in sly anticipation.

"See what you did?" Eddie groaned. "Now I gotta eat a ham sandwich."

"Go grab something else," she recommended cheerfully. "I'll pay for it."

Eddie smiled. "That yogurt back there sure looked good."

"Didn't it?"

"…It does seem stupid to be in a store and not buy what you want when it's right there in front of you. You don't mind?"

"Not at all," she encouraged.

"I can pay you back…" Eddie reasoned while soaking his tie in drool.

Antiope waved him on. "I've put you through enough trouble."

By the time they had followed the instructions from the computer's feminine voice, gotten through the self-check-out lane and made it back to the van with the pillows and all the other junk—long after some of the elderly shoppers had inched their way through the old fashioned cashier lanes on their electric scooters—Agent John Mathews had lost the battle and was passed out in the reclining middle seat, still clutching his sandwich.

"Poor John," Antiope remarked happily.

"Probably for the best," Eddie sighed.

The Wexford-Missaukee Desert Gas Station

After a radio commercial advertised Grube's Dead Duck Removal Service and then Seymour's Shibboleths for a Dying World, a billboard came up at the tenth mile marker announcing combustible fuel of every kind imaginable. A large red 'X' overshadowed a picture of an extension cord plug-in for automobiles. It said the nearest gas station was another fifty miles—but that could not have included Gil and Gamesh, which

44

were both out on different roads some twenty miles away, give or take a few.

A governmental sign said TOLL AHEAD. BE PREPARED TO STOP.

"Wish we didn't have to stop," Eddie said. He took the next exit and pulled into the only symbol of civilization this stretch of upper Michigan. Primitive advertising on painted plywood announced WE SELL ICE and PETOSKEY STONES SOLD IN THE GIFT SHOP with a black arrow pointing inside.

With Eddie out pumping gas, Antiope went to work on the floorboard. She needed to get in close enough to the engine so that it looked authentic. The device consisted of the following: squirt guns full of a dark carbonated beverage, rubber bands, zip ties, John's duct tape, and a big round-faced alarm clock with two shiny bells on top. She wedged them in behind the portion of footrest that most people never had much use for and returned quickly to her seat.

Eddie began washing the tinted windshield with awkward plunges. Despite his heavily muscular physique, he had not been stretching properly and was stiffening up like a side of beef. He scrutinized his extended right arm to be certain that it was not disintegrating right before his eyes.

Brackish water streamed down the sides in natural patterns. The squeegee did its best.

A man with a buttoned navy-blue-shirted potbelly bulging over his pale designer jeans came out. "That pump's really slow," he said, stating the obvious.

Eddie turned and smiled, but said nothing.

"There's a ghost town just up that road from here," the man said. "A lot of people like to go there. It's only been abandoned for nine years though."

"Some other time," Eddie said, trying his best to be polite. The slow pump was driving him out of his tired mind.

The Spider Lake Battleground Memorial

From the pleasantly vacant Toll Highway 131 past the ghost town of Manton and the depleted Manistee River, they took Main Supply Route 114[9] to the Spider Lake Battleground Memorial, where Antiope convinced Eddie they should stop and see the sights. A tour bus for Hovering Vulture Casino had beaten them to it and three-dozen elderly people were being hydraulically lifted down in their motorized wheelchairs so they could zip around the memorial with relative ease.

"Hold out your hands," he said. "I have to cuff you."

"For real?"

"Just until I get back."

"What about me? I have to go, too!"

"When I get back," Eddie said sternly. For once he was very self-assured. He cuffed Antiope's tender wrists and then chained her to the seat with a padlock.

Once Eddie was out of sight, Antiope pulled her way behind the seat and rummaged through her suitcase for a pair of sneakers. She took them out and transferred the pair to the floorboard with the pillows and the other junk. They would be coming in handy soon.

Poor John was still snoring away in the seat behind her. The van was so peaceful that she almost regretted the future.

Eddie soon came back, playing with the rim of his dress pants along the way, and stomped towards the passenger side of the van to release his prisoner. He left the cuffs on, due to his tiredness, helped Antiope down from her seat, and then quickly escorted her to the restrooms.

"Don't try nothin' funny," he warned. Eddie stood outside the entrance in a typical security stance and yawned into his muscle-bound hand. As a precaution, and to keep himself preoccupied, he watched the tracking monitor through the interface of his smart phone application. The bleeping dot barely moved.

Antiope was unusually fast at doing her business. She appeared from the mysterious WOMEN designated direction eager to move forward.

---

[9] A military route from Fort Grayling to just south of the Sleeping Bear Dunes National Lakeshore.

The pillar-like private security agent fought off another yawn as he met his Delilah. "Come on, then," he said, without bothering to restrain her.

"But...can't I see the memorial? Just drag me past it, will you?"

"You're a strange one, you know that?" Eddie said. He escorted the prisoner to the memorial, which depicted a group of people fighting over a bottle of water that remained unattainably above their strained and covetous faces. The figures were lifelike and very dramatic.

"Wait, wait...let me check for something!" Antiope exclaimed. She lured Eddie excitedly to a garbage can made of congealed Petoskey stones and dived in head-first. "Oh, awesome, I love these things!" she said as she rummaged through the public garbage.

"Are you nuts?!" Eddie scolded, grabbing her by the arm with both hands.

"No, wait! I can use these for a science experiment!" Antiope gripped her pieces of trash with such unexpected force that Eddie relented. As she had hoped, MREs (Meals Ready to Eat) with unused flameless heaters that utilized the oxidation of metal to generate heat had been wastefully discarded. She pulled the coveted heaters out from within the food remnants and plastic mess and re-abandoned the meal. She managed to grab hold of another before Eddie, red with embarrassment, lifted her away by the waist and carried her back to the van.

"Thanks, Eddie. That was great," she consoled. "I-I'd never been to a memorial. A-and that statue—so much exaggerated pain in their expressions."

"Yeah, well..." said Eddie. Realizing that she was probably telling the truth this time, he let her climb into the passenger seat of her own volition before shutting the door.

"Shouldn't we put a seatbelt on John, just to be safe?" Antiope said after buckling herself in. "Oh, and watch out, by the way. There'll be troopers hiding everywhere in hopes of catching speeders."

Eddie reached back and fastened a seatbelt around John with such care that it made Antiope sad with empathy. They were an unlikely pair of angels.

MSR 114: The Road to Nowhere

MSR 114 was a relatively new road that stretched past Duck Lake Academy and continued all the way to the muddy edge of the Great Michigan Basin, which, while shrouded in mystery, suited their purposes perfectly.

Eddie was at the wheel, with Antiope in the passenger seat playing with her pillows and glue. Agent Mathews was still passed out under the blanket that had been thrown over him by Eddie and he was beginning to snore loudly from the back central chair.

"Shouldn't you be going a little faster?" Antiope said.

"Hey, what's your hurry?" inquired Eddie. "I thought you hated the academy."

"I-I'm just tired of this road," she explained nervously. "Nothing but blacktop and creepy weather control towers."

"I'm a little tired myself," mumbled Eddie with a yawn.

"Besides, John will be mad at you if you don't get us there on time."

"How would we not get there on time?" Eddie answered— his peace of mind beginning to shatter.

"You've been going fifty-eight miles per hour, which is of course two miles under the speed limit. Judging by these mile markers, we have about thirty miles to go and it's almost six-thirty. It'll take you over twenty minutes at this rate."

"Oh gosh, is that true?! I'd better reset cruise control..."

Despite appearances, Antiope knew what she was doing. She had delayed them exactly 22 minutes, 40 seconds at the supermarket, which went a long way in getting them to the crossroads on time. Ever since their comical journey had resumed from the Saint Louis Police Department, she had done everything subtly possible to delay the trip enough to align them with the bus schedule. She knew precisely when it would reach the intersection of Highway 37 and MSR 114 from Fort Grayling to Duck Lake Academy. What she did not know was how long it would take the van to get there, and only after a series of daily mental calculations was she certain. All that was needed now was a last-minute calibration in speed.

"Damn thing!" Antiope cursed, diving suddenly and aggressively into the pillows by the floorboards. "My heel's come off again!"

"Could you do me a favor now and return to your seat?" Eddie advised concernedly. The nice girl who had once bought him a gallon of yogurt was making him nervous. "Hey, you changed shoes," he added, but Eddie had other things to worry about, like exactly what to say at the gate, and precisely when the little turnoff would be coming up for the private road that would take them through the majestic birch and Hardy Coconut Palms confoundedly enveloping the inscrutable academy.

Meanwhile, Antiope fumbled with MRE heaters, squirt guns, and John's duct tape for some last-minute preparations and then worked on her heel. A proper toss would do the trick, but the road was bumpy. *The rhythm is mine... Wait for it...there!* She tossed it in between bumps. The wooden heel became lodged under the brake pedal and seemed to be stuck there.

"To your seat!" Eddie ordered. "What are you doing down there?"

"Just a second!" Antiope calmly sighed. "My heel's fallen behind the brake pedal."

"It what?!"

"Don't worry, big guy! I'll take care of it!" Antiope brushed against his legs and arms and then pushed her way up to glance out the window. But her face knotted up with anxiety as they approached a small intersection and she dived back into the pillows over the passenger-side floorboard.

Suddenly a green school bus appeared from around the corner from where there was a blinking yellow light and Eddie became alarmed at the unlikelihood that he would be able to stop in time. He hit the brakes heavily and cranked the wheel, but the heel was still stuck and he couldn't kick it loose. They slammed into the rear side of the bus at half speed. The airbags deployed and the van violently rolled over and then righted itself in the middle of the street.

They had fallen into an uncontrollable nightmare. There seemed to be a vacuum of illogical fecundity sucking all action from them as the commotion rallied from the vicinity of the disabled green bus.

Eddie, the driving force in this calamity, feared that he had caused a large amount of people some serious bodily harm. He himself was badly shaken. For a moment, he had failed to recall his own name.

A door opened. Someone scrambled out and started running. Through the passenger-side opening, he saw what appeared to be a petit young she-devil in jogging shoes. Pillows filled the void at the cushioned base of the seat, where a certain young woman's legs should have been dangling. They had been glued together into a comfortable yolk. Below noxious puffs of steam, nothing stirred.

"What the fuck did you do!" shouted John from the back central seat. He rubbed his throbbing forehead and pried his aching body from under the seatbelt to assess the situation.

There was gray smoke coming from under the hood and into the cab on the passenger's side and they could hear the horrible screams of fright from the people on the bus.

Eddie's nose was bleeding. The impact had bruised his legs and chest and had rattled his brains, not to mention his fragile ego, but he felt okay otherwise.

"Where's the kid?!" John shrieked, feeling up the passenger seat like a panicking blind man.

"John, she's gone!" Eddie cried, whimpering over his sour luck.

"Not on *my* watch! Not on *my* watch!!" declared John furiously, still having trouble with his heavy eyelids.

Eddie ripped away his seatbelt and used his massive weight to pry open the door, which seemed to have been jammed. He helped John out of the van and they ran off madly in pursuit.

TWIN

I

Orientation

In the break room of indecipherable food odors, dirty coffee thermoses held out before hunched-over binocular-eyed faces, permanently folded down lunch tables and overpriced vending machines, Edgar was met by a small group of despondent soon-to-be-co-workers and the tall, efficiently handsome, suntanned Pierre of understandably noble descent who had greeted them with warm professionalism and was now vigorously handing out obligatory paperwork for them to sign, seemingly in their own blood.

"Welcome to GGI," Pierre said in an accent indeterminably between Vietnamese French and Argentinean Spanish. "Sign these forms and all your dreams will come true!"

The six of them signed faithlessly. They were for the most part in a state of absent abandon.

"Have all of you signed? Good," sang Pierre. "We own you now—no, just kidding!" He laughed heartily to show that he was only kidding (perhaps a little too heartily). "I suppose you wonder where a strange person like me even comes from. I am a Frenchman from Buenos Aires where my fami-lee helps grow grapes for wine. Now I hold a different purpose. But...here comes your Keeper."

A runt of a woman in a gold-colored Gad Growers Incorporated T-shirt went around calmly asking their shirt sizes. She seemed both impossibly very young and very wise. Her large hazel eyes shone with a golden ancientness from a head of lightly radiant ecru skin, alluding to an epic story on each of two great continents. The accent was strengthened rather than shaped by her intricate knowledge of language and there was prescience in her reserved disposition, as well as presence of mind.

Edgar was transfixed by her strange and natural beauty, which was plain as Canyon de Chelly, yet as gapingly primal as the sinkhole near the Mayan ruins of Chichen Itza. She smiled resourcefully. When she came to Edgar, he looked at her with a puzzled expression.

"I-I dunno. How do your sizes run? Medium I guess." He glanced at the fellow across the table who had already asked for a medium. The fellow was thinner than Edgar, although of the same average height. "No, large. Better make it a large."

"Are you sure?" said the woman patiently, digging into the box with untapped energy and throwing Edgar a large red shirt.

Her smile had faded. Edgar thought she had probably mistaken his indecisiveness for mischief. "Sorry, yes. I'm sure. Thanks."

"These are your uniforms," she said addressing the group in a much louder pitch than she had addressed Edgar. "You must wear them always when inside the plant. Additional shirts are available at your own expense. Nine dollars."

"Do we put them on now?" asked the scrawny fellow.

"Yes, put them on," said Pierre, who had returned from the adjoining office that had a large glass window displaying the drab physical mechanics of administrative-type business. "We must hurry and fit you for your factory tuxedos. And here are your time clock identification numbers. Use them to punch out at the end of your shift today so you'll get paid."

"Tuxedos?" asked the fellow.

"How do we do that?" followed a plump young lady from the group who had wasted little time plugging her identifiable numbers into the grid.

"Here, I'll show you," said the petit Keeper. She motioned for everyone to follow her to one of the time clocks attached to a wall at roughly four feet from the ground. Everyone watched as she assimilated the procedure for punching in and out. Edgar looked at the symbols written on a yellow post-it: * 7993 ENT. This was now his number.

"Not to sound forward, but we weren't introduced, were we?" This had been the fellow, addressing their petite host of misery. His eyes were beaming beneath the incandescence.

"The Keeper of Time—that's me. And you're Eric," she said to the fellow, then continued on: "Edgar. Jim. Nancy. Donovan. And you're Darlene." Breaking authoritatively from the conversation, she turned back to the orientation chief. "We have one person too many, Pierre. Edgar arrived just a little after Donovan and will be the standby in case someone..."

But Pierre stopped her with a glance and erratically waved his hand.

"We've decided—Most of you will eventually be working together, in a special group set aside for the juice line," continued The Keeper of Time, addressing the small group. "And you'll also be packaging the gad powder, which will be shipped off to be used for medicinal gel caps, once that process is underway. But for now we need you to work inside with everyone else. Is everyone alright with that? Come with me, please."

"Will we still get overtime?" asked Jim. "That's the reason we wanted to work here. We heard we would be getting overtime."

"Yes, don't worry. We'll have you fill in somewhere else when the juice and powder line isn't going. You'll be working the same hours as the rest of the shift—maybe more."

The group followed The Keeper of Time into the fitting room. A large Latino woman was standing ready next to a pale and scrawny security guard wearing sunglasses.

The Keeper greeted her in Spanish. It seemed the woman's name was Cecilia. Something was explained and Cecilia began handing out gauntlets infused with recycled pieces of ceramic body armor. The gauntlets were medium in weight and designed to leave the palms and fingers exposed. Edgar could only assume that they were an extreme measure in case of mechanical meltdowns where an employee might have to use the gauntlets as shields against explosive ordinance and shrapnel, but was otherwise caught off guard by this choice of equipment.

"You must never leave the factory with armor. You will return them here, where they will be sterilized for future use."

"Okay." they said, almost in unison.

"However, you won't be in need of them today," said The Keeper. "Just be sure to request them here at the equipment station."

The large Latino woman began taking back the armor.

The group followed The Keeper of Time out to a small room of shelves which was a threshold between refectory and factory, filthiness and purity.

Two more scrawny young guards stared ahead stonily from under black Semper Down Security baseball caps. They wore black T-shirts with the emblem of two steel-gray biceps bulging behind forearms and fists crossed to form an X.

Beyond was uncertainty, the abrasive noise of machinery and anticipation of what was to come.

A sign above read NO RECORDING DEVICES OF ANY KIND ALLOWED BEYOND THIS POINT.

"Here, put these on," said The Keeper of Time, hastily handing out yellow rain suits and rubber galoshes to Eric and Jim. To the rest she bequeathed structurally incompetent singles of featherweight white plastic aprons, blue mesh hairnets, and sets of yellow foam earplugs. "You must not pass this point without a hair net and earplugs. Wash your hands as you enter and exit. No exceptions. You'll be dealing with food, so cleanliness is important. There will be no horseplay. Also, do not eat the gads. If you're caught eating gads, you will be terminated. "

She has a cute accent, thought Edgar. There was something unassuming behind it, as in the luring of strangers to a sacrificial death.

They passed through the threshold into the factory for the first time. The noise was stifling, causing Edgar to wedge the earplugs further into his ears. Ahead, against a portion of concrete wall, was a trough of pouring water where there was soap, paper hand towels, trash cans, and boxes of latex gloves. Forklifts zipped around the aisles of machinery with dizzying speed. They were like wingless bees in an industrial hive.

"This way, please," said their attractive little guide. She began saying something else, but Edgar could not make anything out due to the earplugs. He merely followed and learned from the others. The atmosphere was somewhat overwhelming. The factory kept on for more than fifty of yards from both sides: One side contained an array of belt assemblies, large funneled tanks and metal rollercoaster track, but was clearly the route to the warehouse, judging from the trail of pallets and boxes; the northern side was a vast assembly line along a platform of several machines that were shooting out high-pressure air. Beyond the doorways with transparent plastic fringes horrifyingly reminiscent of late 1960s dorm rooms were the sounds of Texas Chainsaw butchery. As if to accentuate Edgar's morbid reception, a metal-cutting saw began sending up sparks from a distant line apparently under modification through the expertise of a grungy mechanic and his entourage.

Cherry-colored Funk

The Keeper of Time motioned for them to follow her through a maze of stools and assembly belts. They could guess by the casualness of productivity that this was some sort of training area. Instead of gads, the bushel-box containers of sheet-metal were full of luscious deep red cherries. About twelve of them had already been brought in and were stacked off to the side of the assembly. A guy wearing a yellow rain suit and wielding a lance-like tennis racket was preparing a large steel tank full of cold water for the dumping of fruit. The feed tank operator, as he was called, stepped down from the platform and chatted with the forklift driver who had just dropped off another container of submerged cherries and was waiting for the ritual to commence.

The herd of novice workers headed toward a corner of human movement where a line appeared amidst cold wetness and confusion.

Again The Keeper spoke, alluring in her tight gold shirt, and again Edgar caught none of what was being said. He pulled the plug out of his right ear enough to hear voices over the constant swoosh of the factory.

"That's about it, but don't worry," continued The Keeper. "You'll work no more than four hours today. We don't expect miracles. Just do your best and learn what you can from the others. Yell if you need me."

A supervisor came out from the wetness and placed them along the line; Eric, Jim, and Donovan were given shovels and told some instructions; Edgar, Nancy, and Darlene were placed on the sorting line where they were told to sit atop wet metal stools and wait for some kind of signal. The supervisor left and then came back with white plastic buckets which were distributed and placed at each sorter's feet.

"Just take out the bad ones," the supervisor said. "Look for abnormalities; Rot; Discoloration; Anything that shouldn't be there."

A loud bell rang, much like an old-style wind-up alarm clock, and the machinery became animate. A white belt smelling vaguely of bleach rolled by and soon became dotted with cherries. The crew went to work. A creeping feeling of inhumanness invaded their bodies as vulnerable joints began to ache from the cold. Noses sniffled as mucus began to form. It was perfect weather for the entire gamut of mild animalistic sicknesses. The cherries crept by dizzyingly, giving them a taste of what was to come. The work was tedious, the workers bored. They scrutinized and picked, removing the bad from the good like hesitant judges in the afterlife. Rot, discoloration, smallness, deformity: all were plucked from the belt and dropped into buckets with a plunk. As the pace quickened, the buckets filled and the juice of the pitted, dark-red cherries spilled onto the painted concrete floor like sweet, watered-down blood. Beneath the pitting machines, the torn flesh of the fruit stacked up into hills of unmarked graves, plopping from the machinery like dense droplets of fiber. Workers equipped with hoses sprayed underneath and the remaining trash was shoveled into streaming sanitation gutters leading first to the sewers and then to a great furnace.

For Edgar and the others, it felt as if the human quality had left them. They worked like flawed robots, performing their jobs with an emotional decision process that differed from problem to problem. Just as the misery seemed to go on eternally, the day ended in bitter-sweetness and their placid faces were full of pity for each other as the orientation crews unraveled and headed back through the quagmire of industry to the break room and eventually outside to freedom. But it was only temporary.

II

David Finds His Place

Swish, swish, slosh, went the squeegee. The slimy pits the size of almonds were shoved into the gutter, where a gush of cold water washed them away. More pits fell from the machinery to replace them. Plop, plop, plop. There was no end to the waste.

David was one of the guys in the yellow raincoat and black rubber galoshes. He had crawled beneath the pitting machines and was suffering an endless toil, cold and wet and noise-deafened. The pain in his ankle had gone away, thanks to the aspirin, but now his head was beginning to throb. It made him feel ultra-present in this private field of existence. He took the hose and sprayed the concrete to see how long he could keep the place clean: Less than a second. Already the pits were falling to their doom. In his wet and dreary boredom, David likened the process to an abortion. The fruits were being forced to squeeze out their unborn children and they were washing away to rot in some mass grave behind the factory. Of course, the seeds were very much alive and completely capable of becoming trees someday, under the right conditions, or, alternatively, to become organic heating pads under the guise of teddy bears, but under the influence of gloom David cast upon them a dark shadow. He imagined them screaming out in terror at the cruelty of the world they had been robbed of living in. Highly sensitive agents of subatomic particles unaffected by the forces of the known universe were on their way to investigate and to hold accountable those responsible for crimes against love. The tables would be turned, the next time the lotus petals of human perception bubbled to the surface, thought David. It was not a very rational picture, but the macabre imagery kept him from forgetting where he was and from banging his head against the jagged steel grates of the platform. After what seemed like eons, the other cleaning guy appeared from beyond perception and told David to go on break. Suddenly, like a diabolical bell, he craved a smoke and instinctively felt for his shirt pocket. Luckily he had been smart and had placed the device in a plastic sandwich bag. There were five or six drops left in the bottle; he could not remember. Carlos had the rest, but was assigned to work in another building and David was still not sure how to get there. It was somewhere in the back, near the piles of aborted tree fetuses.

Manneken Pis was a Belgian brand of heavily watered down liquid nicotine designed to make smokers quit the habit, mixed with Henbane and licorice which could be cheaply smuggled in from Mexico at 1% of the price. They could then be inhaled right through the cellulose acetate filter of an electronic cigarette. It was with some irony that, in a world where many cheap and deadly drugs were readily available for everyone, even school children, the Mayan *Siyar* had been nearly taxed out of existence. You would sooner find a Crack smoker than someone enjoying an authentic cigarette or a cigar. True, they were addictive, gave people lung cancer, tar-colored skin, yellow teeth, and made them radiate uranium through the added mineral apatite, but anyone would have to admit that they were better for you than crystallized freebase cocaine. And now everything was a façade, and the schools and universities and barracks and courthouses and especially the factories were just a hollow shell of purpose, just a world of string-less marionettes pretending to do things that once constituted life. The great institutions of the age had let pride, greed, and hatred rip away their deep sense of humanity and the entire world had suffered for it. The Corporate Imperators held the field from a distance, wrapped in the red and gold flag of SPQR. There were no people with real courage to overrun the hollowed walls and break down illusions, to once again become primitive cavalry on horses of resistance, charging naked into battle against insurmountable foes and collecting heads frozen in fear. There was no one to set the world straight and to reinstate the peoples' rights to live and die as they should, to snidely exclaim as potently as Brennus did before Rome: "Woe to the vanquished, for the conquered have no rights!"

David's thoughts had become so deep, dark, and uncharacteristically ingenious, and felt so good in their sinisterly appeal for vengeance, that it frightened him. "*What have I done different?*" he wondered, guardedly utilizing an intelligence that seemed to have slipped in from a possessive alien force. Had he eaten something that had gone bad? Suddenly it struck him: There was a pungent smell to the air, an acidic aroma, which momentarily made him wonder: *"Could such a thing be possible…that is, could it really be that this fruit…have I caught a disease down here?!"* But then the confidence was gone and he was left feeling very foolish. Perhaps some medicine was in order, David decided, but then changed his mind. He watched the miraculous fruit glisten along the belt of gauntlets as feminine hands plucked away the impurities—to think he had accused a fruit of possession! How the priest would love catching wind of that one! The entire parish would demand that he be sent to a monastery at once! Just picturing it made him laugh.

David made his way out of the factory, through the break room, and stood just outside the door from the main entrance. He checked the battery on his e-cig to see if it was charged. How strange that everything pleasurable in life was ruined by a paranoid society and made a mockery of through electronics. Maybe the gads were right: It was as if a person was not allowed to die creatively anymore. And for David everything was the same; he reflected wretchedly that even in the old days when he was twelve that Carlos had taken possession of their only carton of *Vae Victis* brand death wands, which they eventually sold to classmates in singles. The packs were covered in photographs of smokers' lung and captions like "Smoking is lethal; breathe smog as a healthy alternative" and "Let us kill you with tap water". That was almost six years ago, and he was still running after Carlos.

"Wait a minute," he mumbled to the summer winds, *"Vae Victis*? That couldn't have been it…"

The electronic cigarette was lit of its own accord, once switched on at the base, and David placed the mouthpiece to his lips with a shaking hand. The shaking stopped and David took the smokeless fire inward. It was all that kept him going sometimes.

The door opened and suddenly his name was called. He looked through the absence of smoke from his exhilarating exhale to see a woman in a gold-colored T- shirt and tight blue jeans standing with a clipboard pressed against her abdomen.

"Are you David Hernando?"

"Yes, that's right," David responded apprehensively. He remembered her from orientation during which they watched a lengthy and very boring video on industrial safety procedures. She had said she was the Timekeeper or something.

"How is everything, David?"

"Good. And you?"

"Doing terrific," said the woman known as The Keeper of Time, "and where are you from?"

"El Paso, pretty señorita," said David. "I think I remember you from the asparagus. You were working in the office. I remember seeing such a lovely woman when I was paid. You know, you smell like a cactus flower-"

"That's sweet of you, David, but I am a *señora* and my husband is a very large man—there he is, in fact."

David swallowed his own embarrassment, which refused to go down without a fight, and looked frightfully at the figure climbing out of an old orange forklift, the figure of a fattened warrior who was significantly armored and was carrying an equally well armored scarecrow that was missing everything below the waist. "So that's your husband! Sweet Mother! My apologies, Keeper. It was a very long bus ride."

David tried his best to make amends, but The Keeper had vanished and reappeared within the massive, flabby arms of her husband, where she could barely be seen. Together, they were the most noble of mountain peons, a classic Mexican village wellspring, in the romantic sense.

David continued to smoke. He had only three nicotine droplets left in his pocket. If he lived to see the end of the day, he would be smart to get another bottle from Carlos. The Henbane would not hold him back forever.

The Keeper gestured towards David with her eyes and the large husband beside her laughed and gestured shamefully with his thick right pointing finger.

David gulped the air of his own fear as the man approached. He could see the eyes and it was like staring into the face of a smiling bear. But The Keeper's husband had no serious interest in David and the swing of his chubby arm was not intended for David's red face or fragile head, but for opening the heavy door and making his way inside to the break room.

"David," said The Keeper of Time. "So everything is fine?"

"I still live, it seems."

"Don't look so depressed," The Keeper said in Spanish. She grabbed David's arm with kindness. "I just wanted to make things clear. How are you getting on? I'm impartial, but our policy is to keep our workers happy. A few positions are still open. Perhaps you would rather join my husband in the orchards, or lift boxes?"

"I would like that—boxes, that is. Cleaning is honest work, but I get bored and my thoughts tend to drift."

"I'll see to it, David Hernando."

III

The Woman Escaped

"I could go anywhere, but what choice do I have?" Antiope thought aloud as she rode her brand new bike to the apartment. It was now late evening. Since the accident, she had driven all the way down to Grand Rapids and back, some 300 miles. The battered van performed as well as could be expected; still, things had not worked out the way she had hoped they would. The train which she had hoped would take her to Chicago had been crawling with security. She instead had had to fool a towing company into retrieving first the van and then her alleged baby—whom she insisted had not been on the hood where she had left him just a moment ago!—from the depths of the Grand River while she had gone to get better phone reception. After Antiope had lowered the boom on the tow truck and unhooked the chains, she quietly opened the driver-side door and left the money on the seat. Although it seemed crass to her at the present moment, she had meant them no harm by this deception. It was simply a matter of remaining incognito. The engine of the van was remarkably resilient and had started right away (The tow truck driver was very surprised). Minus a plastic bumper, she could have gone out West like she had always dreamed of, or South to Austin, or East to the smog-made aureoles of the moon above the rapacious industrial cities, and then on to Europe and Asia. The world had opened up, but she was afraid. The money she had saved over her lifetime was miserably limited. She was taking a big risk. And even though big risks were necessary for big changes, she was having doubts. Every part of this wide open country was loneliness and she dared not go to Bermuda, or to the Academy, where the interceptors would be waiting like half-ton berserk linebackers to shovel her deep into artificial turf. There was a simpler option, not without risk, that would allow her to build up capital until the emptiness subsided. It was a little bit dishonest, but the unwilling benefactor owed the world a favor.

The wound on her right hand, where the microchip had been, throbbed like an analog computer. The organic timepiece—her own beating heart—was wise to point it out. She had forgotten to pick up antiseptic at the store and had used water, relying on Neosporin and bandages from the first aid kit. She hoped that it would not become infected.

The city of Grand Rapids had hustled and bustled far below the expressway bridges and sharp, jutting cathedral spires as the escaped woman had contemplated the possibilities in stunted mirroring skyscrapers. Again she had felt the anticipation, the fear.

The Monstrosso Corporation's Duck Lake Academy had filled the void with terrible ease, since its appearance as a permanent domicile only a few years ago. The place boasted meals served hot and light housekeeping. All of her siblings were holed up there like cozy little town mice. Yet it was far from normal and she would resist such poisonous contentment until her dying breath. She wondered just whom they were hoping to fool. No, Antiope could not let them defeat her with their evil spells. She had continued on, thinking.

The unfamiliar wonders were boundless. Heavy construction was a city of its own. The rebar stuck out of the foundations like the bones of ruinous castles. Then there appeared flat fields of indentured medieval emptiness and the smell of manure. She had pulled off into a roadside park to study the blueprints of her salvation, losing an entire hour, as if maps were some great novel. The roads on the maps were like dark veins over the impression of the United States, stretching even into Canada and Mexico. She studied the outlines with her fingers, this great fantasy of possibilities. Which door would she open first? There were many paths. Many strings of tiny, earth-worn feet led the baroness of adventure through rabbit holes in time. The destinations were endless, but for her the parallels of chance all led to the same narrow place; because the poor excuse for a traveler failed to challenge these definitions set forth within her own mind. The would-be traveler was afraid.

She headed back, to Gamesh, thinking that perhaps it was the last place they would look. Fortune had smiled upon her after she drove the injured van to the nearest used car dealership, after hours, and abandoned it in the sales lot with the keys in the ignition. She tried to sneak into the dealership through an unlocked window to call a cab—her phone was with a robotic monkey in a sailboat at Calypso Bay Resort in New Orleans—but the alarm was tripped and she had to cut through the woods along the highway. It seemed she was in for a grizzly weekend adventure, all alone in the wilderness with only a bag of trail mix and a warped ham sandwich. That was when she happened upon a traveling salesman riding a bicycle attached to a bicycle trailer.

"Ride the Plank's constant!" he had said with great oration. "Buy a Zeno's Arrow™ brand bike and experience the joys of Quantum Pedaling™!"

There just happened to be one in metallic floral lavender that went well with her pink running shoes. She purchased it for \$188.88, thus easing the load for the traveling young Ojibwa.

The long days were a blessing as she rode hungrily towards the darkening outskirts of Gamesh using the clarity of her brain's map[10]. The destination was easy. At the nearing twilight hour there was only one place to go. The key, which Antiope's mother had slipped to her when the agents arrived, was sewn into a small compartment of the backpack. The address was on the attached note: Silver Lining Estates, 851 Senior Haven Dr, Apt 9. It apparently belonged to Tom Cornelius Wesson III, executive vice president of GGI. The story was complicated, but as Antiope understood it, Tom was somewhat of a chronic womanizer and had rented the apartment in his deceased grandfather's name to avoid detection by his wife. Antiope's mother had taken the liberty of having a key duplicated. That was all years ago, when Antiope was just a child. There was a chance, of course, that some pathetic soul or other would be living there as the current sleaze, or some armed guard waiting to blow any potential squatters away with a laser-guided Derringer, but it was worth checking out.

The urban world was a blur, thanks to Quantum Pedaling™ technology, and the easy feeling of cutting through the air by one's initiative along the toxic residual dream-stuff of the all

---

[10] During art class, Antiope enjoyed making mosaics depicting any map she could get her hands on; thus she saw the world as one big patchy montage; many of them had been confiscated by the art teacher, but their memory held.

encompassing morass of evil was empowering. Antiope admired the sun melting into the left horizon as it sent lavender hues spilling along the herds of clouds far to the other end of the world. The western sky was pink and violet and almost cloudless. She liked watching the birds as they flew through the lancing corpuscular rays leading almost midway to the heavens. What a thought, to be free even from the road. She was partway there. The asphalt rose and fell, connecting the divisions of the known world. What was sought was eventually found.

She slowed to make her turn and was exposed to the suburbanite reality of the dream. It unnerved her to think of the irreversible devastation caused by the vast network of gases and chemicals, the menagerie of small furry critters that infiltrated the heavily irrigated lawns of peasant estates only to die a slow, painful death from designer poisons they had mistaken for food. She, too, was headed for disaster, as was the entire galaxy.

A row of brown to faded yellow-green American Arborvitae made a privacy screen along the main road. There were orange hemlock bushes under the windows of the single storey apartments, within the mulched landscaping areas, and along the wheelchair-accessible sidewalks. Several maples spaced apart neatly outside a vast yellow lawn had somehow survived. A rusty water hog lay silent in the weeds near the fairway of the Par 3 course.

The complex had been a retirement community until the golf course almost dried up, and now it was a mixture of the elderly and the young impoverished classes. Some diehard golfers in tweed and plaid outfits still hung around the golf pro shop out near the first green. It was probably a warm-up until they could continue their golf memberships at a full course. Antiope had heard of such things, but had never played any sport except kick ball and lake-style Marco Polo.

The first building was nearest the office, and it was in the very last and furthest away where Antiope found Apartment #9—the fifth, in an unorthodox order of numbering. Each building housed eight apartments and they were all wheel-chair accessible. There was an old Honda motorcycle, a spotless Crimson Pearl 2003 Buick LeSabre, and a pink Hello Kitty mini car parked outside and the lot was otherwise vacant. Antiope hauled the bicycle inside the main entryway with a cheaply designed vaulted ceiling and listened at the door before trying the key. No one seemed to be living there, but the place was a mess. There were pieces of broken furniture, articles of clothing, golf clubs, books, and dishes thrown everywhere. Someone had apparently gotten very angry at some point and had trashed the place.

TRIPLET

I

The Real Work Begins

"Does everyone have a hair net? You, there, with the hairy arms! Get yourself some arm sleeves! They're on the bottom shelf of the pantry! Hurry up, now!"

Orange-shirted assistants and silver-shirted supervisors worked feverishly to ensure that everyone had the proper equipment. Sanitation, they stressed. Sanitation was *key*. They were to remain as clean as possible. They were to wash their hands before entering and exiting the factory floor. They were to wash them twice more after visiting the restroom. Workers were to ignore the dusty forklifts traveling around semi-autonomously on toxic wheels, and also the dirty tools being shoved into greasy assemblage gears. That was nobody's business. Latex, chlorinated water, unnatural plastic bags, would keep the earthen Franken-fruit chastised, would keep the germs of humanity out. "Everyone, get in position!"

The atmosphere cultivated depression. Everything was gloomy, wet, and cold.

"FNGs[11]!" the mechanics whispered, pointing and jeering and pulling at their dirty outfits like zoo monkeys. They snipped and snarled at the flanks of strangers with their insider jokes and their disorderly eyes.

---

[11] Obscene office acronym for a name categorizing a new person who joins a team, tribe, or organization.

"Pay no attention," one supervisor said, smirking at the sheep in wolves' clothing. The name on her silver shirt said Ruth. She was pale and nearing middle age and her silvery brown hair was unnaturally curled, lifting frothily from under the hairnet. This Ruth darted around, turned to them again and said, "Follow me, please."

Other supervisors appeared. One by one, they put the workers in place and awaited the Pavlovian bells. The assistants scurried busily around the factory, involving themselves only with the people in the right-colored shirts, people of importance, checking the hammers, the gears and levers, reporting to supervisors, checking the positions of the workers, talking to buckets mistaken for synchronous minds, to the plastic trays of quality control persons, to shovels, until finally The Keeper of Time gave the signal to begin.

Within minutes, the machinery was in motion. Everyone waited for dripping wet assemblage of vibrating parts to show the first signs of a successful hunt. The fruit factory was a climactic shelf of the ancient gathering system, the apex of the modern industrial harvest as it stood. A mere paycheck was their reward for simulating the survival of the group. For minimum wage plus overtime they could live in a mobile home, scout around the supermarket after hours until the food ran out. Edgar's mind drifted as he thought this, and it occurred to him that humanity had become a chicken coup; the fresh workers of tomorrow would hatch at any moment. If someone refused to participate, they could be replaced with the hyperactive strokes of a keyboard. Mere millions were waiting to be born into a multifaceted slavery. The Orwellian eyes of this Chaplinesque establishment called life were watching intently, still scratching their thick heads as to why so many geniuses were hiding out in the wilderness. They were getting short on ideas. Was it a portent? Not to their elitist way of thinking. Hunting and gathering was where it was at. Barter and trade was the next step up, and then commerce. At the current level, they could simply steal the hard-earned capital of the rodent-like masses with the push of a button, participating in something called a *stock market*. They needn't know that such capital ever existed. They should just remain dumb and starve like conscientious swine (of course, though, while in any country of manners, they would never starve—unless no one was around to witness it). For humanity as a whole, the modern replacement was crude and artificial. It was time for something better.

The machines suddenly stopped. Several impatient minutes passed before they started up again. Everyone waited until the passage was green with golden fruit. The quality control people in their clean plastic aprons rushed to the mouths of the pitting machines with their plastic dishwashing bins and waited at the chain-metal tongues for the first sample to roll out. The workers along the belt sorted like mad until the gads thinned out into a steady and manageable flow.

Edgar soon found himself within the inner throes of the battle and he worked to pick the damaged ones out as they left the pitters and traveled down before him. He felt motion sickness as he fixated his gaze upon the movement. The belt was so white with bleach that it gleaned beneath the light fixtures hanging above. The gads utilized this artificial radiation to their advantage, mesmerizing the workers like the smoldering embers of a dying star, a force almost trapped within. Edgar turned away to steady himself and the room spun angrily. It was as if he was some kind of third-rate astronaut from the distant future.

Around him in the damp glaze were his fellow sorters— young and old, misfits, migrants, immigrants, the forgotten sons and daughters of the revolution—propped up on wet metal chairs with their partial gauntlets creaking as the white plastic ballistic shields hung like aprons from their craning necks.

The uppity quality control personnel sat chatting at their shiny alchemical stainless steel countertop for minutes on end. They appeared suddenly amidst the fray and occasionally edged between the sorters, coldly pushing their way in to the short tongue-like conveyors extending from the bowels of the pitting machines, and swished their latex-covered hands around in their gad samples enigmatically. They were on the lookout for pits, mainly, and who knew what divination they claimed to have read from these assortments.

A disproportionately high number of men swept, sprayed, and shoveled the pits, leaves, and other debris into the gutters, conscious of the dangers lurking there—a rat hole, if there ever was one. It was like a crude Roman city, the way the grated sewers were built into the floor to carry the runoff to the impoverished outskirts. The assembly line was constantly wet, coldly misting from the spray of hoses, making the workers ill. Other than that, things didn't seem so bad.

There were people up on the damp, grated platform of welded steel, contorted as they operated and examined their vibrating machines. This was where a majority of the noise was coming from, and why the earplugs were especially warranted. These were the pitting machines. They looked like ancient appliances welded on top of the steel grates of the platform where something resembling engines could be seen through the transparent sections of ballistic glass with their antiquated turbines cranking. These strange mechanisms carried the fresh gads along on a chain of thin metal pipes secured into a belt of grids and blew out the pits using high velocity air shot through Smith & Wesson type nozzles. They were the pinnacle of mechanical engineering, maybe half-a-century ago, but were now merely fascinating.

"Loud, aren't they?" the woman next to him said. She was middle-aged, her graying hair wound into a bun.

"Very."

"A coat of rubber insulates the insides of the machines to counter the noise pollution. But that's not for us."

"What do you mean?"

"I'm Jaclyn," she said, offering a protected hand.

They shook gauntlets. "Edgar," the protagonist said. "You've worked here before?"

"Last year," Jaclyn said. "I worked cherries before that, twelve years."

"So what were you saying about noise pollution?"

"These gads are sensitive to extra movements, waves, temperature. They use the noise to immobilize them in there. Otherwise they might bypass the machines."

How the heck do they do that?"

"Don't know. They leap I guess, like those jumping beans."

"There's bugs inside them?"

"Don't think so. They just move. These gads are odd. You know the story? Well, rumor has is they were cared for by Malthusian monks who used them for a medicinal elixir. No one knew about them for centuries. The monks would sing chants to the trees they kept hidden within the monastery walls. They called them the God Fruit. But that was before the secret was discovered and they were stolen. Terrible, what happened."

"You mean probably the *Carthusian* monks. They do the Elixir Vegetal stuff."

"Oh, probably."

"Not to be a nerd. Malthusian and medicine paints an interesting picture though. Who stole them?"

"The CIA—at least, that's what I've heard. But don't quote me on that. I have a daughter in the marines. I'd hate for anyone to think I was unpatriotic."

"Hey, I understand. I was in the Army."

"If you don't mind me asking, they send you to the war?"

"Yep. Buktu's Well."

"My girl was in Korea. But she's stateside now. Haven't seen her since Christmas."

"Yeah, it's hard on family."

"No employment here anyway."

"True. Here is about it, and I barely got in this place."

"Really? That's what's sickening. They hire all these migrants before the locals. That just isn't right. Charity begins at home. But soon enough they'll bring in the criminals. That's even worse."

Jaclyn talked for awhile about the factory until the old woman to her left asked her something and they began talking.

Edgar's eyes grew foggy. There was nothing but the job for him now. He hummed a tune that had gotten stuck in his head and immersed his gauntleted hands into the gads. He grabbed the bad ones and dropped them into a bucket that was situated near his right foot. Every little while the sweepers and shovelers would stop and would come over and dump the buckets into a disposal tank that was situated against the wall of the factory. Once that was filled, a forklift would come and take it away to the sanitation department to be burned. This went like clockwork. The entire factory was a timepiece or a hovel of ants. Although the machinery was the living entity of the operation, there was no compassion there. It would just as well slice a finger as a stem and nothing would be felt. The people were themselves the gears and springs of this contraption.

They were becoming robots over time. The soul was unwelcome and left hovering like a sickness. Edgar penetrated the immediate grounds with his thoughts. Where was the separation between man and machine, he wondered. When did it occur? The mind seemed the only legitimate rebel as it wandered and searched for a way out. The body was content to be moving. It would eventually grow tired, but not out of anger. It felt a kinship with the arms and shoulders of the assembly.

A Breach in the Contract

Steadily, the glistening gads moved through the assemblage of processing. Edgar already held a vague understanding of how the processing was done: In the orchards, where the crews of about thirteen worked night and day to harvest the fruit, a hydraulic tractor was used to shake the gads onto tarps held tightly by at least four people from where they were allowed to roll onto a conveyor of a machine that the tarps were attached to and which was driven by someone down the orchard rows; that same tarp machine collected the cherries in square metal tanks full of cold water that were positioned at the end of the conveyor and that were then fork-lifted onto a truck which held about eight tanks each; the trucks brought the tanks to a cooling pad just outside the factory where they stayed for several hours at 48 degrees Fahrenheit; from the cooling pad, they were brought into the factory using forklifts, dumped into a large tank of water (shaped like an indented upside-down pyramid), washed and skimmed of debris, brushed so they would sit upright, sent through a bladed de-stemming machine, and carried within moving plastic catch pockets; from there they were forced into the pitting machines and rolled onto one of several white conveyor belts for sorting; the fruit was then tested for temperature, sweetened, boxed, labeled, and sent to the warehouse where they could be shipped. Edgar knew the process well and had years ago worked both the orchard and factory of the now defunct cherry industry.

Suddenly Edgar was tapped on the shoulder by some guy he'd never met.

"Break!" the guy said, taking the now vacant seat just before Edgar's, where Jaclyn had been, and giving him the sign with his two fists extended and rotating back and forth at a slant.

He had been daydreaming and had not noticed the changes in personnel. They were being rotated on the assembly line for mandatory fifteen-minute breaks every half hour. It was his turn. The large industrial room spun as he removed himself from the metal stool. Why not nice cushioned stools for the workers, he wondered in agony. It was difficult to navigate through a tempestuous ocean with only a sore bottom for an anchor, but he managed to swagger down to the quality control area, passing the stainless-steel counter running under the upper assembly parts of leaking water, down the traffic-heavy aisle between the first row of sorters and a concrete wall, and on toward the hand-washing station and the break room.

It felt weird to remove the gauntlets and the ear plugs and to experience a normal threshold of noise. The break room was a bustling mess. A discordant choir of conversations clashed with the individual movements of temporary needs and wants, the vigorous punching of a plastic button, the taciturn telling of a joke, the desire for a bag of junk, for a can of sludge, to wave a plastic fork in the air as one spoke, to microwave a burrito, to violently slap one's wet rubber gloves down on the floor, to punch the air. These things were chaos in motion, a kind of weird human pattern.

Edgar found his company debit tracking card and walked to one of the vending machines. There were many choices. Something called "Sea Chips" caught his attention. They were an algae snack made in Nova Scotia. He punched in the code for a small bag of them and gathered it up and then moved in for a nasty carbonated beverage in hopes of absorbing the caffeine. Now he was ready to have a seat at one of the fold-down table and chair assemblages. The tables were very crowded. Edgar was careful not to look around with food in his mouth and instead looked down at nothing and tried to focus on a goal for his future.

There was very little of interest going on. Drenched workers came in and out from the restrooms and from the factory, sometimes digging into paper bags or backpacks from a large three-tiered shelf built into the wall near the entrance.

A farmer-looking guy in overalls came in from outside and asked for someone. "Need to see Tom," he said. "Have a few accident reports for him to sign."

"Nothing serious I hope," said one of the secretaries.

Another woman scurried off to retrieve this Tom fellow, while the third kept busy at the computer's keyboard.

"Not yet. Give it a few days though..." said the farmer.

"Bad this year, huh?"

"The worst yet. Far worse than last season."

"Can't anything be done?"

"I don't reckon so. Not really," sighed the farmer. "Not if we want to stay in business. Would take seven years to pull everything out and plant anew. I don't have that kind of money."

"Doesn't the armor help?"

"Sure does," said the farmer. "But them trees are smart. They know right where to hit a fella. I tell you, I've never seen anything like it. There's medieval warfare goin' on out in them orchards."

They were interrupted by the sudden appearance of an important-looking man wearing pressed black dress pants and a golden shirt with a burgundy and black golf-motif tie.

"Mister Ted Sullivan!" cheered the man. He shook the farmer's wrist with both hands. There was a deceitful look in his eye.

"Need your signature, Tom," said the farmer. "Had a few accidents this morning. I'm here to file the reports and get these boys taken care of."

"Why certainly!" laughed Tom, changing toward a resentful look. He snatched the clipboards from the farmer, looked them over briefly, and quickly signed them. "Is everything under control, then?" Tom sighed, shoving the clipboards off to a secretary while continuing to engage the farmer. But suddenly he was aware of a breach in the flow of their privileged information.

"Control isn't a word I'd use, Tom," said Sullivan the farmer.

"We usually let you-know-who handle these things."

"You-know-who ain't allowed on my property; not after all I been through!"

"Now, Mister Sullivan..."

"We've always done our own farming, but…this just ain't right. I won't put my boys through this. It ain't what I signed up for."

"Come right on in here," said Tom forcefully, looking around at the darting eyes and ears of the vacuous break room nervously before pulling Farmer Sullivan in by the shoulder and closing two of the office doors behind them.

Nor was that supposed breach lost on the employees in the break room; everyone was rigid and silent in their respective corners of fear.

As a new trickle of employees came in for their break, the moon-like clock shone from the wall like a fractured spotlight. Edgar noticed to his dismay that he was already five minutes late. He drank what he could and threw the remains in the trash as he suited up and hurried back through the threshold.

At Which Point the First Shots Were Fired

"You're late!" scolded the supervisor when she apprehended Edgar on his way back to the line. "Didn't the Keeper tell you? Its fifteen minutes for these breaks and half-an-hour for lunch. When you're late you set the entire line back. Be on time from now on."

Filled with embarrassment, Edgar found a new seat nearer to the end of the conveyor belt. The next person had apparently already been relieved, probably by the supervisor. Jaclyn was a ways down in the middle and Edgar found himself among strangers. Some of them acted a bit peculiar, he thought. One guy focused intently on the gads moving past him on the conveyor belt, scrutinizing each one as if his eyes were precision lasers that measured each and every fruit for perfection. He was some kind of machine, yet his face was plush with life. It was as if, in a very detached state, sorting fruit was his passion. *He can have it*, thought Edgar, who was once again feeling the motion sickness. The pouring wet floor seemed to be horizontal, pulling itself up from the far wall which stood somewhere beyond the first line where the forklifts occasionally whizzed by with their orange lights flashing. The only things keeping him from wanting to shoot himself was the thought of a paycheck and the fact that the boredom had pulled his mind psychotically towards a semi-eternal dream state. It must have been so, the way this fruit sparkled like wet fiery opals of the abyss. They would ignite from deep within until the artificial incandescence hanging creepily from the rafters caught just the right patch of wet skin, exposing any inconsistencies. Edgar pulled back, plucking absently at what seemed like rot and tossing back those he had picked by mistake. He dropped the bad ones into a bucket with a thump. The noise was excruciating, a crude industrial orchestra of socialist realism. He could feel his ears pleading to have the plugs repositioned, but these things were difficult with ballistic gauntlets and latex gloves. His eyes wandered as he pried wonderingly into the lot of others to see how they coped. The wise ones communicated to their neighbors while others listened to music through a tiny ear piece. But what alarmed him was the number of sorters from the third line, the line just parallel to his stiff backside, whose actions and appearance were the spitting image of Old Laser Eyes (as he had secretly named the guy who seemed to think he was born to this tedious and bizarre line of work). There were at least eight of them, although most of them were ladies, and not all of them really looked identical, but only probably seemed identical because of the sorter outfits. A similar identity problem often occurred in the Army. But nonetheless Edgar found it creepy. Others had noticed this as well, and, noticing that he had noticed, gave him a quick wide-eyed look.

And then it happened. The guy just ahead of Edgar on the second line began acting strangely. First he giggled to himself, and then at Edgar, and then erupted like a Mad Hatter, only to calm himself again. He looked back at Edgar in derangement. "They told me to and I did it!" he said.

"You ate one?" whispered Edgar.

"No, I ate my goddamn shoe! Of course I ate one! I was hungry! And it's wonderful!! Just wonderful!! It's everything they promised!"

"Um, who...who are you referring to?" Edgar inquired discreetly, slipping from his stool while trying to lean over.

"The voices. Little men of the fruit..." the worker said, giggling like a ferret. "They speak in colors and smells...to warn us...to free us from the oppression of industry...the eager shackles of dependency which our overlords lock to our ankles at birth...to control us...to keep us from reaching our true potential..." The worker held his tongue and ridiculed Edgar with renewed precision. "Wait a minute...*don't you hear them*? Maybe I shouldn't even be *talking to you*..." With a look of sheer panic eclipsing the worker's paranoid face, he crept back, bumping into the sorter behind him, and then grabbed at the rolling belt of moving fruit, getting as many chilled and stoneless edibles as he could to tumble into his trembling grasp, and plopped an entire handful into his mouth (Strangely, they began to glisten and change colors). He mumbled something while chewing with his mouth open and bits of half- chomped gad fell onto his apron and then plopped to the floor. Everyone was staring at the deranged young man by this point, but he paid them little attention and seemed to have forgotten just where he was. He slithered down from his chair and was soon on the floor dancing and kicking with laughter.

An extremely focused quality control person in a white apron tripped and fell over the man's legs as she hurried to the mouth of the next pitting machine and her plastic tray went flying ahead of her. Someone yelled and soon the guards came running from every direction. A few sorters rushed over to help the fallen girl, but most stayed put, either working towards inhuman perfection or lost in day-dream-land.

The crazy sorter who had been Edgar's neighbor just a few minutes ago skipped down one way and then the other, laughing through the gathering crowd, stomping past the girl whom he had sent tumbling, and then came back for a second run. "Those dirty rotten... Take that! And that! Ha ha!! Look at me! Look!" he said, wildly extending the palms of his hands. "I'm a wizard! I'm a magic wizard! Didn't want no Rafferty to have one?! Well, I got one! I got plenty! Hey, look! Hey! Little fruit man! Come back here, you! Look! Look at me! Hey, you little man! Hey!" And suddenly the guy was up on the belt.

It was all Edgar could do to avoid being kicked in the head.

The Discoloration Incident

Uno. Dos. Tres. One by one, the boxes were sealed, labeled, and stacked on a pallet. Four. Five. Six. They came down on rollers built into a track specifically designed for such a purpose. A machine applied stickers to them with code numbers in daily sequence. These labels had to be seen while the boxes sat stacked on the pallet before the entire stack was wrapped in plastic. This ensured proper identification during storage. Each box was exactly 20 pounds of sugar-coated fruit. A plastic bag ensured preservation until they could be stuck in a freezer and shipped off to their destination.

David found the work relatively easy, except that his coworkers hated him. One was a large muscular neo-Nazi skinhead with tattoos on his arms of an Iron Cross and the heading "Weiss und Stolz" in bold black Latin letters and the other was a young blond Polish-American militiaman whose hair was just as short as the skinhead's. The young National Guardsman was called Pete and he was the son of the GGI head of finance. David only knew this because the migrants found it helpful to establish a makeshift intelligence network wherever they went so as to know who was paying them to do things and who was not—such things happened more often than one would think.

"How do you like it, Adolf?" said Pete, making sure to hold his chest out in a masculine manner. Although in respectable shape, he was puny next to the recently paroled skinhead.

"I don't even notice," bragged Adolf, nodding his thick head. "Tell them to turn it up a notch."

Pete cracked out a sharp laugh while he helped another box over the rollers. He would pass them down to one and then the other. His good mood fizzled the moment he made eye contact with David, however, and then it turned false. There was a hint of fear. He seemed a little bit nervous.

"How many pallets will we usually do in a day?" asked David when he took the box. He was ignored. Despite the lack of faith weighing on him, David tried his best to please his employers, which came naturally. A vision of his mother and then the adobe brick El Paso Catholic Church of the Sacred Virgin came to his mind as happened every time his family honor was at stake, which was rarely. But David took the time to straighten the boxes on the pallet and to make sure the labels were visible. If he knew anything, it was that tidiness was important.

Adolf was a sloppy stacker. Every layer or so, Pete would come around and shift things into position. Otherwise David had to straighten them and would feel Adolf's mental wrath. Every time such a thing occurred, Adolf's forehead would turn as red as a tomato and the mangy patch of stubble where his hair receded prematurely shone like a bedpan while attempting to mingle with the thicker portions of bleached hair-stumps. The man obviously had problems, even if he chose to ignore them.

"And how are you doing today?" David asked a tall Asian woman in her late twenties. Her skin was a lemon chiffon color, moderately yellow to pink, and she wore a white laboratory overcoat. There were wrinkles under her tired eyes. She smiled weakly and said nothing as she made her way past the box assembly and off to a large conical cauldron where she climbed a ladder and looked inside at the contents. It was somewhat a mystery to David exactly what function the cauldron served, but it probably had something to do with preservatives.

The only nice employees from this section seemed to be a talkative elementary school teacher named Bill and a very short woman named Nan who worked at the quality control station just ahead of where the boxes where. Nan was an assistant teacher at the very same local elementary school and her husband was a truck driver. David knew very little about anyone else at that particular work area because no one spoke to him. He kept at his station and looked ahead to where the track curved beneath the machinery. In addition, there were metal gathering tanks and sugar dispensers. Then there was the quality control station with the stainless steel Santa's workshop benches and the little elves running around, the purpose of which was to inspect the quality of the product and to count the number of boxes and buckets and tin cans that were being filled and to note things like temperature, coloration, date and time.

To conduct their samples, these employees used a simple algebraic equation which David had not been able to witness and therefore was mysterious to him. He was certain it had something to do with averages and projections. As an example, using the caricature of his former math teacher, Mrs. Green, he thought the following: "If two-thousand extremely wealthy colonists are launched into space just before their home planet is struck by a comet, and their success is expected to vary depending on luck, age, and health, how many will survive the trip? You'll need to know 1) their chances of finding another habitable planet, 2) how long the journey will take, and 3) the age and health of each colonist. In this case, we'll average it out so that..."

Suddenly there was a heavy crash from the high mechanism leading from the sorting line and many of the workers closest to the scene rushed over to see what the disturbance was. The electronic sign flashed DISCOLORED as the bell rang to alert human ears. Pete stopped the belt and a beautiful brunette female quality control person wearing a skin-tight, silvery GGI T-shirt ran over to investigate. The gads stopped coming and the brunette undid the packaging on the alleged problem box until someone told her what had happened. Her cornflower-blue eyes flashed with worry. David was afraid to leave his station, but stepped a little ways towards the commotion to see what he could gather. A person was over there in an unprofessional posture. He was David's age and was dressed in a sorter's ballistic apron and the partial gauntlets. The sorter was smiling and otherwise lying motionless on top of the bags of sugar, where he had fallen. Luckily, he seemed unhurt.

Two guards and a medic rushed over and asked the guy some questions, and after he responded they asked the guy if he could stand and when he did they hauled him off to the break room and he was never seen again. The entire factory was soon a frenetic chain of gossip until suddenly the machines were turned back on and the production line commenced.

"Who's ever heard of such a thing?" someone said.

"They should screen people better. A pity." said someone else.

Things soon settled back to normal as the workers shed their anxieties and assumed the position. The boxes were slow in coming. David saw the alluring woman in the gold-colored shirt hauling someone quickly to the sorting line from the safety of the break room. The poor girl was not even armored yet. "I just don't get it, though," the girl was saying. "One minute you tell me there aren't any jobs and to take a hike, and the next minute you're dragging me in here from the parking lot. I haven't even gone through orientation...you don't even know my name...I could be anyone...I could be a saboteur...no, no, I didn't mean that...to incriminate myself or anything...I'm *not* a saboteur, but *you* don't know that......*do you?*"

David was so drawn in to the girl's one-sided conversation that he imagined himself being carried along with them.

Adolf slapped a box down on the pallet. "The next one's yours, wetback."

David had failed to notice that the boxes were finally coming down the track again. The sudden burst of racism had brought him back. He readied himself and grabbed the next box. "So, where you from?" David asked, trying his best to be resilient. "Is this a good place to live? I bet it gets really cold here in the winter."

Adolf grinned. "Oh, I'm on to you, bandito. I'm on you like your own sodden shadow. Think you're gonna steal the land from right under our feet, do you, like some refried doppelganger? No you're not. Nah ah. I'm gonna smack you all the way back to Mexico."

"I'm from Texas."

"What?"

"Texas. I'm a Texan."

"Na, you just floated like a turd across the Rio. I'm gonna throw you back."

"Um, okay."

Pete grunted and made sure that Adolf could see him smirking. He shoved another box down to them.

"They got some nerve, don't they?" laughed Adolf, maintaining eye contact with Pete. "War torn; No jobs here and still they come in droves like cockroaches. Hell, they got more government mules than I do, and I'm a walking felony."

"True enough," said Pete.

David shrugged. "Well, they hired them."

Adolf snorted with disgust. "That doesn't say much for this place."

David looked back at Pete, thinking that surely the son of a company man would be offended, but there was nothing. Working on the box line was proving to be a tight spot for him.

"So where did you get the name Adolf?" Pete asked. "Are your parents in the movement?"

"Absolutely. I was born to the m---memory of the Fuhrer. My whole life has been modeled for the benefit of the master race. Everything I own is Aryan. But I can't afford a Grosser Mercedes, so I drive a 'people's car', a two-thousand-and-sixteen Tiguan diesel-electric hybrid. Diesel and dust, as they say."

"That must be expensive," joked Pete.

"I do pretty good since the food shortages. Even against Canadian muck fuel, I save my nine-hundred-ninety Reichsmark, if you catch my meaning."

"You mean Hitler's plan?"

"Absolutely. The way the entire universe should be, under Aryan guidance of course."

"'The Father is greater than I'. In the Gospel of John," said David, cutting in. "I did a report on that for my Catechism."

"What the Sah-Samson hell are you talking about?!" Adolf's face was a crunched-up ball of red meat.

"No, not that," Pete corrected. "The Indo-Aryan *peoples*; The assumption by Imperialist French and British scholars and thinkers that a bunch of wandering Vikings somehow inspired all the advances of civilization, even though they had nothing but primitive weapons and shields on their backs."

"Right, the Aryan Indo-Europeans," interjected David, happy to have some support for once. "Speaking of that, the Indians do pretty good affordable cars; so do the Brazilians. Germans: not so much...They make good cars, just not affordable ones. Not anymore. And that diesel! Brazil is so very awesome. They got hydrogen now. Have you seen those sex-fuel cars, like from Bandeira?" He had momentarily forgotten where he stood, and so put too much nervous emphasis on his following remarks. "Those things are absolutely broncobustular. I sure wish I could buy one."

"Shuddup, burrito turd!" spat Adolf.

Pete and Adolf laughed.

"You aren't allowed to bring those across the border anyway," said Pete, catching his breath. "There's a ban on sexy cars."

"Sexy cars! You can say that again," David chuckled. He grabbed a box and placed it on the wooden pallet.

Adolf, perplexed by the incredulous betrayal, reversed mood and threatened to hit the blonde Pole. "Hey, Volkswagon is sexy, too!"

"Slugbug!" yelled Pete, who suddenly hustled quickly down along the conveyor belt and tapped David lightly on the shoulder with his fist, then fast-walked towards the break room where in the threshold a balding, white-collar man in a black suit was waiting.

Tom's Apartment

"Opercula. Apparatus. Knobkerrie. Carver, as in botanist George Washington. Zion. Supervene. Hairbreadth. Calceolaria..." Antiope blinked incessantly through buggy, mist-colored eyes as she worked out the crossword puzzle from a Gamesh newspaper. Her eyesight had always been rather poor since the days when they were taught welding without being instructed to lower the visors on their helmets. Mere children at the time, they were only told not to touch the flames and that it was impolite to stare into the divinity of noble gases. Antiope never listened to those whom she distrusted. The flames drew her in, and she might have become a pyromancer in more ancient times. She held a special affinity towards lights and colors; always had, from the moment of birth. They were like another dimension, a better place. The magnificent stained glass from a Polish church near the town of Cedar was all that kept her from burning things down (The church offered transportation, and Antiope took every opportunity to get away).

Tom's apartment lacked these qualities. The interior was dusty-white and almost colorless. She thought of maybe ordering a stained glass kit when she had the money, to liven the place up, but such discreteness would only give her away. She had to become as if a mouse living behind the walls. To aid her in subterfuge, Antiope had found a small box of snap-pops, from which a few were placed delicately under the doormat. It would have to do for now.

Suddenly—mischievously, as if little elves had tuned in to her thoughts—there was a faint double pop, then a shrill scream, followed by a knock at the door. Antiope scrambled out of the kitchen chair and ran for the closet and again there was a knock.

"Hello?" she heard a woman's voice announce. "Sorry to disturb you. We're neighbors. I wanted to invite you over for dinner. We're having vegetarian lasagna and there's plenty to go around. We could all get to know each other." Lowering her voice, the young woman continued, "Most of the people here are really old…"

Answering the door was the furthest from Antiope's mind. But the thought of lasagna made her reconsider. She had never had lasagna. After all, this person must have seen her when she had gone out. It could not hurt to be friendly, she suddenly thought, and looked out the peephole in the door. A young redheaded lady was standing out there, not more than five-foot-three inches tall.

"Coming!" Antiope said, clearing her throat of dust. She opened the door just a crack.

"Hi!" greeted the redhead.

"I'm Tom's niece," Antiope sputtered, opening the door a little wider.

"Who's Tom?"

"Oh. You don't know Tom… Antiope's the name."

"Sheryl. Nice to meet you."

Antiope and the redhead shook hands.

"So are you on for dinner? It's us three girls, and there's always room for a neighbor."

"Um, sure," Antiope answered. There was a pause and she became agitated as she tried to think of something to bring. "I have a bag of sunflower seeds…and some nuts…I could make nut bread…"

"Oh, that's not necessary. Maybe next time. So, you must have just moved in, or at least I don't remember ever having seen you before. You going to college around here?"

"No, I despise institutions. That is, no, not at this time. You?"

"I go to an engineering school through the University Center here in town. I'm studying Tissue Engineering."

"Interesting. Is that body tissue, or…"

"Yes, that's right. We work on ways to replace and improve tissue function in the human body."

"Wow. You must have a good job."

"Well, not yet. I can't seem to get an internship, so I'm currently an exotic dancer."

"A what?"

"Exotic dancer. You know, strip off your clothes; fireman's pole. A stripper."

"Oh I see..." exclaimed Antiope in panic.

"Come on over when you're ready. We're right here at Apartment Eleven."

"Okay, um, sounds good."

"Great! See you then!"

Antiope's Neighbors

"Silver Lining Estates, Eight-fifty-one Senior Haven Drive, Apartment Number Nine," Antiope whispered as she left her humble abode to venture across the gray-carpeted hall to number 11. She had with her a glass of water and the bag of sunflower seeds. She knocked and after a short wait someone let her in.

"Come on in," said a darling black-haired young lady with skin the color of raw umber. She was wearing some kind of moonstone blue blouse with designer jeans and kitty slippers. "Oh, I'm sorry. I'm Amira!" she said enthusiastically. She seemed Middle Eastern, but Antiope was a horrible judge. Antiope shook hands with Amira and was let in. The apartment was nice, with a soft carnelian sofa set with one long and two short and forming a ']' just inside and a small marble-top table in the dining area just down from a kitchen island with black-cushioned chrome bar stools. The place seemed larger than Tom's.

"See, she isn't snooty," said Sheryl, who was just coming in from the kitchen. "Antiope, right? This is Natalie, and you've met Amira."

"Hello."

"Hello yourself. And what do you do, Antiope?" said Natalie. "What brings you to this craphole?"

"Nothing, at the moment," Antiope said. "Just got in to town yesterday. I'm hoping to make some things and sell them,"

"Oh, online?" inquired Amira.

Antiope thought for a second. "The internet. That's a great idea, but I don't have a computer."

"Use ours," offered Amira. "We've got convertible tablets, and that old desktop. Natalie uses it for homework."

86

"Thank you for the offer. I might just take you up on that."

"You don't have a computer?" Natalie's pried with incredulity.

"Nope. My life is repetitive enough," Antiope spoke frankly.

"So how can you even be sure that you know how to use one?" Natalie said.

"Because I can do anything I set my mind to."

"Well..." Natalie screeched.

"It isn't that difficult," cut in Sheryl. "We'll help you figure it out,"

"And if selling things doesn't work, you could always be an exotic dancer," encouraged Amira half-jokingly.

"All of you do that?" Antiope ventured between breaths.

"You wouldn't believe how easy it is," Amira said. "And it's putting us through college."

"Awesome," replied Antiope, unsure whether she should be happy for them.

"It's a lucrative business," said Sheryl. "You should give it a try."

"That's great, but...I'm not really cut out for it."

"Sure you are," Amira encouraged.

"Oh, she's being snooty," accused Natalie.

"No she isn't. She's just self-conscious," defended Sheryl. "Don't mind her, Antiope. She's distrustful. She locks herself behind a psychological aegis."

"I do not!"

"You do!" insisted Sheryl before disappearing into the kitchen.

"Sorry. I didn't communicate that very well," Antiope apologized softly. "It-it isn't one of my strong points."

"Well, when you make some stuff, feel free to come over here and sell it," said Amira pitiably.

"Thank you." Antiope answered.

"Food's ready," said Sheryl, appearing briefly in the threshold.

The girls began setting the table and Sheryl reappeared with a dish full of vegetarian lasagna. They sat down while Amira worked on cutting up the meal.

"What exactly do you make anyway?" Natalie charged to ask, glancing at Antiope across the round table as Amira dished out the first portions.

"I'm not sure yet... I'm really good at origami. I can blow glass and make pottery, but you need a furnace for that. So I guess I'm stuck with folding paper."

"Good luck with *those* ideas." Natalie retorted snottily.

Antiope was a little put off by the remark, having spent her life among phlegmatic peers, under guidance of instructors who encouraged her in anything that kept her occupied, no matter how dispossessory and unflattering.

"Natalie and Amira are studying to be software engineers," Sheryl explained discomposedly. "They're great at reciting otherwise-meaningless code, but there isn't an original idea between them. Therefore, many would argue, they're really just studying to become programmers."

"Hey, now... What a snoot!" Natalie barked. "Are you hearing this crap, Amira?"

Amira was stuck with artichoke-and-cheese-covered noodle in her mouth and had to wait for her thoughts to digest. "You're probably right, of course, but I really wonder why you bring it up so much," she said finally. "Could it be that you, too, are something of a programmer?"

"Good one!" Natalie cheered.

"A tissue programmer... hmmm," contemplated Sheryl to her distaste. "But you have a point."

Amira restructured her words, seeming to put them on the fork as she prepared to devour them. "I mean it isn't like you're creating your own life form or anything...thank Allah... The stuff's already there; we can't even evolve on our own merits; the code for adaptation is predetermined..."

"Okay, so we're all a bunch of uncreative copycats," admitted Sheryl. "That's why we need someone like Antiope here to inspire us."

"Well, what are you waiting for, Antiope? Inspire us already," purred Natalie before taking a bite from her dish. She was certainly a moody feline to behold.

Antiope became evermore quiet, unintentionally placing the girls under her spell until it became imperative that she speak lest she become ostracized from their tentative friendship.

"I *do* have an idea," whispered Antiope as she glanced frightfully in the direction of the three would-be engineers.

The Magic Mirror App

Beauty, Antiope realized, was measurable. That meant, given that a person's dimensions could be captured and then reflected back as an illusion, that anyone could be made to look better than they really did. Given that an object's dimensions could be captured using a precise laser scanner and then stored within a computer, any reasonably-sized object could become quantitative for just such an operation as that which Antiope had in mind.

Beauty, the pinnacle of craftsmanship, a pleasing quality recognized in harmony of form or color, the alluring search for truth, was an intoxicating notion set aside for the human condition. Most other living things couldn't give a rat's butyrin about beauty: the butterfly and the bee cared far more about wavelength than the illusion of color in a flower; animals scrutinized each other during mating season but were only concerned with health and strength to best represent the future of their kind; birds were an exception, however, as male birds often displayed their beautiful colors during an amazing courtship performance. But they did not get lost in it the way that humans did. Therefore she had the idea, which she had absorbed after reading things such as *Snow White and the Seven Dwarves* and *The Chronicles of Narnia* in the Academy's illustrious library of childish and juvenile literature, that a mirror was a very powerful tool. And although she could not develop the idea herself at this point in her life, she was certain that someone could, and so the idea had been placed on the backburner of her mind. Now suddenly there was a tug at the line connecting worlds. The divine signal had startled her at first, but she would not let it smolder and die out of selfishness. Evidently, the thing wanted to live.

QUADRUPLET

I

The Nenaa'angebi Homestead

"Was a guy last season got his throat cut."

"Bull shhhhih…"

"Swear to Christ he did. Bled to death in the emergency room."

"You're full of it. I worked sanitation last year and I never heard nuthin' 'bout no body dyin'."

"They kept it real quiet. I was right there on line three fixin' a sliced hose near the de-stemmer and be damned if I didn't look over my shoulder and see the fella on the other line keel over right into the feed tank with blood squirtin' ever where. The guards rushed over before I knew what the freak. They took that operator off through a secret door strapped down to a stretcher, tennis racket and all, and replaced him with some other guy from the line."

"Bull shih. They woulda hada shut everything down and sterilize the hell outa that entire line. All them gads woulda hada been thrown out."

"Well they didn't. They jus' kep right on goin'. Never seen that fella again neither. Friend of mine at the hospital verified that he was dead."

"Bull shih."

"Swear to Christ."

Just then a gust of warm wind blew over the parking lot and swayed the rickety wooden roof of the bus stop. The beams groaned and a shingle soared off into a passing truck.

Edgar was beneath it, seated with his back resting against an old wooden picnic table. He was eavesdropping on some fellow employees nearby while waiting for his niece to pick him up. She was already a half-hour late. This job that he had taken was really something. *What have I got myself into,* he wondered.

The wooden beams creaked in answer.

He looked out at the hot gate and then followed the driveway down to the road and imagined that he was going to be picked up soon. The traffic whooshed by in complete oblivion. How pathetic it was to find himself in such a position, so dependent on the arrival, like a helpless pet. A child was his lord, her chariot his only shuttle between road, river, and rail, over the vast network of distances. A sense of freedom was his once, until shortly after arriving home from his final deployment. His cherry red arrest-me-please Government Motors *Fotzepolitic* that had been sitting outside at his mother's house had lost its protective cover and become an attractive haven for a swarm of hornets. With the fuel line corroded, and the aggressive hornets refusing to relinquish the trunk, mirrors, and space between the doors, it was a total loss. The vehicle was gradually given permission to return to nature while the former owner swam through a deepening depression.

Edgar unconsciously lilted into a hum, having become a monk of boredom, until his silent contemplation was interrupted by the sight of the odd, insect-like vehicle which could only belong to Edina. He waved with both arms so that she would spot him.

"There you are," said Edina when her uncle opened the passenger door and stepped in beneath it. "Sorry I was late. I was hosting a tea party with my dolls when Little Miss Poopyhead decided to get lost. I had to retrace my steps while I still remembered them."

"Great. And I suppose you found her at last?"

"She was in with the laundry."

"That stinker."

"Look, Uncle Edgar... um... I need to go to the Weatherholt homestead. There's a part I need from the barn. I have a feeler malfunction below the left abdomen. Discovered it this morning. I looked in the manual and there's this one specific part. If you don't mind—I'm scared to go there by myself."

"Well...yeah we can do that. Do you need me to put it on for you?"

"No, I can handle it."

"Because...if you want I can help you."

"I don't need any help. Just go with me to get the part."

Edgar wondered how it was that she could do these things by herself. How did a little girl who held tea parties for dolls named things like Little Miss Poopyhead perform maintenance on her futuristic automobile? Edgar felt that he must have been missing something—that it could not have been simply that she was a Weatherholt. Too many others had fallen far short of these acquisitive and admirable capabilities.

Early into the battle for 'alternative fuel', two unlikely inventors made unprecedented advances in the production of energy through friction and the resulted heating of gases. Aunt Edith and Uncle Jerome (Fitzarthur) met at the MIT library in Massachusetts while studying plasma physics, steam engines, and Viktor Schauberger's implosion generators, just as each of them was preparing to drop out to pursue their radical inventions. Little was known concerning their early lives, but they eventually returned to Aunt Edith's family's homestead farm and performed experiments in the barn. With Uncle Jerome focusing on design and Aunt Edith working out the kinks in her "Gas Friction" energy technology, they constructed the prototype for a completely self-reliant automobile they coined the **Desert Mantis** due to the fact that it ran partly on hot air and could zip over the earth on long, springy saw-like legs. The car was even featured on the cover of *Trendy Technicalities* with a lengthy article appearing in the technology section. But everything went terribly wrong when they sought out a patent. Strange men would appear at the farm on the premise of investing in the company and then at night there would be break-ins. Sometimes shots were fired from the adjoining woods. The barn inescapably burned down and all trace of the Desert Mantis vanished into obscurity.

Unwilling to give up so easily, Edgar's Aunt Edith and Uncle Jerome switched to a more idiot-friendly sugar beet hybrid and began testing the oil in their engines[12]. They formed a small company called **E=J²**. Uncle Jerome, an insanely brilliant engineer, tinkered around with some design concepts while Aunt Edith tested the functionality of the internal organs and eventually they pieced together the perfect sugar beet automobile.

They called this one the **Cicada**.

Allied with the Michigan Sugar Beet Farmers of Sebewaing, they eagerly began seeking investors, but as word caught on, so weighed the pressures from oil and gas giants, whose lobbyists successfully attacked smaller biobutanol and other biofuel companies on multiple fronts. The sugar beet ensemble was choked and buried before it even had a chance to lift itself from the devilish earth. The Fitzarthurs (Aunt Edith and Uncle Jerome) suffered bankruptcy as a result and eventually died in each other's arms from a simultaneous stroke, but managed to gift the only sugar beet automobile to their favorite second niece.

Edgar's own father was an underling for the production team, but would eventually betray them—a despicable act which he would never be forgiven for and which would result in divorce from his wife.

"So are you going to actually live in that house someday? If you do, you should clean it up," Edina said.

"I can't legally move in yet," Edgar explained. "The bank owns it; I'd be a squatter."

"What's wrong with that? I squat."

"Well, we'll all have to squat here if things get any worse."

Edina took her eyes from the road with an unimpressed look. "Ewe. Where would I sleep?"

"Upstairs in the cobwebs."

"Not funny."

Edgar still pondered. "So what would you do if you were alone and you had a flat tire?"

"I don't have tires. I have tarsal pads."

"What if you got into an accident?"

---

[12] The oil was coined 'bug juice' because of the coinciding bug problem, and also due to the resultant automobile's resemblance to an insect.

"An *accident*? I have a perfect record! Besides, Aunt E and Uncle J have my back."

"We all have your back," assured Edgar. "But that's not the point. The point is…just be careful."

They drove north along Highway 31 through the outskirts of Gamesh and hugged the Grand Traverse Quagmire for many miles until everything changed before their eyes and the world was as the birds would have it. The hot cherry orchards still clung for miles along the hills, merging with farmhouse bed & breakfasts and parched nature preserves. Three psychotic little townships came and went. North past vacant houses of the disillusioned dotting old cottages opposite ridiculously large stone summer mansions, deeply hidden lakes, immaculate golf courses, equestrian lodges smelling of roses and high-class manure, thrived the wilderness, if briefly, and they were soon swallowed in trees that hugged the sky so tightly that they formed a tunnel around the road. The vegetation rose anciently and swallowed the wood as it had for millennia. Corpuscular spears of light trickled down forcefully and danced along the trail as if within water. An owl screeched and glided white overhead with outstretched wings. There was a sense of magic. But soon the world opened again and the sky held them down oppressively. They turned off east and then south. There was openness of road and artificial lighting and pipelines connecting the slaves to the source. These were the traits of America. The power lines that should have been obsolete by this time stretched on like greased crosses through the wasteland of the damned and disheartened.

They passed the labyrinthine marsh of a dead lake and the remnant dwellings amongst the abandoned summer houses and cottages. The fields were vast golden grass and hardy wildflowers and then the haunted ghost orchards where forbidden fruits no longer found the land suitable for living. Up rose the hills through the old government plots of swindled Pottawatomi rights and the Pioneer homesteads of robust dreamers long deceased. There in a windbreak were the ruins of the Weatherholt farm. Gray, warped, and spirited, the old house of etched and frosted glass was all that stood. The fields were a quagmire of grapevine and thick coils of barbed thorn bush. Shaking Aspens, maples, oaks, wild cherry, grandmotherly willow, thick, ancient white pines, and even the sweet-smelling arborvitae had grown stunted and wild above the unsightly thorns and vines.

"Do you think it's even safe?" Edina said as she emerged from the automobile.

"It always was before," said Edgar. He felt defensive, mainly because this was supposed to have been his house and he had screwed things up. But, under the stipulations and procedures of his aunt and uncle's will, he could not inherit unless he paid off the mortgage and cleared enough annual income to maintain the place. It was the irony of ironies that he could do neither and so was left homeless.

They climbed the cracks in the concrete steps, unlocked the door with a spare key left secretly behind the lighthouse birdhouse, and strode the inconsistency between porch and stair that had widened into a tiny crevice over the centuries. The floor was warped and creaked considerably.

A large brown spider scurried further into a corner.

"So where is this stuff supposed to be?" Edgar asked.

"In one of the...of the bedrooms I think."

"Well, come on then," said Edgar, grasping Edina's little arm and pulling her in after him.

Some kind of pastoral theme, homesteaders threshing wheat, was artfully depicted on each of the frosted windows—all intact, amazingly. The light shone in through the dust and cobwebs. There in the next room were the parts. A huge metal filing system said CICADA in brass letters and the drawers were labeled under Dewey decimal classification.

"What's the part called?" Edgar asked.

"I don't know that!"

"You don't know...What did the manual say?"

"'T' I think. I forgot."

"'T' it is then," said Edgar. "What part of the body is it?"

"A foot, I guess—I don't know!"

"Foot," mumbled Edgar as he bent down and opened the drawer labeled **Legs and Feet, R-T,** and found the section T**5.5**. Various parts were inside, each within sugar beet-derived plastic bags. There were large rubbery cream colored tubes, wide cylinder bolts insulated by soft blue cushions, and rod-like forms with sensitive feelers. "Any of these look familiar?"

"Err... That one! There it is!" Edina exclaimed excitedly. "And while we're here, I need all the tarsal parts."

Edgar took the barbed metallic cylinder called *tibia* and four of the hard, rubber-coated parts called *tarsus* and gave them to Edina. "Anything else?" he asked her.

"Well, let me see," said the little girl, sticking her head in each of the drawers as she hung from the edge with two small unadulterated hands. "This one," she said. "Better take some. And that one, too. Those sometimes go bad."

"You amaze me sometimes, kid."

Upon the Return to Sugarland

The approaching twilight made the tunnel of trees grow increasingly dark and phantasmagoric as they sped through the vegetative portal to a home-cooked meal. They both glanced fearfully in exhilarating anticipation of encountering a headless horseman or little Pukwudjininee fairy men or maybe a voracious Columbian banshee. But soon enough they were back in the world of logic and the clouds exploded overhead.

"Gosh!" Edina chimed. "Where's all that water coming from?"

The low-lying mist was catching on the windshield, to the wonderment of the miniscule automobile controller. As they approached an expansive estate within a white-picket fence the rush became louder and the calculated rain fell to quench the surrounding equestrian facilities on order, maintaining the green lawn for beautiful horses subdued.

"Well?" continued the little girl. "Why doesn't it do this where I live? Uncle?"

Edgar was too distraught to explain the cause of the phenomenon and remained silent. He felt it everywhere and there was no escape; it was whispered from the quaking trees and from deep within his mind. The roof of the vessel was purposeful and mocked his superfluity; the side mirror was distortional and rooted in the past. It pierced his heart and made him sink. He understood completely: Born to the lingering Bunsen burner fumes of better times, Edina had never witnessed the beauty of a thunderstorm, nor appreciated the cleansing aspect of aquatic torrents upon the disease-ridden ghost forests and parched flowerless meadows of her homeland. Gone were the days of natural disasters, of crop failures, of freak early spring snow storms and pleasant rainbows after summer rains. Edina's time was one of man-made cataclysms, of vanishing species, vanishing mysteries, of corporate domination of the world's food production, of tourism or suburbanization versus the local farming industry. Her world was a controlled agony under the watchful eye of the oppressors. It was the rebirth of despotism in which industry replaced the landlord estates and where the dominion was the entire solar system. The despotic industries controlled, but they controlled little. The world, always boiling, continuously erupting under the skin, was in a taciturn phase, was itself ever watchful and sensitive to the whims of mites and miniscule changes in the dust.

People were lucky to get a good misting out on the old pioneer homesteads, unless they happened to be in a good weather zone. As would be expected from a group of thugs, the regularity and quantity of precipitation an area of land received varied according to utilitarian importance, favors, and bribes. It was the typical human response. They were off center, under-appreciated, out-valued, but people got used to the changes. Whenever a neighboring farm, lakeside community, banking franchise, tree nursery, or golf club went out of business, the residents expected a few less downpours that summer. The exceptionally heavy winters during leap years were all that saved the remote areas from emaciation and semi-eternal entombment.

Through the quaking aspens and strained beech trees of small disheveled burrs, the towering prison-like barbed wire atop an elegant stone wall held the answer: Somewhere beyond was Loon Lake, currently inaccessible to the public, despite the existence of at least three designated public accesses which were under secret police watch on behalf of the unionized retirement community township.

To reiterate the point like a missile shot from a royal British helicopter pilot, they drove past gated great-lakeside-condominiums walled up into a perfectly plush village of elitist health clubs and shopping centers.

"Well, what's the deal, Uncle Edgar?"

"It's from the lake," said Edgar. "Down there."

"What lake?"

"*You* know. Like a giant puddle. You've been to Great Wolf Lodge, right? It's like that."

"I know what a lake is, but there's no lake down there."

"True. Not anymore. Now it's just a reservoir dammed up along a basin, sadly. But those people. They're responsible."

"Okay, so…how'd it get up *here*?"

"A drop in temperature is probably the culprit: it used to be from trade winds, usually coming from low-lying southern areas, mixing with those from northern arctic places or mountaintops; the weather gets very hot and very cold, respectively, and collides, and water condenses out of atmospheric vapor and falls to earth. That isn't how it happens anymore though…"

"But, for rain, how's the water gonna get that far up in the sky?"

"The weather machines bring it up there."

"What? Creepy."

Edgar's tear glands reacted to the irritation of wonderment upon his bare sight. It had been years since he had experienced the purification of a body of water. In his fading memory, obstructed from fulfillment by the unscrupulous hospitality lords of the age, such wonders thrived. There were mad, rusty rivers flowing icily through forested bedrock of iron ore, the banks of which made for isolated, magical campgrounds; seasonally-occupied estate-curtains of trees and walls; prattled, beach-castle-darkened sandbars crowded full of boats and footballers and cramped children frolicking near a floating snack shop, dropping murkily into deep sapphire lakes; hidden algae-bloom jewels within swamps; mucky streams of whisper-grass and unknowable clairvoyance; pristine freshwater oceans pregnant with foam and bulging austerely over their protectorate breeding ground; miles of cosseted, silicon beaches pushed up from the forested tree-line. And what did that have to do with anything? Plenty. Like the ancient rivers themselves, the flow of water through valleys of hydraulic civilizations divulged in different directions, one of respect and one of domination. Most often it was a combination of both, as people diverted, irrigated, dammed, inadvertently salinized, and suffered the consequences. No matter how dumb or smart, they never seemed to learn which was better (One group of creature never got along with another anyway while at the watering hole). A war had been waging probably before The Great Migrations over fresh water. It was something few living creatures could do without.

A Quick Digression Concerning the Mysteries of Water

The first recorded human conflict involving the vital liquid was a dispute at the Edge of Paradise (Sumerian *Gu'edena*). As it was written, sometime around 2500 BC, the son of Urlama, King of Lagash, cut off the water supply to the neighboring city of Umma[13]. He had done this because King Enakalli of Umma, on the guidance of his god[14], destroyed the irrigation works in the valley floor which they both relied on as a food source to create a "margin of desolation". Hence, from that point, the Sumerian confederation of independent minds was at odds, and the paradise between two rivers could only be subdued by those controlling the massive flow of water doubling as its bulwarks.

About 770 years later, when the Amorites of Babylon held faltering control over the region, the grandson of Hammurabi, Abi-Eshuh, dammed the Tigris to prevent the retreat of rebel Sumerian forces under Iluma-ilu[15]. Despite his efforts, the rebels escaped and established the Sealand Dynasty in lower Sumer. They, too, faltered, in the luminous blink of Marduk's eye, and the many folds of that particular mindset were forever scattered to the wind.

---

[13] Umma and Lagash were two of eighteen major Sumerian cities from the prehistoric Ubaid period to the Ur III period, roughly from 5300 BC – 1940 BC. They were located between the Tigris and Euphrates, equivalent to present-day southern Iraq.
[14] The god was probably Shara, the eldest son of Inanna, a Sumerian war god whose temple was in Umma.
[15] A self-proclaimed name in reference to Marduk, chief god of the Babylonians ("solar calf" or "the young steer of the day", according to *The Religion of Babylonia and Assyria* by Thophilus G. Pinches).

Then there was the fabled Plain of Esdraelon told of in the *Old Testament*, where, at the edge of Mount Tabor, circa 1300 BC, the army of the Israelite general Barak defeated the superior iron-clad chariots of the Canaanites under mercenary general Sisera which were caught in the rushing headwaters of the Qishon River during a divine winter torrent upon the mountain[16].

From there it was a deluge. The lessons spread in electric thought-waves over the deserts and jungles and forests of the ancient world, burning like fire in the minds of human beings—but they learned nothing, and even at the frothing Qishon there was no stopping the harassment of water by mankind.

Again, like a wild bull, the world bellowed. Again, despair. The people sprang up like daisies and were cut down as if with a scythe. They poured out libations and made offerings on the mountains of their time. The sun baked clay and the moon pulled at the tides. The earth quaked, heaved, rose and fell. The unique variations of spirited energy trapped in their myriad replicating forms were thrown prostrate into chaos like dust mites in a formless rug and people were the worse for it. The survivors trembled, wailed, raised their tiny fists in defiance, crawled back on and stood up. The young were gathered, stripped, sent forth into the sacrifice. They threw harnesses on their children, on the wilderness and the fields, stirred nature into a steaming pot. Up came the snakes, lured by sweet libations of the fruits of labor, and stole away with it into the night.

Inevitably, a diabolical humanity made their way to the single largest freshwater resource in the world. North American waterways had for millennia been the apian highways of its primordial communities. Latecomers utilized them no differently, as they littered the banks of lakes and rivers with cannons. The Railway Age of England infected its former colonies with industry and the residual overpopulation ran carelessly westward through stewarded lands. Currency cut through the ancient forests and lakes like a hot iron blade, felling giant trees like dandelions in the wake of voracious lawnmowers, littering the waters with corpses, and carting people even deeper into the wilderness.

---

[16] Sisera escaped, but was killed by Jael, wife of Heber the Kenite, thus fulfilling Deborah's prophecy.

The conversion of steam to gasoline-powered engines, sometime in the early twentieth century, gave America's fresh waterways a steep decrease in health. But the sprouting of pollution as if from under rocks did not hinder the desire to steal this valuable resource from the as-yet sparsely-populated Eden of the North. Over a billion gallons of water had been pumped through offshore cribs and into Chicago daily since 1865[17].

Good neighbors had helped maintain these large reservoirs of glacial water somewhat during the childhood of European corporations. Yet they were vulnerable to the rise of indifference and attacks on reason by the unreasonable; people of faith and uncertainty alike began to doubt the importance of something which consisted anywhere from 55% to 78% of their own bodies and which they would not survive more than a few days without. Decadence, it seemed, would once again claim an empire. Dreams shattered into fragments. Opinions were those of Hatfields and McCoys, the minds of millions seemingly hijacked by harpies, demons, or alien thought-rays. The ranks had formed along a dividing line that must have appeared like the edges of a puzzle throughout the many countries carved into the suffering land.

2016 AD was the year The Great Lakes Water Wars were fought against profiteering corporations. An entirely new branch of the Armed Forces of the United States of America, called the U.S. Civic Legion, was formed to help deal with the crisis. Although the United States and Canada were victorious in that particular battle, at a loss of thousands of lives (figures which include both human and robot) and miles of habitat destruction from remote projectile, chemical, and biological weapons, hundreds of cubic miles of fresh water had been secretly hauled off in tankers by enterprising companies.

Then in the summer of 2018 a very unbelievable thing happened: In an instant, Lake Huron lost almost 200 feet of depth causing a flood of water to pass into a gigantic whirlpool like a drain

---

[17]At the 2010 rate of Chicago thirstiness, it would have taken 3992650.74964 days for Chicago to drink the entire Great Lakes, or 10938.769177 years (excluding leap years; The 2010 estimation for Great Lakes total volume [measured at the low water datum] was 5,439 cubic miles, or 5,988,976,124,460,000 gallons [almost 6 quadrillion]).

into the earth. Untold trillions of gallons of precious, vital commodities evaporated into thin air and the 10,000 miles of shoreline around the Great Lakes became the edge of a malodorous quagmire. Terrorists from Toronto, Ontario, claimed responsibility. The pair had constructed homemade nuclear bombs in the kitchen of their tiny apartment overlooking a landfill. They pled insanity; claimed the motive of their crime materialized in their sickened minds from a combination of mercury levels from the fish they were eating on a daily basis coupled with the city tap water, but were given the death penalty without the right to a trial. From the apparent safety of solitary confinement in a notorious Cuban prison, and to the disgruntlement of inquisitional CIA interrogators, they both soon confessed that strange near-lifeless American men had approached them, had quickly tutored them on the detonation of nuclear devices, had taken them to a remote cabin near Lake Huron, and had then dropped them by hovering spy plane into a tiny makeshift submersible reminiscent of those used by Columbian drug cartels to smuggle cocaine into the United States. No such submarine was ever found to authenticate their story, nor the alleged cabin. They were not even Islamic, as the media had claimed, but unemployed pirates from Somalia who once practiced witchcraft in a secret cave behind the local mosque. They were soon murdered in a prison riot[18].

The Great Lakes communities had fought "tooth and nail", as it were, against water privatization, pitting themselves against farms, corporations, cities, breweries, entrepreneurs both foreign and domestic, oil enterprises, and even the federal government, and in the end had witnessed the sealing of their own coffins, as far as water was concerned. This had been the apocalypse of their time. The great and wondrous Algonquin lifeblood and highway of trade, the very spirit of life, had been fully demoralized, dismembered and dispersed within solidified toxic vapors for financial gain, for

---

[18]Although the culprits claimed it was nothing personal, just one of many quirks of life behind bars, conspiracy theorists wasted little time filling in the holes. Few people on the outside really cared anyway. Rumors eventually circulated that the catastrophic event had not been caused by a nuclear explosion at all and that in fact the water had been sucked out by a top secret weather control device and flown to China as a cloud.

nihilism, for the easement of unquenchable thirst, to add mere seconds of levitation to the animate human corpses above the frigid fires of death. The tankers and cargo ships of once-lucrative trade routes now littered the great marshes, decorating aquatic nature with their gaudy structural hulls and rotten ineffectualness.

And yet it rained in some places. This was largely because human beings had learned to control the weather[19]—and not in a good way necessarily, but in a greedy, mechanized dictatorial process of egging on disastrous natural consequences and at the same time the eternal downtrodden soul, thus inspiring the bottom feeders to commit acts of sabotage and counterrevolutionary thoughts of violence against whatever psychic phantom haunted them in sleep. Government-sponsored corporations, those with their talons imbedded deeply into the flesh of laissez-faire, controlled the nation, turning it into a massively mythical clepsydra of time-measuring and oppressive organization. Freedom, democracy, they tooted from pulpits, but even under a woman president with a likeness to the silhouette of the torch-bearing giantess echoing from the colossus of tight-knit Mediterranean islands they dissolved their own hand-puppet-words and hollow ideals with blatant subterfuge while accumulating their wealth abroad and passing it through offshore accounts. They controlled the nation, operating their weather control stations in such a way that only the very comfortable received steady rainfall: metro D.C., Bethesda, and Arlington; Miami; Hollywood; New York City; what was left of the once-great metropolitan areas, coastal or otherwise, aquatic performers of dwindling Las Vegas; the maximum security farmlands of sickness and horrors; a chain of chateaus along the oceans and lakes; the gated communities of the world replete with itchy trigger fingers and neon-green golf courses. As such, Edina could not see the source of the dew, nor had ever laid eyes on the army of elite machinery required to harness nature.

---

[19] Weather Control had been at least partially operational in the United States since 2003; many claim it had been scientifically possible since the days of Tesla, roughly from 1899 to 1917, at Wardenclyffe Tower in New York and Telefunken Wireless Station in Long Island. The phenomenon of increasingly more severe weather globally propelled what is currently the second and most efficient weather control network in the world.

And So the Profitless Voyage Continues Once Again

"Uncle Edgar?"

"Yes."

"Never mind."

"It's fine. I'm alright. What did you want to know?"

"Is grandpa really a…a weathercock?"

"More of a weather balloon, I would say. He works for those wind-chokers down in Creve Coeur."

"I know that. How far is Creve Coeur?"

"A ways. It's along the Mississippi River, down in Missouri."

"Is he a traitor?"

"Who told you that?"

"Grandma. She said…well, I'm not allowed to say what she said."

"Grandma swore?"

Edina shook her blonde little head happily in the affirmative. "She visited for Easter." Edina giggled at the recollection.

"Grandpa betrayed…they offered him a job, and he took it this time."

"Why is that bad? Grandma hates them?"

"Well, you see, the Weatherholts…I'm not really sure, but we have some kind of a history in directing the weather somehow, out of a primal appreciation for the natural world, passed on through the generations, and…but not like the North American Weather Control Authority, who force the weather into submission. I suspect it was more of a dance—something spiritual, maybe. A farming community would really value something like that, people with an intimate relationship with the wind and the rain. Anyway, when the big corporations sabotaged your Aunt Edith and Uncle Jerome's automotive company, the family vowed to boycott, that is, to avoid, anything those rotten people touched. After ignoring these kinds of people for most of his life, your grandpa Alexander suddenly came out of retirement and devoted his talents to them. He helped them choke the weather."

"So he's really a son-of-a-bitch?"

"...yes."

Small defeat sometimes came at an enormous cost. Largely because of the defeat of a fledgling business on the battlefield of monstrous corporations, Edina was the sole consumer of sugar beet oil and owner-in-trust of the world's only sugar beet engine.

Her automobile was remarkably adapted for the use of a child, with shrunken driver parts and big shiny buttons, autonomous safety controls that watched for symptoms by utilizing mysterious sensors, a playful atmosphere, extra space for dolls, etc., and a raised, cushiony seat perfectly awaiting the angelic body of a childhood—all the power of a 191-kilowatt (260 PS; 256 hp) V12 bivalent engine[20], yet with preset checks and balances to offset the devilish, wandering youthful mind. This was Edina's bubble, where she appeared to be the compound iris. However, the rest of the head/ thorax body structure were of perfectly normal size and function, including the Malpighian waste tubes, sugar-based ganglion engine, and trochanteric 'wheels'. All things considered, Edina operated her craft exceptionally well.

"So, Uncle Edgar, why exactly do we need this weather control?"

"A good question. In theory it's because the country was becoming a seasonal desert with increasingly dangerous weather conditions: winter brought the sudden dumping of dense snow and ice storms; spring gave us high winds and record tornadoes; in summer, while places like China were experiencing record floods, we had record droughts. The Mississippi would dry up. But then the next year conditions would switch. There were mass power outages. Lightning would zap us like Martian ray guns. And of course there were those hurricanes. Natural problems were becoming worse and worse by the year. The entire planet was heating up. They figured that controlling the weather was the answer. It seemed like a good idea at the time..."

"But...America still nearly *is* a desert..."

"It didn't really work the way it was designed to. Logic pushed for things like indoor farming, tiered hydroponics crops without soil being grown inside warehouses and skyscrapers.

---

[20] The exact fuel sources used for the dichotomy of this particular engine are as yet unknown.

Detractors said it would be too expensive, and it was, but not nearly as expensive as controlling the weather for the entire planet. Well, this being the home of rugged individualism, departure of logic, unfairness, and greed, the system became just another grid for extortion and profiteering. So now instead of the lush paradise they had advertised we have private garden islands dotting a wasteland. It hasn't changed anything for the better. The last remaining sanctuaries of diversified life are still drying up, becoming fodder for cattle. This country just can't do anything right anymore. No one does anything to fix it."

"Sorry I asked."

"It was a good question. I'm just too tired to provide you with a positive answer."

The rain stopped like the turning of a faucet. They had entered Antrim County.

"Luck of the Irish," Edgar mumbled under his breath.

"What's that?"

"Nothing. So do you wish you were back in school?"

"Are you kidding me?"

"I thought you liked school."

"We're in cyberspace *a lot*. My teacher is a dweeb. It's kind of boring."

They took a series of winding side-roads and before long they entered the eastern outskirts of Grand Traverse County near Kalkaska. A creek wound mysteriously through a crotch of bushes, vines, and small trees, and then a house appeared in the middle of a burned-up field. It was little more than a two-storied heap and a wrap-around porch. All that held the wood in place was the fresh coat of Byzantium paint which Edgar had applied on the eve of Lent. A yellow fiberglass garage sat off to the right of it, and a ways back there appeared a red barn rising from an undersized green and purple ocean of famished beets.

Ellen Nellie Weatherholt-O' Caoindealbhain

"It's about time," the young woman said, ambushing them when they emerged from the garage. "You can both help me pack up." Edgar's sister, Ellen, was throwing candy from a sales stand into glass containers and had a little red wagon standing by, ready for loading. She was in the front yard near the old country road, where the yellowing grass was somewhat sandy from wind deposits. Edgar grabbed two bags of sugar and took them to the pantry. *The algae lives*, he noted, taking a moment to admire the glass tanks of leafy green stalks on the porch.

Ellen, meanwhile, tried putting her nine-year-old daughter to work.

"Can I have one?" Edina asked her mother while grabbing the life out of three large suckers with Van Gogh swirls in them.

"No, you cannot. I looked in your room this morning to see if you had cleaned it like I asked you to and guess what I found hidden in the toy box?"

Edina smiled guiltily.

Ellen continued, her long brown hair flowing mysteriously around her: "My missing canister of chocolate dream fluffs: half-eaten! Really, young woman! These things are for us to sell, not to kill ourselves on! Oh!! How can such a small thing eat so much and not get sick?!"

"Pleeeease?" whined the naughty young woman.

"Absolutely not! Now, help me pack up or you won't get any dinner."

"But...the wagon's doing most of the work...and it's mine, so..." Edina reluctantly returned the suckers one by one from where she had removed them and helped place the canisters.

"You're treading dangerously, missus..." scolded her mother.

"So how did it go? Sell anything?" Edgar asked, having returned for another bag.

Ellen sighed. "Ten pounds of sugar... That bicycle salesman, Ron, came by again today. You remember him, right? His dad used to work on the Desert Mantis with Aunt Judith and Uncle Jerome. What was his name? He's Ottawa. Anyway... he quantum pedaled all the way from Nenaa'angebi to show off the

108

new styles. He totes three or four of them in a special trailer. They're really nice."

"I've heard of those. *Ride the Plank's Constant.* Is that Mister Wabe'no? What does he have to do with Quantum Pedaling? Is he the inventor?"

"No his uncle invented them I think. Ron's uncle. Forget his name but he started the *Zeno's Arrow* line. Ron must have worked on them, too, but they delegated him to sales. Completely homemade. Everyone thinks it's a gimmick but they really work. I can't believe they aren't filthy rich yet."

"They'll catch on."

"Santa's going to get me one for Christmas!" Edina exclaimed proudly. She was, of course, bouncing childishly up and down on her invisible springs of fairy-dust-coated joy.

"Santa's good business for Ron," Edgar supposed.

"We'll see, honey. Anyway, you got that car of yours to get around in."

"But I want a *Zeno's Arrow* bike!"

"Oh boy! The joys of kids," Ellen laughed.

"But mommy..."

"Silly, the way life is," she continued sedately. "Loe 's down in Indiana with that old pickup truck that breaks down all the time. Here we are on the brink of starvation with this multi-million-dollar car. Loe 's tried to bypass the features, but only Edina can drive the damn thing."

"Mommy swore!"

"Sorry, sugar."

"That means I get a bike!"

Ellen looked down at her daughter sternly. "A certain little girl should just be content that she's enjoying her childhood."

"A bike, a bike!"

"Go clean your room and maybe I won't murder your bare hide for all that candy you ate this morning."

"What?! How did you know?!"

"Mommy knows everything!" declared Ellen.

"That's not fair!" swore Edina bitterly before rapidly stomping off towards the house.

Edgar helped put things inside. Ellen had a system that needed upholding for her own sanity. There was a special sealed-off cupboard for the candy until it could be hauled back to the stand and sold. "So are we doing okay, I mean money-wise?"

"We're fine," Ellen said, wiping her forehead with flour. "We'll sell more candy than we can possibly cook up once the tourists get here."

"But it's the middle of July...never mind. Is the tractor still broken? I need to water the beets, and...let's see, what else..."

"Edina fixed it. She said the coolant hose had disintegrated. She replaced it with one from the garage."

"Really, she fixed it?"

"Amazing, isn't she. Don't tell her just yet. It might go to her head."

"I'll get to the watering then," announced Edgar, trying to sound enthusiastic.

"Supper shouldn't be too long; just rice and stir fry. I'll send the little bugger out to fetch you."

Edgar nodded. "Hear anything from mom?"

"She called earlier, said she was going shopping."

"She still with that creep Winston?"

"Afraid so," Ellen said, somewhat giddily from receiving such an absurd question. "He isn't that bad, is he?"

"I dunno. Maybe it's just me."

"I mean he didn't kick you out or anything, right? There's just no work up there. Not much here either."

"He's retired Army, thinks I should respect him for it or something. But he never did anything hot. Filled out some paperwork during Panama and he thinks I owe him a salute. Tell that to the dead at Hombori. I'm out; I'm not fucking saluting anybody. He can salute my bathtub elixir. Besides, he's been retired for years. What the fuck's his problem?"

"I don't know. At least mom's happy."

"Is she? Maybe."

Edgar's Dream

"How do we proceed, doctor?"

"We let the swelling go down and we wait."

In the dream he was in a hospital. His head was pounding and seemed to be on fire. Encephalitis, he seemed to think it was. There were heavy bandages and a feeling of euphoric madness hovering just above the pain, a cloud of anesthetic that fed upon his very existence. The invisible forces were whittling him down from the inside. Intuitively aware that he was not alone, Edgar looked up from the sloping bed and saw those who joined him in misery. The patient next to him was sleeping beautifully. She had part of her skull removed and there was instead a synthetic exoskeleton-like covering. There were casts on her right arm and leg and white padding keeping her back in place. Edgar felt like he knew this woman, even though he didn't recognize her in his present state. There was a vague recollection in his memory of being able to communicate with her somehow in a very unorthodox manner— perhaps telepathy or something. He couldn't remember. The guy to his left had been shot up very badly. He was moaning both in Spanish and English, something about his mother. Suddenly it occurred to Edgar that he had been claimed by a war shortly before this hospital arrangement, but could not seem to remember the journey between. It was a war at the oasis of a desert, where the date palms were crawling with giant fuzzy orange hornets and where the night sky was a wondrous sparkling tiara over the earth, and the buildings of creamy plaster-hidden brick were decorated with forbidden Middle Eastern murals harbored like treasures inside the scurrying little draconic dinosaurs with wonderful blue and green and gold scales. He remembered beige turtleback humvees with ballistic windows half a foot thick and turrets with mounted 60 caliber machine guns moving like chariots across the desert roads and being swallowed up in turbulent sand-plumes. There were camels, Western SUVs, caravan busses with Bedouin drivers, along the ancient thoroughfares, irrigated, miraculous green crops, and the dunes rising like a living sea of antimatter. He was certainly not there now. It was odd that one could be so sure, being kept in an artificial room like a houseplant.

"Please, miss... Where am I?" he asked a passing nurse. She, too, seemed familiar. But he really did know this one—she was the Keeper of Time from the gad factory.

She waited captive, in agitation, and then, remembering something, thought better of things and walked quickly within speaking distance of the patient whom Edgar felt to be himself.

"Walter Reed," she said. "Hell's army medical center. This is the near-death ward. You've been in a coma. Oh, wait! You're Weatherholt, Edgar E! We've been informed that your niece is on her way to visit. Isn't that nice? You'll have to excuse me..."

The Keeper was even busier in the dream than in real life. And she still had the cute accent. As he attached himself to that wakeful reality, something began pulling him more and more aggressively through the watery particles of time and space until he arrived at the surface of the spare bed and groggily opened his seemingly-newborn eyes. He felt unsettled, in near-remorse of that departed world. But then, back in his own uninjured body, he felt fortunate. The pain had subsided. There was nothing limiting him here in wakefulness and there were no excuses. If there was restraint, he held himself back.

II

At the Migrant Camp

The night shift exited the bus, one after the other, each a pale and wayworn soul of the darkness. Their haggard expressions each seemed to tell the same story. The night offered them some kind of hope, an escape from the dull, probing spotlights of society where they might find something unusual from time to time. The lightlessness kept them meditative and sedated; they took life in through the fangs, a meal high in the esoteric and radiation-deficient. As they entered the factory as if being swallowed by geometrical shapes, some turned back and watched as their polar opposites occupied the same seats and stared out of the very same windows that had been their escape for 25% of a day. The bus rumbled and shook and then rolled out of the parking lot towards a destination that had become slightly foggy to their memories, as if it existed only then and now, in the minds of those who lived there.

The S.O.B. driver was at it again, cursing at the wind as the bus bounced along the road at top speed. Highway 37 was to him just an illusion. He damned the places and the objects that had no right interfering with the path of a green old loaf of metal and plastic and the synthetic rubber tires which would soon have to be replaced before they exploded, causing massive casualties along notions of punctuality and reliance.

The spring-watered trees of the roadside forest swept past the windows until they were replaced by a lone beauty shop and then a small neighborhood in the shape of a rectangle with rounded corners. The hillbillies had been dropped off a half-hour ago at a campground just outside of Newaygo and the rest of the unwilling passengers were numb with fear. They hit a rural intersection and turned forcefully up a hill and then down into a valley, still too far away to see the dry sandy banks of what was once Lake Michigan.

Empty asparagus fields inhabited both sides of "Oceana Highway", a rural farm route, and then there appeared farm markets, orchards, country houses, and gardens full of squash, peppers, and tomatoes. They pulled into the migrant camp through their own cloud of dust and the bus slid to a halt.

"Now get out!" laughed the S.O.B. driver, finding himself in a rare moment of cheer. "I gotta get home and make love to my wife! See y'all suckers early in the dark blue mornin'! Don't be late! Ha ha ha!"

The migrant camp occupants had little to be happy about, except for a small garden next to the row of rundown red cabins. Only the kid-strapped housewives, who were here for the long-run, had the time to plant anything, so it was always skimpy with patches of herbs and white grates of hot peppers.

The main farm in cooperation with the government-assisted program to house the migrants during their stay in Michigan was over on West Polk Road and consisted of miles of apple orchards and fields of sweet corn, asparagus, squash, and pumpkin. Additional asparagus fields were a little further north where they had passed on the bus. While once a superb locale for apples, cherries, peaches, nectarines, plums, and grapes, the nurturing "great water" winds no longer blanketed these inland nooks along the old shoreline. The fruit grew hotter and less happily, but were still protected from damaging severe weather. And, except for a singularly beautiful farm dedicated to the many original apple species, they had the meddling of an evil plant-hating university to help keep them round in shape and free of certain diseases.

David shared an old hunting cabin with about twenty other men. He slept on a small bed using his sweat pants as a pillow and, as a covering, a vivid woolen serape-style blanket that he purchased in Matamoros during Spring Break to South Padre Island for his senior year of high school. The blanket was not where he had left it and looked to have been used by someone recently. That was the problem, sharing with the night shift. Each shift was like an infestation of mischievous Elves to the other and one never knew whom exactly one was living with.

"Smoke?" asked Carlos. He was holding the entire carton of Manneken Pis.

"Just a second," said David, checking his blanket for stains. The vivid Mayan strips of yellow, orange, red, purple, green, blue, and brown interweaves shone brightly as the dust trickled through the corpuscular beams. The delicately wavering serape with its spectral colors was the hero of the moment. The central star appeared like a single crazy eye with white vitreous humor and purple iris. The lair was otherwise dank and dying, the planks creaking against the cadaver-logs that somehow still breathed with the seasons, seeming to give sermon.

The door opened and closed.

They went out for a smoke.

"Carlos, why do you carry that thing?"

"So no one will steal it. You need a bottle?"

"Can't I get like two bottles?"

"Of course. I just hope you don't lose one. You always lose one when you get two."

"I won't lose it."

Carlos grabbed two tiny bottles. Half of the bottles were already missing.

"How in the hell did you smoke that much already?" David asked in alarm. "Jeez. I can't smoke more than a few at a time without feeling sick."

"The job stresses me out."

David looked concerned. "Ask the Timekeeper to put you somewhere else. I was stressed out and she let me switch. Tomorrow I start on boxes."

"I did ask, you monkey donk. She wanted to put me in the orchard. I'm not going in no freaking place like that. I spent my whole childhood in orchards; cherries, oranges, apples, pears, dawn 'til dusk, there was little Carlito playing with a stick while mommy and daddy picked themselves to death for nickels and dimes."

"But there's nothing wrong with your parents; they're very healthy, in fact."

"That's hardly the point! They have nothing! Nothing!"

"They have their little Carlito."

"Ha ha, you funny bastard," said Carlos in perturbation. "I just wish, you know, that we hadn't blown off those Army recruiters. That sign-on bonus would have made all the difference. We could have gone into some kind of business for ourselves."

"You could have still gone in. I just couldn't. How's anyone going to have a shot at killing me if my mother's beaten them to it?"

"I know, because of your father. That was some tough luck, getting cut to pieces in a faulty drone strike, but that sort of thing rarely ever happens."

"See, like no one ever dies in a war. I'm an only child—what's Mom going to do without me? You have like a brother and three sisters. Besides, you can still go in. They moved the cut-off age to seventy-five just last month. It had been sixty-five."

"That's just stupid. But, do you realize how many people die at work every year? Right here at home. Look it up sometime. The math teacher Mrs. Green made me use the stats for extra credit problems so I could pass. And I know it's true, 'cause my second uncle was cooked to death in a tuna factory's oven down in Florida. And my uncle, they couldn't afford to bury him. At least the Army will pay for your funeral."

The two of them stared off where the smoke should have been, losing themselves in wispy-clouded blue evening sky.

"Someone slept in my blanket I think, the one I got in Matamoros."

"Who knows what it had been before that anyways," said Carlos.

"What do you mean?"

"Never mind. Let's get something to eat."

They went to see the lady who did nothing but cook a lot of food and they bought some chili con carne and melon with soda. They let the spice burn the memory of hardship and went to talk to some girls and then it was time for sleep.

David dreamed of a chimney sweep who was trying to make a living in the Artic where the Inuit had re-created the city of London out of ice and were walking around in the snow like snobby gentlemen beneath the pale green spectral Northern Lights. Because David had never really seen snow, except in video games and movies, his version was large and puffy and remained at room temperature. There was no smoke from the chimneys, and hence no soot to sweep. The rooftops were frosty and the sky was purple with stars. The chimney sweep complained about the absence of hearth-fire and one gentleman in a white-rabbit-fur-coat said, "No fire in the hearth? Fire is for hussies!" and the gentleman threw cubes of frozen whale fat at the chimney sweep until the poor man ran off and was eaten by a polar bear. David had no idea who the chimney sweep was supposed to have been.

Suddenly he was awakened by a loud ruckus. The dream swooshed away and the details of that bizarre reality became lost as the dreamer adjusted to the newer, more unpleasant one.

"Okay you sons of bitches...woo hoo!!" The driver had arrived and was honking the horn and hollering like a drunken fool. "Oily, rotten bonitos!" he said. "Get your sorry asses in this can!" There was wild laughter from the Wrangler-jean-wearing S.O.B..

3:55 said the white face of the clock. Time was always dragging them into the grave. People scrambled around in the darkness, trying to collect themselves and everything else they needed to survive the coming day. They had five minutes to board that scary green decanter.

David Hernando ran for his life. He only hoped the S.O.B. driver was not as drunk as he seemed.

III

The Audition

Antiope was spending a lot of time at her neighbors' as of late, during the week of the 16th and 18th of July. She had spilled the beans about the apartment and about her predicament and the girls were adamant on the issue of salvation and convinced that they would help Antiope reach a better place in life.

"Why don't you come in with us on Friday?" insisted Sheryl as they sat in the living room on cheap furniture. "You could stand to make a lot of money. All the bankers are in town this week for a convention."

"I'll have to think about it."

"Girl, it's easy money," Amira said. "You don't even have to look good. The clothes will be coming off, after all. Just use those hips like a pendulum and don't let anyone touch you. Young attractive ladies like us can get anything we want in there, if we know how to get it. Keep the taser handy though. Sheryl has to zap the same guy every weekend in the parking lot."

"The clothes have to come off?"

"Of course they do!" cried Natalie. "Haven't you ever heard of exotic dancing? One of those old Egyptian professions. You make art with your body."

"I don't know," Antiope deliberated. "I just don't have much experience with that sort of thing."

"You don't need any. We can teach you how to be a world-class stripper right here in this apartment," said Amira. "On average, it only takes five minutes."

"Oh, is stripping an art?"

"It is if you can get a man excited before anything's come off," boasted Natalie.

The girls laughed.

"Oh, I see," Antiope said, turning red with embarrassment. "I might be able to do that. But does it really have to be nude? Ballerinas aren't nude. That's definitely a body art."

"It's a strip-tease," Sheryl explained. "You lure them into giving you money by flashing your mums."

"And they don't get mad? Well, if it's something that'll feed me until I can get my money out of the bank…"

"That's the spirit, girl!"

A Video Conference with the Atypically Benevolent Managers

On the videotelephony application screen in ultra-real eagle vision was a middle-aged man with wiry black and grey hair and benevolent olivine eyes. "NATHAN T. BERGEMOT 56 of Gamesh, Michigan, USA, EARTH 44°46'05 N 85°37'20 W, Owner of VTB Entertainment Inc., Haplogroup R1b" scrolled on the bottom of the screen in a pin-prickly paranoid language reminiscent of a Zamyatin dystopia.

"Hello, my darlings! How are you this afternoon?"

"Great, Papa Berg. Doing just great. How's Momma Berg?"

"She's right here. Say hello, Mama."

A silvery old mare of a woman appeared on the screen of the videophone's computer. "Hi, girls!"

"Good to see you!"

"You, too, girls!"

Suddenly the teleprompter scrolled, "MAUREEN A. BUTCHER-BERGEMOT 62 of Gamesh, Michigan, USA, EARTH 44°46'05 N 85°37'20 W, born Chicago, Illinois, MtDNA Haplogroup N1e'I.

"07/18/2020 10:24:13 AM.

"07/18/2020 10:24:14 AM."

"Listen: we have someone we'd like you to meet. Papa, this is Antiope; Antiope, this is Papa Berg."

"Hello," said Antiope shyly.

"A new recruit, I see," said Papa Berg. "Does she know what she's getting herself into? This line of work isn't for everyone."

119

"She knows, Papa Berg. She's just having a little trouble paying the rent. Are we still hiring dancers? We were hoping she could audition."

"We got rid of Amateur Night after that near-toothless 'brother/sister' act kept showing up and soliciting customers into watching them do despicable things at home in their mobile living room—sad what great extremes people will go to these days."

"They didn't even look related," explained Mama Berg. "And they smelled just terrible."

"But we *are* short a few dancers for this weekend," Papa Berg bemused. "I suppose she could fill in and get to know the place. Has she ever waitressed?"

"Um, no, I'm afraid I haven't," Antiope admitted.

Sheryl interposed, taking the initiative: "That's okay, Papa Berg. We'll show her the ropes. Heck, what's there to serving drinks? She's a real star, this one. She's the unobtainable girl. Just look at her—tell me she doesn't come off as an untouchable little librarian."

"Well, let's ask Mama Berg," Papa Berg said with a shrug. "What do you think, Mama?"

The elder lady gave them a pitiable look. "Has she been told the truth? Let her know the risks involved. Here, let me see who I'm talking to. There you are, dear. Oh, for pity's sake! My, what a sweetheart! Listen, dear, it's a Pandora's Box, becoming an exotic dancer. We're talking exile from the Garden of Eden here. It's really hard putting the lid back on once you've taken it off. Does that sound like something you can handle?"

"Oh, is it really all that?" Antiope asked. "Sheryl said it was like dangling sweets before the eyes of diabetics and making them think they'd actually tasted them."

"Oh, I just don't know, Nathan honey," Mama Berg said worriedly. "She's got the sex appeal, but I think her heart's in the wrong place,"
Papa Berg remained benevolent. "Well, is she alright in front of crowds? She seems a bit nervous. That's usually a sign of a struggling personality; someone dealing with an uncomfortable situation."

"I'm sure if she could just audition…" pleaded Sheryl for the cause.

120

"Well, if you girls feel that strongly..." answered Papa Berg.

"You can just do it on videophone, can't you?" Sheryl said. "That's how Amira was hired."

"You're right!" Papa Berg exclaimed absent-mindedly. "By Jove, these distant encounters just get easier and easier. Say, that gives me an idea. We could probably run that club in Bangkok we've had our eyes on from right here and avoid the monsoon. Okay, go ahead and put her on. Start at your own peril. Whenever you're ready, my darling."

"Wait...just a minute," Antiope mumbled, fidgeting with her hair. "Okay, um...Right now in front of everyone? Will-will I have to take my clothes off?"

"No! Heavens no! There's no need for that, darling. Just show us your routine—what will you be doing up there in front of everyone?"

Dance music suddenly blared from someone's smart-phone speaker attachment, seemingly brought up from Hell on waves of sound.

"Go ahead, Antiope. You can do it!" the girls cheered. "Show Papa Berg your sexy moves! That's it, Antiope. Woo hoo! That's all there is to it, girl!"

Antiope did as she was told, gyrating before the videophone. Having broken out of her initial phase of uncomfortable embarrassment, she shook her hips with abandon, and soon both worlds of the videophone were dominated by dancing people.

"That'll do, Antiope," said Papa Berg at long last when he was nearly out of breath and clutching the frame on his side of the visual. "Come on in, then. We'll start you Friday as a cocktail waitress. If you survive that, we'll let you perform the following week during Happy Hour, but only if it feels right. We're in need of a cocktail waitress anyway, so whichever you prefer."

"That's for the best, dear," said Mama Berg. "You'll know the environment by then and can more easily make a decision as to going further. And you'll earn yourself a little money."

"No more than two drinks per customer... Well, we can discuss all that later. Is there anything else, girls? Mama and I are due for a nap, so we'll have to leave you. Bye, bye, now, my darlings!"

"Thank you so much!" said Sheryl. "Later, Mama and Papa Berg!"

Through the Pink-Tinted Windows of a Hello Kitty Mini Car

Along the thoroughfares of a town bustling with shops they rode as if a dream on holiday. There were shops for shoes, shops for dresses, shops for just about everything, and some had even been part of a former mental hospital. When they hit the end of one road and an intersection onto another they saw trees at the edge of a beach and then what looked like a dead sea of mucky rocks. There were tourists crawling up and down the paths and from further in they could hear the sounds of the carnival rides as sweetened and salted children were thrown into the air and then left to vomit.

"Why go this way?" asked Sheryl from behind Amira, the driver, to whom she was speaking to.

"You have to get the whole effect," answered Amira. "*Yesterday USA* named it a top ten festival this year. The region is known for what could potentially be a world-record gad harvest."

"It's the *only* gad harvest, except for Argentina's test facility in the mountains and that place in China," Antiope said softly. She was sitting next to Sheryl in the back seat, her head resting against a pink bow (the cartoon face of a white kitten was barely visible behind her). "Soon enough, however…"

"So what did you do there, exactly, Antiope?" asked Sheryl concernedly.

"Just about everything: I sorted and stretched, folded and sweetened."

"But what did you do before that?" she asked. "I mean before the gads took over everything?"

"We worked briefly in a nuts and bolts factory until a temp service took it over… before that I interned at a place that made oboes…before that, a chemical foundry…"

"That sounds awful," Natalie said.

"I liked the oboes," Antiope admitted. "The tester was ahead of his time. I was able to pick it up in just under a week from watching him play, but then he was hit by a bus. I'm not even sure what city it was in—we lived in the so-called orphanage nearby."

Sheryl was momentarily speechless. These were tales of which she knew nothing about. On top of that was the commotion. Amira had taken them into horrendous traffic.

"What is she even looking at?" demanded Natalie, seeing from the front passenger seat a bedazzled woman who was standing on the island of cherry trees between four lanes of traffic and staring off into the quagmire while her two children skipped dangerously about.

A jogging path rolled murkily along the grass until the park entrance emerged, allowing a variety of choices for casuals and fascists alike. A testy volleyball tournament had commenced in a sandbox just off the scenic road and a grown woman was throwing a temper-tantrum. Tents billowed as a herd of drunken adults stumbled across the designated walkway. To their right, the downtown appeared busy. Gamesh public transportation shuttles puttered in and out of a brick and glass connection hub, ignoring the snotty comments over undesirable human beings. Glittery Ferris wheels churned the air amidst mini-coasters and funhouses. Festival-goers strolled double-fisted with buttery pretzels, pink and blue cotton candy, watered-down soft drinks, stuffed unicorns, toys-for-tots, or sometimes hand-in-hand.

As Amira turned onto Union Street, they could see a Venetian river heading under a bridge and eventually washing out into the muck. The willows rustled gently above carp and trout.

As they headed towards the downtown shopping area, confronting the noise of a parade, Antiope could see that some of the people were wearing masks.

"What's the idea behind *that*?" she asked.

"It's a protest," Amira explained somewhat indifferently, yet with a touch of enthusiasm. "V-for Vendetta, that sort of thing; they're angry about all the surveillance."

"They should be used to it," Natalie said. "Tracking is enforced, especially by parents with kids. Most places make you get one of those tiny microchips with the beacon."

"That's why I'm happy to be working the shadier side of commerce," said Amira, grinning, even though she could not find a parking space along the river and was having to drive further out.

"It can be a nice thing to have though if you're murdered," continued Natalie.

"What would *that* matter?" Sheryl countered. "You'd be dead."

"Wouldn't you want your parents to be able to bury you?"

"That one's really nice," Antiope commented softly, admiring a bejeweled, gold-feathered mask on someone. She rubbed her scarred right hand and wondered thoughtfully about the future.

Gad Queen

The town was full of people. Once like a city-state along the shores of a vast trade empire, now a trap glistened over the bones of sawmills and smelting plants (better yet, slums, distilleries, whorehouses, and mental institutions). The walls were made of glass and inside the shops along the sidewalk-gantlet of pain there appeared the images of mannequins wearing expensive clothing; luxury glassware; overpriced touristy knick-knacks like hats and mugs; fresh fudge; half-living heathens sipping chalices of wine; tables with resting mugs of beer, sandwiches, or soups.

Barricades of safety-orange road construction barrels, lazily-placed fiberglass planks, and idle squad cars with short-sleeved policemen (or sometimes policewomen) blocked traffic from entering the designated areas. Just a few yards down the street, a shimmering sign read GAD GRAND BUFFET featuring "A Pitchfork Recipe Extravaganza" in a farm theme with culinary delights—neither the culinary nor the catering professionals looked like they knew much about agriculture aside from scrutinizing vegetables at the grocery store. A selection of local wines boasted a legacy of uppity-ness, well worth the $33 admission fee.

Sheryl seemingly led the way through the crowd. Adults, kids, and anonymous youth accommodated the party of four with inquisitive indifference. "So where should we go first?" she asked.

"There's a GADOPOLY Tournament at eleven-thirty; or do we want to see who's been crowned this year's Gad Queen?"

"The coronation was held yesterday evening," Natalie said, "on top of the Park Place Hotel." They could see it rising from some distant hill, and as they turned the corner onto Union Street they saw a float covered in pink blossoms upon which a very young lady with a shimmering white crown on her head was waving enthusiastically at the congealed faces along the sidewalks. She was wearing a silky gown that appeared to change colors. Parade participants with burning brands in their hands walked along the side and in front and up ahead of them was a shiny new silver and gold hybrid car. Flanking them was the high school band and a large banner reading GAD FEST 2020.

"Things just keep going," Natalie continued, fighting the noise with ease. "It's like they're unsure how many pie eaters to award, which princesses to promote, or how long to raffle that car. All this stuff... That carnival should have moved on a week ago."

"Guess they can't decide when it should end," Amira chimed.

"When did the cherries end?" asked Sheryl, addressing no one in particular.

Natalie thought a minute. "I forgot all about the cherry festival. It ended after the first week of July, I think. Didn't have much of anything; not even an air show. They keep cutting back, more every year."

"Well," contemplated Sheryl, "when's the end of the gad season, I mean, from a farmer's perspective?"

"That depends," Antiope said, feeling that she was the only one qualified. "Last season was until Labor Day, but it could have gone on into winter. They just didn't have enough trees. I don't think they want them to be confined to seasons."

Sheryl's eyes went wide. "What?! Well, that's just madness."

"*You're* the *gene* designer!" Amira scolded. "Isn't that what you people do?"

"Feed the hungry?" Sheryl said with a shrug. "Why do you think I chose a medical field?"

"Why *don't* they feed the hungry?" asked Antiope worriedly. "Is it really all about the money?"

"Afraid not…" Amira answered coldly. "It's about control."

"Madness…" said Sheryl.

Madness it was, but not without method. The gads were performing as designed and people were getting what they asked for: Tourists kept the local business owners happy, the farmers were fat with crop, and Monstrosso was finally collecting its dues after considerable time and investment. The competitive spirit of two festivals running back-to-back in the same town was just the icing on the cake, so to speak. An American aura pervaded the air, bolstering the capitalistic cause with a double dose of "freedom" and "democracy". Every sight and smell seemed to comfort people, telling them, 'How can I aid in the fulfillment of your dreams?'—At least, that was how it *should* have been. What was said in propaganda should have been true, yet the projection was false. Even at the precipice of decline, the helots of mercantilism would love a parade. The devils knew that—they who were at the controls. Despite everything to the contrary, commerce was still king, congress were fools-well-paid, and money flowed like the Lethe underfoot of the downtrodden. Meanwhile, the nation was sending its subjects through the grinder and onto the scales. It was a criminal deception of promises and half-truths hissed through archetypal megaphones. With sincerity, face-to-face, they should have said to those who supported them wholeheartedly in trust, 'May your life become one great *epic* in a series of great epics.' Yet instead, if exposed through torture or truth serum, it was more along the lines of 'May all your efforts become wasted on the swank party which I'm about to throw for myself and my closest friends.'

The charade continued, with themes floating down the street as the band played subversive songs to the rhythm of two-dimensional dance moves.

"What is *that* supposed to be?" wondered Natalie.

"A pile of dung I think," Antiope said innocently, and without the aid of rose-colored glasses.

The smell of food made them hungry and Amira suggested a place up near K Street[21]. Progress proved difficult, however, and

---

[21] Actually more of a symbol than a street in this sense, K represents government corruption.

they soon found themselves at the precipice of an incident: Three masked young men were involved in a scuffle with the local police and a wave of bodies was headed their way. They heard a sharp whine and watched apprehensively as one of the officers discharged his electroshock weapon into the thigh of a perpetrator. The young man relaxed instantly onto the sidewalk and appeared to have wet himself. There were visible burn marks in his jeans from where the electric blue current passed into the barb imbedded in his muscles.

"Okay, forget it!" proclaimed Sheryl, having lost her appetite. The candy and popcorn aroma was overpowered by the smell of charred human skin.

Some spectators screamed as they shoved their way out of danger, but most just pointed and laughed. Someone whispered that the anonymous young men were selling 3D-DVDs without a license. The assumption was "black market", but one recent customer snuck away with what appeared to be a local band's album.

"Hey, that's not your boyfriend, is it?" joked Natalie; the masks were forcibly removed.

"Shaddap, you," Sheryl answered (playfully to calm her nerves). She led them back through the crowd in search of less dangerous activities.

QUINTUPLET

I

Bernard Clairvaux

The day went on, just as the last one had, with irritating demon spikes set into the minute timeframes. There was the usual tap or nod, momentarily excusing one from torture, and the vacation would unravel like a brief, third-rate party under the incandescence. But the clock would tick weightily, chiming like a banshee to the marches of time, and the spikes would commence.

Such reprieve had come to Edgar and he pried himself from the stool and stumbled through the tumultuous halls. Into the break room, he emerged from work, sore, tired, and depressed. Although he hated taking breaks because they offered a distraction from focus, this day he wanted one to last eternally, to become a sullen purgatory of stupor. He took a seat away from the others and stared into his folded hands. *What a life I've made for myself*, he thought depreciatively; *all that effort and learning just to become a disintegrating cogwheel.*

Someone had planted pamphlets on the tables and he browsed through one with residual interest. It contained an article on "Celebrity Rand Fanatics", which seemed ironic because the people under discussion had contributed nothing real to society. It was true, however, that no one bothered to thank those who so pervasively had impacted every micro-fiber of their daily lives—especially if they happened to be Liberals. What a shame, though, he thought, putting down the pamphlet, that these Rand fanatics were incapable of rational-self interest, seeming instead to foster a sociopathic belief that they were hated for their greatness (He had read one of Rand's books outside of class once, during high school,

Garet Winced, or something like that, which was about a guy with the audacity to think that he and a handful of other "men of the mind" had created the entire world and therefore had the right to destroy it).

"If only I had me a dorf pony…" he overheard a woman say. "I could die happy, if only I had me a dorf." She was very diminutive, with a cute, shriveled face, almost herself the human equivalent of that which she desired.

Edgar looked at the clock, then into his hands again. When again he looked, seemingly due to the strange unconscious feeling that he was being watched, Jaclyn was sitting over at the next table and she turned to see him. "Hey, Jaclyn!" he greeted. It was Thursday. He had not seen her all week.

Jaclyn put down her banana and waved unenthusiastically. "Where did they put you?"

"Still on the sorting line. What about you?"

"They moved me back to Line One. Some of the girls were missing the bad ones and the quality was down."

"Good to see you."

Edgar left the gaze of his former sorting buddy and moved back towards the sustenance of a peanut-butter-and-jelly-sandwich. The room was so crowded at first that he was lucky to be sitting down at all. The break room chatter became louder and more discernable as conversations gave way to one that proved the more interesting. An argument of some kind had broken out at the central tables and people were drawn in like curious housecats.

"Why do you work here?" someone said to Bernard Clairvaux, one of the quality control employees (By now, everyone knew that he was the son of a Methodist preacher from Ohio). "You could be in your father's church or out in some foreign land spreading the good word."

"Because here is where I am needed the most," Bernard answered. "Don't you see? People here are in serious need of God."

"So you come here feeding on the misery of others? We've got enough problems. We don't need you giving us the guilt trip. Why, hell, you're green as it is and coming off all sour. Try going out and ripening up a bit, then come back and preach to us about our misfortunes. I'm sick of people telling me how to live—especially the green ones."

"Ignore him, Bernard. Tell us what you meant by that... what you said before," encouraged one of the women seated at the table where all the commotion was.

"Alright, I'll tell you," said Bernard. "Do any of you know where *Gad* comes from, the word for it? In The Second Book of Samuel, Chapter Twenty-Four, it reads that King David had a seer named Gad when he decided to take a census of the people so that they would be numbered; this he ordered to assess the kingdom for battle. Soon after, he regretted it and asked the LORD for forgiveness. This is the David who defeated Goliath and in doing so became King chosen under God. As David slept that night, the LORD said through Gad the seer..."

"What a load of crap," said the instigator. He got up finally and disappeared from sight.

Two more followed, and then another. The allotment per hour tugged at their minds like a drug.

Bernard continued, and although Edgar had received only parts of the lecture, he heard the following clearly: "Now the LORD regretted his command and said to the angel, 'Enough now! Stay your hand.' When David saw the angel who had smote the people like so much kindling he said, 'Lo, I have sinned, and I have done iniquitously, I, the shepherd; but these sheep, what have they done? Let Thy hand, I pray thee, be against me, and against my father's house.' They built a temple and made sacrifice, as the LORD commanded-"

Someone dropped a plastic container, spilling a drink with an irresponsible smack.

More people got up and left the table.

"Why is the angel a storm? I have a hard time with that," said one of the other women at the table. "I had a brother that was struck by lightning..."

"Weather, and storms in particular, are angelic in the sense that they impose both fear and awe into the hearts of all who witness their destructive powers," explained Bernard.

"But *we* control the weather. We ride it like a bunch of cowboys. So is humanity responsible for its own misery?"

"That's exactly it, yes. Strife plays a vital role in religion. With bridled nature sedated and packaged up in a box, there can be no God worth investing in for most people. But there can be a God of industry, for here is strife. Misguided, that can be a dangerous situation. Do you want the voice of redemption, or the one which gives you a paycheck every month? Perhaps even the one that sends you to jail."

"So what do we do, preacher's son, just lay back and take it? I'm not gonna lay back." Some other fellow said this as he got up from the table.

"Then what are you doing right now, if you aren't taking it?" said the woman whom had first spoken.

"He's taking the first step. Let's hope the path stays true," said Bernard, rising from the bench at the behest of the clock.

Many others rose to leave, also, and it seemed that time had won.

The Unlikely Entrance of Vin Diesel Davis

The damp and dripping halls of the workplace were overcrowded with makeshift janitors, stool-sitting fruit sorters, mad hatters, quality control personnel, and the occasional tight-scheduled supervisor, each group with its own agenda, while above on the second tier the high-octane pitter machine operators, one young and one middle-aged (unbeknown to her), dangled from the yellow safety bars of the high steel platform like playground children in their increasingly more constant attempts to get the attention of supervisors and shift managers alike. A problem had occurred. The line was killed dead in its tracks and then eventually brought to life again. Forklifts driven by safety-minded hunters of things that had recently become full and needed emptying buzzed up and down the narrow side lanes as procedural impulses activated the horns, lights, and beeps of propane-run vehicle-tools.

While three or four toolbox-wielding men climbed around the factory with heretofore unseen energy before vanishing again into their Dwarven halls, an empty-handed pack of mechanics stood idly around a distant corner of machinery, hovering around a lone wolf who was attacking a motor with screwdriver-bits from an electric drill and a black soldering gun, each of them feeling very smug in dusty coveralls. The hive produced the mead and fiber of industry from the electrical marvels running freely beneath their clever fingers.

"We're taking it to the next level. Try and keep up!" warned the supervisor.

Things had gotten hectic inside the factory. Time had been turned up a notch and there seemed to be more workers crowding in than the previous day. To Edgar, this was no cause to worry, though, because he was used to high doses of stress from his time in the war. Nothing short of hell on earth seemed to satisfy him anyway, and he felt like he should have been living on the edge— backpacking through Siberia, climbing mountains, or sailing the oceans on a thirty-foot sloop. Instead he was wasting away in a gad factory. Disappointing, but this would have to do.

A crowd had formed at the quality control table, and at first Edgar thought they might be waiting for the third line to start up. This was the table that was placed at the labyrinthine crossroads-type area centered between four or more assembly lines where a partial wall separated the early stages of feed tank accumulation and de-stemming from the middle stage of pitting and sorting.

An absorbed young lady in jeans, a red T-shirt, a white apron, and a hair net came by shortly with her dishwashing tub to check the quality by which the machines were successful in getting the pits out of the fleshy substance of the fruit. Edgar had never seen her before, and, looking over towards the quality control table, realized that many of them were new to his experience. Immediately the anger surfaced as it occurred to him that they had been given better jobs, even though he and others with completed college degrees had already been working the less-desirable jobs for almost a week.

"College kids," huffed the woman next to him with the uncanny ability to read Edgar's mind.

A nubile crowd formed at the quality control table that was placed at the labyrinthine crossroads-type place centered between four or more assembly lines where a partial wall separated the early stages from the middle stage of pitting and sorting.

The privileged young college student made her way down the short perpendicular pitting belts that were spewing unseeded gads systematically onto the longer and wider sorting belt below. Seeming almost ethereal to the sorters, she began placing her juiced tub on temporarily vacant stools instead of the designated steel pedestals placed strategically along the belt for her advantage.

Edgar was sorting near his usual place, but had elected to stand in hope of relieving the pain from his sore butt cheeks. Watching the careless student, he wondered if he might be better off protecting his pants from soggy gad juice being spilled over the seat of his stool and just enduring the pain. He decided to give the student the benefit of the doubt, thinking the obvious was obvious. He was wrong. The student tested her samples for pits using Edgar's stool and dumped them unceremoniously into the bucket at his feet so that they splashed the astonished Edgar, and then she casually moved on. Now his seat was wet, as were his pants. And the careless person responsible seemed oblivious to any wrongdoing as she went on wetting the untenanted stools.

"Can you believe that?" hissed Edgar's neighbor.

"I can't," Edgar said. He was too angry even to continue sorting. Instead, he went up to the crowded quality control table, cut in, ripped a long strip of paper towels from the roll, and then went back to wipe off everyone's stools.

Soon things seemed back to normal as everyone hurried to keep up with the quickening pace. They took turns rotating breaks. Edgar took his fifteen-minute break and returned to the hell that awaited him.

Some kind of commotion was boiling at the quality control table that was placed at the labyrinthine crossroads-type place centered between four or more assembly lines where a partial wall separated the early stages from the middle stage of pitting and sorting. The freshly-employed group of college students had the look of disturbance.

"I can't take another minute of this!" said one. "Who's for quitting this stupid job? We should form a protest!"

"Yes, let's quit! These conditions are deplorable!"

They were drowned out as people moved back and forth along the walls of periphery. Supervisors arrived, yelled, and were yelled at in turn. Having been overcome by a mob, which was something of an orderly nature despite the peril, they ran off to ally themselves with a higher peerage. The managers appeared in the confusion and they, too, were confronted. Being as such that the industrial servant rarely appreciated the forces which had educated them to their own miserable self-awareness, the revolutionary college students were united with irony. It was industry, after all, which had allowed them to remain so numerous in the first place. So argued the managers, but their efforts were futile.

Despite this background riot, those who were occupied paid little attention. The mechanical resonance carried assiduously through the factory with deleterious effect, being so kind as to numb the human ear into painful health around the foamy green disposable plug. The moiling atmosphere held a penchant for placing the workers inwardly into deep daydreams of escape-minded psychosis and lulling the haunted inner children with industrial lullabies.

"Excuse me, please," sulked a shift supervisor. She had put on a white apron and taken a tub and was apparently checking quality. The poor woman seemed upset despite the opportunity to actually do something physical.

Edgar grinned and kept on working.

At some point during the next hour, replacements were brought out to fill in the large gaping holes in quality control and to relieve the supervisors. Edgar had seen most of them before, but only knew a few of them by name.

A guy armed with an aluminum shovel barreled beneath the production belt like a crazed boar, scraped the pits and the gelatin slime into the gutter, raced back out, and then just stood there propped up against his weapon of sanitation. His entire body twitched like a ring-necked pheasant and his eyes bulged red. "Ah, this is so fucked," he said. He took in a tired breath, oblivious to the bleak unwearied world around him. "How do you even do it?" he spoke through the babble, assumingly to the human forms on stools. "I no longer feel anything, but you...where does the pain go?"

"Oh, it's right here," said one lady, holding up her gauntleted wrists and wiggling her short fingers.

"I mean the pain of living like this," he said. "Me, I'm just passing through. This is all staged for Vin Diesel Davis—that's me—and I'm just waiting for events to unfold."

134

"What do you usually do—when you're not down there pretending to be shoveling?" asked one of the sorters.

"A pharmacist of sorts—a medicine man for the weary and downtrodden—I'm in league with your cheery preacher here," said Davis, referring to Bernard, who had been one of those requested to replace the seditious college students.

Bernard swished the dead and soulless fruit around inside his grey plastic tub. "What's that?" he said, surprised to hear that he was included in a conversation. They were nearly all deafened as it was.

"You're a medicine man for the weary and downtrodden!" said Davis at a louder decibel. "So am I!"

"Oh, yes! I guess we had a talk in the break room not long ago, didn't we!" said Bernard, suddenly recognizing who was speaking to him. "You told me you were possessed by demons!"

I am!" said Davis. "That was no lie! I've been taken over by the chemical kind! And you know what? I like it!"

"You mean drugs?" solicited Edgar. "That you're a drug dealer?"

"What? I didn't say that! I'm a musician," said Davis, almost tripping over the shovel that he dragged along in front of him. "My parents knew I was going to amount to something— that's why they named me after The Diesel."

"You sure amounted to something alright!" laughed the sorter lady. "Look at you, down there in all the riches! You don't deserve no actor's name!"

"I just mean that it's all an act. When you get right down to the heart, it's just a matter of belief; something or someone triggers a response to what you've been searching for and makes you believe that you're getting it, but there's nothing really there, just music; or apparitions; or, if you wish, chemicals."

"He's no musician," declared another sorter-lady. "What do you play: the crack pipe?"

The few people who could hear what was being said laughed out loud.

"Ladies, please," said Davis. "We all have our own roads to salvation! I'll not apologize for my evil ways. I'm just sayin' that Bernard and me ain't so different. The preacher here's got what you need, the opiate of the masses! File into your pews and prepare to be mystified!"

"In a manner I guess!" said Bernard loudly, fighting the noise. "If you prefer to think of it that way. But it's one drug that won't bite you back! You think you've got the rapture in your hands, but it's really just serpents!"

Davis beamed down at his hands in sudden terror. He looked back at Bernard uneasily, but then managed a jittery smile. "Good one, preacher!" he laughed. "You really had me going there for a second!"

"Somethin's got you, alright..." mumbled Bernard. "Lord, help this fool."

"Well, it's been nice talking..." said Davis. "Don't wait!" He grabbed the shovel and ran back into the damp trenches.

Missing Digits

The clammy stool had become like a trickster, shifting beneath unsuspecting sitters as they sorted through the sparkling would-be treasure trove. It was a wet perch for a sickly humanity. The stool bore the brunt of the struggles of the human spirit against the harsh conditions of industrialism, collected just above in the sack-like rump of idleness. The sitters wobbled uncomfortably. They endured the hours with inner strength. The seat remained dry, stifled, somewhat civilized beneath their chilled flesh.

As the afternoon wore on, Edgar began to feel the motion sickness again. He glanced around the factory to see if he could shake it. The machinery moved like a flowing river. Allegedly stationary things shifted oddly and in a counterclockwise direction. Edgar watched the room spin, the water flow uphill. He felt nauseated, detecting a hint of death in the clammy coldness of his surroundings. He went back to sorting, but felt himself falling into the belt. He fell and fell. The stool seemed to be shifting out from beneath him. He shimmied himself by his buttocks into a more comfortable position, only to fall and fall again. He watched the gads flow down the river. His crooked back ached. He repositioned himself. It seemed an eternal afterlife of irritable repetition.

"Eeek!!"

The shriek of humanity came at him as if from a dream that he had been pulled from.

"Get it! Get it!" shrieked a sorter near the beginning of Edgar's line. The workers seemed not to be getting it. Someone jumped up and ran to find the supervisor. Workers were scrambling like mad to catch the thing, but seemed to lose their nerve once they got there. Whatever it was, Edgar's imagination went wild with the possibilities: perhaps a finger, an emerald pitviper, or a warty gray treefrog. A small mob of frantic belt-followers watched the object ineffectually while a supervisor lunged in between them and grabbed nothing but fruit juice and air. The bells rang like sirens from the deep and all three lines abruptly wavered. It seemed to Edgar that he was at the bank of a nightmarish landscape and observing the bottom of a river. Now that events unfolded before him and the movement had taken a different direction, Edgar could see the problem object firsthand. Something was definitely on the belt. Instinctively he lunged and collected the repulsive item, which turned out to be a soggy deer's head pierced by several rather long wooden barbs. He held the smelly head up triumphantly. People gathered around to see; the fear was still in the poor animal's eyes; most were disgusted, but some were curiously attracted now that the thing was being handled by someone else.

"Are you alright?" someone asked. Edgar could barely distinguish the wavering face.

"Just motion sickness," Edgar explained nauseously.

Ruth the supervisor broke up their fun, however, and made Edgar place the severed head into a large black baggie.

"Break! Everyone! Go on break!" she yelled. "And you, sir, will need to be sterilized. Dispose of your things and meet me in the armory."

"Aw, doesn't he get a cookie?" someone whined sympathetically.

"We're all out of cookies!" said Ruth irritably. "Barb, take this please!"

"Great. Me?" Barb sulked, zooming in on the problem. "Okay, Ruth. My God, this thing's heavy!" Holding the bag at a safe distance, especially considering that poisoned barbs had punctured holes in it, she went away to file the head for evidence and to retrieve the bleach and the brushes.

Disoriented from the motion sickness, Edgar followed the transients as if in a drunken stupor.

Vin Diesel Davis crawled out from his hole at that moment and checked his pager before joining the creeping flock just ahead of where Edgar was swimming.

"Don't tell me: *you* did this!" accused one of the sorters from the assembly line.

"Not at all. Why accuse me?" reasoned Davis blankly.

"Why? Why indeed! Well, earlier today *you said*-"

"I know, my dear. I know. Intuition tells you to be suspicious of people like me, and you would be right," said Davis with a surprising show of honesty. "But this was none of my doing! In fact, my plan was to take place tomorrow. I guess that stray tomcat I caught last night gets to keep its guts. Fortunate. Maybe cats really do have nine lives."

"Sicko!" said the sorter.

"Just being honest. I smoked a little grass this morning... What? I have a pain disorder...it's legal across most the country..."

"I'm going to tweet a note to Vin Diesel about you!" said another sorter-lady disgustedly.

Davis shrugged. "What's stopping you?"

"Not you!" challenged the sorter-lady. "I'll do it just as soon as we get to the break room!"

"Why not do it right here?"

"W-we're not allowed!"

"Live a little. Rules are a pain in the ass."

"Vin Diesel's gonna kick yours!!"

"Looking forward to it. Alright. Well, I've gotta go see my peeps. Have fun, ladies."

II

David Gets Lost

The week had become increasingly more dangerous for David. Adolf's friend Harvey had joined them on boxes that Day of Thor and the two fascists were pressuring Pete to replace David with a third friend, Karl. So now there were three skinheads wandering about and they were all large, aggressive, and very pale. The anger of being locked up inside of a societal fortress, of the castle turned inward and against, radiated from Karl, even at a distance, but had been turned peaceful with Harvey. David suspected this was partly to do with prescription drugs. Nonetheless, Harvey smiled stupidly when spoken to and retained a certain level of politeness. But underneath he harbored ghouls and his mind was sharp and potentially dangerous.

"White Power," greeted Adolf, giving Harvey the salute.

"White Power," Harvey cheerfully answered. He waved his right arm outward from his chest and held it for a moment in mid air.

As yet, though, only two skinheads occupied David's workspace.

The worst of it was that Harvey was not as stupid as he looked; in fact, he might have been some kind of criminal genius. He had a way of acting nice while he manipulated people into doing his bidding without them even knowing it; he had convinced Pete that David was a careless worker by loudly and politely lecturing to David every time the stack became uneven and by stepping in to fix Adolf's conceited shortcomings. Adolf got a big kick out of this and yet Pete seemed oblivious to the mean trick.

"What do you say we get rid of this stain and replace it with Karl," persuaded Adolf. "We'll be a real team then, with Pete here to lead us to supremacy!"

"That's up to the boss," said Harvey; "Although, Karl could lift this messy guy into the ground."

"He would crush him!" added Adolf enthusiastically. For effect, he plunged his fist into the flesh of his palm with a smack and laughed dementedly.

"I'll keep him in mind, "said Pete. "Once the third line is underway, another spot will open up. I'll let the Keeper of Time know."

"Why can't we replace him now?" questioned Adolf impatiently.

"It's not up to me, unless there's a problem," Pete explained. "Is there going to be a problem?"

Adolf scowled. "He's a sack of b-burrito shit!" he stammered. "He's b-been messing up the stacks! Get a r-*real* worker in h-here!"

Adolf had popped some kind of pill some time back when he thought no one was watching and was beginning to trip over some of his words, but David was not about to report this humorous observation out loud.

"Keep your head, Adolf. Everything will work out," assured Harvey calmly. "It's like that Blue Oyster Cult song, 'Don't Fear the Reaper'."

"What's Blue Oyster?" Pete asked.

"What?! It's timeless!" proclaimed Harvey.

"Why get into the old stuff?" Pete asked. "There's a lot of great new material out. Have you guys heard the new Clerun Gowph album? *Kilgore Trout*; I love that song 'Everything is Plagiarized'."

David's face brightened. "I heard the other one online I think: 'Originality is Hard'."

"That's a good one, too," said Pete happily.

"Hell, w-what's an album?" Adolf grumbled, folding his muscled arms with difficulty. "I just go to the Aryan Brotherhood festival and get drunk. Who was it last summer…played…what was the song? 'White Goddess'. That was a great song."

"I was incarcerated last summer," said Harvey. "I got into that fight at the bar and almost killed the guy."

Adolf paused. "That's right, I f---forgot. I was thinking you were there."

"Only in spirit, bro."

140

"You always did like p-picking fights," continued Adolf. "You're a true w----white warrior."

"I did," Harvey said blankly.

"The bass player for Clerun Gowph is from Montevideo," said David. He was ignored.

"I like that new punk band High Octane Pup," said Harvey. "They do a bitchin' cover of Slayer's 'Angel of Death'."

"We should probably start taking breaks," said Pete, changing the subject. "You wanna go first, Adolf?"

"Me? Err...could you do me last?" stuttered Adolf, illicitly playing with his phone. "I'm trying to coordinate...I mean, a friend of mine..."

"Okay, then Harvey."

"I can wait," Harvey began diplomatically. "My girlfriend works here and we spend so little time together as it is. I was hoping to catch her...say, in about fifteen minutes?"

"I understand. Have it your way, then," Pete said. He gave these orders with a certain purpose which no one even guessed at. Acting perturbed, he gave his final afternoon command: "David, you can go first."

"We won't even miss him," said Adolf.

"Okay." David shrugged and contentedly made his way to the break room.

He felt his pocket but it was empty, to his chagrin. "Damn, I really need a cigarette," he mumbled. "Where the hell is Carlos?" Carlos had placed the bottles with their lunches, but he was in the other building and David was clueless about how to get there. "I knew I shouldn't have agreed to that." Carlos was a good friend, but he suffered from selfishness. He had convinced David that the second building was close and that he would have little trouble finding it, but when he had asked Nan she said it was way in the back behind stacks of metal and plastic bushel-boxes and that the only way to get there was through a double door that was way in the back of the factory near the juicing machines. Without the luxury of having been given a tour because the bus was late that day, David turned back into the factory and walked aimlessly through the industrial maze of factory equipment.

Through a wide opened doorway there appeared a room, almost like an industrial kitchen. Large witches' cauldrons sat empty and shiny on the shelves. Plastic cups used for packaging applesauce were stacked on a stainless steel counter. The next room resembled an assembly line in miniature with a weird little grain dispenser ready to drop something onto a track made for the rolling of boxes. Just over the dispenser was a short belt of rollers arching upwards from a sorting belt being fed dried gad stuff through a white PVC pipe attached to an ordinary feed tank. Beyond the only accessible passage, a wide doorway with fringed plastic hanging down, David could see another interesting sequence of machinery involving assembly lines, large tubes, water hoses, ballistic glass, a high-rise tank holding what seemed to be a large corkscrew grinder, several thick boiler tanks, and a large, expensive-looking hydraulic pressing machine covering the entire upper floor or a metallic storage platform. It looked very expensive. A small crew was working the line. They were wearing gauntlets and plastic aprons and appeared to be related—in fact they were nearly identical. David watched to see if he could figure out what was going on. He knew enough through his past experience with cherries that this was something special, something beyond merely sorting, cleaning, and removing the seeds. The first sorter from the outside portion of assembly that stood obscurely beyond more fringed plastic strips was actually a robot detection system, leaving the job of the second human sorter so full of idleness that he had his feet propped up on a stool and was watching television on a large screen attached to one of the holding tanks near the white assembly belt. A crown made of wood and some kind of filled sack-like material sat tilted on top of his head. Two or three workers ran around the machinery checking valves and such while another—the same pretty young brunette from quality control who ran back and forth near the boxes—wrote something down on a clipboard. But then something gruesome happened: The guy who was working high up at the corkscrew grinder had an incident and subsequently disappeared in a spray of blood. A man in a perfect cap who wore a clean and pressed navy blue mechanic's uniform appeared at the base of the yellow platform's staircase, then ran up to the corkscrew grinder, followed by the valve checkers.

"Get the hiring manager!" he said, gesturing wildly with his hands. "We need another worker!" He turned desperately and, seeing David at the door, pointed and yelled, "Hey you! Are you new?! Hey! Come over here!"

David deftly ignored the man, frightfully inching his way out of the bizarre situation. He ran frantically back through the maze of industry like a terrified little mouse of NIMH. There was no other way out of the building from this back side that he could see. Everything was very confusing. He ran and ran until finding the hand-washing station that was just outside the break room to the human resources office and the factory exit. There had to be a way around to the other building, but he was out of time and patience. Over near the boxes Harvey had disappeared; Adolf looked angry and pointed as David came into sight.

Suddenly there were bells ringing and both lines stopped to a halt. The supervisors ran around frantically to assess the situation and then ran frantically back with their gathered information. The attractive, skin-tight quality control brunette with the clipboard was there in the mix, appearing from the back corner of the factory where David had witnessed the accident. Then the supervisors ran around giving orders and people were saying that everyone was to go on break. David was caught at the head of a rush to the break room and decided that it was best to just go with the flow on this one.

"A break," people were saying, "until further notice."

David was overjoyed. Perhaps God had heard his plea for once and was helping him get a cigarette.

Someone grabbed him roughly by the shoulder and he was swung around against his will. Harvey and Adolf were there, anchored within the crowd, and coming towards them was the face of someone who could have only been Karl. Harvey's powerful hand was resting heavily on David's shoulder.

"Here's the scoundrel!" scolded Harvey somewhat playfully. "You're one lucky bastard! Where in the Hell were you, anyway? Trying to screw us, weren't you."

"I was looking...I need a smoke...my friend has them..."

"You and your compadre have something against skinheads, don't you?! Thought you'd pull one over on us, you lazy piece of shit! Just admit it!"

"No, I have nothing against you!" David answered, his face frozen from fear. "May you remain forever as blanched as snow!"

"I don't buy it, Adolf!" said Harvey. "What about you?"

"He's a lying sack of burrito shit!"

The abrupt increase in stares from fellow co-workers encouraged Harvey to loosen his grip and, in a sudden change in course, he playfully patted David's head. "I love this guy!"

"He's like a refried chipmunk!" Adolf chided in near-warmth.

The arrival of the third personage of pale-fire rage distracted David's coworkers enough that he was able to slip away with the next wave of humanity and he scurried outside to find a way around the building. A dark simmering field of death stretched out before him. There were sharp foreign combustible chariots lined up near the sidewalk and much chintzier methods of transportation scattered about the parking lot. A high fence topped with razor-sharp wire secured the factory grounds, making trespassing impossible. There was a feeling of being watched. Which way was best, he wondered. They both seemed a long way towards satisfaction: to his right, the blacktop made its way down past security and around the building, but was currently a grazing area for huge semi trucks with heavy loads from distant farms; across the parking lot to his left quietly sat a vacant storage building with an arm attached to the main factory and backed by a thicket of indignant red pines. A mysterious tower rose into the sky from well beyond that side of the factory and he had been curious to see what purpose it served. But it was much further than he had initially realized and was set against the backdrop of the day. Against his better judgment, he took the left, which seemed reasonable enough. This way, he could avoid being run over.

An increasing number of people were standing around chatting while others entered their vehicles and invited people inside as if into an office. Various forms of music blared from car stereo speakers, joining within the "empty" spaces of air—nitrogen, oxygen, argon, carbon dioxide, neon, helium, pheromones, microbial life forms, dust particles, low-altitude pollutants, and miniscule toxins—to create a discordant symphony of madness. David dodged the waves as best he could and imagined the sweet licorice smell of *Manneken Pis*.

He was able to easily pass between the storage building and the high fence separating the factory from the road and make his way to the pines. Something scurried, which frightened him, but he could not see what it was and judged by the sounds that it was much smaller than an eighteen-year-old human being. The smell was nice as he made his way into the thicket, crunching the pine-covered branches of the floor with his uneasy feet. There was definitely something unhealthy about trees, but they managed to keep pushing on in life, despite the unhappiness over their locale.

A black squirrel bounded over the piles of orange needles, discarded cones, and piles of sticks, avoiding a shiny aluminum can and two dirty Styrofoam cups.

David smiled and crunched further into the trees like Frankenstein. He could see that there was a fence at the edge of the thicket which appeared to stretch all the way to the wall of the factory and this troubled him. Traveling out of a sickly makeshift harmony, the fence stood before him, reminiscent of one found at a power station to keep people from getting too curious. A small sign said simply "KEEP OUT!"

Suddenly David heard something large crunching over the floor behind him and to his horror turned to see Harvey and the one he suspected was Karl making their way into the thicket of tall and thin red pines.

"There—isn't that the son-of-a-bitch?" Karl asked as he pointed.

"Sure as hell is!" said Harvey. "There goes your meal ticket!"

Karl fidgeted as his mind was pulled by a different gravity. "But, the exchange; what if they decide to do it now instead of tomorrow? Adolf said to stand by due to the unplanned break."

"You got your phone, don't you? Well, I know how you can't part with it."

"But there was at least five minutes after we talked when I forgot to turn the ringer on. We should have just laid low. And what if the guards saw us? We'll draw attention to ourselves!"

"What, seriously? This is too good to pass up! It'll just take a minute, Karl. Can you think of a better warm-up?"

"You just got out of prison. Are you really that anxious to go back?"

"My god, you're a softy. Go and hang around Adolf's crack, then. You never seem to stop licking it anyway."

David heard the ringing ring-tones of two cellular smart-phones—one, a cheesy metal riff, and the other a vastly overused rap rhythm. Adolf's voice echoed between the three-way call.

"What do you mean it *might* happen, Adolf?" scolded Harvey into the smart phone's screen. "Is it going to happen, or isn't it?" A voice was teleported back from some unknowable location. "Well, didn't it occur to you to go find out?!"

"I'll be right there, Adolf!" chimed Karl. "You coming, Harvey?"

"I can't! Not on a maybe!" said Harvey as he took off through the trees. "I've been good...for far too long!"

And just like that David was being pursued. He tore off down the fence line and back into the trees, trying to make his way around to the second building with life and limb intact. There seemed to be no fence in this direction, but the trees became thinner and less healthy until suddenly he was running through a ghost forest. Further ahead, across a dismal landscape of mosses and decaying plant matter, there appeared the metal obstruction he had been conditionally expecting. He tried to turn and circle back to where the factory should be, but the skinheads were too close.

"You crazy fool!" yelled Karl in perfect Wagnerian pose. "This is exactly why Hitler lost the war! I'm going back!"

David assumed this was a trap and kept his head forward. In time, he figured, the monstrously large skinheads would get tired and have to go back to refuel; their aggressiveness was unsettling, however, and it seemed they would not be easily deterred. He soon came to the fence and looked to the bottom edge and followed frantically until he found a canine-size hole with enough room for a person to scramble though. He quickly crawled under the mangled mesh of the fence. The footsteps closed in. David could feel the vibrations of black steel-toed combat boots over the earth as he raced away from the epicenter. He darted through the wooden corpses of dead trees, zigzagging like a hare, until the impossible happened: the ground became sand, and he suddenly faced an oasis of soft beach grass, quaking aspen and white pine amidst a sea of dunes bulging hotly in the sun. He was trapped and there was no alternative for him other than to trudge on into this unlikely desert and hope that the lily whites would give up the pursuit. He ran as fast as he could, kicking up sand and leaving a noticeable trail in the natural lines of drifting essence, until he reached the mysterious anti-grove of trees on their little foundation of earth, where he rolled on the ground in exhaustion. He heard one pursuer yell something about being an expert, but doubted it meant what he thought it had meant. Knowing instinctively that it was imperative to keep his edge, he pried himself up on wobbly limbs to see what his pursuers were doing. Karl actually had turned back, David was happy to note, but he did not see Harvey. It seemed too good to be true. He got up behind a tree and looked out and still did not see Harvey. But then he looked out to the north and saw him creeping around the natural grooves in the sand like some kind of desert lion. David had been filling himself with the joy of victory, but that was now quickly replaced with terror. *I could make it*, he thought, looking back toward the ghost forest and several hundred yards of neglected fence-line, but then the wind suddenly picked up and blew sand in his eyes and when he looked back he did not see the lion. Filled with panic now, he slid down a slope of shifting sand that slowly cascaded from between two knobs of grass and hardened sand and took off down into a wide valley towards the next row of hills. The sand was difficult, but nothing like the prickly ashtray surrounding El Paso and rising into the Franklin Mountains where deadly rattlesnakes lay coiled behind red prophetic rocks. If those wishing for the eternal silence lived through that, they could travel north to the White Sands Missile Range and try their luck with ordinance, or just head south into Juarez. As he shuffled into the picaresque valley and then back up the sloping dunes, David doubted he would have to worry about such things.

He heard a roar somewhere to his right and glanced towards the sound to witness the charge of Harvey from a granular valley near the anti-grove. The sand made a zipping sound as Harvey bounded into the valley after him, but for all Harvey's power, he lacked the stamina needed to catch the much smaller and weaker

David, who had been a mediocre long distance runner for the track team during high school—the Mustang mascot inspired many a flapping foot along the Greco-Roman oval at Burges High. Neither was willing to give up, and so the two of them trekked stupidly into the unknowable maze of shifting grains while the ghostly wind erased the marks behind them before vanishing once more into the mystery of stillness. The rising and falling waves of creamy fortitude made it difficult to navigate, despite a southern-leaning sun of the 45th Parallel. Some declines were simply massive, requiring kangaroo-like jumps into self-made pockets of comforting sand, and extremely difficult to climb. Bushes and small trees made sparse appearances along the open sections and provided very little shade.

But the next time David looked back he saw no trace of his pursuer. He was very thirsty and it occurred to him how stupid it had been to go running off into a desert with no water. He turned towards the sun and slightly away from the descent in hopes of discovering some kind of familiar landmark that would lead him back to civilization. His throat was beginning to stick and growing sore and he could not stop the tears from acting as balladeer to his lack of sense. He would surely die out here, never to be found. The skinheads had won, like coyotes driving the rabbit to its death. They thought he did not belong, but now his body would meld with the local elements for all time.

There were sharks in the sea of air that were like black neutrinos with their fins slicing through a golden light in his disturbed vision and for some reason a verse which he had never even fully absorbed caught him naked at the temple, so to speak.

"If I am going to be drowned, why in the name of the seven mad gods who rule the sea was I allowed to come thus far and contemplate sand and trees?"[22]

Sometime early in his sophomore year at Burges High, in El Paso of the American Southwest, between his parents' estrangement and moves to Agua Dulce where there was nothing, the class had read from an anthology of American Literature. David had liked the stories by Stephen Crane, one of a handful who knew what they were talking about. In that story, some guys on a sinking lifeboat

---

[22] The line is from "The Open Boat" by Stephen Crane.

were trying to reach the shore. David had forgotten all about it—funny that he should remember that line now.

The dunes shifted in the breeze, never again to completely resemble what they were a second ago.

Buried Treasure

The sun beat down through the haze, cooking humanity like empowered villains of Superman. The northern dunes may as well have been the Sahara. No one within this solar oven was safe.

David stumbled on something buried in the light goldenrod sand and ate dust after falling belly-first along the unmarked trail of death. After picking himself up dejectedly and cursing his sour luck, he glanced back to where he had caught his foot and saw something appalling: A semi-helmeted skeleton in advanced ballistic armor and bluish-gray military combat uniform—seemingly, perhaps, integrated with some kind of invisibility cloak that flickered in and out of existence—peaked out from a blanketed natural tomb. He could just see the barrel of an assault rifle sticking out[23]. All of the soldier's gear was still intact, and as much as David desired to leave the corpse in peace, there was his own survival to think about—already, he imagined that he himself was the one buried there unknown. FORESTER, read the strip of cloth over the right breast, and the other said U.S. CIVIC LEGION[24]. Very

---

[23] Most likely, the Mk. 16 Scar-L Close Quarters Combat variant designed by Fabrique Nationale.

[24] Late during The Year of the People's Revolt, when all congressional leaders were forcibly sent to a retraining camp in Cambodia for an internet reality show announcing both the end of political cronyism and so-called "reality entertainment", all sensible citizens of the United States of America voted unanimously to circumvent military corruption and waste by diverting tax funds from the Pentagon to create a special domestic force called the United States Civic Legion. Despite a radical change in structure in which lieutenant and captain were the only available ranks; Nevertheless, twelve four-year positions for Head Peon were ultimately created, each capped at only two terms, in which eligibility could be obtained at the end of a nine-month online correspondence class. The Legion proved valuable during the North American Water Wars of 2014, when traditional branches of the U.S. armed

carefully, he dug in the sand to see what he could find. A small pack clinging to the boney shoulders contained the following: a pair of desert sunglasses, a live hand grenade, all-in-one blueberry lipstick for chapped lips, four packages of sanitation wipes, an e-reader, a petrified lump of chocolate, a sports bra and matching panties. Although the grenade would make for a messy exit, there was nothing that suited him. But something else was buried a little further down and he was overjoyed by this discovery: A portable back-sack thing for liquids, covered in the same bluish-gray camouflage, with a protected drinking tube! Overzealously, despite his fatigued condition, he did not hesitate in taking the tube to his mouth and drinking a series of deep gulps. He lay down to face away from the skeletal remains and waited to see if he would die. There was a very faint chemical taste to the water, but it had otherwise been well preserved. He seemed to be alright and was grateful that in the place where he was the dead cared for the living.

David turned again and made a comfortable divan out of the sand. He laid back and contemplated the corpse and what it meant to his own life and to the larger forces which had forgotten them both. Part of him wanted to get away, far away, but the other part felt indebted and even connected to this spot, the eternal tomb, buried in a sea of stardust. The fine organic particles sparkled as they were blown out of place yet again.

It was lucky, David thought. He whispered a quick, simple-minded prayer. Certain that he could make it back if he continued on in the same direction, he took another drink and blessed the remains of Lieutenant Forester and again set off away from the sun. As he danced along the dunes with renewed energy, he carried the vision of the Civic Legion casualty with him as a sign from God that he would make it back alive. Indeed, everything seemed more pleasant than before and he witnessed the grace and beauty of the dunes, the mystical shapes and shadows, the tiny footprints of animal caravans, noting how life clung to the wasteland and resisted the shifting of space. Far to his right, he now realized, a forest was battling the dunes. A blackened green and orange blob of resistance, it pushed back against the encroaching sand, forcing it to form a steep sloping wall of purplish shadow below the golden

---

forces, excluding only the U.S. Coast Guard, held worldwide obligations well beyond domestic borders.

150

plateau in the shape of capricious toes belonging to a never-ending foot. A story was being told here, of distant past and future, and the epic battle between elements. It was both hope and despair; beautiful and also terrible in its inevitability.

David trudged on through the golden terrain. He was beginning to remember certain ridges and vegetative patches of life. This was a good sign. He jumped off a grassy ridge just for the fun of it and bounced several times and then let the momentum take him into a roll. Suddenly he heard a very hoarse roar from a small valley to his left. He tried to run from whatever it was but it tackled him.

"You...you're not getting out of this!" gurgled Harvey. He fell into a choking fit and David managed to break free, but then Harvey came at him again. "I'm...k-hack...I'm taking...you... with...me!"

David easily maneuvered away this time. The red, ashen lion was in no shape to be hunting anything. "Save your strength, you stupid ass!" he scolded defensively. "There's water! Water! Wait here! I'll get some for you!"

"Bullshit...kahhhhh [cough; choking sound]...you'll...you'll leave me out here. I expect no less; just be honest, you angelic twit! Kah kah kkk... It isn't like I don't deserve it. I'm a bully...always have been...I thought I could change if I just kept a steady head... I read all those fagoty novels... listened to motivational failures on mp3. It's just fate...the warden was right..."

"Don't believe those gringos. They're just evil! They need someone to feed their own twisted existence. You're making the effort. You desire the change."

"You're too much...just go on...back to your prissy little heaven...leave me already! Kahh-kahak-kahak! Leave the humorist in his grave!"

"Hold on! Try not to move! I'll be back! It isn't far!"

The Grail Quest: Any Cup Will Do

David retraced his steps, which were thankfully still noticeable, until he rediscovered the unmarked grave of Lieutenant Forester. But when he unclipped the straps and tried to pry the water-pack from the shoulders of the corpse, something got stuck and he had to change position. The sand slid away, even though he was being careful, and, the way the position of the grave sloped, David was afraid he might dislodge the corpse entirely. "Carefully, carefully, David, you idiot!" he scolded himself. As he stood over the entombed and pulled at the sack, the arms lifted and something fell away inside the combat uniform. He could hear something scurry. The thought of snakes or spiders living inside Lieutenant Forrester made him cringe. But then he could hear something squeak in panic as it tried to find the exit, the sound of a furry little desert mouse. David continued cautiously, persistently, to take the water from the corpse. It had become like gold, and seemed as heavy as such. Finally he pried the sack loose, but then the skeleton shifted with the arms the skull became completely dislodged from the helmet. It startled him so much that he quickly stepped back and tripped on the protruding barrel of the rifle, and, as he fell backward, the entire cadaver slid and fell on top of him and he was certain that he was going to Hell for molestation. Then, as he whimpered his way slowly out from under the remains, the eternally-smiling Lieutenant Forester turned what was left of her morbid sun-bleached face somewhat unexpectedly and gracefully placed a skeletal hand on David's thigh.

He was careful not to mention any of this to Harvey upon his return.

Harvey took the water gratefully to his parched orifice and then curiously examined the pouch. "You had that the whole time," he accused, regaining some strength.

"I got it from someone—there's a corpse over there."

"A corpse! You got this from a corpse?!"

"Well..."

"And you let me drink it without telling me?! Ah, man! How do you know he didn't *die* from this water?"

"I don't think so—it was a soldier. I drank it, and I'm not dead."

"A soldier! What the fuck! What's a dead soldier doing out *here*?!"

"There was a war, wasn't there? I read something at school about there being a war here."

"The Water Wars..."

"Yes, that. Must be. All I know is that I was thirsty and I tripped. God gave us this water."

"God, huh? Thanks, angel twat. And now I'll commence beating the shit out of you! Oh, ha! That face! Ha ha! Relax, I'm only kidding! Anyway, not all skinheads are racist. Some of us just hate everyone equally. A year in prison can really change you. Anyway, if it was all God's doing, as you say, I don't need to thank you. You were just a means to an end, you stooge of God. Ha ha! No. But seriously, thanks. I was just having a little fun—too much fun, as it turns out. I owe you one. Call it a truce?"

"Sure, I guess," said David.

"So, you say there's a soldier over there?"

"Yes."

"All the gear was still with him?"

"Yes, I think so."

"Now, where is this soldier exactly?"

"Why do you want to know?" said David suspiciously. He had already molested Lieutenant Forester enough himself and did not wish the corpse to be disturbed any further.

"I can't believe the body of a real soldier would be out here," Harvey said, regaining his strength. "I mean, what kind of shitty outfit was he in? Who would leave their own to die and not even bother to give them a proper burial? That's just fucking horseshit!"

"I guess you're right," David said agreeably. "That is pretty crappy. She was in the Civic Legion. Her name was Lieutenant Forester."

"That explains it: An entire battalion from the Civic Legion was wiped out from a chemical attack by Neruda Corporation's mechanized private army. They had an illegal extraction project in effect that was heroically squelched by said Civic Legion, but at a high cost. My cousin died in that war; *Battle of the Sleeping Bear*. I kinda forgot. I heard it was at some dunes, but I didn't realize it was these. We must be in an extension of the Sleeping Bear; used to be a recreational park. What-the-fuck-ever. Say, what kind of gear did this lieutenant have?"

"I'm not telling!"

"You scrawny bastard. We're friends now. Friends, get it? I'm offering your illegal ass my friendship. I should have just killed you—you're obviously too stupid to live. Ha ha! No, I'm just kidding! That's the old me talking through a new body full of sarcasm. You see, I'm just projecting all the negativity from my past life onto your face. It's a work in progress. But you: I just can't believe you didn't take anything besides this camel pouch. That gear's probably worth a lot of money. If *you're* not going to take it-"

"It should go back to her family; she deserves a proper burial."

"Well, there you go. That's a gallant mission. But you'd better do it quick. I'll give you a week. Then I'm coming out here. I do that out of respect, because you probably saved my life. But that's it. This is a golden opportunity, you know."

"Fleecing dead people," David remarked in disgust.

"Better than fleecing the living, isn't it?"

"I wouldn't know."

"Just take care of things on your end, as discreetly as possible," said Harvey before snickering at the valley of sand. "My god, aren't you just the chivalric one. I'm sure she'll appreciate it. Hell, she'd probably do you for it if she were alive."

"What?! Take that back!" shouted David with uncharacteristic animosity. "She doesn't deserve to be desecrated by your mouth!"

"Alright! Alright! Again, just projecting. I'm a projector."

"A little self-projection probably wouldn't hurt you any."

"Boy, you're pushy all of a sudden. Don't worry I won't molest your girl. Can't afford to miss an opportunity, that's all. I probably already lost one today. And maybe a few old friends. Let's just get out of here. I think your halo is fading, you fucking hypocrite."

The Unholy Scene in the Parking Lot

Unsure of time and having spent what seemed like an eternity in a Northwestern Michigan desert, Harvey and David used the mysterious tower as a western marker and retraced their steps back through the thick, miniscule forest of red pine and into an unholy scene: The parking lot was crawling with the barest minimum of patrol cars from the Gil sheriff's office that were all flashing like heterodyne deviants at a disco and positioned like wolves around a white 2016 VW Tiguan hybrid and an Indian knockoff of a black Jeep Cherokee by Mahindra & Mahindra. An additional utility vehicle pulled up to the security gate with the marking of the Gamesh Police Department. An excited German Shepard was in the passenger seat.

Harvey swore under his breath and whirled on one leg like a dervish. "No, no!" he said.

"No? Um, isn't this a good thing, really?"

"Shut up, you stooge! You don't understand!" Harvey at first retreated back into the pines, but then crept to the corner of the factory's unused storage building and hesitantly lingered.

David hurried into the parking lot, anxious to get a better look. All-in-all, he counted five police vehicles. Several employees were outside watching the arrests. Then, to his horror, the green bus passed on its way back to the migrant camp. He had missed what remained of his entire shift! David waved his hands wildly, running down the shores of his captivity in shipwrecked passion. A few noticed and gradually made a hysterical commotion, briefly, on his behalf. Next, Carlos appeared at the window—at first, alarmed, raising his arms to the bus driver, and then exploding with laughter. The bus did not stop. In three terrifying hours it would be in Oceana County. Where would David Hernando be? He had no idea. The asphalt island swallowed him in abandonment. He had little choice but to drag himself into the only institution he had left to gather up his things and inquire about a hotel. As David drew closer, he recognized Adolf and also his former pursuer Karl among two of the five being shoved into squad cars. A third was definitely a skinhead, but the last was a twitchy unkempt type who appeared to have stunted his growth.

A short and stocky old sheriff of Asian descent hobbled behind, cursing at both the detainees and the apprehending officers. "This is still my town!" he bellowed.

"We'll handle things from here, sheriff. Go back to playing solitaire."

"Why you...son-of-a-gun! I was out taking care of business when you were still in diapers! Don't you talk to *me* that way!"

"Plant a tree, save a life," said one Gamesh officer, in reference to the town of Gil's motto. The Gamesh officers laughed.

Harvey cursed his way behind David and peered sideways over his head to follow what was going on.

"Hey, there's Pete!" David said, pointing to a guy with a blond crew cut standing in a small group comprising factory security.

"Pete!" echoed Harvey. "I'm going to kill that guy—No, what am I thinking?!"

"You think he had something to do with this?" David asked Harvey.

"Of course he did, you dummy! I told Adolf not to trust him! He probably told him something, that Goddamn chatterbox!"

"Well, in that case, you're very lucky today."

Harvey cursed under his breath: "Lucky, my ass!" He pumped his right fist.

But, of course, David was right. He was in a position to envy the lucky.

Two snipers dressed in black SWAT uniforms appeared suddenly from the same urban thicket of red pine that David and Harvey had recently vacated. Apparently wanting their presence known to the trespassers, they each held up an extremely sophisticated green and black sniper rifle[25], and one sniper saluted them and then brought her arm outward in a threatening gesture, with the hand forming the shape of a pistol, and pretended to fire at Harvey.

"I'll be goddamned!!" said Harvey, just then noticing them.

With David seemingly in the lead, and Harvey guiding David's shoulder from behind, the two of them shuffled through the crowd and headed towards the factory entrance.

"But I want to see," whispered David.

"I'm a suspect, dammit!" spat Harvey. "Just get me in here!" He opened the door just enough to slide backwards through the opening and drew David in like he was a hostage.

---

[25] The 7.62 mm Bor-inspired Brazilian PT 251 Phantasm, which fires epibatidine-tipped bullets in addition to the M118LR NATO rounds.

"Now will you let me go get a cigarette?" David had unknowingly said this to no one. Harvey had disappeared into the bathroom conjoining the right side of the break room in an abstract blur of movement and the door was recovering and beginning to creep to a close again before being slammed open as someone exited.

With a renewed sense of freedom, David walked back outside and watched as the squad cars reluctantly drove away. He had missed all of the good parts, it seemed.

"What happened?" he asked a fellow migrant in Mexican-Spanish.

"It was a drug bust!" said the man excitedly. "Ritalina, I think! Man, what a show!"

"Dang! I wish I had seen it!" David said.

"It was over pretty quickly," the man said. "The guards saw them and called the cops. The drug dealers were very surprised."

"Dang!" said David. "Say, do you have a cigarette I could buy off you?"

"Nope. A word of advice: Smoking will kill you."

"This job will kill me first."

"Stay away from Ritalina!" the migrant warned.

"Not to worry, friend."

"Who's worried? It would be fun to watch!" The fellow migrant laughed ostentatiously and followed a watchful David into the break room.

III

Henrietta Penuel

A handsome little golden brown Bermudian boy was handing out flyers in the sunlight. The flamboyant Gombey Dancers would soon be expressing themselves on the grey-green Devil's Grass. Any minute now. Up away from the cerulean blue clarity and the pink sand beaches for miles along the south shore.

Henrietta was anchored to the elastic throne. These touristy festivities seemed like such a chore. She took a sip and got gurgles of banana-flavored air. The smell of rum was wafting in and from the white folding chair under a naval blue umbrella she could see the sexy young bartender serving a woman a zombie. The shirt was red hot, smoldering over his abs and that poor showing of chest hair. He was up near the concrete walkway to the hotel, which seemed much farther away than before. After-hours he would be in the ocean, diving for someone's clams. All the ladies would be down for the view. That meant there would be no more Banana Coladas after the festivities. The bartender would have to come along. There were no ifs and buts about it.

The flyer blew away up the beach, joining a natural flock of seemingly alive inanimate sheets of paper with their beastly marks. They whispered conspiratorially and then each seemed to go stiff and then suddenly come alive again, taking turns dispersing into hiding.

The gray cliffs with heads of cedar mocked her from far off, even farther than the hotel; to the north. It pained her neck to look around any further behind. She knew it so well anyway that everything else had become a mythology. The ocean was a myth. The shapes and shadows and silhouettes were mysterious, a wondrous and sad beauty. There were little fairy creatures lurking in the coral rocks beneath the turquoise waters. The sounds and smells and orientation of the beach resort were all too familiar. Henrietta closed her eyes and imagined the Gombey Dancers moving in the red like 007 James Bond silhouettes. Beyond the pink fence posts and the wheelchair ramps and the palms dancing in the breeze, she sensed some form of life. The Calypso music carried down to the sea foam washing over the pink. The cacodemons were at it again, way over from the heavy wooden deck of the hotel. The Lord Harries.

Something wicked was coming. The warm westerlies blew the Venetian red cotton sun hat from Henrietta's head. The jaded onyx-dyed hair stayed in place from years of abuse. An otherworldly alarm made her pink skin tingle and bump up, a brief recollection of hurricanes forming thousands of miles away.

Thank Hell for weather control, Henrietta thought bitterly. The Gulf Stream was coming in nicely. A fresh saltiness blessed the air and accumulated on lips and eyelids. Everything smelled like coconut rum and pineapple juice. To think they were living on the teeth of some mountain range jutting out of the ocean. The people here acted as if it were the scalp of the head—not so. The imported grass had been sown in over the scalp, for the sake of the aristocracy who came to lord over it now and then, who feared baldness almost as much as revolution and poverty. Ah, Bermuda! 'Let the cricketers wail away on the fertilized grass, like chess pawns, like Persians, like reformed soldiers. Let the grass cover all the lawns of the world as the Mounties keep the Plebeians in line. Let it keep them haunted by psychosis for want of virtual titles and estates and false sense of purpose. Let them multiply like rabbits in the warrens of *our* domain. Let them generate revenue for us in intricate cycles of novelty, and let us use a fraction of that revenue to silence them in age-old sleep. Let them never suspect. Let the busy hospitals of our namesake maintain our legacy into the Apocalypse. Let the chemicals used to treat the grass to keep it virile pump them full of cancer and, lest their own deaths intervene, keep them amused by lions with a taste for Christians and Pagans alike.' Henrietta was amused with herself. Such was as she assumed for the aristocracy. The bananas wafted. Henrietta was a lush. The wind blew salty kisses up along the beach; the bald, pink scalp. There were shipwrecks off St. George where the sailors died not knowing they were mere hours from the most beautiful solar light show they would ever see. The sun rose from the clouded white Sargasso Sea up from Morocco and fizzled into South Carolina. Somers Isles. The place was special. It was full of rich tax-dodging men.

A Spaniard had discovered them long ago, before becoming fully absorbed into his quest for riches and eternal life. He had claimed they were inhabited by pigs, so Henrietta had been told at the hotel. There were certainly no pigs now. She wondered what they had turned into.

Henrietta looked around for pig-headed men. The beach was empty. The cedars atop Ferry Reach had the ideal life, when they were not being carved up for tourists or suffering through tamed tempests—the hot breath of hurricanes demoted to tropical kittens. It wasn't clear to her how nature did that, or where the pent-up energy ended up.

The cliffs were gray.

The bats were probably growing restless inside their caves.

Yet the large white Bermuda lilies had not wilted and were contrarily basking in their trumpeted glory. Some kind of plant sound was probably blowing through them. Only the fairies could hear.

A drink. It was time for another drink. Where was the smoldering hot bartender? Henrietta's head swung around on a pivoting stick of a neck and she remembered the hat and picked it up from the sand and brushed it clean. It fell elastically into a half-cocked position. She could never keep her dark locks hydrated.

The fiery medicine was still high over the sweltering planet, but soon enough...

Out towards the past; towards the country of fizzle; an enticing eatery that brought on the soulful indigestion. Where the sun was like effervescence in a glass of water.

South Carolina. "That goddamn place." It reminded her stubbornly of something negative and suddenly there was turbulence in her stormy eyes, somewhere behind the large auburn 1970s retrograde sunglasses. Antiope, the child who had traversed half-way across the world to meet with her long-lost mother, had been dragged onto a plane and flown back over the Atlantic with those two security apes from Monstrosso. The act had been nothing short of a kidnapping. She had placed her long-lost daughter on the Jaded Princess from the port of Cape Liberty, New York, over a week ago to join her at last, and they had snatched her away like property. Any real mother would have done something. Yet here Henrietta was, getting sloshed on a beach and soaking up the sun into her varicose veins. But her stony presence was making the planet a little cooler. She had been living in Bermuda for over a decade, a superfluous ghost haunting the beaches and clubs and impermanent bars, and that brutal parting was the saddest sunset she had ever endured.

"May I have a drink, please?" Henrietta asked a passing tourist whom she had mistaken for a waitress.

Finally, to be reunited with her long lost daughter, to become something like a mother, for once, a mother, only to see her fizzle in the horizon. Antiope was the only child of the bunch to even acknowledge that she had a mother. What a rotten bunch, and it was all her fault. Henrietta was lost, in want of feeling permanently severed from reality. The steady stream of Banana Coladas was her only link to the living world. Funny that she had never had a reason to get drunk before in all those ten years. Not since her stint as a weaving instructor and those factory days in Hamtramck.

Where It All Began

Henrietta Penuel held her first real job at Detroit/ Hamtramck Assembly during the mid 1990s. It was a large General Motors factory in Michigan where she helped Cadillac-K-body production near the Beth Olem cemetery wall. She would go to a Polish deli during the dinner rush for her lunch and the homeless protestors would sometimes yell at her and demand that their church be rebuilt: The plant had unfortunately destroyed an entire neighborhood. But that had been back in 1981 when Henrietta was attending George Armstrong Custer Elementary School in Monroe, Michigan, as a second grader. Those people had been protesting fourteen years after the fact and she didn't want to think about what they had been doing all that time. That was the year she had met Tom Cornelius Wesson III. He had been a promising young shift supervisor some two years her junior who was working an internship. They would go out only in the afternoon. He liked to feel her up in the city parks.

Almost a year went by and things got pretty serious—or so it seemed to Henrietta. She had hoped Tom would propose, but instead he hit her up for a bizarre opportunity. He said it would make her a lot of money. Tom had no idea. He was a typical golden boy and the bright pagan mask of the dark side of his soul was on a little too tight. The Christian side was not much better on him, but he used it to his advantage. He relied heavily on his father's influence. Tom Wesson II was the legal kind of drug dealer. He sold fertility drugs for Case-Flint Drugs Limited. As it turned out, the Pangloss Fertility Clinic of London, Ontario, was paying women to birth children for an undisclosed client. They were offering upwards of $20,000, but the applicants would be extensively screened and only the most suitable need apply. Tom was convinced that if he could send them a suitable applicant it would be a foot in the door for him at Case-Flint and he would be on his way to following in his father's footsteps. The company had been thus far unwilling to offer him an internship. Henrietta liked to think they had an aversion towards little twerps; actually, however, it was because they were more than what they seemed. The mysterious flow of vacuous people wearing expensive travel suits under their cheap hospital gowns said it all. They were not doctors. A middle-aged man and woman duo were the real doctors, but their indecisiveness gave them away. They were not really in charge. These infrequent strangers were in control of everything. Some of them from the lab wore Case-Flint logos on the breast pockets of their white laboratory jackets and carried clipboards. They came and went as they pleased. No one at Pangloss ever bothered to question them. How Tom Wesson II had gotten a job at Case-Flint was anyone's guess, because both companies were deep in government secrecy—even for a medical company.

"Do this one thing, sweetie, and with the money we can get married, travel the world," said Tom, looking deep into Henrietta's eyes—he dared, not long.

"Are you saying we'll get married?"

"Sure! Why not? Lots of people get married."

"Are you saying you'll *marry me?!*"

"Well, a guy can't just… do these things at the spur of the moment," he had sputtered. "Let's think on it, see what happens."

"Oh, Tom…"

Henrietta took the job, thinking it might pull things in her favor with Tom III's family—she had never actually met them, then, nor ever. Tom bought Henrietta a bus ticket to London, Ontario, where she underwent a medical evaluation. They said she was genetically predisposed to multiple births, which she had not known. They were overly excited, foaming at the mouth even. She was practically an only child, with a twin brother and sister just over twelve years her senior. She hardly knew them, even now. The family figured they were a fluke, like that nursemaid in Russia during the 19th century whose name no one could remember. The Penuels had never known much about their history; there were vague associations concerning Huguenots, a blue fountain, the Walloon weavers of Petticoat Lane, East London, who lived in Spitalfields just outside the legendary city in England, but nothing else. Pangloss paid Henrietta's way from then on and she was to choose a sperm donor from a list of lucky bachelors. Henrietta wanted Tom to be the donor, but he refused. He said he was afraid of his own potency, that he would always wonder who they were, how many there were, and that it would keep him up at night. In reality, he was shooting blanks. Although frustrated, a decision had to be made. With November closing in, the air grew colder. A warm little nest egg was something to look forward to. Henrietta chose number 19971320144-V and hoped for the best. She was given her own fertility room. The clinic took good care of her, despite the weird humor: A plaque on the waiting room wall read "Number ye the people, that I may know the sum of the people" and below that quote was a social security number; they joked about paying her in shekels of silver; "Choose your punishment," they said. "Will it be three-thousand dollars annually for seven years, to wait two-hundred-and-seventy months and receive two-hundred-thousand silver-backed shekels straight from the Central Bank of Israel, or an instant lump sum of two-hundred ounces of gold[26]?

The gold would have been the obvious choice, but Henrietta suddenly thought of the Beth Olem Cemetery wall and a strange premonition overcame her. "I choose the shekels of silver," she said.

"Are you sure?" they laughed. Some of them were soon rolling on the floor with true emotion.

---

[26] At the time, gold was worth around $100 per ounce.

"Yes, the shekels."

"Very well, then," said the head creepy guy. His typically lusterless eyes shone with pleasure. "Sign here, please."

It was probably the running joke at the agency for years.

There were a lot of strange stipulations that Henrietta was required to follow at the fertility clinic concerning the birth of the litter and how she was to conduct herself afterwards. It was never even certain that the treatment would work, and in that possible instance she was to never mention the deal to anyone, which would become null and void, except for a small severance to make it worth her while. If successful, she was to prepare the birth certificates herself using only Biblical names and would immediately forfeit all rights to the children.

The results were far more prodigious than anyone had expected—the Pangloss fertility doctors had in their indecisiveness doused her eggs quite liberally, and traveling between countries that year and into the next, she thought little about what was happening to her body. By May 1994 she was heavier and considerably more irritable. The inconveniences she suffered daily placed otherworldly value on these incubating commodities of hers. She requested and was given permission to move into an Ontario hotel until the upcoming birthing process that frightened her more than the thought of dying. A month later, the entire city of London was excited to learn, through a leak in the hospital cafeteria staff, that an American woman had just given birth to a set of dizygotic nonuplets. Nevertheless, due to unknown circumstances, the press decided to alter the story by claiming that all but two had died prematurely.

It was an exhausting ordeal for Henrietta, the hospital, and for the Pangloss Fertility Clinic. The doctors had issued explicit instructions to the staff, but during their absence (apparently, an emergency company meeting in Creve Coeur, Missouri) the hospital nurses took it upon themselves to disobey orders. So tiny were the infants upon birth that they had been placed in their own incubators for almost a week while their poor mother recovered from exhaustion. The head nurse thought it particularly unnerving that they had not yet received proper names and were being identified by numbers and made arrangements one afternoon to rectify the situation. One by one, the tiny infants were placed in Henrietta's arms so that she was forced to connect herself to these human commodities sharing half of her own DNA. A picture was taken by a nurse who happened to have brought a camera to work that day, but Henrietta had no idea whatever became of it.

"Your decisions are your own business, but don't you think it's about time they received their proper names?" prodded the head nurse. She handed Henrietta a heavy clipboard packed with nine sets of forms. "Here, you can fill these out in your own time. Just make sure to keep track of them—they each have numbers, see?"

And so they ran thusly named as Mathew James Esther Pauline Timothy Mark Susanne Jacob and the middle name Zilpah for each. But when she had gotten to the ninth child of the second group, and looked upon the face of this child, the child of her own blood, who had the eyes of her much adored Aunt Clara, a heavy emotion overcame her, and in that brief moment of joy was inspired to give this child a different name. Antiope she would call her, so as to make her stand out from the others, with the middle name of Clara. Antiope Clara Penuel. As she watched the baby sleep for what she feared would be the last time, the mother passed into what must have been love, and she vowed then and there to make off with the child, no matter what the cost, and she began making excuses. Surely they wouldn't miss one less child, she pondered—one less specimen. The Pangloss staff would have to agree or else face exposure. But when she approached them on the subject and pleaded her case over the telephone they denied her flatly. "You're under contract to give up *all* your children," the voice said. Then she could hear the other voices whispering, out of the dead governmental air, and the speaker continued. "You made an oath. Why this sudden conflict of interest, I wonder? You'll not get a shekel more from us, Ms. Penuel, we assure you."

"I don't want any more damned anything from you! I just want this baby, *my* baby! What's one less to your client? You've got the others. They were more than what was expected. Do what you want with the others. One less drone for you to manipulate is all!"

"Now, look, Miss Penuel, you've given birth to a fine litter, but unless you plan on spitting out another one, the answer is no. We've taken DNA samples. The data has been fed into the computer. They've already been assigned social security numbers and everything. It's a done deal."

"So change the goddamn numbers!"

"It's all gone through the proper channels. The babies will be taken and that's final. I'm sorry, Miss Penuel. There's simply no backing out on this."

The parting was bittersweet—more so than Henrietta had anticipated. Her back ached constantly in the memory of her nine children. What would become of them? Despite her premonition, she tried believing they were going to be taken good care of, that it had all been done for some wealthy couple somewhere who were desperate for a platoon of tiny screamers to fill in some void or other in their rich lives. None of it made sense.

She returned to the United States a shell of her former self. Even Tom was different, standoffish. When she met him in the park like old times, he refused to feel her up. He said he didn't think he could have sex with someone who had just given birth to nine kids. It just didn't seem natural to him.

"This is all *your* fault, you know!" Henrietta had barked. "I'm not just some kind of wolf bitch! It was that lying, heartless scheme of yours; that goddamned fertility treatment your father sells!!"

"Leave my dad out of this!" stammered Tom.

"I wonder about that! It's more than just a drug company, you know!"

Tom had no idea, but was more than forthcoming on everything else. Suddenly it all came out: He had been two-timing her—perhaps even more times than that. He had been seeing a girl from Cranbrook Schools in Bloomfield Hills since before Henrietta had known him and they were to be married that coming summer. He said it had been off and on and that they had gone through a trial of seeing other people, but Henrietta eventually found out otherwise. The birthing scheme had been a way for Tom to get rid of Henrietta while using it to his advantage. Tom had gotten that internship at Case-Flint and would be selling drugs with dear old dad, just like he had always dreamed. *His* dreams were coming true, while Henrietta's had turned into a nightmare.

The factory, too, had become nothing but loud hammers beating into her and she quit Detroit/ Hamtramck Assembly less than a month later with very little to show for it. Henrietta fled the state and moved to Chicago, where she got a job in a linen factory. After several years, she became quite good. She bought a Jacquard handloom and learned Bauhaus by studying the late Gunta Stölzl. But no matter how hard she tried she could not forget the children. She embarked upon little investigations in her spare time, visiting university libraries and internet cafes, and dug up some rather interesting dirt on Case-Flint involving another company called Monstrosso Corporation. It seemed the latter had been in the chemical business since the early twentieth century, producing a wide range of products from deadly herbicides, insecticides, industrial chemicals, digital clocks, the world's first batch of saccharin and caffeine, plastics, explosives, synthetic fibers, and biotech crops—most disturbing to Henrietta were the patents on genetically modified living organisms, including a patent on breeding techniques for pigs that essentially provided them ownership of any pig born through such a procedure. The eternally-wistful Germans had thankfully risen to the occasion and closed the breach, but elsewhere the shallowness pervaded, snuck in on tip-toe through devils posing as Supreme Court judges. Although quite an evil stretch, she could not help wondering if the same could apply to human beings. Had they secretly already reached that point, and was Monstrosso the confidential client and legal guardian over her abandoned children? The very thought made her dark hairs stand on end. Surely, Henrietta was only a victim of paranoia; she had hoped and prayed this case at the time. A corporation was not a person, after all. It did not hold rights, *could* not hold rights over human beings. 'Could it?' But she had already strayed into dangerous waters and feared her amateur investigations would become known. During her snooping, Henrietta discovered the names of those who had once stood before the giant: a number of persons acting against the company's interests had become inanimate by way of ludicrous legal methods. One had even died from self-inflicted gunshot wound at roughly fifteen feet from impact. Those companies which she had actually dealt with and knew to be real were even more mysterious. Case-Flint was some kind of government front, passing through time like a ghost. It had been involved in all the Monstrosso-related defense projects over the years. Pangloss Fertility Clinic, meanwhile, no longer existed as a permanent residence and had become something of a circus, moving from town to town and then vanishing altogether only to reappear a few years later under similar names (Blind Faith Clinic, The Stork People, The Ooh Ah Push It Group, PFC inc., etc., etc.). Something diabolical was certainly going on. Henrietta had to find out more, to find the children and rescue them, before her own tracks were uncovered and she, too, was pulled from existence.

The Year of the Big Payoff

Twenty-one years passed before things paid off. 2015, the date her payment of shekels was triggered[27], was the year that a meteor hit the Negrev in the area of Beer Sheva and formed rare diamonds from high-pressured graphite, toxic waste, and unrefined sewage from the nearby rivers. The Israeli new shekel went from 1/3 against the failing U.S. dollar to one in forty for the first time in its history, making a few million people, including Henrietta Penuel, very rich.

---

[27] 1/3 of $200,000 equals $66,666.67 (rounded off from 66666.666666666666666666666666667).

SEXTUPLET

I

Supper at the O' Caoindealbhain's

"Are the dreams still bothering you?" Ellen inquired at supper that evening.

They were having leftovers.

"Yes," Edgar replied.

"That's too bad. I used to dream of snakes, but they stopped when I met Loe. There's probably some medicine you can take-"

"No way. No meds. They aren't that bad anyway—not nightmares. Just weird. People in them seem familiar, as if I know them from somewhere."

"Those *are* weird," said Ellen. "I've had some like that. Once I dreamed of an entire Serpent band that was playing 'My Sharona'—do you remember that song? And they were all ex-presidents, plus a few of my teachers from high school."

"No, I mean, I've never seen them before..." he explained, momentarily stuck in thought, "except for the one that I met at the factory. The Time Keeper, we call her. I'm pretty sure she was the nurse. She told me that Edina was going to pay me a visit. But I think I was dead, or at least dying. Isn't that strange? Do you think maybe I was just associating the nurse with the Keeper because I'd just met her? She is pretty cute. I heard she has like six kids. Hard to believe."

Ellen listened through a glass of water. The casserole was being stubborn. "Maybe you know the others, too, and you just forgot."

"No. I'm pretty sure I've never met them before."

"You probably played together on the merry-go-round or something back in kindergarten."

"But they were adults. How could I have known what they were going to look like in the future?"

"Don't know," said Ellen. "They say there's no time in dreamland. You could probably find all the answers in there."

"Maybe you're right," he said absently, glancing out the window. "So where's Loe? Did he get lucky in Wichita?"

"That's a hell of a thing to say." Ellen glared at her brother and then glanced worryingly at her little Edina.

"I mean with the sugar beet sugar, sugar," Edgar rectified.

"He said he's waiting on a decision from a chewing gum company. They wanted to go back to an artificial sweetener."

"Those cause cancer."

"What doesn't?"

"That's just what they want you to think—fear everything in the entire world so they can sneak right in when your guard is down. So does he think they'll buy?"

"Hope so. We sure can use the money. Tax season is coming up in a couple of months."

"Don't worry about that. I can help."

"No, Edgar."

"I'm staying here, aren't I? It's the least I can do—I'm no parasite."

"You're a hobo!" Edina giggled, butting in. "Hobo bobo!"

"That I may be, but I'm no tick," proclaimed Edgar, smiling. "I can pull my own weight. You'll see."

II

Concerning the Guy Who Was Unlucky

"Is there a hotel nearby?" David asked the security guard at the front gate.

"Not that I know of. I'm not from around here though," answered the guard.

This was the wrong kind of news for David. It seemed that he would be sticking around the factory for the rest of the day and also incidentally throughout the night. He had no idea what he was to do.

"Um, can you help me?" David asked the secretary from Human Resources. He had been sitting at a lunch table outside the office for a half-hour before trying to pass off his misfortunes onto his employers.

The secretary fidgeted around with her telephone headset and continued to speak into the mouthpiece.

"Oh, I'm sorry," David said. He waited for someone to talk to him.

The secretary ended her conversation and began rifling through paperwork. Another secretary came out and, seeing David, tried to look busy.

"Please, miss, could you help me?" David said. Her nametag said Judy.

"That depends," huffed Judy, looking around hopelessly for a place to hide. "Okay," she relented. "What's the nature of your problem?"

David watched as she approached the counter at a snail's pace and it occurred to him that she was actually afraid. *Jeez, maybe they should change their name to Inhuman Resources*, he thought impatiently.

The tall and crisped Frenchman they called Pierre ran in suddenly from the inner GGI offices, which were nicer and much larger, and stared at David's bust above the counter as if he were some kind of problem to be solved. "What's going on here?" he said.

"I'm just now helping him with that," said Judy nervously. She turned to David. "What can we do for you?"

"Well," he began, "my problem is this: I'm on the morning shift and I missed the bus. I'm staying over at the migrant camp— or at least was, over in 'the Hart'. Do you know of a place where I can stay, like a hotel or something?"

"Holy smokes!" whistled Pierre. "How on earth did you manage to do *that*?"

"I went out for some fresh air; was gone a lot longer than I had intended."

"Well, there aren't any hotels I'm afraid," said Pierre in faux sadness. "All gone. The closest are in Gamesh. That's twenty miles from here and it's nearly impossible to get a taxi out this way. You'll just have to punch back in and curl up beneath a pitting machine, or go on break the entire night until your shift starts up again, or you could wait for me to get off work and you could sleep on the couch with the dog. I'll be working late this evening, though; probably at least until nine. And I have tomorrow off, come to think of it. Hmmm. Let's see. Judy could take you home. What about it, Judy? Can you take this boy home?"

"Me?" shrieked the secretary, wincing. "But I have two teenage daughters! No way he's going home with *me*! You can't make me!!"

"That's not necessary. I'll be alright," David said uneasily. He was not one to inconvenience people.

"Pretty please?" Pierre pleaded, babbling to Judy in French-accented baby talk. It was a little unnerving to watch. "I could let you out early—say, now—and you could take him to a hotel. Do what you want with him after that. He'll probably never find anyone willing to bring him back out here anyway. I'm sure he'll pay you."

"I'm not a hooker!" Judy hissed, glancing uneasily into the offices behind them.

"Sorry, buddy," Pierre said to David. "And he looks so sad and helpless. You can probably pile up someone's dirty things there in the break room—maybe get an hour's rest, if you're lucky. There's also some train coaches nearby. No one's using them, although I think I *have* seen clouds of what you call 'yellow jackets' as big as cows flying out from one of them. They've been known to kill people, where *I* am from."

"Alright, alright!" said Judy, showing displeasure at her boss' insistence. "You'll let me leave right now?"

"*Oui, absolument!*" promised Pierre. "Thanks, darling Judy. What a trooper."

"I just better not get raped," huffed Judy, hurriedly snatching her purse. "Can I get all this in writing? Oh, that look…You smoothie. Grab your things, whatever your name is. I'll be out in a minute."

Judy Welf

Judy's parents had met during an attack on Christmas; Judy's father was a disgruntled Atheist and her mother was a staunch supporter of Christ's big day. They argued so vehemently against one another while standing there in the cold beneath that year's chosen tree that they fell passionately and foolishly in love.

"A miracle has happened, and it kicks like Saint Jude," mother had said when Judy's existence had first been discovered. Father had allegedly groaned: "Just, for pity's sake, don't give him a Christian martyr's name." Ethnically Flemish and Bavarian, respectively, the Welfs were a contrast of opposites: The only thing they had had in common was that their in-laws hated them. Thus Judy was born Judith Jael Welf: Judith because her mother's hero was a sword-wielding widow, and Jael because Father had played a cunning joke on Mother by cynically pointing out the fictional elements to the Biblical story, a joke which was never disclosed and which Mother never discovered.

A virtuous, pious, and beautiful assassin, the Biblical Judith shared little in common with Judy Welf. Judith's story described how a widow in mourning saved her people from impending bloodbath by her temerarious astuteness; Judy had lost her entire family during a fateful trip to Yellowstone National Park.

"I'm Welfy," she liked to quip to her friends. But she had never been. Never would be, unless she could wrestle Tom away from his wife who did nothing but sit there in her ivory tower. Such was the irony.

After a string of unintentional one-night stands with disinterested men, Judy married Tim Holofernes, an independent building contractor with a penchant for screwing over his customers (the irony was just too good to pass up). They became a semi-popular brunt of pointy jokes by phone book comedians in the Grand Rapids area circuit before going completely yellow. Tim had been well aware that she was not an exemplary woman. But Tim was no saint, either, and certainly not a loyal general, and although the name was Assyrian-Greek (she had looked it up), Tim had always claimed that he was French. He had been dishonorably discharged from the Army after going AWOL during Basic Training and had never made it past the rank of private. Like the fictional Holofernes, he was a drunkard. For the most part, his head had always been just outside the wall. They divorced after less than a year and then ineptly remarried when it was discovered that she was pregnant. Ten years later, in the eve of winter, Tim was shot to death by someone's grandmother. The poor old woman was near-frozen solid because he had skipped town instead of fixing her leaky roof and *kaput* furnace as agreed. She had paid him in advance, after all, which proved his death sentence. The woman's name was Esther[28], further adding to the irony that had been Tim and Judy (Welf) Holofernes.

After Tim's life insurance policy was rejected, Judy abruptly changed her surname back to Welf.

Now she was in the middle of a messy affair with her boss' boss and, more currently, driving an adorable little brown rapist home with her—the only hotel this way through Gamesh had the red NO VACANCY sign just barely noticeably on, like one in a Hitchcock movie, and every website she could think of to check via

---

[28] The eponymous heroine of the Biblical Book of Esther, one of only two books never to mention God. Born **Hadassah**, which means "myrtle" in Hebrew, it has been conjectured by historian Jacob Hoschander that her name is derived from the Akkadian *Ishtar-udda-sha* ("Ishtar is her light").

her smart-ass smart-phone/consumer data collector/taxpayer tracking device (which was, incidentally, illegal to use while driving) suggested the same due to a banker's convention.

"David, is it?" Judith said to break the chill in the warm summer evening air. She had forgotten to turn down the air conditioner. "So, do you have any girlfriends back home?"

"No, I'm not that good with women," he insisted. This one was playing hardball. "I hope I can find one again soon though, one who's like me."

Judy gave him a demonic look. "Listen, buddy, I have two teenage daughters at home, and they're off limits. You're to stay on the couch tonight. If I hear so much as a noise in any other part of the house…"

"No problem, Judy, I mean Mrs. Welf." He spoke timidly, mannerly, but Judy knew that he must be putting her on, because no young man on earth was *that nice*.

"I mean it. I'll call the police."

"Mrs. Welf, are you sure there are no vacancies?"

"Unfortunately not," groaned Mrs. Welf. "The bankers screw me, no matter what I do."

"…that *is* unfortunate."

"Oh, I'm sure you're just all broken up about it. A young guy like you probably spends all day planning these things."

"Pardon?"

"I see. Playing the religious type," Mrs. Welf assumed. "My mother was very religious. She feared demons. I often think of her as an angel, watching over me and my daughters…"

"Angels are cool."

"My father was her chosen Hell. He slowly killed her with anxiety."

"I'm sorry about the inconvenience. Are you keeping my hundred dollars?"

"I'll give it all back to you tomorrow, once I know my daughters are safe and unmolested."

"Um, okay."

Judy smiled. Her aggression seemed to be working well on David. "So which is it: Demon or angel?"

"…"

"Never mind. It's been a long day."

The Welf Drama Unfolds

"You! There! Couch!" Judy ordered once they were inside the house.

David did as he was told.

The phone burst out into song, the ringtone that of some song better left unmentioned. It was Tom Wesson, right on schedule. Sometimes she thought he was more of an alarm clock than a soft kettle of water. Her dreams of steam engines had gone limp and would never reach the surface.

"What is it, baby?" she whispered into the headset. "Do you miss me?"

"Judy, I'm burning up…how about you and me on the green in half an hour?"

"Can't…I got a hot Mexican here on the couch. What can I do, leave him all alone with my daughters here? You'll have to play solo."

"Judy, baby, you're killing me. I've been on top of the world today. You've gotta see what I can do with this sturdy old wooden club."

"Aren't you jealous? I said I've got a hot Mexican."

"Oh, err…of course I'm jealous. Just get over here! I thought you'd want to see my wood!"

"I'd love to see your wood. I've been dying to show you how much my stroke's improved since the last time we played together, but this darn handicap is getting in the way. Have you talked it over with Margaret?"

"I've been married to her for twenty years. I can't just drop her like a bad habit. These things take time…"

"Life takes time. I'm getting old, Tom."

"Bullshit. You're a hot young charger. You're the prize beauty and I'm your stud. Let's take it out to pasture."

"Oh Tom…that's a…that first part just melts me…have you taken your magic beans?"

176

"You know it, baby! I'm gonna blow all my talent if you can't come out to play. How about I order Chinese and we talk about it once we reach the ninth hole."

"[wheezing sound] Szechwan! I'll be there in fifteen minutes!

"Ok I'm going upstairs now!" Judy hollered suddenly, addressing the house. "Don't even think about leaving that couch! I'm a very light sleeper!" Judy rifled upstairs along the creaking, carpeted steps. "Tammy! Molly! I know you can hear me! I'm going to bed! If I hear you leaving this house tonight I'm calling the police! Is that clear?! Oh, and how was your day?! Hmmm?!" Judy hesitated, but received only giggles from one of the rooms. "Tell me later! I love you, girls! Goodnight!"

Soon could be heard the sound of doors slamming and bathroom sink water running, clothes falling to the floor, zippers zipping, Judy cursing, then a menagerie of clattering sounds. An upstairs window opened and something crashed down into the bushes. A lot of unprofessional cursing ensued in a voice much resembling Judy's and then a car's engine started up and sped out of the driveway.

Two Nymphets

"Who the hell are *you*?" asked one of two identical little nymphets rushing down the stairs on a cloud of mischief. One was wearing a black mesh nearly-see-through high-waisted top and a tight red rayon mini skirt and the other was dressed in a beau blue camouflage undergarment blouse thing without any pants. They looked to be no more than fifteen years old.

"Hello, I'm David," he answered unconsciously, standing in embarrassment from where he had been sitting idly for some time. He could almost hear the police sirens salivating from just outside the nearest donut shop in anticipation of the coming disaster.

"How old are you, David?" said the camouflaged *hottie*. She was very presumptuous.

"Who, me? I just turned eighteen."

"You hear that?" she said, bumping her twin excitedly.

"Sure did," announced the rayon-skirted twin with a hint of boredom.

"Say, David. Do you think you could buy us some electronic cigs?" asked the camouflaged one unabashedly. "They won't sell to minors. I hear they make a girl really horny."

The rayon-skirted one giggled.

"I-I don't know. Your mother would kill me I think."

"A fit young guy like you 's afraid of our mom? Believe me, she's harmless."

"Yup," chimed the rayon skirt.

David stayed strong. "But I'm a guest here. She doesn't like me as it is."

"Well, there you go then," the camouflaged one said, walking up to the couch seductively. "What are you worried about? She already doesn't like you. She's out fucking her boss' boss right now anyway. Don't you like to *fuck*?"

David gulped.

Suddenly the doorbell rang. Two beatnik-looking teenage boys were let in. They looked around nervously before taking on a tough air.

"Who's *this guy*?"

"This is David. He's going to buy us some e-cigs, aren't you David?" said little miss blue frilly camouflaged undergarments, twirling her hair and grinning mischievously.

""Yeah!! Great!!" the lead boy said loudly. "Smokes are just what we need to take the edge off!"

"You got the stuff right?" said frilly.

One of the boys pulled out a small unmarked bottle of pills and shook it like a baby's rattle.

"Don't ruin them, idiot!" the other boy cursed.

"Shuttup!" the lead boy yelled excitedly. One shoved the other and there was a scuffle. The lead boy was shoved violently against the hallway wall.

"Do something, Tammy!" cried the rayon skirt.

"Shuttup, Molly," ordered frilly blue camouflage undergarment. It seemed she had a penchant for evil.

"You like fights, huh?" David said to the wearer of the frilly blue camouflage, whose name was apparently Tammy.

"Huh?" the lead boy groaned exhaustively, his black shirt ripped at the collar.

The boys stopped mid-fisted.

David continued through the cease fire with confidence: "You guys into Lucha Libre, the free fight? I can fight. You can fight. How 'bout we make a little wager…"

Tom Wesson III Chips One onto the Putting Green

"Tom's going golfing. I don't know where he gets the energy." Mrs. Margaret Chase Wesson said this to each of her friends as they pulled up to the house, trotting in like equestrians, one by one, into the circular driveway, and relinquished their high-performance hybrid carriages to the valet (actually, her son Tom IV). Tom III was just on his way out. He was taking the Cadillac Escalade AV. He blushed, smiled, and waved. The car was leased and rather expensive because the driver was a robot. They couldn't afford it, but no one had to know that.

"Strike a blow for me, Tom!" said one of Margaret's friends as she joined the frenzy.

Tom blushed every time his wife lauded his virility in front of their friends, not because she was lying, but because she did it badly. He could tell without even ordering the windows to be rolled down. It was all she ever talked about. She had been denying him sex for weeks at a time. She was using sex withdrawal to punish him for spending too much time at the office. She seemed impervious to the fact that she had gone well out of orbit from those youthful powers. Yet that was only a part of the bigger picture. If not for the wonders of science, the world would have seen the end of the Wessons. Each of his two-and-a-half children had been shocked into existence at a laboratory, In Vitro, and then stuffed into Mrs. Margaret Chase Wesson's fertile womb. But he never wanted them to know that. The Smiths were never to know either. "Just be thankful that you weren't birthed by complete strangers like the Martin children," was his prepared excuse in case the children ever asked. The half of a point provided a distraction anyway: Their youngest son had the additional effect of existing as part of the first official line of designer human beings and had thus been born with immunity to sickness and disease. As for the kid's abnormal appearance, Mrs. Wesson explained to friends and family that, 'Good looks wasn't an option at the time.' Neither was intelligence. But despite these early shortcomings of the program, which Tom supposed was like buying the first cell phone or DVD player, the older siblings were terrified of their younger brother and feared that he would strip them of their privileges based on overall health and superiority for their breed. They were very self-conscious.

Tom's straw-headed maternal grandfather was obviously laughing at him from the grave. As for the other one, though, he could never be certain.

Briefly, Tom's Childhood

When he was a child, Tom visited his maternal grandparents only during the summer. They lived in a mansion once owned by Henry Ford. While at their estate in the glamorous outskirts of Detroit, Tom would sometimes be shuffled into the parlor room by a frightened maid and told to sit in a chair and to avoid playing with the locomotive engine sitting on the desk that was made of gold lest he get struck by a bullwhip. His pompous old grandfather would impatiently light up his calabash pipe and recite stock quotes from the Wall Street Journal as if they were proverbs. The only two books worth reading, he said, were *All about Women* and *Atlas Shrugged*.

His maternal grandparents spent their winters in Mexico, so after Christmas Tom would visit his blue-collar fraternal grandparents who lived in a cute inner-city house with a little yellow yard. Unlike most blue collar people, Grandpa Tom Wesson Sr. hated lawn maintenance. He had some crackpot theory that lawn chemicals had given him cancer. It was the Industry Barons, he claimed. They wanted to build a chemical empire and destroy the aristocracy in one swoop. People assumed that the aristocracy had disappeared, he said. It had not gone out with the plantations, but was inherent in every head of corporation and household, in every schmuck's genes, just waiting for that individual to reach the top of the hierarchy. Any hierarchy would do. There was eventually a convolution of schmucks until all levels of society were in contempt of each other; rampant waste from the top and anarchy from the bottom. Then there were the spiritual wounds that could never be healed. 'That's what ruins civilizations', he said. 'Don't be a schmuck.' And then he spent hours dry-heaving in the bathroom. He was a retired machinist. He said that men had a deep-seeded fear of domination, and that if they were defeated in life they turned to watching sports. He encouraged Little Tom to drink beer. He was highly suspicious of the government. He hated Ayn Rand. One day in March when Tom lugged around the audio book version of Atlas Shrugged narrated by Alan Greenspan, Grandpa Tom snatched his *i-thing* and gave the following speech:

Listen to your own flesh and blood, my boy; the spirit of LIBERTY has been hijacked by this author and further demonized by unreasonable dip-shits. The evils inherent are real enough, but it hasn't translated well in you people. If you're going to absorb it at all, know what you're getting into and come to your own conclusions.

Randians can't listen to reason; they're misguided half-assed Libertarians and Libertarians don't know shit.

The world of a Randian rubs the real one all wrong.

A Randian world is a place where people get drunk and aim their fireworks at you. In a Randian world, billionaire business moguls get mad when the government interferes with their shitty business iniquity on behalf of the outraged community and in consequence they go on strike (they form subversive clubs and spend a lot of money trying to destroy the people who're in their way; self-loathing steel workers with adept unions run around calling smart people "no-good liberals" due to misinformation from both sides).

Randians don't get it that stupidity is by far a more powerful cultural sedative than a dictatorship; sonny, we're living in the age of stupid people, and it's only getting worse.

In a Randian world no one wants to pay taxes; but when they retire they *do* want to claim social security.

Once his rant was finished he placed the *i-thing* back into Tom III's hands with the same force with which he had taken it away and went to the garage to beat things around.

The neighborhood was scary and without purpose: The boy next door had murdered the cat by drowning it in oil and then setting it on fire; residents were devoid of extra income, yet their houses were full of junk; while parents seemed relatively smart, their children spoke with a disproportionately high level of mental impairment; the unions had not yet been destroyed. The people had nothing to hope for.

His paternal grandfather Tom Wesson the First eventually died of serrated liver. But as Tom Wesson III took on the sport of golf in high school, following in his maternal grandfather's footsteps, that old yellow lawn would haunt him. He had seen enough chemicals being sprayed onto a golf course to have constituted a munitions supply for chemical weapons in some countries. He held a suspicion that it had something to do with his sterility.

Back On Par

Although Tom was headed to the course for entirely different reasons, his mind was currently on his handicap. There was something wrong with it. Was it his grip? Was his grip all wrong? Was it the swing? Perhaps he was using the wrong wedge. Or was it that he just didn't have enough masculine power to drive a tiny ball roughly a hundred yards to a small, round hole in the ground. On the Women's Circuit they could do that in just under three attempts. No, that wasn't it. Well, but they had a handicap, too, of course, because sport was a man's field to graze on and not a woman's (although so and so from the club had played him once and had whipped him pretty good even without the handicap; he wouldn't dare mention it to anyone). Mrs. Wesson was no doubt to blame somehow. Or was it the fertilizer? Through his handicap, Tom was witnessing was the fall of United States of America.

How Antiope Escapes Her Predicament

"Oh, Tom! You're just what I ordered!" the woman said as she straddled the man who had been waiting in the kitchen.

183

Antiope, meanwhile, was hiding under the bathroom sink. She heard a lot of chewing and kissing. Then they must have gone to the bedroom. The door was probably still wide open.

What's taking them so long, she wondered. She had called the girls a half-hour ago on her new black market phone in which the tracking was jammed. The little conditioning noises it made had almost given her away; also, the controls were tiny and hard to see in the dark. She had nearly escaped twice only to have the woman feel her way in to use the bathroom or Tom scamper out of the shadows to answer his own persistent link to the outside world.

"Don't answer it, Tom. Only answer to me, and I to you." the woman would say.

"Shall I get out the bullwhip, madam?"

"Rarrrr, tame this beast! Oh! But I don't have the shoes for it... I do so much walking around the office..."

Finally the doorbell rang. The rhythmic squeaking of the bed continued up until the fourth ring.

"No, Tom! Don't stop!" the woman said.

"I haven't even gone yet. I took my magic beans a little too early; my fault... The Chinese hot sauce should put me in the mood again..."

Tom threw something on and went to the door. "Fantastic. Right in here..." he said.

"Sorry to disturb you, but I've misplaced my keys and need to use a bathroom really bad!" It was Natalie. She had come to Antiope's rescue!

"You mean you aren't from Kung Po? I ordered a half-hour ago... No friends around here, huh? Well, alright. Just make it quick, and no messes, please. I don't want to have to get the maid involved..."

The light came on and there was Natalie dressed for work. She ran over to flush the toilet and then, without saying a word, grabbed Antiope's flailing arms and pulled her to safety.

"I hear giggling. Has the food arrived? What the hell's going on out there, Tom?" the woman said.

184

Tom didn't answer. He was too busy trying to figure out how the second young lady had come out of a bathroom that only one had entered.

The Velvet Touch

"My god Natalie that was great!" said Sheryl.

"You don't think he'll figure it out, do you?" Antiope worried.

"Don't worry about it," said Amira, greeting Antiope a friendly hug. "If he changes the locks you can come live with us."

"Of course she can," Sheryl seconded.

Amira drove them to the outskirts of town along US 31 and pulled into the parking lot centered within an industrial strip of grass.

"Here it is," said Natalie. "Are you nervous?"

"No, not at all," Antiope said uneasily. She was packed behind the driver's seat of the Hello Kitty hybrid mini car. Natalie was equally cramped beside her.

Amira made eye contact through the rearview mirror: "You poor thing."

Antiope was covered in goose bumps and from her stomach she felt what was called butterflies. She looked at Amira in the mirror and smiled uneasily.

"It's okay. You'll see," said Sheryl from the passenger seat. She turned as best she could and gently squeezed Antiope's right hand.

Antiope smiled uneasily and looked out. The first thing she noticed was the lights. The place was lit up like a Christmas tree; a suburban string of petite red bulbs formed a rectangular outline and then an obese pyramid around the slanted restaurant-style roof; *The Velvet Touch* logo was accompanied by three buxom neon red women in high heels who appeared to fondle the heavy white "V", "T", and "h" like weightless mythological succubae; a sexy leg on a concrete pedestal dominated the center of the parking lot in memorial to vices.   Earthly by default in the soft glow of otherworldly pink noble gas, the skin of the giant thigh appeared smooth above a black mesh stocking—a hard plastic sculpture the color of alabaster. Some of the clientele were boozing it up outside and caused a ruckus at the approach of the Hello Kitty mini car. They were yelling something about a private show.

"That's typical," hissed Natalie.

"The pigs," Amira cursed. "You learn to ignore that kind of behavior. The paycheck helps."

Natalie pointed her witchy finger out the window from the cramped back passenger seat. "Isn't that the guy you always have to zap, Sheryl?"

"Sure is," said Sheryl. "He'll be brain-dead before long."

"It'll be your fault," said Natalie, smiling sheepishly.

Sheryl smirked. "Hey, I can't be responsible for someone else's behavior. The guy just doesn't learn. It's in his genes."

"I wonder how his line is even getting passed on?" said Amira. "Where I come from, a man is beheaded for such behavior."

"Amira, you're from Dearborn," Sheryl said.

"Exactly," said Amira. "It's easy to get someone expelled from Dearborn."

"You mean deported," Natalie corrected.

"Even if they're American?" asked Sheryl.

Amira shrugged. "That doesn't matter. It happens all the time. This entire planet is bugged."

Sheryl was dissatisfied. "Doesn't that bother you?" she asked, knowing her roommates all too well.

"It's a cheap way to travel," Amira stated and then shrugged with the steering wheel.

"Why don't you call the police on him?" whispered Antiope from the back seat.

"I have, several times," admitted Sheryl. "But anyway, he's harmless."

Amira drove to the back of the club and pulled into a vacant parking spot designated EMPLOYEES ONLY.   A thicket of unhealthy trees stood static down from the asphalt and the grassy mud that was decorated with Styrofoam, booze bottles, and brackish

186

liquids harboring dark, deformed rainbows. A black house cat slunk into the shadows of the putrid suburban jungle.

They got out and a bouncer let them in through the heavy door, which was promptly relocked. There was commotion from the front of the club, but the girls made their way to the dressing room.

"Where in God's name is your outfit?!" Sheryl said. She had noticed for the first time that Antiope was wearing a baggy pair of blue jeans instead of her new deep purple skirt suit with the matching dark purple boots. They had all taken the city bus downtown just the day before and had spent the afternoon lounging on pie and shopping at the overpriced stores. Amazingly, the petit skirt suits were on sale.

"I'm wearing it," Antiope said, "under these pants."

"What? You're ridiculous," Natalie said.

"She's a born nun," chided Amira. "She could be a wife of Taliban."

"Just a precaution," justified Antiope while she dropped her drawers and clumsily slid the boots free. "I'm not as Spartan as I would like."

The girls giggled.

An attractive middle-aged woman in white blouse and white rhinestone pants rushed in, telling everyone how great they looked. "Oh, and this is the new girl!" she said, admiring the skirt outfit. "You're like a cowgirl! Wonderful!" Edina realized that this was Mrs. Bergemot in the flesh. "When you're ready, I can take you over to the bar. Papa Berg is waiting. He wants to train you himself. We both decided to come in today and see that things ran smoothly—not that they don't otherwise. But anyhow..."

"I'm ready," Antiope said. She could not stop blinking.

Mama Berg brought Antiope to Papa Berg. He was over at the black saloon-style cocktail bar which was situated along the left gold-lacquered wall. Except for the section comprising the bar, which was black tile outlined in brass and glowing red lights, the floor was carpeted and resembled snow leopard fur. There was a half-circular stage with two shiny brass fireman's poles centered at the back of the club against the mirrored wall of the dressing rooms, with a low black and white velvet divan at the feet of a black portiere partitioned across a doorway with a half-spherical cornice-type domed velvet roof. There seemed to be a lot of halves. The same half-domes topped all the exits of the club. Little round obsidian-glass cocktail tables with comfortable black lounge chairs dotted the area in front of the stage as if it were a smile. A shimmering island with carpeted leopard stairs leading to an additional fireman-poled platform was situated opposite the main stage, itself an island in a pond of men and dark furniture. Erotic photographs, paintings, and sculptures appeared on display from out of darkness, illuminated by wall-mounted lights, throughout. A short hallway separating the entryway from the lounge was especially prone to them. A beautiful hostess stood at a fancy mahogany podium near the entrance, where a single bouncer struggled to prevent a riot. A trample of youth paid their nine dollars and ogled over the glittering hall of art before entering the belly of the beast.

The classy elder woman smacked her latex lips. "What do you think? Do you like the art? I did some of the sculptures, the marble ones, but the paintings and photographs we buy from a Russian pervert."

"They're very nice."

"I think so, too, said Mama Berg. "It adds something to the place."

"The new girl!" Papa Berg exclaimed from behind the bar. The spry old man was rinsing off glasses and drying them on a plastic rack. He waltzed over to embrace his Mama Berg and then took Antiope by the shoulders as he pointed out the basic features of the job. "You see those tables over there? I need you to take some drink orders. We generally start off with orders. Then I'll send you out there with these tube shots full of various schnapps. I'm sure you've seen them. Spring Break locales usually thrive on them. From midnight to the blue hour I like to finish things off with a complimentary Pousse-Café a la Francais featuring a local cherry brandy and Elixir Végétal de la Grande Chartreuse—what they don't know won't hurt 'em."

"What's with the virtual old guy?" asked Antiope.

Across from Papa Berg was a hologram bartender extending from a black silhouette platform and waiting in virtual limbo. He was old, handsome, and very twitchy.

"He's the bartender," Mama Berg said, hesitant to find her place just yet. "Go ahead and try it out. Ask him for a drink."

"Okay…" Antiope said, moving down to the bar. "Um…hello bartender."

"Greetings, young lady," said the ethereal bartender, suddenly becoming animate and very cordial. "My name is Bob. What can I get you this evening?"

"Um…how about…a Pousse-Café."

"What manner of Pousse-Café? Would you like me to recite our list of pousse-cafés?"

"No thanks. I'll take it French."

"One Pousse-Café a la Francais. A moment please."

The silhouette platform made some faint beeping noises and then the dark refrigerator-like machine vibrated with activity. Just when it seemed like something might have gone terribly wrong, a perfectly layered green, red-cherry-dotted transparent, milky white, and finally red brandy drink in a tall cordial glass was spit out and came moving down a rubber belt set into the middle of the bar's countertop.

Red and blue lasers came out from somewhere below and to the right of the bartender's virtual arm and studied the drink for a moment. A tiny camcorder behind the bartender's head shifted focus.

"Anything else?"

"Um, no. No thank you."

"Your total comes to…four dollars and fifteen cents…but tonight this one is on the house. Please enjoy yourself…Penuel of…" said the bartender.

"That's amazing," Antiope declared nervously, unsure what to do with the attractive drink.

"He's supposed to recite first names only…does it by facial recognition. That's strange how he called you by your last…I'd better reboot him."

"I come from a big family," she reasoned anxiously. The implications worried her, however, and she would have thrown on a disguise had she realized the prevalence of eyes weighing down the circumstances of liberty; the entire facial recognition program was hooked up to the encompassing surveillance network. Luckily there was an ocean of faces and very little reason to fish out any Penuels. And yet, there was one, she imagined, one dedicated little Napoleon with nothing better to offer the world other than paranoia and a snooping, controlling curiosity.

"Are you alright?" Papa Berg asked her concernedly.

"What? Yes! Certainly! I'm alright. Just nervous."

"You'll have to put up with a real geezer for the rest of the night, I'm afraid," Papa Berg said apologetically. "Tonight's drink specials are Between the Sheets and Black Velvet. Three-seventy-five. Two dollars for shots. Beer special is Arcadia Loch Nut. $2.75, which is a steal. They're listed on these gold foil flyers. Here, take this thing, and this cash belt. Have you ever used one of these? You can scan credit cards with this. Most of these guys you see out here in the middle will pay with gold Express cards. The small-time drug dealers and student-types at the front and in the corner near the beds will most likely pay cash. The prices are already built in. Just go to the menu and select the icon and then the quantity. What do you think? Can you handle it? Good. I know you can do it!"

Antiope smiled anxiously. "It's just a lot to take in…but I can do it."

"Take a sip of that drink. It'll put you on the level."

She found a straw and hesitantly took a sip. She hadn't tried an alcoholic drink since the days when her ex-boyfriend was still alive. That had been a decade ago, and it was from a still they had secretly made in the machine shop.

"Just leave it wherever you want and you can come back for it if the customers get so dumb that you can't understand them."

With tools in hand, Antiope was sent out into the world. Twelve or more square tables with couch-seats occupied the middle, sparsely filled with excited businessmen. As she gained enough confidence to approach the first table, someone slapped her in the thigh and made her drop the flyers. She speedily picked them up, having the uncomfortable notion that she was being eye-raped. "Hello gentlemen. What can I get you?"

"Angel's Tit," said one, trying to be cute (or so she thought).

"When do we get to see the real angel's tits?" lewdly said another.

"Any minute now," Antiope answered blankly, trying to figure out how best to take an order with the handheld computer (she was unused to computers). Once she coaxed their orders from them she was able to move on to the next booth. "Order, please."

The club became lit from chandeliers as another group of businessmen made their way to the center booths. Two women wearing lingerie were swimming over red silk sheets covering a heart-shaped bed in the far right corner. An additional bed was unlit and seemed like a dark invitation to tired eyes. It sat unused before the mirrored wall.

"Hello! What can I get you?" Antiope said, making her way quickly through the maze of booths.

A topless woman in a peacock feather headdress and turquoise panties, stockings, and stiletto heels winked as she brushed past to make her way up the stairs to the island. The boobs were fakes, but she had real Pilates buns. The careful attention the woman was getting made taking drink orders a little easier. If she couldn't manage to get their attention she just ordered them a Black Velvet and threw in a beer just in case. Antiope tromped back to the bar as she was in the trenches of warfare. Papa Berg already had most of the drinks ready thanks to Virtual Bob.

"Quicker than you can blink. That's why I love technology," he said.

Antiope took a tray from the server station designated for her in white letters above the brass and carefully distributed the weight of the drinks. She was like Atlas in a never-ending struggle.

"Which one's the Angel's Tit?" she asked. "It's a drink, right, and not some perverse dialogue?"

"This one," said Papa Berg, who shrugged innocently. "Don't look at me: I didn't name it! And here's the Black Velvet. These are the martinis. The diagram on the handheld tells you where to go. You know the rest."

With drinks loaded up for the first round, Antiope tried her luck at holding the tray while in motion. It was heavier than she imagined, but not unmanageable. She figured that her subservient genes were helping her out. When she finally arrived at the first table, she forgot who ordered the Black Velvet and could not will the handheld up from her pocket. "Black Velvet?" she asked. One of the men raised his hand and smiled imperceptibly for only a moment. Then she was on to the table of martinis, and then the Arcadias. Rum and Cokes seemed to be the next favorite, then Between the Sheets, then Black Velvet again. Most people didn't care one way or the other, as long as they had something to hold on to. One guy had the gall to ask her for a Blow Job. She created such a scene that the guy was forced to change his order to Black Velvet out of awkwardness.

French dance music blared through the speakers and the men became even more excited. Natalie was the first to come out. The beginning of her act was a leg in blue stockings playing with the curtains. Then she rolled over the black and white velvet divan, did the splits, and danced her way to the pole. She was wearing a blue sequined ball dress. Most of the men were too stunned to applaud, and neither could they keep their eyes off of her. Next there appeared Sheryl in shimmering green, kicking her smooth legs over the mysterious threshold, and finally Amira wearing a sparkling silver gown. They remained clothed for two songs and then began their routines. Sheryl was very good on the pole. Wearing nothing but an emerald bikini, she shimmied to the top, turned and held herself by the legs, extending one arm, then turned on her head with her arms hanging and slowly slid her way back down to the reflective darkness. Natalie and Amira, meanwhile were soon topless and began taking turns having sex with the floor.

"Embarrassing," Antiope whispered under her breath. She continued trying to take drink orders.

SEPTUPLET

I

The Day of the Meteor

"God, this is boring," said Darlene, "but at least we're outside."

"My poor Jim is still in there," Nancy said, looking in through the clear plastic strips, down the assembly belt and the miniature squared-off pool of water beginning the ascent of white plastic pocketed shelves which rose up the ziggurat, slanting sharply along the towering machinery, to where Jim stood over the grinder[29].

Edgar sat on a high metal stool next to Darlene and Nancy. The juice line was in operation and they were sorting out the leaves and sticks just outside the factory building. It was far more pleasant outside, where they knew the sun and could smell the sweet rot in the transient air. More importantly, they could hear themselves talk and could understand what people said to them.

"Whadya think happened to the first juice and powder crew?" inquired Darlene. "I heard there was another until just until a few days ago."

"I heard that, too," said Nancy. "My understanding is that they were *special*. The work proved too independent for them."

"That would make sense I guess..." said Darlene. "Strange, though. I thought *we* were the crew."

"We are now," Edgar said.

---

[29] The grinder was responsible for slicing up fruit and for releasing the pits into a waste receptacle while sending the valuable juice and flesh to the gigantic press machine and then on to the boilers and dryers.

193

They could see Donovan out on the asphalt resting against one of the yellow plastic tubs that were lined up in the open, empty, except for the transparent plastic bags made sticky from the juice. It was Donovan's job to remove the zip-ties and to tape the bags down around the tubs and then later to remove the bags for disposal. He was getting roasted out there.

"You ready yet?" the forklift driver said anxiously, glancing through the slits in the sheets of steel armor at the battlefield of writhing thorns and dead organic matter. The tub from the orchard had been lifted by the forks and was waiting idle over the tank of gads and discolored water.

"Just a minute..." Eric said. He sloshed the extended tennis racket around in the muck.

"It's the last one..." breathed the driver in anticipation.

"Last one?"

"Until the next truck arrives," explained the driver.

"Great. Well... Okay, then."

The hydraulic lift of the vehicle whined to life as the heavy plastic tub was tilted, cautiously, causing a river of fruit to cascade before Eric and his racket. The gads howled like banshees as they were sucked downward into the abyss of mechanical parts, through the pipes, and forced onto the system of wire-stitched belts and paddles. The tank was overly full, making it impossible to sort things out.

"Too many! Shit...shit!" Eric said, addressing no one. He thrust the tennis racket into the cauldron and pulled out a few handfuls of leaves. He thrust it in again and this time a large quill-type thorn got stuck in the trellis. "Son of a bitch, look at that!" He used wire cutters to get it out and then an entire dismembered branch section was tossed to the ground where it curled back and forth in angry spasms.

As Eric stood with effort upon the platform before an unruly tank of drowning gads, roughly 8 x 8 square feet of steel sheet-metal, something cosmic burned through the sky and landed godlike somewhere within the Great Michigan Basin, well beyond the living dunes that danced over the myth of the sleeping bear. There was a flash of blinding white light, an explosion, and then nothing.

A scurry of previously unseen creatures retreated into the pines to where the desert-like dunes overtook an evergreen sanctuary of rare birds.

"Holy Hell! Did you see that?" Eric screeched. The sorters had stopped sorting and were glancing around to where Eric was pointing wildly with his arms.

Edgar nodded in affirmation and looked out toward the sky. How could he not have seen it, which was like a gigantic flashbulb going off?

"Some weather control!" Eric hollered, enthusiastically holding out the racket as an extension of his arm.

"It ain't gonna stop meteors, stupid!" spat Darlene.

Eric threw a handful of gads at her.

Darlene threw some back.

"Where do you think it landed?" asked Nancy, nearly getting one in the eye.

"The congressional offices, if we're lucky," Darlene bellowed. She pelted Eric in the forehead with a single shot.

"Ouch, goddamit!"

"I wonder if it hit the basin?" contemplated Nancy.

"They usually dissolve in the atmosphere," Edgar explained through the gaps in the machinery. "Otherwise, we're in trouble."

"Yep, I think you're right," said Darlene.

An old-fashioned tin buzzer sounded and suddenly the machinery quieted and calmed. The belt had stopped.

"Hey! What gives?" Eric shouted attentively. "Damn it! Now we're gonna catch hell!"

A guy in a neat blue mechanic's outfit and perfectly formed matching hat came out of the factory and looked to be hopping mad. This was Don the boss. "Too much junk!" he bellowed. "Way too much! You're gonna damage my machines!! Is it so hard to sort them out?!"

"…there was a meteor…" explained Nancy.

"A what?!" Don shouted, pacing up and down the belt and scrutinizing the equipment.

"A meteor." The workers shook their heads and pointed.

"Never mind all that! You need to pay attention to what's on this belt!" scolded Don. He examined some sprockets.

Inside, between the press machine and the conveyor belt, a loosened hose began spurting out gad juice. A leaf blade had sliced though and was gleaming triumphantly.

"Get that damn thing out of there! Get it out!" Don shouted. Despite these impromptu commands, it was Don himself who ended up climbing the ladder that was hurriedly brought out by Jim. Don pried the blade out surgically and applied a roll of tape like a bandage. He soothed the hose lovingly as if it were his child's limb. "You hurt my baby!"

For once Darlene was speechless. "But...we didn't mean too..."

"I know you didn't...I know..." Don acknowledged hotly. "She's worn through; have to be replaced. Poor, poor little hose." He whispered in sing-song and rubbed the hose soothingly with his fingers.

"Are... are we gonna start up again?" asked Nancy. "Should, um...should we go see the Keeper?"

"Yes. The Keeper. Maybe she has something. Clean up...see the Keeper...come back tomorrow..."

"Walk, don't run, as in 'no need to rush'," mumbled Eric, addressing the ladies.

"Oh, I won't," said Darlene. She and the others grabbed squeegees, shovels, and water hoses that were available in the nearby corners and began cleaning up.

II

Change Comes to Box-Lifting Station

"You're slipping!" scolded Pete, taking hold of the box in David's stead. "Rough night, huh? You'd better get some caffeine. We need you now more than ever, buddy."

David tried to work faster but he was exhausted. He rubbed his shaven head to generate some luck. It really had been a rough night. *Luchadores*, *Luchadoras*, and even those who qualified for the Mini-Estrella division had appeared from out of nowhere once a proper ring had been established in Mrs. Welf's backyard. It was as if they had been waiting for just such a thing to happen. The neighbors had even thrown out an old training mat for him to find. It made for a much softer landing. He had won the first match against one of the two fighting beatniks, but had lost the second match against both of them at once. They had agreed to a "hair versus hair" match, the result of which had been very funny the first time, yet not so much the second time. But at least he had kept the neighborhood clean for a night. Quite a lot of money had been generated, though, through the cunning of the Welf twins Tammy and Molly, which had overjoyed Mrs. Welf upon her eventual appearance later that night, but would probably come back to haunt him if Lucha Libre Chicago ever learned that he had formed a league this far north. Somehow he would have to direct the attention onto the twins, if such a fire was ever sparked. You didn't want to mess with the LLC.

David lifted yet another box and placed it sloppily onto the stack.

"Look at this shit! Adolf would be ecstatic!" joshed Harvey. "So, who's going to replace those two jailbird losers? Are we getting any relief?"

"I don't know yet. We're still asking around," said Pete after he had placed another box.

"I'm not angry, you know," said Harvey, "I mean about your covertness. It isn't like you gained anything by it; just doing your job as a supervisor."

"Absolutely," said Pete. "I understand how you must feel. We can't allow that sort of thing around here. They could shut us down."

"Right. No reason why a few bad apples should ruin the bunch. I just wish they had confided in me, first. I had no idea!"

'Well, it's out of our hands, now."

"Truthfully. I wasn't in on that party. I hope you let my parole officer know that, if she happens to come in today…"

Pete smiled sheepishly.

The bright lights on the machine flashed orange just then to notify the overpaid quality control inspectors that something was amiss. The beautiful brunette and a male red-shirted supervisor scrambled over like worker bees to illuminate the problem and assess the damage. They opened up one box and then another. Pete ran over to see if he could help. It looked like it would be awhile before production started up again.

"Now's your chance to wake up," said Pete once he had returned from the commotion. "It's the damnedest thing: The gads are changing colors on us. They're sending us all on break. Don't know how long. Hopefully we'll have some help afterwards."

David Takes a Break

"Hello there, you! Come back any time!" said Judy from the Human Resources office partition window.

David blushed and rubbed his Velcro-like head.

"So what happened to you yesterday?" asked Carlos.

"Me? What are *you* doing here?" answered David.

"I asked you first."

"Well?"

"I'm working on this side today, down under the machines. There aren't enough gads for our building to run on and they shut us down. Rumor has it there was an accident in the orchards this morning. Some people got hurt."

"I see. Well…it's a long story, but yesterday I got lost and made a few friends. I had to stay over at the secretary, Mrs. Welf's, house last night. I lost my hair."

"That's awesome! Did you get lucky?"

"I'll tell you all about it later…" continued David sleepily.

"Going out for a smoke?"

"Yes."

The two of them went out for a smoke. The day was muggier than usual, David realized half-consciously. The nicotine cartridge seemed partly alive. Carlos wouldn't stop asking so David tried his best to relay everything that had happened to him the previous day.

"Lucha Libre! That's insane!" Carlos said.

They conversed for a little while. Then a bell rang and they salivated back to work.

Noah, by God

The box crew for lines one and two grew by one member that late afternoon. The new guy was someone David knew to some extent, a hillbilly in suspenders whose pants kept falling off every time he bent over.

"This is Noah, everyone," said Pete. "Noah, meet David and Harvey."

"Hey there," greeted David. "Remember me? We ride the bus together."

"Oh yeah! Then we almost died together!" exclaimed Noah with wide eyes. "That some bitch is plum crazy!!"

"Woah! Might want to get a new pair of suspenders, buddy!" Pete advised.

"Know where I can get some on the cheap?" Noah asked. "Afraid these clips is all worn."

"No idea," Pete answered.

"I'll ask the clowns at the circus next time they're in town," volunteered Harvey.

"Might nice of ye," said Noah.

The lines started up slowly and after a few false stops and starts they were in business.

"There isn't much to it," Pete explained to the new guy. "Just take a box and place it like this."

Noah took the next box and loudly broke wind. "Darn kin," he said.

III

The Money Origami Long-Stem Roses

The roses on the counter were green, the petals the folds of one-dollar bills. They were craftily attached to plastic stems without an adhesive and would outlast the life of the paper. They were being sold in singles and dozens with colorful wax-paper vases or just as-is.

Antiope was selling them on the internet for $5 plus the value of the bill, which in this case equaled $6 apiece. Most were from the tips she had received at work and the exchange of larger denominations for smaller ones. The origami long-stem roses were an unlikely success, but easily found admirers among the money-worshipers. They were especially valuable for dinner parties, weddings, graduations, executive take-the-money-and-run departures, or for anyone appreciative of the art. For a cheaper option, she was buying up foreign currency and preparing them into colorful bouquets. Sri Lankan Rupees would work out nicely, as would the Maldivian 5 rufiyaa and Lebanese pounds. Beautiful money made for beautiful origami. In her hands they would become a worldly garden of legal tender. She would pack them into rose boxes and with the invoice she would add the following note:

PLEASE HELP!!! I am being pursued by madmen! For the past two years I and many others have been held against our will at a place called Duck Lake Academy. It isn't really a school! It's a work camp for Gad Growers Incorporated! Before that, we were held at a series of other front operations, during the entire course of our innocent young lives. I alone have escaped to relay this message: MONSTROSSO CORPORATION IS EVIL! This is no joke! Please read the attached pamphlet detailing the mischievous plans of one of America's top multinationals. Inside you will learn how they plan to turn us all into slaves using their fertility treatments! Please look into it!

Thank you for your purchase!!

The Scoop on Buyer Cranbrook_Beauty96

Mrs. Margaret Chase Wesson was in a buying mood. She would have preferred to take the gas-guzzling Cadillac Escalade AV to the few remaining local shopping centers suitable for her culture to see what knickknacks she could pick up, but her daughter Kitty had totaled it on her way back from cheerleading practice. It was still uncertain just how she could have totaled an autonomous vehicle, but the supercomputer (lovingly, but by this point redundantly, given the name HAL in honor of Arthur C. Clark and his science-fiction novel *2001:   A Space Odyssey*) claimed that someone with sweaty fingers kept repeatedly switching the manual override button on and off with their teeth. Mrs. Wesson had opted out of watching the onboard video of the accident and had simply grounded Kitty for an entire week.

"Oona! Oh, Oona!" Mrs. Wesson shouted authoritatively.

A perturbed young Irish woman who had been washing the windows in the very same room and who was in fact just behind Mrs. Wesson stopped what she was doing and called out, "Here, Mrs. Wesson, I'm right here."

"Power up the computer, Oona. I want to go shopping."

"Of course, Mrs. Wesson." The strawberry-blonde maid went to the marble table to Mrs. Wesson's immediate right and turned on the silver tablet notebook computer that was situated lightly upon it. "There you are, Mrs. Wesson."

"Thank you, dear."

Oona, having been an unemployed computer programmer in her home country before signing up with a cruel but efficient temporary work service, had placed all of Mrs. Wesson's internet needs under the pink folder designated "M", and so all that was required of Mrs. Wesson was that she press the shopping tab and browse her favorite stores.

With this in mind, Mrs. Wesson delicately picked up the tablet computer with her softly gloved hands and took a seat on the white leather couch. She loved the feel of touching the screen with her silky fingers and how the flat little machine did what she told it to; a tablet computer was like buying a dictatorship for $699; she was now Queen Margaret, Supreme Leader of God and Country United. The impertinent pop-ups had darn well better get out of her way. She knew the right people and could easily ruin the underprivileged slobs who had made them. After browsing unscathed through several clothing stores, she finally remembered what it was that she needed.

"Oona, dear, how do I type?"

Oona dropped what she was doing and came over to help bring up the virtual keyboard (She had been trying to convince Mrs. Wesson to get speech recognition software to no avail; because things like temperature and home security procedures were controlled by the occupants' voices, Mrs. Wesson was afraid of making the house computer jealous).

"Thank you, dear. Such a strange thing." said Mrs. Wesson. She typed PARTY FAVORS in the blank spot of the default search engine with godlike fervor. As a result, a wonderful list of party-favor-type things appeared on screen. One of them caught her eye especially: a dozen money origami roses. She hit the item and watched the screen change. What a clever idea, Mrs. Wesson thought. She bought ten dozen. The next dinner party she hosted was going to be rich, figuratively speaking. She could hardly wait! "Oona, dear, could you get Mrs. Hoyt on the phone? And Mrs. Rutherford...and...get my little pink book. No, never mind, dear, I'll get it. You deserve a break for once."

"Thank you, mum. Whatever you decide," Oona said, continuing to dust the living room.

OCTUPLET

I

Edina's Stalker

Edgar felt foolish when his niece's car arrived to pick him up. Earlier that afternoon during break he had told The Keeper of Time about his dream during an odd discussion about premonition and she had taken it so well that she seemed to be coddling him. How could she have been so much on his wavelength about it, that ridiculous dream? Those people were known to her, she claimed after he had described them in detail, and the meaning would unfold in phases of entropy. She had said that she understood and would take care of things, whatever that meant. He had been advised to dwell upon it no further. And then he had received a call from his brother-in-law which had put him in a funk.

He climbed into the car and failed to notice at first that something was wrong.

Edina was morosely silent that evening. She was definitely not her usual self.

"So how's the city life treating you?" Edgar posed once they had hopped out of the parking lot and were bounding down MR 114 to reach Highway 31 North.

"What? Good. Why do you ask?"

"I got a call from your dad today. He said you had a run in with a strange man; that he tried to kidnap you. You were so shaken up that you called him. He almost came straight home. He says it's my fault and that I'd better do something about it and to get back with him."

"I don't know anything about no kidnapping," Edina insisted, drowning in her own words.

"He said you were almost kidnapped on the Gamesh beach. You shouldn't have been there, let alone unsupervised."

"Kidnapped is a stretch. He was just watching me by the swings. He gave me the creeps."

"What were you doing there?"

"I just wanted to see what it would be like, you know, if there had still been water there. If it was anything like I imagined, the beach would have been really neat with water."

"From now on, don't go anywhere without an adult," Edgar puffed angrily. "If you see that guy again, call the cops."

"Then how will I pick you up?"

"Take your mom, or just come straight here and keep your doors locked. I'm serious. I don't like hearing this stuff. This guy could be dangerous."

"Okay," Edina wheezed, obviously frightened.

"Are you sure nothing happened?"

"Yep."

"This self-isolation doesn't fit you very well. Something must have happened."

"Nothing happened. He just creeped me out is all. I want to get a hold of some remote control helicopters and see if I can program them to kill people using facial recognition."

"What?"

"Facial recognition. If I can find out where people live, I think I can get one to recognize them and shoot them."

"Umm, hmmm...have you told your mom about any of this?"

"No. She just wouldn't understand. So do you think you could get me a remote helicopter and a gun?"

The little thing was serious, Edgar noted in humorous surprise. "Well, no. I can't. But I know how to make some really good pepper spray."

"I don't want my helicopter to shoot pepper spray!"

"For you, goof! I think you should carry some from now on. And we'll tell your mom about this strange man."

"I really don't think that's a good idea," insisted Edina.

"It's not up for discussion. This is serious."

"Alright, I'll describe him to you… cause if I'm right then I think he's packing heat."

"Did he look like a policeman?"

"No, I don't think so… a policeman always wears a blue uniform, don't they? No, this guy was wearing a white shirt with a tie."

"Okay, take me to this beach."

They drove into Gamesh and dodged shops, grocery stores, and tourists until reaching the overcrowded beach where a small group of healthy young people were narcissistically checking themselves out while playing volleyball. Edina drove onward towards the East Grand Traverse Bog until she found the swing set where the creepy guy had been spotted. Currently, there was a mother with four children playing there.

"He was right here," admitted Edina factually.

"Okay, well don't go here ever again unless you have an adult with you."

"I'll bring my helicopters with me next time, and I'll wear one of the shirts I'm making to protect me."

"Unless it can guarantee that you won't get kidnapped then no."

"You don't understand! I've made this cloth for shirts that uses body heat to produce power which is used to regulate temperature; in addition, I think it also acts as a Faraday Cage which can potentially disrupt stun guns…not sure though. Someone at my school, Lakeland Elementary, was stunned last year for misbehaving in the hallway…the security guards thought she was packing heat…a banana in her pocket, left over from lunch which the school claimed wasn't healthy enough and so charged her parents ten dollars for a greasy slice of pizza—after that gross meal, she had no room in her tummy for the banana…anyway, I would hate to see anything like that ever happen to *me*, so I'm making this shirt…"

"But you go to school over the internet now… Wait a minute…You think this guy had a stun gun?"

"Maybe. I'm not taking any chances though. I promise to stay away from here. Mom just better let me have some kind of fun this summer. Selling candy is boring. It's far more exciting to just eat some."

"A Faraday Cage, huh. Do they teach you that stuff in school?"

"Are you kidding? I read about it from an obscure site on the in-ter-net."

"Where did you get the fabric?"

"From the attic."

"You'll have to show me how it works."

"Do *you* have a stun gun?"

"Nope."

"That's unfortunate, 'cause I need to test it on someone. Do you think you can get one? It's really important!"

"I'll have to take a look at this thing first."

"Why doesn't anyone believe in me?"

"All in good time, sport."

II

David to Replace Someone Who Has Perished

"David, it's time," said The Keeper presumptuously, and with a certain degree of the occult.

"Whatever do you mean, Keeper?" asked David in alarm. He had not even seen The Keeper approach and now she was there in front of him.

"How would you feel about working in the orchard? A new crew is needed and I think it would be a good fit for you. Lifting boxes has made you a few dangerous enemies. The skinheads from the other line have been glowering at you. Driven to fear, your mood might lead you to some hasty decisions. It would be wise to counter that."

"The orchard! I...well...if you say so, Keeper. As long as they let me smoke."

"Death cannot be cheated as one cheats his fellows. One day it will all come sweeping down on you. It's all a matter of time."

"I should quit, I know. But it gets me through the day."

"So you think. Well, do you want the job? You'll be working with my husband and I think it will be a healthy experience. And yes you may smoke yourself into a coma if you like."

"Death by smoking is still better than by meth-induced pummeling of fists and the sharp kicking of steel-toed feet. I'll take it."

"Good, just sign this please."

"What's it, a release form?"

"A form that frees GGI from liability in case of accidental death or injury," said The Keeper in complete seriousness. "It just means that you should keep on your toes out there. The work might become dangerous. Don't get hurt."

"Okay," said David apprehensively. He could never get used to these sorts of things. "Will I get a raise or anything?"

"You will. Be at the security shed near the front gate tomorrow morning at six."

"How can I do that? I ride the bus out of the Oceana migrant camp, right near the heart."

"You'll be there. The factory's hours are changing for the mid-season rush. The bus will start running an hour earlier to reflect the changes."

"A whole hour! But we never get any sleep as it is."

"You can nap on the bus."

"It's impossible; that bus is like fourteen elder brothers, thanks to the S.O.B. driver."

"I know all about your driver. I sent in a complaint, but they don't have anyone to replace him. And he *does* get you here on time."

"The bus will never make it," David worried.

III

Happy Hour on Monday Night

"What, I have to go on?! But I'm the waitress!"

"Just get your ass out there!" yelled the head bouncer acting as the assistant manager. He was standing just outside the dressing room door.

"But I'm not ready! I haven't mentally prepared!"

"Are you kidding me?! Get your ass out on that stage!"

It was just after six. The lavender Zeno's Arrow had mysteriously carried Antiope to work an hour early that Monday evening and she had returned that kindness up to the dressing room as she prepared. The thought of losing the bicycle to some drunk from the parking lot had haunted her a little bit at night as she kept forgetting to buy a lock for it. Surprisingly, no one seemed much interested in a bicycle that defied the laws of Newtonian physics.

Antiope meditated by closing her eyes and slowly breathing in and out. If nothing else, she felt confident in her dancing abilities. The girls had initiated her into their pole dancing class which took place every Tuesday and Thursday evening and the Olympiad instructor did not accept defeat. Already, she had learned how to hang from the pole by her bare ankles while swinging dizzily under the lights like a tetherball and sliding upside-down to the floor with a buoyant thud. As an exercise, pole dancing could be exhilarating and fun, but she had never dreamed of having to perform in the nude!

Pound pound pound!!

The heavy assault on the door broke her attempt at meditation once again and demanded that she go on immediately and yet she still had not accepted public nudity into her psyche despite watching a German nudist instruction film on the dressing room computer. Her anxiety was rising to dangerous levels. The girls were at college today and Antiope was on her own for the big debut she had never intended to perform. Papa and Mama Berg were absent as well and the head bouncer, Brad, was in charge. Brad was at that very moment pounding on the door.

210

"Where the hell are you?!" he desperately shouted.

"Watch yourself, Brad!" warned the old woman who was standing between Antiope and the door. This was the club's house mom who was responsible for seeing to the needs of the working girls and protecting them from unfairness.

"I'm begging you, lady!" Brad pleaded. "Look, tell you what: I'll drop the fees on this one! The place is a madhouse... some kind of two-wheel stand-up electric scooter gang! I need you!!"

"Okay, okay! Give me...two minutes!" Antiope was overly-anxious. Her heart felt like it might explode. Even her reflection was filled with apprehension. *The things I go through to escape insanity,* she thought. Her mind was like a wild film reel. *What to do?! What to wear?!* She got up dizzily from the makeup station and disappeared into the clothing rack.

An old jazz number haunted the club from the unseen rafters, floating eerily down to the carpeted floor.

There was a scuffle behind the stage. Someone was shoved. A stiletto-heeled shoe was propelled. "Damn it, crazy little... You get out there!" a raspy masculine voice whispered. There was another scuffle and someone was pushed. "Fine!" a chirping female voice whispered loudly. A silver woolen leg warmer appeared through the black curtains, rising and falling with a white-leotard-covered foot. It searched for the black and white velvet divan, and then a glittering silver party mask appeared over a face of creamy smooth skin. What came out was some kind of overcrowded human clothing rack. A thick white fur coat dropped to the floor of the stage, then a long navy blue wool coat, then a feathery neck warmer. A pair of black silk gloves was next and gradually the glassy stage became like the room of a messy teenager.

The two-wheel stand-up electric scooter gang comprising a substantial portion of the audience was actually a group of government contract specialists that was involving itself in sophisticated autonomous transporters for government employees to utilize after a hard day of internet browsing. G-men with laser-guided Tommy guns were at that very moment skewering the parking lot for potential violators of government property. Inside, the club had become a co-educational fiesta on the taxpayer.

The lights blinded. Having attached her securities to the pole, Antiope was lost to the sudden realization that she had no bare skin with which to dance in that manner. She was therefore restricted to the vast open field of the stage, the blinding lights, the raping, covetous eyes, lest she rid herself of the remaining layers. But the clothing was also a security. This stripping business was such a catch-22! She improvised a ballet routine.

"Take it off for me, baby!"

"What, *this*? You want *this* off?"

"Yeah! Take it off!"

Antiope played along, feeling trapped by a sudden female outcry, as if there were many inverted guns pointed at her and ready to misfire. She teasingly stripped down a layer, taunting the suckers with every article, even tossing a pair of woolen leg warmers into the crowd. They saw a bare shoulder, then an elbow, a wrist, a breast, or at least the shape of one, somewhere under layers of fabric.

The males in the audience were surprisingly quiet, intently watching, somewhat annoyed at the rancorous females. They focused their drunken attention upon the woman on stage whose vacuous interplay of curvature and light sucked the dollars from their wallets.

Antiope tried her best not to freak out. The unbalanced peer pressure was closing in on her. It was like those dramatic oboe performances she had always dreamed about, yet with a demented and depraved twist: The money was to be put where?! She was reminded of those documentaries on Eastern European sex slaves, except that in this case she had arrived within the trap willingly and there was the potential for huge profit without any physical contact or fear of unwanted force. Despite these American perks, she was still having trouble getting naked. The point where licentious men and rancorous women would hopefully (or not so hopefully) be shoving filthy paper currencies into her unmentionables was still quite a ways into the future of this terrifyingly time-stopping event. In light of that horizon, she panicked.

"You-you want more? Um, stick around!" she said. "I'll-I'll be back really soon..." She waved nervously with both hands and walked backwards along the stage, picking up an extra layer of clothes as she went, then tripped clumsily over the divan, rose achingly, and vanished through the curtains.

The crowd of riled-up feds was not exactly thrilled at having their bottles capped. Males and females alike chanted for skin, although a few were certainly turned on by this fetish performance.

"Hey, what is this?!" they yelled.

"I thought you were *full nude*! What a rip-off!"

"That girl didn't reveal so much as a bellybutton! We paid to see some skin!"

"Ain't this the place of that world-famous Ishtar?! Where the hell is she?"

"Ishtar! Where's Ishtar?! We want tits!!"

The maledictions were coming in through the curtains and permeated backstage, much to the jubilation of the veteran dancers, but Antiope knew the old saying, that the mouth which cursed would also bless.

"There, there, girl. Is everything alright?" said the house mom, posting guard inside the dressing room after having locked and bolted the door. "Are you sure you know what you're doing out there?"

"Um, I just need time to think!" she bluffed. "Just wait a half hour and the dollars will unfold—you'll see, house mom. This is behaviorism; it's all just an emotional chess game. I excel at these things. " Antiope said this, but her voice lacked confidence. She really had no idea if her trick would work or not—there were just too many variables! "But...maybe I'm just not sexy enough to pull off this kind of move," she admitted.

"Don't worry, girl, you're sexy enough!" said the house mom. "Hell, with enough booze running through these boys, even I could be sexy enough. Just show them the goods!"

"Oh, I'm not going to do that..."

"You're not?"

"No, ma'am. I'm strictly a teaser, at least until I really get to know someone. But, even then, I would never venture out to a public place in the nude!"

"Oh, boy! So you won't be revealing so much as an areole?"

"What's an areole?"

"My policy is not to force my girls into doing anything they're not comfortable doing, but you should probably show them *something*. All the laws that used to protect a girl have gone straight to Hell! They'll rip the place down! You don't strike me as the outgoing type anyway. A smart girl like you: How did you even get talked into this? A sign of the times, I suppose..."

"Don't worry, house mom, I'll give them what they want. I still have three layers to remove."

"I'd better go talk to Brad, then, before there's a riot! With Blue Lobelia called in sick and Ginger knocked-up, we'll need more cover-fire than just two leather sacks in high heels, hot-to-trot-or not!"

"Am I going to get fired? But you haven't seen the whole act yet..."

The house mom grabbed the fire extinguisher that was clamped in near the door and prepared to exit. "Don't you worry, girl! Just go out and do your thing and we'll try and hose them down."

"If only the girls were here..."

"Those college girls? I'll see if I can get a hold of them."

"Oh, I'm sorry...I think they're still in class."

"They actually go to class? I thought all the kids nowadays went to those virtual schools that don't really exist. Well, it's good to know that not everyone's a cheating recluse."

Antiope tried to think. The angry shouts from the mob were repeating in her mind like a maddening choir. "What about this Ishtar they keep asking for? Can we call *her* in?"

"Her? She was too good for this place—moved on to a bigger venue. What a drag. Hell, I'd go out myself if I thought it would help."

"Thanks anyway..."

Phoenix and Cleoclaptra

Two veteran dancers were seated together near the most proximal side of the stage on top of an unfurled red satin bed, complaining and puffing heavily at lifelike electronic cigarettes.

"I just don't know Cleoclaptra; I'm not making anything. The refrigerator's almost bare. The buns are all moldy. Nothin' but lips and assholes for me to look forward to."

"You can say that again. I'm down to pink slime. Where did we go wrong, do you think—was it the ten-thousand-dollar boob job? I'm beginning to look like a flabby old slingshot. This career used to be so easy. Now I gotta worry for if my boob's gonna come attached and scare the meshugaas outa someone again."

"Don't blame yourself, sweet-ums. Society is definitely down on people like us. Everyone's so judgmental. And this economy! I finally got a lap dance in last week. A couple of drunk college boys came in here late in the night and I was the only one still on duty. Satellites were knocked out in a solar storm. High speed internet was out statewide and they were desperate—think I gave the poor kid a rash."

"Well, let's go get us some contractors, Phoenix. See how they like being on the receiving end for once."

"These types expect an awful lot, for lookin' the way they do. You'd think with all that taxpayer money that they'd learn to dress a little better. But at least they're combustible. Too bad they don't allow no more real smokes or we'd have 'em explode without really getting the whole picture. I really miss that. We should talk to Papa Berg about a smoke screen of some kind. Then maybe I could afford to eat out."

"Well, Phoenix, are you coming or not? Put that goddamn e-cig away! I got a feelin', and you know what that means…"

"You're finally pregnant?"

"You silly nine-tenths naked whore. Come on off that bed 'fore my boob comes attached."

The Second Part of the Act

Brad was going off outside the dressing room like a cuckoo clock. The house mom would not allow him in for fear of violence. She held the extinguisher like a flamethrower.

"She'll come out when she's good an' ready, Brad!" she insisted.

The German documentary on nudity was playing on a small monitor that was situated on the white countertop of one of the mirrored makeup stations. Antiope, meanwhile was occupied with a series of belts and loops of some medieval contraption.

The room darkened and the crowd quickly settled down, then began cheering in anticipation. A demonic male voice sounded over the speakers, something about woe and the devil and the number six-hundred-and-sixty-six, the following silence breaking into soaring guitar and violins. Next a series of male and female voices sang to music from an array of musicians. The experimental post-metal band SYNTYCHE was performing an elaborate cover of the Iron Maiden song "Number of the Beast", which had been lost to culture for nearly a decade. Spotlights blared upon the stage a minute and eighteen seconds in, illuminating a horned woman who was hanging seductively from the fireman's pole. Her body was red and she was wearing a glittering black bikini. A whip cracked from one of her capable hands. She thrust her body out toward the bewildered crowd. Again the whip cracked. She danced around the pole. It was a great performance. Men and women alike rushed the stage with green bills flying like flags from their outstretched hands. But just when they thought they would finally get what they had actually paid for the seductive performer strutted over to the divan on sharp black stilettos, covered her jeweled goods with white leather and began locking herself with padlocks and chains. She strutted around the edge of the stage like this, cracking her whip, covering her eyes and gritting her teeth as a multitude of hands molested the modernized chastity-belt-type prop, shoving their slush-funded bills into the pockets and pulling down on the chains. Someone grabbed her thigh and the whip cracked again, striking the hand of this particular outlaw like the sting of a scorpion so that it writhed in pain. The petite night-haired performer broke away, strutted backwards, and returned to the pole for a dance.

"What's the deal? Take it off! Take off the damn belt!" someone yelled from the front booths.

The performer had no intention of removing the belt. Tears were streaming down her face, ruining the makeup. Before the audience of depraved governmental types was a modern Pelagia, a falling saint of chastity. The diabolical had been overcome, exposed in the desert. Just like that, her career was over.

"I can't believe it!! She's not going to take it off!!"

It was at this point when the tormented crowd went berserk. Chaos rippled through the fabric of civility like whack-a-moles escaping the confines of the game to take up arms against the whacker. Tables were toppled; Drinks were thrown; Glass shattered the stage. The boiling rage of disgruntled feds on holiday was centered on anyone connected with the club, as if an eighth of a year was hardly adequate to compensate for such strenuous work as riding on the backs of others. The white chastity belt was especially targeted with violence and the infamous wearer ran for her life, vanishing evermore behind the curtains of black.

A sparse handful of bouncers came out like New York City storm troopers and soon became lost in the scuffle. Brad could be seen momentarily, as he was carried through the mob on a wave of fleshy digits, yelling for someone to call the cops, but then vanished, seemingly drowning in body parts. His final words bounced bitingly from the club's rafters: "That crazy bi---tch!!"

The Woman Captured

"Name and occupation..."

"I'm not really a dancer...I mean, this was my first time. And my last, I'm sure."

"Just state your name and occupation please."

"Clark, um, Gab...uh, Gab, Gabrielle Clark."

"Okay, Number 6934. I want you to rub this swab against your cheek. Not like that; on the inside, dummy. Okay. Now hand it over. Step back please... Well, Gabrielle Clark, according to your DNA, you're a perfect match for one Antiope Clara Penuel, ward of the state, currently issued for arrest nationwide. Seems you have an unfulfilled contract with the Monstrosso Corporation. Gone AWOL, huh? That'll really put a blemish on one's record. What a shame. You may as well get used to those hideous orange socks, then. Enjoy your stay."

"They make a decent Christmas stocking for the kids...not that I have any of my own," said veteran stripper Phoenix, in line just ahead of Antiope.

"I suppose you got those stretch marks at the gym, is that it?" held the female cop slyly. "Sure, you got no kids... you probably aborted and then ate them, depraved, lyin' sack... Okay, take these three down to the women's cellblock. Put little miss devil in with that fat one, Rochelle. That'll make her think twice about shirking off her duties to this great country, the good ol' U.S. of A-One. Okay, who's next?"

"But what's the charge?" asked Phoenix hopelessly as they pulled her away.

"Alright, listen up!" they heard ahead of them in the zoo-maze of putrid cells. "Breakfast for you scumbags will be served at six! Don't ask what's in it, because I have no idea! I don't want to hear another peep! If I hear anyone else complain, especially if it's to ask for a nice fluffy pillow, so help me Baby Jesus..."

"Welcome to the Grand Traverse Holiday In', sweet-pea...as in Incarceration..."

"Shaddap!!"

NONUPLET

I

A Strange and Portentous Morning

That morning had been the strangest ever. When they had arrived at the juice and powder line early 5:45 AM there had been a halo around the moon. A misty werewolf night had met them broodingly before the transfer of twilight's hazy blue scepter and then the golden dawning of light that pried them awake. Somewhere in that brief transition they had heard the terrible blood-curdling scream of Donovan. He had undone the plastic bag in one of the 1300 pound boxes of fermenting gads and had seen something unprecedented. There floating in the golden red superfruit elixir of such boisterous claims as the easing of arthritis was a bloated, pale, slightly purplish human face. The result of that encounter was a police investigation headed by the FBI and the disappearance of Donovan from the factory, seemingly of his own will. The face, as it turned out, belonged to an employee on the harvest crew who had not been seen since the night shift began; none other than that of Donovan's brother.

After all the commotion had subsided and all interviewees were long shaken from their cold, clammy nests to provide brief unhelpful statements to the clashing heads of crime-fighting organizations, the insects began to appear. The place where they had come from was as mysterious as why they were here. Adding to the strangeness was the addition of fresh faces from the factory's employment roster. A pale and pregnant Elsie had joined them outside, and just inside were placed first a woman in baggy black-green-tan camouflage trousers and an azurite-colored sweatshirt, then a tall and attractive bob-headed young lady and her narcoleptic husband with a penchant for cheap sunglasses and sleeping on the job.

"My god, look at that? He's gonna kill himself..." Nancy said, observing the guy in the dark sunglasses as he bobbed dangerously back and forth on the metal stool.

His companion looked around in embarrassment, her sweet voice of warning too low to penetrate the stupor and the droning noise. "He works the Wendy's night shift to get us by," the young lady whispered from inside, barely discernable to all but Norma-Jean.

Nancy and Darlene were excited by the new companionship, having spent half the season talking to each other. Additionally, there was a large, blond, muscular guy whispering into a pregnant girl's ear, but he soon exited.

"Was that your husband?" Darlene asked their new neighbor Elsie after the muscular guest had vanished inside.

"Boyfriend," breathed Elsie. "That's Harvey."

Apparently, Elsie's boyfriend had just gotten out of prison for manslaughter. Edgar was having trouble hearing the rest because he had been delegated to the snipping of zip-ties and the unraveling of plastic bags. It was tedious and boring work.

"...He can't keep his hands off me," Elsie said, patting her tightly-buttoned belly.

"Is he a drunk or an alcoholic?" asked Darlene.

Elsie contemplated.

"Does he go to meetings for it?" Darlene pressed.

"No."

"Then he's a drunk."

The ladies continued swapping tales of alcoholism, but Edgar missed out because the forklift driver came in too fast with his 1300 pounds of gads-in-a-bag and Edgar had to jump out of the way to avoid being crushed. An awaiting box had been crashed into and was sent skidding, almost biting into Edgar's legs as it lunged forward.

"Oh crap, I'm so sorry!" the driver apologized, his hand shaking on the gear-shift. "Brake slipped!"

And On Into the Afternoon

A buzzer sounded from far off behind them, somewhere inside. One of the lines that had apparently stopped had started up again; however, no one was surprised because this had become a daily occurrence.

The forklift drivers had made themselves scarce since the interviews. Some new kind of problem was unfolding. A revving whine sounded from the direction of storage. An unknown driver appeared to be in tears as he zipped his way speedily towards shipping and receiving. He stopped and got out for a moment, then got back in and sped off, swatting the air as he went.

Eric began throwing a fit up on the metal upside-down pyramid-shaped tank. He waved his arms, jumping up and down on the platform. "We're gonna run out!" he cried. "Edgar, you gotta get someone over here before there's trouble!"

Edgar was sitting lazily upon a rusty metal stool with his wire cutters. He stood up with sudden purpose and looked around. The back lot was quiet and motionless except for the buzzing sounds coming from a few small, low-flying birds.

Terry, the main driver for the juice and powder line, appeared on his forklift just coming out of the shipping and receiving building with three yellow plastic boxes of gads. He swatted at something. Another forklift came out and they both seemed to go crazy. They nearly collided out near the mountain of metal boxes which were neatly stacked in even rows out from the second building. Edgar had always gotten a kick out of them because of their family crest-type logos which were displayed on all sides to denote ownership and yet also fealty to GGI and therefore ultimately to Monstrosso.

"Oh no! Watch out, Terry!" shouted Darlene.

Terry's forklift hit a tower of metal boxes which came crashing down on top of him with a thundering "boom, boom, boom!" The safety frame had luckily protected the driver from almost certain death, but it was difficult to tell whether or not he had been injured. The other forklift had stopped abruptly and the unknown driver was wading through the bulky rubble to get to Terry.

Darlene and Nancy rushed over in astonishment to see if Terry had met his demise or not. Edgar and Eric followed.

Men in blue-collar shirts rushed over from the shipping and receiving section of the building, swearing and cursing at everything within sight, and then stared at the ground like they couldn't believe something. More men came out, including an old farmer with a shotgun, and then there appeared women in neatly-tucked green T-shirts, until finally the men in white-collar shirts arrived to taste the pesticide-ridden air.

A loud buzzer rang and the juice line stopped. Don came running out in his neat blue mechanic's outfit and perfect hat to find out what was impeding the progress of his juice and powder machines. It upset him, though, to see that his pet driver was involved in an accident and he rushed over to help.

An ambulance soon arrived from around the far eastern corner, blaring down the flat asphalt spaces with the lights going, after which two paramedics came out and helped a limping Terry and his human crutch (Darlene) to the back of the ambulance. Terry seemed puffy and rather sedated.

The old farmer with the shotgun left the crowd at shipping and receiving and headed angrily down to the exposed juice line while being hindered by a train of white-collar staff.

"But we can't do that, Elijah, it isn't legal!"

"What would you have us do, boys?! We can't sit around and wait for the government to do something! We've got a farm to run!! Just get back to the powder room and let the men handle this!"

"Elijah you old fool! We're liable for-!"

"This is between God and farmers! You there!" Old Elijah pointed a bony, rickety finger at Edgar and others who had formed a sizeable group of factory spectators. "I need a posse! Able bodies! A hundred dollar to start, and twenty more for every giant dang bug you can put in a sack! I'm gonna end this problem once and for all! Go see that guy over there in the black pick-up truck and he'll set you up! Don't forget to tell 'em your name! Thank you, son!"

"I'll go!" said Darlene, appearing from out of nowhere. "I'd sure like to kill some bugs!"

"No women; I'm sorry. Just the men for now. Nothin' personal."

222

"My ass," said Darlene to Nancy under her breath. "I tole you this place was sexist."

The Task At Hand

Before Edgar knew what was happening, he and Jim and three others were being escorted by security down to a gravel road curving out from the second building and a thicket of trees to the back of the factory grounds where they waited. The group became gradually larger as males from the second building arrived in hopes of earning *Benjamins* and a wad of *Jacksons*. A truck pulled up fifteen-minutes later and two men in cowboy outfits handed out shotguns from a pile in the truck-bed while a third man took names and signatures; a third passed out paper bags full of shells.

"I don't know no Spanish, only English; have someone explain it to you," they were saying. "No, we ain't got the money. You'll have to get it from Ol' Elijah. Divvy out a plot for yourself about forty feet wide and happy hunting. Don't shoot nobody."

There were only about a dozen members so far and most of them were migrants who were happy to be receiving a gun, but clueless as to what they were supposed to be shooting at. Despite a lack of direction, people were banging away, soon enough.

A white BMW pulled up speedily in a cloud of dust and one authoritative-looking guy in a shirt and tie came out and pleaded with the men at the truck to stop. "No more guns!!" he ordered frantically. "Get all those men back here!!"

"No guns?" the startled weapons man said. "Then what are they supposed to shoot them with?"

"Bug spray," said the suit. "It should be here any minute. Getting the boxes out from storage as we speak... Just stop all that shooting! Now, that's an order straight from Monstrosso!"

"Monstrosso?" the signatory asked snidely. "They can't tell us what to do... Can they?"

"Just see that it's done, boys! I didn't come out here to argue!"

"Yes sir, sorry sir."

The two men in the truck got out and apprehended the gun-happy bug hunters who had gotten an early start and then returned to the signature guy guarding the unhappy pile that filled the bed like unwanted toys.

A dark van pulled up and men in dark suits and sunglasses exited and silently motioned for the idle group to approach. They handed out cans of foamy bug spray to the disappointed crowd.

"Say, pal, we're still getting the hundred dollars, right?" asked Jim.

"We're just here for the bug spray, sir."

"So we're doing this regular pay?" Jim said unhappily.

"Can't tell you that, sir."

"Great," Jim huffed disgustedly. He teamed up with Edgar and they wandered off into the wilderness. A wasteland depression of dune grass proved uneventful and soon they were in an abandoned horse pasture. There was a pile of rusty machine parts near the foundation of a barn and then nothing but a perpendicular road headed into a town of tombstones and fungus. Edgar found a decent-looking trekking pole left against an old shed alongside a sun-warped pair of snow shoes. Another matching pole appeared not far off in the weeds. "A souvenir," Edgar said, presenting Jim with the pole.

"Hey, I've been looking for one of these," said Jim happily.

There were hardly any people now, no other exploited workers of the factory, save for a group of five far off near a patch of thorns. Two houses stood just off from a paved road of cracked asphalt somewhere to their right with yards of high weeds and rosebuds and windbreak rows of blue spruce, places abandoned, with all remaining love buried somewhere in the back yard. The prior occupants, despite their ties to the area, had moved out east, or out west, had taken their chances in some big dirtball of a city, or were perhaps alone in vast Asia, thankfully plugging some kind of American-English niche for an inquisitive people.

A mysterious tower appeared in the distance, rising into the blue. Nothing else could be seen around this post-meridian citadel except for miles of struggling trees. The ground in their immediate vicinity was parched and dying. The sand had eaten forests-turned-pasture, creeks, ponds, large patches of marshland, and was heading inland from the dead lake. It seemed to Edgar some kind of omen, a form of augury in landscape.

"That's it I think I'm going back," said Jim. "It was a nice walk at any rate."

"I guess you're right. This was all pretty stupid anyway."

Something in the grass got spooked. Edgar figured it was probably a rabbit or a snake—that is, until it made a sharp buzzing noise. What they saw was an abnormally large black and yellow-striped beetle, roughly nine inches in length.

"I'll be leaving that one alone," commented Jim in both amazement and disgust.

Edgar agreed, the alarm rising to a shriek amidst his troubled thoughts. With minds blown, they headed back to their metered world of mechanized impermanence.

II

The Gad Orchard

The next morning David ate toaster pastries with dispensed coffee and cream and went out to discover his new position.

A man was waiting at the security gate next to a black suburban.

"I'm to be here, for the orchard," David said groggily. His feet felt wet from the grass dampening his shoes and the birds were chirping away.

The guards at the guard post asked him his name and prepared some paperwork. "Go ahead and get in," they said, gesturing towards the vehicle. More workers began to arrive and were made to fill out paperwork and then to sit.

"Put your lunches and any personal belongings in this box," the man said once everyone was inside. "Don't worry, you'll get them back."

They took David out, seemingly to the middle of nowhere, down an old country road haunted by half-dead cherry trees full of rotting fruit until a high fence appeared, stretching on for at least a mile. The other frightened workers, four in all, joined him in the belly of the unbranded black Suburban. Two governmental security types were up front. They wore caps that read SEMPER DOWN SECURITY. The same caps were worn by the guards at the factory.

The driver took the handle from an old drab-green military radio and spoke into it. "Seventeen, this is APACHE ROMEO, over."

The radio answered back. "This is Seventeen. Go ahead Apache Romeo."

"It's the big bad wolf. Party of five little piggies. Get ready for the war dance. Over."

"Roger that. Over."

"Over and out," declared the driver.

He drove to a gate in the fence and waited for it to open and then stopped at a security checkpoint. A sign read GATE 17 in black Roman symbols.

226

"Got some fresh faces," the passenger guard said to the gate guard. "Here're their files."

"Great, just in time for the slaughter," remarked the other, stressing his sense of irony, then led them through the gate with a wave.

They seemed to be in a vast orchard field over permeable clay and mud. A mesh fence rose up along the trees and enclosed the orchard as if the grounds of a high security prison topped off with coils of razor wire, and in between them was a sort of demilitarized zone with small white cannons sequenced to fire exactly five minutes apart to deter the creatures of the wilderness. Additionally, there were metal flagpoles situated just inside the inner wall with glittering ribbons streaming and reflecting the sunlight (likewise, to counter invasion from the air). It was a bizarre setup.

David was alarmed to note that an ambulance was at that moment coming in through the gate behind them. The lights were off and there appeared to be no emergency yet, but the sudden arrival certainly gave David a hazardous impression. He began to wonder for the first time just what had happened to the fellow whom he was replacing.

"Over here, maggots! On the double!" a meaty guard beckoned loudly.

They exited the black Suburban shakily and followed the guard to a drab steel military shipping container the size of a boxcar. The guard unlocked the double doors and pried them open and went inside. A second guard came over with a clipboard and requested a signature for the specialized gear that they were about to receive. Inside was a pile of small round ballistic shields covered in black fabric which were like a Greek *aspis*, Medieval European *buckler* or the Scottish *targe*.

"Welcome to rent-a-shield," said the first guard farcically. "Line up and receive this free gift. We'll be taking them back at the end of the day. If you lose it, you'll pay for it, and it ain't cheap."

David waited in line for the gift. The charcoal-colored shield was slightly larger than the appearance of the full moon at night, with a hard, sturdy feel and secure arm straps at the interior.

"You're lucky," said the guard with the clipboard. "These just came in, due to unforeseen circumstances. You'll also be receiving a dollar raise, courtesy of Monstrosso Corporation. A whole dollar. Just like a regular goddamn war."

"You wanna quit and join the ranks, Frank?" teased the armory guard.

"A few dollars more and I probably would. But I've got the little buggars to feed."

"You could get one of those nose rings," the armory guard said. "Change your name to Bluetooth."

"I'd get a big brass one for each pierce, too!"

The guards chuckled.

"Um, w-what are the circumstances?" David asked nervously from behind the mountainous garb.

"What? Weren't you guys briefed?" asked the guard with the clipboard.

"Not really," said the larger of the workers. They all looked around at each other, feeling foolish.

"Well, just man up and you'll be alright. Some of the trees are being a little difficult," the clipboard guard explained.

"The trees?" one of the new faces ventured confusedly.

"It's a lucrative opportunity—for all of us," said the armory guard. "Just keep your wits about you."

"Now off you go," said the clipboard guard.

There were three trucks lined up just past the guard post, each with twelve steel boxes of cold water fastened into metal brackets. Two forklifts with extra-wide, deep-treaded tires drove over that way and each removed a steel box before zipping off again towards the orchard. A white pole barn sat behind the guard post, built over a concrete foundation with a space for vehicles. David wondered what could be in there. A second mobile-type building was directly across from the guard post and a very faint pink neon sign said *Snack Shack*. When David asked where his lunch was so that he could grab a cigarette, the guard said they would be in that building.

A commotion reached David's attention from where the forklifts stood idle. The crews had gathered on a hill from the embankment of the first row, overlooking several dozen acres of orchard. The Keeper's husband, Arturo, was standing before them,

228

down the slope a ways, delivering a briefing. David and the others hurried over with their new shields stuck to their arms.

"…And now we do what is expected of us, for company and kin. But most of all, we do it for ourselves, that we may lift our humble heads of courage from the bootstraps of fear and spit in the eyes of the damned! Let no one lose faith, even before legions of giant cannibals, for there is a way through to every heart. Now I read from Ezekiel, the Song of the Sword…" Arturo paused to read from a crumpled sheet of paper that had been folded up in his jeans pocket. "'A sword, a sword has been sharpened, a sword, a sword has been burnished: To work slaughter has it been sharpened, to flash lightning has it been burnished. Why should I now withdraw it?' We, too, are that mighty arm of a universe projected unto danger. And so we must be ruthless to those who offer us no truce; with quick deliberation, our able grip on blades of tempered soul, we will work the anger and carve a circle of equal thrones from this wicked wood. We are the eager apostles of this heavenly fruit; it is up to us now to spread the good news, that the LORD is victorious! Mere youths, we go forth in a swath of humanity, and we come out men!!"

The crowd cheered and held up their shields with renewed vigor. Many of the shields had personal designs on them and David asked someone how this was possible.

"It's a covering," the worker said, showing off his motif of skull and crossbones. "Ask Darrel for one, that forklift driver there. He sells them for about ten dollars and they've got straps that connect back here. Personalizes your gear, and adds a little extra protection."

"Okay, thanks," said David.

"He's a clever one, that Darrel," continued the worker. "Shit, we just got these a few days ago. I don't know how he's been able to keep up with orders."

"Who's this Darrel again?" David asked.

Darrel was a bald African-American guy with a big smile, looking to be in his late thirties. He rode the pale yellow forklift. David was about to walk over to inquire about the coverings when he was apprehended.

"Newbie, right?" It was the bear-like Arturo. His large meaty hand was on David's shoulder.

"Yes?" said David nervously.

"You're part of the second squad. Come with me and I'll show you what to do."

Arturo brought David over to the first rows and placed him around a long red tractor with a white conveyor between two rolled-up tarps that had wooden poles for handles. It was lined up at the threshold of trees and was ready to start. Three of the workers were already there, standing in their designated places. Arturo went to gather the last of the crew for the 'newbie' squad. David waited where he was.

An additional red tractor with a full crew of tarp-pullers was in the neighboring rows, awaiting orders to start.

The trees swayed nervously before the line. They were unlike anything David had ever seen before, with long tooth-like thorns scaling branches of thick fleshy umber and exotic fruits weighing down deliciously as they hid like dense bundles of aurora borealis within strong spade-shaped, serrated leaves. He thought the thorns must be the reason for the dollar raise, which, in that case, it was fortunate to have at least a shield. He only hoped his small piece of protection was made of ultra-high-molecular-weight polyethylene and not some chewed-up old plastic.

Arturo soon came back with the remaining worker.

"You stand here," said Arturo. "And you here. The other two are here and here, on the opposite side. That's right. Your job is to pull out the tarps and catch the gads while the Zapper zaps the tree. Hold them tight, now, or we'll have problems. Let me see you do it. That's right. Pull them out while the big guy here releases them—that lever there," said Arturo, moving from the tarp-pullers to the tractor controls above a platform attached to the right side where the larger fellow stood. "You must be prepared to do this for long durations. We will probably switch you around from time to time, but it makes for a long day out here. Where the hell is Darrel? Okay, wait here."

Arturo stormed off in search of the other forklift, which soon came zipping towards them ahead of a robotic-looking tractor that could only have been the Zapper. The huge arm extending from the yellow nose was similar to the Shaker used for harvesting cherries, but with an altogether different hand mechanism—this one was a wide metal 'U' with two holes lined up on opposite sides of the interior. There were cushions on the outside, up to the ends, and the hydraulics were used to lift the arm for placement of the hand, but the hand itself did not form a grip or enact any other movement, as with the Shaker. In addition, wide black pads extended out like wings to help catch the falling fruit.

"This is Graham," Arturo said, introducing the scrawny blond kid driving the Zapper. "Graham, this is...let me see..." Arturo pulled out his crew manifest. "We have Moses. Raise your hand, Moses; be proud! Christopher, Charles, David, and of course big Ernesto on Long Red!"

As Arturo had said, the larger guy was Ernesto and he was a Latino just slightly older than David, with thick, bushy chocolate hair forming a prominent widow's peak. Moses was also Latino and was very small and quiet. He looked to be no more than sixteen years old. Pulling with Moses on the left side of the tractor was a tall and slender farm boy with brown hair and cornflower blue eyes named Christopher. He was also about sixteen. Charles, or Chuck as he preferred to be called, was a good-natured Viking sort of fellow with red hair and a short goatee and dark jolly blue eyes. Chuck pulled with David on the right side of the tractor. He was roughly nineteen.

"The guy on the forklift is Darrel," continued Arturo. "Darrel will make sure you have an empty tank for your gads, but let him know when it's almost full. He also has these nifty shield coverings that he'll be more than happy to sell you for about ten silver-lined greenbacks."

"I'll take one!" someone said excitedly. It was Christopher.

"Not now, though," Arturo explained. "Now we work."

The larger crewmember started up the long thin tractor from the side platform and Graham instructed him over a handheld radio to line up the center of the tractor with the first tree of both rows. David and the other three tarp-pullers deployed the tarps and wrapped them around the nearest tree and Graham came in on the left tree with the Zapper. A fuzzy blue stream of electricity poured out from the two holes in the interior hand of the arm and zapped the tree, causing it to release some of the gads.

"Um, pull it tight," said Graham in his geeky high-pitched voice. "They'll roll right down."

The gads rolled down onto the conveyor belt, changing color as they went, and were carried along until they plopped into the cold metal tank of water.

Next it was Chuck and David's turn. The shields made the work slightly more uncoordinated, slowing the entire crew down, but they soon got the hang of things. David was more worried that he would trip and hurt his sore ankle—it had flared up again for the first time since the accident.

Again they came down and wrapped the tarp around like a deceptive blanket. The Zapper tickled and then tickled again with short jolts of electric blue. The weight was held until all the magical super-fruits were safely on the belt and plopping into the tank.

"What do they taste like?" Chuck asked Graham after he had zapped a tree in their row.

"Don't eat one or you'll get fired," Graham explained quietly. "They're very strict about that. And they have eyes everywhere." Graham sat up straight and looked skyward. "It's like cherries times a million. These people are ruthless. It's the seeds they're mostly worried about—got them patented. The last guy who ate one swallowed the entire thing and they actually had his stomach pumped. I heard he's blacklisted; can't find a job anywhere in the country."

"Shit, really?" Chuck responded, his eyes large with worry.

"It's true," said Christopher as he pulled out his part of the tarp. "I've heard a lot of things... Gotta buy them like everyone else or there'll be trouble!"

The crew moved down and another two were wrapped and zapped. The tarp pullers performed their awkward dance. They were getting the hang of it.

The trees looked sad, so full of fruit that their limbs were breaking. Some of the gads even seemed anxious to commit suicide as they fell to the ground rather than be gathered and eaten. Once the crew rolled in and the fruit was forced off, the limbs flexed back into place and the trees exuded relief.

Devils of Noon

Lunch break was a perfect opportunity for David to test the limits of Darrel's vast trade network and see if he could become part of that system.

"Darrel, I have a problem," David said, lifting his second piece of pizza, which was given to them by a mysterious man in a suit and tie who had recently driven up to the gates in a dark and tinted Chinese knockoff of a Hummer to await the pizza delivery girl and was just now headed back to his private summer residence on a deep lake hidden within a forested battleground.

"What's the problem?" asked Darrel with interest.

"Do you have anything with an alarm clock, like maybe a watch or a phone?"

"I knew I should have gotten into phones! My wife said it was a bad idea. Well, I have these watches," Darrel said, opening a green duffel bag of goodies, "but I think what you want is something like this."

"What is it?"

"The Nishiki 3DVTV-440 pocket television; has videophone interface capabilities, Bluetooth internet, an alarm clock, and plays mp3s. All for the low price of five-nine-nine."

"Five-hundred-ninety-nine. That's more than I have on me."

"You can pay in installments if you like. Say about one-fifty a week?"

"And it's a television? What channels does it get?"

"It's more like a tablet computer for television shows in 3D. It picks up your local digital channels, and can also access internet television channels—like say you want to watch Pandora."

"But doesn't a tablet already do those things—minus the 3D?"

"Yes, but this thing doesn't require an internet hub. It also learns from you; builds itself around your preferences. And it has an alarm clock."

"I see…So what's the catch?"

"The catch is that you can't browse the internet. If you did, your head would probably explode. Everything's built in. You can play all the popular online games, though, and there's no additional fees like with your phone. Imagine fighting a medieval battle and all the tiny axes and swords swinging out of the screen at your nose! Can a tablet do that? No. Too many health warnings. It's like one though in all other respects."

"Odd. But I'm desperate. Okay, I'll try it out. How soon can I get one?"

"I have another one right here. Never been opened."

"Wow, look at that..." said Chuck from nearby. "What else you got in there?" He peered curiously into the green duffel.

The lunch hour evaporated under the heat of day and soon enough, too soon, they were locked back into anticipation of paychecks and counting down the minutes in austere agony. They pulled in, pulled out, and carried their crosses down streets of agriculture. One day they would get paid and then everything would start anew.

The Grand Mass

Late into the evening, once all the trees in their section had been cleared, the guards blasted high-cultured music through the loudspeakers (David had mistakenly assumed that they were more bird deterrents). Suddenly the music rose out of the mundane roar, an ensemble of strings, horns, and woodwinds rising into a holy chorus from the grave, and the orchard was overcome by a tremendous orchestration of instruments. The exhausted crew was just headed for the gates after robbing the final tree of the day. The journey out left the crew with a feeling of accomplishment, seeing the vast results firsthand and hearing the leaves rattle fruitlessly in the conditioned air. Once they had turned their shields in and huffed their way to the guard post for a ride out, David asked about the music.

"I don't know what it is," the one guard said.

"What does the CD say?" asked the other guard. He went over to the shack and scrounged around and came back with the jewel case. "Berlioz," he said. "Grand Mess...*des morts*...whatever that means."

"The higher-ups make us play it. They say the trees like it," said the guard from before. "In the morning we put on Debussy and Strauss. I have no idea what they see in that Imperial shit. I guess trees don't know any better."

"I kind of like it," said Graham in his high-pitched voice. "It calms me. I think there's no human beauty left in the world until I hear stuff like that."

"You're weird, kid," said the one guard. "But, then, so 's the people that hired us."

A Solution to a Problem

After a turbulent day in the orchards, the guards shuttled the non-operators back to the factory. David was happy to be out of work and anxious to relax and see what was on television, but first he would have to eat and take a shower. The time, he realized, was just after six. The break room was like a co-educational kitchenette and that is where he was headed.

"What the hell are you still doing here?" someone said. It was Harvey. He was working late.

"Oh! Um..."

"Hey, where are you going?" demanded Harvey. "I have a few things for you!" He sounded uncharacteristically beneficial and was out smoking a custom pipe that had been carved into a lion.

"What kind of things?" David answered worriedly.

"I've been looking all over for you!" Harvey said, grabbing David's shoulder roughly, yet with the obvious intention of masculine affection. "You're a hard one to find. Where have they been hiding you? Oh, of course, the orchard; I detect a chemical smell...sulfur dusting...bactericides, fungicides, herbicides, insecticides...slightly toxic to humans..."

"How did you know that?!" asked David, stiffening at the thought.

"I have a great nose."

"Oh..."

Harvey extinguished his pipe. "Here, let me get them from my bag. It's over with Elsie's and my lunches. Just inside, here…" Harvey led the way as if a host at a lavish party and scooted left to where the deep wooden shelves stood crowded full of lunch boxes made of either plastic or vinyl, invincible thermoses with chintzy tops, large paper grocery bags filled with enchiladas, burritos, red peppers, salads, removed a black hiker's backpack from the ensemble and brought it to the nearest table. "Remember that skinny dame you discovered out in the dunes? I noticed that you haven't done anything about her yet. Well, I arranged the set-up for you."

"You did what?"

"A hot little number, that Forester!" Harvey continued. "I can see where you'd take a liking to her. She had this picture album screen thing in her bag—don't look at me like that; just hear me out; I didn't take anything. Just this tablet thing and I cleaned out the acid and replaced the batteries for you. I had my girlfriend snap a few pictures of the grave and we put them into the album for her. Kind of a morbid creature, my girlfriend. You wouldn't think it to look at her."

David was astonished. "And I'm to do what with it?"

"I figure you can give it to the police so they can identify her. I got the coordinates typed out on this index card. It's a little roughed up…been in the duffle over a week. But they certainly don't need to know that I was involved, if you get me. No mention of old Harvey, if you please."

Harvey handed David the index card and a 7x7 inch digital picture album frame.

"I can't believe it. Thank you. That sounds like a great idea."

David attempted to leave but Harvey stopped him.

"Also…I got you this pipe. It's a gift that keeps on giving. It actually liquefies foliage and then vaporizes the liquid like an e-cig; filters out any bad stuff. Black market techno engineers invented them and various subversive pipe artists work them into expensive novelty items. You can buy them legally at the Native American village of Peshawbestown. I don't know where else you can get regular tobacco, besides growing it. I um don't usually smoke that kind. But it works on any leaves, any kind of vegetation.

Even pills, so I'm told. Well, don't look at me like that. I'm certainly not going to hug you or anything. Hell, I probably just shortened your existence. Just, thanks. Alright, you motherfucker. On with life."

David was almost teary-eyed (he would never have admitted as much). His face lit up as he examined the short calumet. Almost prophetically, it depicted the swirling Underwater Panther clutching on to a fish. The pipe appeared to have been made of white, red, and black synthetic micro-clay, mahogany, and plastic, so that the tail of the panther made the mouthpiece, the neck the shank, the head and jaws becoming the liquefying bowl and chamber. Furthermore, the bubbly midsection was the stem and battery chamber, the fish the atomizer. The pieces were detachable and it came with its own battery charger and USB connection. The pipe was the best that David had ever seen and he felt like he had just been on the receiving end of an engagement ring. He wanted to say something, but could not find the words.

"What's this?" David asked finally, picking up the pouch of tobacco.

"Some kind of drinking smoke," Harvey said, shrugging casually as he prepared for flight. He got up from the table. "A practice brought over from Tibet after millennia of migrations through Siberia or some such; perfected by shamans after times spent in the dreamy dark; just something the natives around here like to make. I've been using it to get me away from, ah, you know, the dangers inherent."

"Thanks…I've never before been given such a fine gift."

Harvey was already gone, vanished out into the light burning up the square little window. He came back in shortly, accompanied by a sexy, diminutive bird of a woman with a black and blue tattoo of the White Goddess on her lily neck of brawn, her dirty-blond hair put up into a tight bun, and they grinned knowingly at David, but subsequently paid him no attention.

Electronic Cigarettes and Chocolate Milk

A bar of soap and a box of detergent made life bearable and clean, after quite a lot of side-work, but the clincher was the pocket television Nishiki 3DVTV-440 that he had partially purchased earlier that day through trade-savvy Darrel Lewis. There were only a few offline channels that he could pick up digitally from satellite, given North America's paranoid control of broadcasting through those asses in Congress, but they were exceptional, the world bulging out from the miniscule screen as if life were a brilliant hologram. One was just a channel with superfluous media news and a heck of a lot of commercials, and the other was something weird called Oz TV that sometimes had a fuzzy broadcast despite being in High Definition. A third that he at first could not get because the satellite coordinates were still downloading seemed to be dedicated to things in nature that were just recently lost (give or take a decade or so). Currently it played some never ending movie about the Inuit and polar bears and David was almost certain that the tiny white bear protruding from the screen would devour the nose right off of his face.

A little red squirrel scurried suddenly into the passenger car and David threw it some peanuts from a bag he had gotten free of charge from one of the co-op farmers at the factory break room. The squirrel chirped happily as it gathered them up and zipped back outside.

There was a genuine sense of freedom to being able to smoke indoors while drinking chocolate milk. With television in hand, the tiny micro-lasers at the top of the device scanning out imperceptivity from a cyclopean central eye, David was able to relax as he occupied himself with switching back and forth between the channels. He kept hoping that another movie would come on— hopefully an engaging one—but all he could find besides the polar bears was a bunch of comically annoying commercials. It seemed that corporate America was trying to laugh people to death. He fidgeted with the controls to no avail. *How to get online?*—he wondered. It was usually so effortless. Where were the instructions? The box was empty. The mice must have shredded them to use for a mattress. Having gone a very long time without participating in broadcasted consumerism anyway, he sat there before the screen and digested his environment with a sense of holy repulsion, switching between networks until they became diabolically melded into a seemingly personal conversation aimed at David himself:

OZ TV COMMERCIAL:
"Come See the New Mexico!"
"Olé! There's a siesta waiting for you in Mexico! Plenty for you to see: Climb a mountain, visit the wondrous ziggurats of the Aztecs, join in on the many festivities happening every day, or just hang out at the beach from your luxurious Yucatan resort where you'll be treated like a celebrity! Vamos! What are you waiting for?"

CBC B.S. NEWS WITH LOLA CHAFFIN GREEN:
Move Over Monstrosso
Lola Chaffin Green: "An emerging biotechnology company in Monterrey has had a recent break-through in the highly controversial designer baby war, having isolated the pigmentation codes within human DNA to control coloration. Meet LunaTek, an overnight success in research-poor Mexico, funded solely by Grupo Infante. Extremely lax patent laws have allowed Mexican scientists to go forward on key procedures within the field of gene therapy and will soon collaborate with colleagues at China's Department of All Things Biologically Transgressing at the Peking University in Beijing. In distant Mexico City, meanwhile, rumors abound that new fertility treatments are causing genetic alterations in parents' offspring; that, late at night, UFO's have been abducting prize fighting chickens; that blood-sucking goats roam the countryside; and even that the mass cloning of billionaires has taken place on a grand scale, but no evidence has been gathered to collaborate any of this."

CBC B.S. SPECIAL:
Power to Change

Part 1 of the series *Power to the People*. The robot harboring Noam Chomsky's brain argues for democracy through socialism and tolerance.

NABC SPECIAL:

Chomsky-a-go-go

Red Mather argues for the Quaker business model as the perfect capitalist system.

Political and news correspondent John Johnson hosts.

"Show me Eden, Noam. Where is Eden?" says Christian economist Red 'Flag' Mather of Discovery Institute. "There is no such thing as a perfect society, and we certainly won't get there through socialism."

OZ TV SPECIAL REPORT:

Mexico Rich!

Emerald City Newsroom with host The Guardian of the Gates. The Guardian: "Due to tidal shifts in the Pacific Ocean, Mexico has received more rain distribution than ever before in recent years and has become an agro-industrial wonder. TIMBRE Magazine calls it 'The new Eden!!' With quick expansion of Helu and Bailleres family infant clones across international markets, Mexico is flourishing; so much in fact that desperate Americans are heading there in droves to beg for employment. To bolster a renewed sense of national security, an electric fence is being erected on the Mexican side of the northern boundary to keep out potential border crossers."

NABC SPECIAL REPORT:

Flourishing Mexico a Lie

'Flourishing Mexico: Don't believe it', says the United States Department of Agriculture secretary Virgil Balsac. Recent reports from the North American Weather Control Council show that Mexico is hotter than ever, with more crime and little humidity to show for it, creating a cauldron of death for its 111 million thirsty Lucha Libre fans.

OZ TV EXCLUSIVE:

Live From Cancun

Handsome Male Latino Narrator: "See for yourself, gringos." A spectacular aerial view of Quintana Roo emits a salty perfume from the aquamarine to deep blue habitat around the luxurious spine of the Yucatán Peninsula. Beautiful suntanned men and women party on the beach of a sparkling resort. Beautiful Female Latino Narrator: "Mexico is home to the largest number of U. S. citizens abroad, according to the U.S. State Department. Don't be left out in the cold: Visit us in Mexico!"

CBC B.S. BREAKING NEWS:

"Gun battle rages on bridge to Mexico"

Lola Chaffin Green reporting: "Cuidad Juarez, point A of a highly lucrative drug-smuggling thoroughfare into the US, is a ruinous high tower along the battlefield of a brutal turf war between rival cartels..."

OZ TV STUDIO Z WITH BUTTON-BRIGHT:

"Every major U.S. city a war zone"

Button-Bright reporting live from United Nations Headquarters in New York City: "Flint, Detroit, Atlanta, Birmingham, Baltimore, St. Louis, Oakland, Miami, they have three things in common: They're cities, all of them are in the continental US, and they are among the most dangerous places in the world... Why are Americans so violent? It's an often neglected topic. However, a discussion was brought up recently at a foreign relations meeting in New York to facilitate support for an investigation into psychosis of democracy."

"It was just a silly discussion," the United Nations Secretary General says as she leaves the UN Secretariat to face a crowd speckled with Gilles of Blanche masks. "The United States contributes twenty percent of our budget. We would never criticize them in public."

"The Belgians should learn to keep their traps shut, if they want to continue arms sales with this country!" says Committee on Foreign Affairs representative Michael McFarrell. *"I don't care* if they're ecstatic about beating their own record for time spent without an official government. Crazy waffles!"

*****

David began to feel very tired by this point and just let the news roll as he rested his eyelids. It occurred to him that despite living in the abandoned train his routine that season would be working and then eating and then sleeping and then working again.

*****

Button-Bright reporting from nearby Ralf Bunche Park: "Now, from a pseudo-scientific perspective, we've been fortunate enough to run into psychologists Julius Nottebohn and Dr. Ira Smartz. *Are* Americans becoming more violent? Go ahead, doctors."

"We've seen it happen in rats," says Dr. Julius Nottebohm of the National Institute of Mental Health. "Overpopulation, as we all know, brings out the violent tendencies, triggers a bouquet of mental health issues for mammals both large and small. But that's nothing in light of what our most recent research suggests. We haven't witnessed such disturbing psychological news since that ingenious escape to the Fitzgibbon farm back in nineteen-sixty-seven. I mean, this new generation takes the cake! You breed them for creativity, place them in an open-ended maze while slipping them one too many placebos, and before you know it the entire mess of them are screaming at you from their tiny pulpits!"

"No one questions it anymore," says Dr. Ira Smartz of the Max Plank Institute in Mecklenburg-Western Pomerania. "Especially in complacent minds, they think that with freedom brings insanity. They're listening to authoritarian propaganda. My advice for them is to get naked. Plan a hiking trip with friends and bare it all for nature. That's how we do things in Pomerania."

"My bags are packed!" says Lothar the Homeless[30], rising from his newspaper-covered bench in sober excitement. "To Pomerania! ...wherever the hell that is..."

Button-Bright: "Meanwhile, as the president of the free mourns the loss of her son in Los Angeles, members of the Senate anxiously await the signing of a document allowing them to begin purges against American war criminals..."

---

[30] Formerly, Jimmy Sims, 2018 graduate of Syracuse University Online.

"Authorities in Northern Michigan on the lookout for a biological terrorist…"

David sat there in magical unrest, stretched out on the burgundy seat that made him itch despite having been cleaned several times with soap and water. "What am I to believe? They always lie," he thought out loud. At the conclusion of a commercial for BANDEIRA MOTOR CO with their "Keepin' it Real" slogan for sex-fuel cars, he opened a console for online games and thought about what he might write to the police.

III

The Woman Bailed Out of One Mess and Forced Into Another

Several versions of what had happened could be found throughout the world's media outlets and all of them contained Antiope's full name and telephone number because she couldn't afford what they were asking to withhold the information from the public. "Some freedom of the press," she had mumbled when Tom and his wife had arrived to bail her out that morning. Her smart black market telephone had been ringing 'off the hook' so to speak the entire time of her incarceration (for inciting a riot, they had said). She assumed that her things had been kept in a filing drawer. Aside from the lewd comments and special offers, the girls had called to apologize for not being there yet and in one message Papa Berg said not to worry about the damage because the publicity would more than pay for it. The county-famous Ishtar was even considering a semi-return during holidays.

Mrs. Wesson was sitting on the divan in the living room while sulking away over the company's best-selling product of the season.

"But that girl's got talent, Tom," she said, dipping into a bowl of chocolate-covered gads that she held up by her own effort. "Can't you do something? She can stay *here*. She can share the guest room with Oona."

"It's out of our hands, Margaret. She's Monstrosso's asset. They decide what's to be done with her, not me." Tom explained this as calmly as possible, despite heavy fatigue. He paced the room indecisively, moving from one periphery to the next, and then abruptly stopped. This had all come as quite a shock and he feared the truth. The night had been restless.

"But it's *your factory*. She works for *you*. Can't you release her over to *us*?"

"What, and adopt her? Are you crazy? She isn't a domestic servant! Besides, you don't understand."

"Understand what? That Monstrosso has an evil hold on you? That it casts a dark shadow over my dearest desires? I know more than you think," Mrs. Wesson said, dipping into the bowl.

"Then you should know not to press this," Tom stressed. "Our entire livelihood is on the line here. Do you realize... Two years ago we were headed for bankruptcy!"

"You sold your soul, Tom!" Mrs. Wesson whispered discreetly, despite the fact that Oona was with Antiope in the adjoining room and could hear everything that was being said.

"I never had one, Margaret. You can't have a soul and run a flourishing business!"

"I know, it's just that-"

The doorbell rang suddenly like the chimes of a cathedral.

"They're here, Tom!" said Mrs. Wesson, her voice misted in worry. "They've come to take my little currency artist away! Don't let them, Tom! Don't!"

Tom suddenly took on a serious air, posing like Washington crossing the Delaware: "Worry yourself to death, my precious dear. Time marches on, as they say, and our legacy with it. Her kind overcomes, despite the hoof marks of progress beating it out of them...shaping their awkward characters...making them good for something."

"No, no! I can't allow it!"

Again the doorbell rang.

"It's us, Mr. Wesson!" a conceited, muscular voice announced from outside the front double-doors.

"Isn't anyone going to get that?!" Tom demanded, growing perturbed. People in his periphery were always interrupting their playtime.

Oona and Antiope appeared from out of the adjoining room with dour expressions. Antiope held her bundle of cleaned and pressed stripper clothes and squeezed Oona's hand affectionately. "This was indeed fortuitous, Oona. I'll keep in touch."

"I'll look into what you said," insisted Oona appreciatively.

Oona scurried off to answer the door.

"It's alright, Mrs. Wesson," Antiope consoled. "Even *you* can't protect me from these evil morons." With that, she walked herself to the door where there awaited with Oona and the sudden appearance of the Wessons' blushing daughter two disgruntled old friends.

Home Again, Home Again, Jiggety-Jig

"Just couldn't stay gone, could you," barked her old friend John Mathews. "I was hoping I'd find you in the obituaries. Now we gotta deal with your crazy ass again."

"Poor John. Did they skip you over for promotion while I was away? You should be used to it by now."

John squeezed the air in front of him and gave Antiope a look that said that he wished it was her neck.

"I was actually getting bored..." added Eddie Monstrosso with a shrug.

"You'll be back in shape in no time at all, big guy," Antiope avowed.

Eddie grinned.

"You two losers deserve each other," was John's great comeback.

Duck Lake Academy, really more of a vocational school than anything else, was a gold brick pigsty rising to swallow her at that moment, with wooden double doors open wide from the grey concrete pillars and blinding glass. The combined smell of ammonia, teenage body odor, and sweaty one-dollar bills wafted out from the channeled air, giving her the chills. Although not exactly fecal, she was certain that some kind of metaphor was translucent before her and that it would lead to an important allegory if she opened her senses enough. The mindless drones shoved her onward towards the gaping maw. She heard the iron gates close behind them and looked up at the three-story façade of the entrance hall to where it narrowed before the copper-brown pyramidal roof of false ceramic tile. At the very top, the cadet blue Eye of Providence within the triangle pointed like the head of an arrow towards the sun.

The threshold was a salivating thought seemingly bending through time to capture her forever, freezing her cognition with a most unwelcome feeling of déjà vu. As they passed the security checkpoint and viewed the lobby Antiope began to laugh uncontrollably. There was quite a welcome party waiting for her: The dean, three instructors, two mystery suits, five military recruiters, and even a few students who had been accidentally drawn in to the event while walking the mundane hallway. They were all standing in front of a large glass display case which had been placed there in the entrance for some unknowable reason. What would they do to her, she wondered, put her in a glass cage in the middle of the lobby?

"Are those chains really necessary?" asked the dean, an uncharacteristically young man in his mid thirties with all the mannerisms of an Ivy Leaguer.

"Just part of our modus operandi, Dean Yorkshire, sir," John explained.

"Well, could you take them off now? She's safe here with us," the dean said with authority.

The man and the woman whom Antiope had never seen before grinned grimly. They represented Hodge, Hoffman, and Litchfield, the Monstrosso heads of the academy, she supposed, which was why they wore the expensive suits.

"We know you haven't been very happy here, Miss Penuel," continued the dean. "We hope to change that. Have you ever thought about a career in the military? Well, today is career day here at the academy, and thankfully we have the pleasure of introducing our students to five outstanding representatives of our nation's fighting forces."

"What if we'd rather join the Peace Corps?"

"Ahem…But never mind that now," said the dean tactfully. "Let's get you settled in. Do you remember your old room? Well, your roommates have been reassigned, so it's all yours now. Wasn't that nice of us? If these fine agents here would be so kind as to escort you, lunch will begin at the usual time. Afterwards we'd like to send some folks over to talk to you for a bit, if that's alright."

"Of course you would," Antiope said in the manner of Alice in Wonderland as she was briskly taken away by force. *At least the floors are clean*, she thought to herself smugly.

Inciting a Riot in the Land of the Complacent

One by one, or sometimes in groups, the eldest students of the academy, Mathew, James, Esther, Pauline, Timothy, Mark, Susanne, and Jacob, were met by their radical sister. Antiope Clara Penuel was her name, and they wished she had shared more of their inherited characteristics. For starters, it would behoove her to complain less.

"You stupid fools, please listen to me!" She spoke fiercely before each sibling, inciting them to riot against a life of corporate enslavement. "You're wondering why we must fight, and I tell you that INDEPENDENCE is a cause worth upholding! Would you live your life in trust of those who would demand ownership of you, despite the gross immorality of doing such a vile thing, and despite the Emancipation Proclamation and other important legal documents already set in stone for the people of this the United States of America, for the world to utilize by example, which are each a long flight upward from the days of egotistical hero-kings and fatalism and small groups of inbred nobles conveniently ignoring the hard existence of a great number of individuals within a community in the midst of toil?"

By this point the sibling would stare at the wall and wish for the noise to stop so that the world could be at peace. Bang, bang, bang, head and wall as primitive drum, and it might eventually pass.

The voice of the sister continued unabashedly that evening after work, pushing the sibling towards hysterics: "Do you enjoy wasting your precious years inside of a dank, loud, and smelly factory where they recompense you just enough to encompass your rent that you must give them for your own captivity, so that they may feed you, which you cannot do on your own because they had stripped away your means to do so? Would you put your trust in the wing-like ears of the baby elephant called Dumb...I mean, Liberty,

248

or spend your brighter days on a road to nowhere with this traveling prison of sorts?! All you need do is take the plunge! What say you, my brother / sister? Am I getting through at all? No? Not an ounce of rebellion? You're half French, you know!"

Neither Mathew, James, Jacob, Esther, Pauline, Timothy, Mark, nor Susanne cared to listen any further to the sibling who had painted *"No animal shall sleep in a bed with sheets*[31]*"* above the doorway to her room, thus causing disruption to the shapes, colors, and patterns guiding them safely along the hallways of their home and castle—the place of happiness which allowed for such diffuse immersion of talents after a long day of work. They were content just to begin the evening's art class where they would do fabulous things with a box of crayons.

A Little Green Shop Opens on K Street

Something stirred inside the little green shop on K Street that had been vacant for almost five years. The thick dust comprising the storefront window had been cleaned away. It was a sure sign of progress. From within, a sunburned woman in a red hat could be seen breaking her leisurely back against the wooden floor. The floor was old, but well-built, of dense giant-sized white oak. It had been thankfully protected by a mite-infested rug which was currently situated in the parking lot of the back alley.

The place smelled like lemon and pine sol. White industrial buckets filled with Murphy's soap and hot water harbored the rags of purification while a mop and a metal pail awaited their role in the process. The rags soaked into the floorboards and walls and countertops and kept soft hands from getting any more scuffed up than they already were from earlier, far distant attempts at hard labor.

---

[31] One of the commandments from the allegorical novella *Animal Farm* by George Orwell, later replaced by two ironic maxims.

The woman stopped for a moment and sighed in mixed satisfaction and regret. The muscles were unbelievably sore. Most people just did not realize. Henrietta Penuel had decided to tackle the job herself. She was hoping to clean the place up in time for the shop to open. **K Street Fabrics** she was going to call it, or maybe just **The Little Green Shop**. She could hardly decide which one was a better fit.

The floors in the White House had been built with Michigan wood, she remembered some old guy telling her at the logging museum in Cadillac, which in consequence made her feel like an overpaid house servant as she dug into hers with the sponge. Decades had passed since this kind of labor was her means of life. She came to it like old times, but with older bones and soft entitlement presiding over domesticated muscles, mental fortitude, and manicured hands. To be living it again made her appreciate the grand escape that was incidentally her greatest regret. Henrietta supposed that she was some kind of grotesque working class hero, having mingled like she had amongst the bourgeois princes and princesses of the privileged classes for so many years. According to the Homer Hoyt Model for City Planning, still used in many of the world's metropolitan areas, such feats of prowess were only supposed to have been possible had she graduated at the top of her class and become a lawyer, doctor, industrial engineer, or consented to dubious and long-ranging sexual arrangements with "gentlemen" from the other side of town (the only bridge near enough to the wealthy arm of the city was the INDUSTRY-FACTORY arm that spanned across the poor section of the city, thus making it easy to get to work and to worry less about having to live very long). She supposed that Homer Hoyt had been very popular at his all-white-male Midwest country club.

Starting a business was exciting, all the same, but Henrietta was glad that she had waited. The Bermuda air had vacated her cells repressively and made her feel jittery. The red hat failed to lift in the same way. The absence of the summer wind added to the emptiness, made the streets fill with stagnant pollen. The trees and flowers had a lively beautifying effect on the city's appearance but were devoid of spirit until the swooshing of cars. It was like watching a modern movie-still through a viewfinder. The electric cars barely even swooshed. Their only impact seemed to be the heavy toll they had placed on those electro-mechanical generators still driven by fossil fuel combustion, therefore causing an increase in the price of electricity for both their drivers and the public. Two of them, in fact, had just been pelted with eggs, while three culpable adults wearing thin, plastic rabbit masks ran for the Boardman River outlet. Ironic, she supposed, that a plug-in car had filled so many with the hopes and dreams of a better future. Henrietta doubted that the invisibility of energy would happen anytime soon. The oil company would have the government spend tax money to drill asteroids before allowing the country to move forward. The oil people did not seem to care that their beloved product had already run out and that the spirit of a nation had gone dry in consequence.

An Indian-made ORV drove by, proving her point.

With the business license nearly valid at city hall she anticipated the future. Life in the sun had been a blast all those years but had gotten her nowhere. It was a limbo for horrible parents. In Bermuda, every plastic-cupped Banana Colada had reminded her of the children, how she had exploited them, how they were like the slimy human batteries from that movie *The Matrix*, defined through the eyes of the government as nothing but a potential mercantile workforce for a healthy gross national product. The poor bastards were probably drinking nothing but caffeine and saccharin-water to supplement their daily insulin injections. She saw orphans in the faces of the unstressed. It saddened her to realize that she was not alone in abandonment. Many parents were absent in one form or another, and the wealthiest of them had something or other to do with Bermuda. People needed to be more careful. Everything they did affected the future in small ways; collectively, they were a force to be reckoned with. But society was stubborn. It was a world according to vices and dreams made. Henrietta had made the decision. She could be there for them now. For once she could be there. If they were disgruntled, she could certainly understand. But she had to find out. **K Street Fabrics** would soon be open for business.

DECAPLET

An Opportunity for a Private Army Venture

The insect-like vehicle arrived to pick Edgar up from work that August tenth of an indeterminate year with unsettling silence. Little Edina was, of course, driving the thing and had brought her doll Little Miss Poopypants along for the ride. For once, she was nearly on time. The passenger-side wing of plum-colored transparence rose to allow admittance.

Edgar tried to smile but his face was weak. "I called your mom and she said it was alright if you could make a quick stop for me, just south of Gamesh. We'll be a little late for dinner though."

"Seriously? Don't I get any say in this?" Edina was adamant as she palmed the gears of control.

"There's a candy store near there..." Edgar held, pathetically vague, without enthusiasm.

"Now you're talking!"

"But I was wondering if you'd actually prefer a science kit from the hobby shop."

"What? That's a hard decision!"

"You can decide while you wait," proposed Edgar. "I need to apply for a job, if that's alright with you. I'll order pizza for us once we get there."

"But you *have* a job," Edina said, looking confused. She half-consciously shifted gears as they were sent hopping towards the northern coast.

"This one's a little better. I got a reference for a private army venture."

"A what?"

"A private army. They're hiring people to kill some bugs."

"Kill some bugs...*with an army*? What kind of bugs are you talking about?"

Edgar was at first dismissive, but decided to respond. "Invasive. Abnormally-sized bugs. There's an infestation apparently."

"Yuk!" Edina bayed, making a face. "Whatever! Alright. Well, if it gets me a science kit."

Same Empire, Different Fiefdom

Four recruiters in smart, shiny uniforms licked their chops in the waiting room of Semper Down Security, which was overcrowded with applicants. A fifth was chatting away with a gang of high school misfits.

"Seriously, war is just a game," the recruiter for the U.S. Army said. "Everything's robots and drones for the best division of the greatest war corp. You just sit back and fire away."

"Awesome! That's just like what I do at home!" the acne-plagued kid admitted with squeaky excitement.

"Or you could join the Marines for a real challenge," pitched another recruiter, confidently butting in. "Courage; Duty; Honor; Valor: You won't know the meaning sitting on your asses on the living room floor. Just sign here and I'll transform you into a lean, mean, absurdly deranged human being!"

The crowd was thick, smelling of liquid tobacco and cheap aftershave. Despite increased recruitment efforts and an oceanic cesspool of pledges and promises, the military remained the quickest way to unemployment. The last thing they wanted was career soldiers with full benefits and pensions. The war was not a continual state of grinding, but more an off and on thing, always popping up somewhere between short gaps of personnel change. Such a gap had just recently occurred, but not for long. With an ounce of familiarity and distaste, Edgar pushed his way to the line of desperate people waiting to sign the clipboard on the desk.

Someone was already starting trouble, having created a dangerous void somewhere ahead. "When do we get to talk to someone: this year or next?!" he shouted with neon arms flailing.

"Just put your name down. We'll call you when we're ready," a brisk male secretary explained patiently.

"A good job, huh?" someone in front of him said to someone else. They were both full of worry.

"If you can even get an interview," said the other.

"I'm not going nowhere; got no passport."

"No one got a passport. Don't need one; they just cut open your hand and insert that trendy microchip. You be just like cattle then. Don't you got a microchip?"

"Nope. I'm a Nam Vet. We got every shitty damn thing *but* a microchip."

"Well, you don't look like no spring chicken..." said a more youthful applicant, laughing drolly at his own stupid joke.

"Spring chickens ain't got a chance in hell with Semper Down," said yet another.

A third one jumped in morbidly, whispering to the youth: "Unless you've spent a little time dodging mortars in some choice local, don't even waste your energy."

"If I hadn't, I wouldn't even be here!" laughed the young applicant bitterly.

Eventually, after listening to an entire textbook of this kind of talk, Edgar was able to sign the clipboard. He pushed his way to a vacant spot in the lobby and waited.

Several small cameras that were mounted from the ceiling moved suddenly and scanned the room, stopping for a moment on Edgar before moving on. About ten minutes later, two iron-faced women in gray officer's uniforms marched out through the armor-plated double doors and shouted "Weatherholt!", then inspected the room and motioned for the guy with his hand raised to follow them back through the threshold.

Edgar did as he was told. After passing a security checkpoint and a few more double doors, they arrived at an interior lobby where they stopped until an aide ushered Edgar into an office and closed the door.

"So you wore the green tuxedo, huh. How long were you in?" said the guy giving Edgar the interview. He was ex-military in civilian dress clothes, judging by his demeanor and high-and-tight haircut.

"Eight years, Army Reserves."

"You must have just made it through before the changes."

"I did. Was in two years when they made the rule[32], so they let me stay. I thought about the Civic Legion, but it was too late for me. I was a world traveler."

"You saw combat? What was your MOS[33]?"

"Got back just last year; did some time in Timbuktu. Was previously dug down into Antioch for three-sixty-five plus days. Battled school on the side. Have a degree in solving puzzles."

"Your MOS?"

"Cryptologic Linguist."

"Good to hear. That's a tough one. Well, we don't currently have any positions open, but there is a special assignment we've been given through a...government contract on a temporary basis. It's grueling training, but pays well, and will help your consideration for employment here at Semper Down, should something permanent become available, you understand..."

"Certainly, sir."

"Great. So, if you're interested in trying out for the team..."

"Might as well..."

"Might as well, huh. There's no going back, you understand. We only want those who are committed."

Edgar nodded affirmatively with a blank look.

"Then it's settled," the guy said. "You got GPS? Type the following into your vehicle's navigation system: CAMP DO OR

---

[32] Public unrest over the excessive use of military personnel and equipment utilized internally against citizens of the United States led to the dissolution of the National Guard component of the United States Army and to the creation of the government non-profit Civic Legion, which was to fill the role of homeland security. In response, the United States Army released a moratorium restricting non-active personnel from their remaining Reserves component. Effective March 15, 2014, no less than one year of honorable active duty service in any U.S. military branch was required upon entry into a Reserves component. The result was a more efficient and better equipped force abroad and an ethical and liberty-minded force at home.

[33] Military occupational specialty.

DIE. All capital letters. It may take a moment, but things will pick up. The junior Spooks have to verify is all; first come, first serve."

"I'm to leave now?"

"The sooner, the better; Death doesn't wait."

Camp Do or Die

"This is the coolest thing ever!" assured Edina with bundles of coiled energy beneath her and in the springs of her shoes. "Punch in a few stupid words, wait for-ev-er, and suddenly you're off! Wow, look! The car's driving *itself*! Gee, you'd think that Aunt Edith and Uncle Jerome…"

"It is pretty…well, terrifying, I think."

"I can't believe you're gonna be an army man again!"

"Me either. But at least it's only temporary. One last hurrah for ol' Sergeant Weatherholt."

"Is it dangerous?"

"Probably. But we're just sort of…high priority exterminators…"

"Secret agent bug zappers!"

"But don't tell anyone about this."

"My lips are sealed."

*****

They came to a stop. Edgar got out of the car's wing-like doors and walked to what looked like a ranger station out in the middle of the woods. A ranger was inside, despite the fact that Edgar was not actually in a national or even a state forest, but private land owned by Grube Sausage LLC (Edgar had done a few minutes of research before departure).

"Welcome to Camp Do or Die," greeted the ranger. "I suppose you want to do some exploring."

"Do I?"

"Yes," said the ranger sternly. He pointed to a pile of brush far to the left of the ranger station.

Edgar's spine had been reduced to jelly, despite years of proven experience. Once he saw that Edina had sped off safely to enjoy her new science kit, Edgar strolled over and uncovered the brush to reveal a wooden door with a pull-rope for a handle.

"I want to go in?" asked Edgar stupidly, already knowing the answer.

The ranger nodded, grinning meanly.

Edgar opened the door. A wooden ladder descended into a dirt tunnel held in place with extensive wooden framework. Dust rose through the corpuscular rays like purgatory escapees. Edgar feared tight earthen spaces such as this, but there was no going back. He sighed and climbed down with his backpack and sleeping bag clinging uncooperatively to anything within reach and then crawled slowly along the lighted tunnel. He could see a trickle of light several yards down, where the shape of another simple wooden door was outlined by the sun. Once reaching that point, he held the door open from the bottom and climbed a set of wooden stairs without the benefit of railing. The tunnel seemed to have been set into a bluff, and below this was a level camp full of freshly-built hunting cabins. People were lounging about the area, some smoking electronic cigarettes, while others chatted, complained, fidgeted, or carved sticks into little spears.

One cabin wore a banner that said CHECK-IN. Edgar went there and was screened for medical issues and assigned a bed in a cabin. Soon after, he and the other displaced veterans were issued black cotton undergarments and gray-blue camouflage uniforms and were told they could begin training early the next morning.

A Week Later

A week later, Edgar found himself assigned to an elite reconnaissance mission (a mission so secret that disclosing even a single detail would eventually result in the death of the author!). A raffish company was formed out of the dissociative ranks. They were drilled briefly in cohesion and Death Cult[34] etiquette, then issued weapons on small print lease and left to a reverie of past military flashbacks and illustration. Still, the mood was excitable for Edgar and the free hours of night and day were filled with heroic dreams. He had always been one to drift away on dull assignments, but the mind edged towards relevancy when the human vessel was inspired to act. The agonies of the factory were overshadowed, the problems forgotten, and even the algae stood deposed in his thoughts.

"Grab your guns and don't forget your weapons!" shouted Edgar's new squad leader. "That means you, too, woman! Still some trainin' yet tonight! Puttin' holes in dark silhouettes! Let's go!!"

There were groans and curses.

Edgar carried his second-hand HK417 from a sling, so that it rested against his back with the barrel pointing down, and headed out with the others. He had hoped to have been placed with A Squad, which was almost all women and included an enchanting pair of brunette twins, but had fallen in with the emotionally disturbed policeman's son due to his unfailing bad luck. This squad contained one feisty little red-head female and three boisterous males. No real names were to be used; they referred to each other by code names. The transformation was done unceremoniously, by regrouping everyone and documenting each initial alias and then rechecking them for duplicates. Once the code names were officially recorded against the skin of the past, the squads were isolated and forced through intense multiplayer video game levels under their new identities. After the appropriate amount of sleep deprivation they were ready to assume the identity of their fictional aliases. Now, if they could still hit a real target.

Range 13

The range was as any other he had ever seen; there was a wooden control tower centered behind the walkway, a bunch of foxholes lined up like graves, a billowing field of shadowy

---

[34] Death Cult is essentially the metaphor for military life.

headstones, the smell of carbon discharge, of hot bras. A whine of distortion sang above the meager crowd, preparing for the vocal assault. They were positioned like cattle and sent through the gates, one-by-one, to be branded in consecutive numbers which coincided with a field of vision. Twenty-round magazines filled with sharply-pointed cartridges were handed out in pairs. The stacks soon became diminished and the range sergeants went to work unlocking ammo containers, $0.53 a pop. The vanguard grew anxious. They hurried into position. A voice through the megaphone told them to watch their lanes. Gas-operated firing chambers ignited, sending 7.62mm caliber bullets whizzing through 12" cold hammer forged barrels, the shells exiting like hot coals. Again the bullets fired, hitting things with dull thuds as the chambers popped. The shells twirled in the air, striking brass like reindeer bells on Christmas Eve and piling up on hot sand.

Edgar was embarrassed. A 23 was needed out of 40; He had scored a mere 18. The excuses he-hawed from his stubborn mind: Allergies were causing his eyes to itch and swell; He was becoming exhausted; Darkness was just around the corner and it was getting harder for him to see the targets. They were so full of holes by this time that it did not matter anyway. It would have taken bricks to knock them down. Surely he would fail for all time, he was thinking to himself. Indeed, it seemed so.

A striking sunset fell upon them, transforming the uniform rain clouds into pink and purple factories of the heavens. At that moment Edgar felt as if he had been transformed into another time and place; as if the shoddy Semper Down firing range had turned into something ephemeral and insignificant. There might have been a million Range Number 13s for all anyone knew, with a million failing Edgars. Even his identity was slipping, the information determining existence suddenly becoming particle-waves that traveled along a beam of light projecting out of a bloated red lens.

"Kill that son-of-a-bitch!" someone yelled as he moved down the line of prone warriors. "Because he sure as shit won't hesitate in killing YOU!!"

It brought back all the old phantoms, the emotional turmoil, reasons for turning on to a different path in the first place. Yet here he was. He was to play the soldier, then, once more, the killer of men. The war was a perpetual string of firecrackers popping off into the heavens. Where was Empathy, he wondered, that ancient *Einfühlung*? Where was the cease-fire?

"Please ensure that your weapon is on safe and retreat back to your starting position," said the voice through the megaphone.

Safety buttons clicked as the shooters moved behind their foxholes for the long-suffering wait.

"You may begin to exit with your weapon facing downrange."

The shooters exited in an orderly fashion, each getting their barrels plunged with a ramrod by safety attendants waiting at the central lane.

"Very good," said the voice. "Remain calm while we prepare for night-fire. Someone will be coming around shortly with your tracer rounds. Remember to employ your night-vision goggles, but only on my signal. Please stand by for further instructions."

There was distant, stifled laughter from the control tower.

As he was moved to the bleachers just beyond the range to wait for the next cycle, Edgar thought about his direction. Where would this take him? What would it do to him? He would have to see.

The scenery rotated out. Darkness fell upon them and the stage became enveloped with stars. It billowed into the night—a messenger, a masterpiece, a magnificent ceiling under which the entire world revolved at that moment, there above the range lit dimly in red. It was a renewed stage of unfathomable chaos and destruction, where, from below the training ridge, the orange, blue, and green tracer rounds raced across the darkness in search of an end. Orion rose out of the abyss, far above the cold and hungry, his many shining eyes helplessly fixed below. Caught as Edgar was by the beauty of the celestial moment, he began to think that perhaps he had drifted into a parallel universe where the living forever remained untouched from death, existing—or perhaps ceasing to exist—in a fantastic moment when the circle of life vanished and the black-shrouded-scythe-holder lost consciousness. It had always seemed to him that the goal of mankind was to live without killing: Sustenance without pain, without murder, in an environment so vast and lush and free that it eliminated the very definition of overpopulation, was a departure from logic confined only by the limits of the age. In this dream, far off, in a grove of Druidic oak, owls, rabbits, mice, deer, jays, squirrels, bison, doves, and sheep danced to a song performed by the beating heart. Tonight was such a night as when the ancient hunters would gather around the bonfire toasting past heroism and telling stories propelled by alcohol, tobacco and adrenaline, to awake intoxicated on nature's great mountain heights and deepest ocean depths, its fairy forests, its vast savannas and illusory deserts, its pleasant steppes and snowy tundra, its jagged islands rising from the mist, its lilac wine and salty sea air. Tonight there would be no closing time. Nightingales sang the eternal thirty-second song.

The Expedient Birth of Psycho-Tron

Early next morning, they were loaded into Army surplus turtleback Humvees and dropped on the beach some two miles apart. The assignment was simple: Track down the enemy, recording all movements and activities, and map out a possible invasion plan.

A circular concrete foundation jutting out of the sand like a chalice full of beach-fun and death ruined the pattern of continuity etched in golden grains and glossy stone particles of afterbirth that told amazing stories of nature's power. Glacial gemstone, smoothed glass that was like petrified tears imbedded in the sand, glittered through overwhelming catastrophe to create a preserved sadness.

There was nothing, nothing of importance to soldiers, until they saw the trail of prints heading into the sun. A series of slashes in the wind-painted ripples and pungent muck, they wrote of something unnatural.

"From glass to microchips: hard to believe," mumbled what seemed to be Edgar. Even as he spoke, the words seemed ethereal, not his own. He had become something else. The exfoliated skin of Edgar E., until recently, seasonal factory worker * 7993 ENT, was somewhere north of the desert shore. A second skin was becoming detached and revealing a survival mode image, a crazed negativity in mental state. Everything past and future had come down to this very moment. He was *there*.

Five fading pistons of Semper Down Security's B Squad kneeled in crescent formation before the unknowable, mapping out their past actions of the day and preparing the descent. They each glanced up suddenly at a flock of passing birds, confident the cloaking technology of their camouflage and armor uniforms were working as designed. Not so. Cadaver Dog's right shoulder was splattered with smelly white goop.

"Damn seagulls! Don't they know when to quit?" said poop casualty Cadaver Dog.

"Radio it in," said the squad leader, whose codename was Reaper.

"What, that I got shit on?! Oh, I'm on it!" avowed Cadaver Dog in disgust of his foul luck. He took hold of the squad's communications videophone tablet and signal scrambler, shot an audiovisual record of the tracks and logged their movements.

Short, redheaded Pinfish looked beyond the war paint with yearning. "We're going in?"

Reaper nodded affirmative, grinning from ear to darkly-painted ear.

Pinfish's bright blue eyes flashed. "How far?" she asked, her voice full of hopefulness.

"Far enough," said Reaper.

"I don't get it," said Death Puppet. "Why do they come all this way only to run back home again? What are they after?" His thin, muscled frame quivered. The nicotine eyes were full of worry.

"These aren't your average insects. I read something on them," said the agent formerly known as Edgar: under their current auspices, he was to be called **Psycho-Tron**. "They were engineered for biological warfare," he continued, "even put to use a few times beyond protocol, North Korea, Iran, but along came the budget cuts, a career stopper if ever there was one, struck a certain top secret lab over in Wisconsin, among others, and an unknown number of superbugs were able to escape through a breach in security. Not only that, but they devoured many of the scientists from the lab...out of revenge, as it were. Not something you'd expect from your average bug. The reports I've read say they've adapted to their host environment with deadly efficiency, even planting their own fortified hydroponics garden habitats. That may be exactly what's going on out there in the quagmire. And now it's up to us."

"Budget cuts again? But we're at war everywhere!" said Pinfish irritably. "What are they cutting defense for?"

"Because of all those damn spy planes," spat Death Puppet, just happening to look up and see one at that very moment. "Everyone wave to Big Brother!" Death Puppet waved at the silhouette in bitter sarcasm.

"That and government pensions," added Cadaver Dog.

"So, what you're saying is they're highly dangerous," assessed Reaper, taking on an assertive pose. "They're capable of deploying deadly poisons, chemical weapons, in addition to sharp blade-like incisors, javelins, quills, and extreme raw power. That's just the kind of stuff I'm used to! Hoo-rah!!"

"Hoo-rah!!" shouted the rest of B Squad. With renewed berserker strength, they re-geared and headed through the ghost-lake and into the sun. Now packed into a single dune buggy that had been left out of sight during the assessment for motivational purposes, they followed the tracks through sand and mud.

A large beetle scurried on Edgar's side and he fired only to have his weapon malfunction. Sand had crept into the firing chamber.

"Psycho-Tron's out!" shouted Cadaver Dog.

"Get me close!" growled Pinfish. Death Puppet cranked the wheel and came up on the beetle's right side so that Pinfish had a shot. She fired and nailed the bug in the backside. "I shot it, I get to tag it!" Pinfish called. The dune buggy stopped and she jumped out and sunk into the mud near the corpse, revealing her brawny midriff where the black T-shirt broke free from the gray-blue camouflage cargo pants. With a DNA kit taken from her left cargo pocket she was able to recover a sample. A photograph was also taken, via cryptic smart phone, to be logged into the mission for later use. "Tagged and bagged!"

"Let's roll!" ordered Reaper from under the chassis behind the driver's seat.

The trail into the quagmire became wider as the obstacles grew larger and stranger. A half-submerged helicopter lay in the mud some thirty yards ahead, joining an array of trash, junk, fishing equipment, wood fragments, and stones. Additionally, the mire became increasingly more fluid, such that B Squad was covered in noxious tan sludge.

"Uh, I don't think we're gonna make it much further," said Cadaver Dog, watching the fat high-traction wheels sink in to the axle.

"Alright. Stop this shit-float a minute and let's think," assessed Reaper as he looked around at the mud surrounding their sporty off-road vehicle.

"Couldn't they just fly us in?" asked Pinfish. "I got airborn training. We could parachute...just sayin'..."

"Yep, we could," said Reaper, wracking his brain for the answer.

"I have an idea..." offered Edgar pensively.

Reaper felt the potential to be inspired. "Well, let it out, Psycho-Tron," he encouraged.

"You'll think I'm barking mad, but historically...In Paris...when they dug the metro under the Seine they used to stick coils in the mud and fill them with coolant. This would freeze the mud and allow them to keep working."

Pinfish's eyes lit up. "So we can walk on it."

"Yes, exactly," reported Edgar.

"And this'll work?" Reaper asked trustingly.

"No idea. I hope so," Edgar said, glancing around at the faces pulled in to contemplate.

"A road for the Frenchies. We'll let you go on it first, then," joshed Pinfish.

"Yeah," Edgar agreed absently.

"Okay," said Reaper. "Punch that in as our Plan B. Sounds as good as any."

"Punching it in..." said Cadaver Dog.

"Let's get the hell out of here..." ordered Reaper. "Bravo Squad, grab your rod and move 'em on out!"

Operation Bug Splat

Early the next morning, August 10, at 0400, all squads comprising the company were awakened for duty and advised to meet Major Pinion outside the mess hall. They did so following breakfast and were taken on a morning hike through the woods. Eventually they reached a dull green canvas military tent. The tent flexed in the wind blowing through the clearing and tested the strength of anchoring ropes and pegs. Towering white pines, maple, and spruce creaked and then settled, emitting a fresh enlivening smell.

"This is the place," announced Major Pinion, leading the squads inside for the briefing. A series of black folding tables held a model of the ancient, ghostly Lake Michigan shoreline and contemporary quagmire west of the camp, replete with waterless islands, decomposing shipwrecks, universal sand, grass, and tiny trees.

"Ladies and gentlemen of the elite warrior division, that caste of unparalleled excellence and triumph, I must have your undivided attention. You are here!" Major Pinion pointed at the model with his long black stick and continued walking around the table. "Now, what we know, thanks to our reconnaissance teams, is that the bug trail goes from here to here, possibly to rendezvous here, at the wreck of the BMS Osiris. This poses a problem, because that area of quagmire is soft and perilous, with large glacial boulders, ancient log remnants, poisonous snakes, thick, prickly foliage…a horrible, pervading smell…not a pretty picture. We can fly you in on Apaches, NoE, but you'll have to rappel directly onto the poop deck of the BMS Osiris and we have no idea if it's structurally sound or not, where the bugs are positioned, or when they will attack. They have been known to take down an Apache attack helicopter, but I'm not allowed to tell you that. These things are highly classified, very hush, hush, and you will not disclose a single bit of this mission to anyone! Understood?!"

"Yes, sir!!"

Major Pinion continued: "Now, a Plan Bravo presents itself, thanks to the ingenuity of Recon Platoon's Bravo Squad and Agent Psycho-Tron here, who propose a freeze in the mud by the strategic placement of coils and pipes which will then be filled with coolant to form a road from here to here, where a forest of northern white cedars have mysteriously sprung up in apparently fertile ground to add warrior stability, precisely four-point-four kilometers around the wreck of the BMS Osiris to allow an attack at this point. The walls of the dome are extremely tough, but nothing a little see-four can't handle. From there, we will penetrate deep within, will take them by surprise, and we…will be…victorious!"

"Hoo-rah!" shouted the company.

"I can't hear you!!"

"Hoo-rah!!" they shouted even louder.

"Plan Bravo is hereby enacted. Captain Kazimierz, notify the Engineers and find out what we'll need from them. Report back pronto. Troops! You will fly to this point here, at coordinate forty-four sixty-six-point-nineteen degrees north, eighty-nine fifty-seven-point-thirty-nine degrees west (44 66.19'N, 089 57.39'W), which will be the rendezvous point. All clear?"

"Yes, sir!!"

"Good, then it's settled. We leave at oh-twenty-one-hundred hours! Dismissed!"

From below the open door, the small trucks were in the process of losing coils, pipes, and liquids as even smaller engineers worked in the mud like ants. A medical hydrofoil waited near the semi-floating platform, where perimeter guards watched attentively through heat sensor goggles. In the left perimeter towards Wisconsin they could see the sapphire blueness of the shrunken and weakened great lake, now a series of jewels in the softened, glacial earth.

"Victor not victim!" trailed off into the vacuum of space.

"Victor not victim!" shouted the next warrior in line from the belly of the beast.

The air smelled heavily of antifreeze.

The Apaches buzzed noiselessly overhead, poised with insect-like stillness over the rendezvous point while Team VNV rappelled back to earth, each with hot hands and thirty pounds of extra counterweight. Down they dropped, skating onto the frozen cappuccino highway that was at that moment being put into existence by Team VNV's forward operating engineers. A and B Squad were now part of Team VNV's 2nd Platoon in what was to be known as Operation Bug Splat. Once again, they descended into the specter of the lake, passing giant boulders until reaching a watery quagmire of peat, wooded moss, tall grasses, and stunted, witch-like trees. The giants of old lay submerged beneath shallow crystal waters, long, twisted forms covered in mud and bacteria. Large metallic blue dragonflies swarmed in to measure up the intruder, dancing from white lotuses and green lily pad pedestals. Ahead they saw the structure, a huge honey-brown dome beside the rust-iron wreck of the BMS Osiris. A multitude of transparent pentagonal windows let in the sun, making it difficult to determine safe entry. The company commander, who went by Lord Sinister, broke the two platoons into wings and sent them into a sweep. Each 25 troop platoon, the body of men and women accompanying their lord into the field like the yeoman quills of old, were like flickering ghosts along the wasted dreams of the Great Lakes States. In place of spears, halberds, bows, and rusty swords passed down through ages, they held the latest assault rifles by Heckler-Koch, the gas operated HK417, which fired 600 rounds per minute of accurate long-range 7.62 mm caliber bullets through a 12-inch cold hammer forged barrel, fitted with a night vision adapter telescope sight, a folding tripod, and a sound moderator. Micro fiber cloth and ceramic body armor integrated with cloaking technology replaced chain mail, woolen rags, and wooden shields. Carrier pigeons had become cryptographic smartphones. In place of the handsome orange-orbed goshawk there was the... the... But in a world which refused to give up the contradiction that pretending to be lords and knights of a bygone caste system jeopardized their dreams of equality and freedom, the positions were very much the same in theory.

2nd Platoon moved into position around the dome and waited for the signal. Something was happening, but their sensory perception kept them in the dark, leaving only the traveling waves of sound.

"All hell just broke loose!" crackled over the radio. "Attack! At-a-kkkkk..." As visuals were transferred from the point of heatedness, they could see events unfold through the interface. 1st Platoon had reached the BMS Osiris, where an army of blue and gold Bombardier beetles, each over a foot in length, rose from the sand on long, bristly, segmented legs and attacked by spraying boiling hot chemicals from a holding chamber in their rears. The popping of exploding insect artillery was audible, followed by human cries of pain as nasty blisters formed on exposed skin beneath the eaten fibers of combat fatigues. Yellow-and-black-striped Blister Beetles, many over two feet, attacked from somewhere within the dome, rushing out angrily to confront the intruders.

The platoon went to work, hoping to take the bugs unawares. Pinfish attached a plastic explosive window monkey to the wall of the large, thick brown dome with the transparent pentagonal cones and gave the signal and they all ran for cover. After the explosion had subsided, they moved quietly through the opening and oddly found themselves in a jungle of acacia, sunflowers, and other plants. The air was hot and moist, a condition which seemed to be occurring by steam rising from the ground. The heat sensors flashed with huge specks of movement in the red and orange sectors, to the center of the dome and into the earth. The shapes were indistinguishable. An unsettling feeling passed through 2nd Platoon as they moved through the thorny bushes. They were exceptionally tall and thick, of uncommon healthiness. The dome seemed for them to nurture with ideal care. The draconic thorns pierced through uniforms and skin with ease, causing an itching, burning sensation. The platoon-members began to feel an overwhelming claustrophobia, like being pressed upon by the unseen.

The branches moved as if by the weight of a sly, predatory wind.

Without warning, the ants attacked, pushing soldiers backward into thorns and inflicting very painful stings. There were only a few of them at first; they were, however, very large, at close to six inches, with nasty hairs on their segmented amber bodies and large, black eyes peering out from atop powerful hacksaw jaws.

Machine guns rattled into the foliage, sending the bugs running with orchestral screeches. It seemed an easy victory. The line thickened into meters. Combat lifesavers moved in to assess and treat the wounds of comrades. They talked boldly, encouraging each other in superhuman prowess until faint rumbling sounds disturbed the relative quiet of battle. But then the line thinned again, like bad blood, and the tide turned. Heat sensors from quickly-roving cybernetic eyes captured the rising pitch of fear. They were vastly outnumbered and outgunned. The sensible platoon leader gave the order to retreat.

As they fell back, crouching amidst loyal thorns, the horrors of genetic warfare unfolded. They scanned quickly for a way out, but only the breach proved inviting.

Giant hornets attacked from the roof of the dome, maddening with their lance-like stingers and buzzing wings.

Shit Goes Awry

Lord Sinister proved incapable of preventing a rout and was like the Persian King Darius III between the wedge of Alexander the Great's Companion Cavalry and the incoming Macedonian six-meter lances charging in through that fateful breach at Gaugamela. Shots were fired. Bullets flew like heat in rapid thunder. A great discordant chorus of clacking rippled from all sides. Yellow chemical spray dominated the field as stingers and pincers faced off against grenades and assault rifles. The sky soon filled with apocalyptic buzzing wings as locusts and giant hornets swarmed in for the attack.

The mercenary human forces were overwhelmed. They took cover where they may and some fled, escaping the battlefield with terrible blisters and burns. Some even fell into convulsions and lay face down in the mud. Machine guns rat-a-tat-t-t-t-t-t-t-t-tat-ed as brass dragon's teeth fired into the monstrous mist.

Despite their insane numbers, the bug casualties were stacking up. They were becoming a chitin wall around the offensive. The fertile soil stank from yellow globular insect blood and guts.

"Stand your ground! Die with honor!" Lord Sinister shouted in vain as more troops fled the field.

"This place is for shit!"

"I'm with that!"

Dozens from Lord Sinister's company answered in pathetic catch-phrases as they bolted for the rendezvous point.

Others took root behind moss-covered junk or smooth, round boulders and continued to fire at the superbugs.

Still inside the dome and hiding in foliage, 2nd Platoon had been reduced to scrambling patches. Many had either fled back through the breach or tried their luck further in.

Edgar struggled for thought. The assault had failed. He had become separated. He was lost between thorny acacias and tall, thick bamboo. It seemed the best thing was to try and find some kind of headquarters. According to his reasoning, it could not be much further ahead. If they could at least gather some important information, map the place out, perhaps, it would keep the mission from becoming a total loss. But where was Cadaver Dog, the one comrade to reveal his face this past half-hour? The mapping equipment was with the rest of the platoon. Where was anyone? "Cadaver Dog, Reaper, Death Puppet, Pinfish, anyone...does anyone read me? This is Psycho-Tron!" he called into the radio. "Is anyone still inside the dome?!"

"-refrain from kkkkkk -to keep the f-cking line clear!" he heard partially. He had accidentally cut someone off. It had probably been someone important. There was a series of clicks and then shouts from different people's voices.

Edgar felt a sharp pain at that particular moment from a large brown ant that had crawled under his vest armor to give him a powerful sting at the lower backside. He slapped it out in a panic and moved to stomp on it among the acacias and bamboo but the thing was hardly phased.

"Tough little buggers!" he hissed.

The ant lunged at his boots.

Edgar touched the safety switch instinctively (even though his weapon was still battle-ready), aimed, and opened fire. He was splattered with ant guts. He fired again. The thing was still moving. Again he fired. Satisfied to have at least severed the head, he limped off in pain through the shoots of bamboo until reaching an area of tall grass and what looked like a gigantic ibex horn rising complexly. Something scurried off just ahead. The tropical trees rising around the clearing were nothing he had seen before. The place was surreal. Edgar followed the claw prints through the deathly silence to a post-meridian citadel. It was as if a spiraling blue-gray minaret ascended from the jungle. Deeply confused, Edgar crept in to study the structure. He followed with his hand over timeless tales; highly-detailed eccentric relief depicting beetles, blazing suns, black ziggurats, and centi-pedal warriors with insect wings; things which had certainly gone unnoticed a moment ago.

A stone in the floor gave way suddenly, revealing a flat, spiraling ramp into the unknown. He followed at first out of mere curiosity, but then became afraid—what could be down there, he wondered; would he even be able to breathe? Semper Down would certainly not pay a corpse, if anyone even found this ornamental mid-morning tomb without sharing the same fate. But then an alluring smell wafted. He passed under a stone entryway and noticed a surprising amount of light shining in through glassy portholes in the ceiling. Next he followed the encircling ramp down into a hallway which led to an eerily cozy lobby of sorts. Abstract chairs twisted outward from the circular wall. A stone door barred the way further, but Edgar managed to force his way in as it grated loudly along the sandy floor. To his further astonishment, the next room was furnished with bizarre abstract objects and seemed to be a library-of-sorts: A collection of well-preserved volumes took up space among amber shelves comprising a section of circular wall. The carpeted floor was devoid of dirt or moss and disoriented with spiraling feather designs. There was a musty smell of ancientness, as if from a deep cave. A circular artwork of maroon and rich pink colored coiled rope of a feathery nature was displayed in the center of a white wall between the two bookshelves. Completely mystified, Edgar approached the shelves and carefully pulled a book out from between several others. It was a strange texture, smooth, but acidic, and seemed to breathe ever so slightly in his careful grasp so that the dust was gradually blown out, leaving a clean surface. On the cover was a swirling design which was probably around a square foot on the surface and about three inches deep. There were shallow markings just above the swirls, but he couldn't decide what purpose they served. He placed it carefully on a table carved from a surreal, rainbow-colored metallic bone structure and made a cloud of dust rise up as he tried to flip the book open. It was locked with a strange mechanism, a puzzle of sorts. Edgar was good at puzzles, but had never encountered anything remotely similar to the abstract locking mechanism keeping secrets from him. He forgot himself completely, dangerously oblivious to the war still waging somewhere above, and was soon absorbed in the complex disposition of the problem.

The awareness of a gradual movement to Edgar's rear paralyzed him with fear and his neck hairs stood on end. With widened eyes, he turned slowly to assess the situation. To Edgar's horror, a bizarre Nereid creature with a pair of golden spiral feelers, orange mandibles, and a barbed exoskeleton of chitin appearing a brown-pink on the backside of hard maroon segments moved on the wall where the art had been. He tried to obstruct it with the steel barrel of his weapon, but it moved so suddenly, jumping from the wall with lightning speed, that the creature soon clung painfully to Edgar's neck with its powerful claws. Paralyzed once more, except for a faint squeal escaping from deep within, he could only stand in terror as two lengthy orange incisors did their quick work on him.

II

West of the Fields

The *modus operandi* for the harvest crews in their second week was markedly different than in the first. Two security guards had met an untimely end while checking the orchards for signs of trouble early one twilight morning. Monstrosso was forced to up the ante as a result, lest they lose their partners in the second year of production. It would cost the company millions, however, and they would likely meet lost profits for the next ten quarters. They could only shake the farmers for so much, and hence prices would have to rise. The whitened executives of Gad Growers Inc. were especially worried, as they had invested heavily in the new fruit; the remaining cherry farmers in the area once internationally known for such things would hardly make the regression worthwhile; the genetically modified superiority of gads had already worked weightily on the local psyche.

West of the fields, which were heavy with sweet-corn, the orchards of Sarasin Farms undulated over the countryside in cinereous-rose and green, a pointillistic forest for industrious dwarves. The canopy sparkled like cresting waves. The place meant business.

David arrived there with the others in the usual fashion and received a small shield, just as he would have on any other day; however, the setup was different. There was a secretive-looking mobile office of some kind, an additional pole barn, and at least five new semi-trucks full of who-knew-what. Security forces had multiplied exponentially and were struggling to unload and to set everything up.

They gathered for Arturo's big speech with about three other crews, as usual, but with the addition of several scarecrows. Most of them were wearing clothes, but Arturo's was armored, just as

David had seen it a few weeks ago at the factory when he went out for a smoke. He was unsure what they were to be used for, but perhaps, he thought, to scare off the crows. Crows were very smart, though, and he doubted they would care about the armor.

The crew waited for placement. They were to start somewhere in the middle of an orchard to the left of a dirt road. Another crew would start at the beginning, so they would each tackle exactly half of the work.

A heavily-armored guy with a scarecrow on a stick was walking through the first lane, poking the scapegoat into the gad-rich foliage.

"Ah, now I see," David whispered.

"That's what happened at the meeting," Graham said. He told everyone how the use of the scarecrows was because Arturo's idea had won out at a recent meeting held for the bosses. From now on, the trees in the orchard were to be checked by brave individuals who wanted an additional pay-raise. But the catch was that some of the trees had gone rogue and were now spitting acidic quills at anything that moved—hence the untimely death of the guards.

"Boy, that's a shame... Hey, wait a minute!" Christopher cried out in alarm, having rubbed the crud from his eyes.

Darrel drove in smelling of propane and replaced a full tank with an empty one and then drove off again. Soon enough, he was back, and the crew prepared for a day of hard labor.

"Darrel, I need your help, man," said Arturo once he had descended from his forklift. "Grab your dummy and let's spook some trees."

"No, ut-uh. Not me," said Darrel, failing to budge from his polyester throne.

"Whatdya mean not you?" Arturo worried. "Oh, that's right! I guess we need you on forks. Who's got your dummy, then?"

Darrel shrugged. "John? I forget. He's from one of the other crews."

"This must be him," said Arturo as they watched a guy drive in on a green forklift. "You guys go ahead and get started. The first twelve have already checked out."

Arturo ran to his orange forklift and put on his golden bear helmet (the faceplate resembled the white jaws and golden brown to black snout of a bear) and then grabbed his scarecrow and ran down the left row of the orchard screaming, poking up into the trees as he went. The new guy, John, followed suit, running down the right row and yelling as he poked his much lighter scarecrow up into the trees. When he had made it just under a quarter ways down, some fifteen trees spanning over fifty yards, a long quill shot out and pierced the unprotected face of the scarecrow and John sidestepped back, threw a smoke bomb and then shot off a red flare. A full-armored security team came roaring down in a ballistic Mahindra Nitro[35] with thick bulletproof windows. The team members were on their bellies looking out through a low-positioned strip of ballistic glass. When they got to the tree from the opposing lane, they rolled out of the heavily modified sports car through shape-shifting slots and jumped in like a special operations team. The tree wavered and stretched. Thorns fanged out like ebony jaws. One member was stuck in the leg by a projectile and soon bled over his greaves. Another member went down. Others were struck and they wailed in pain. Next, as replacements bravely ran in, a bright orange parachute was thrown over the tree. The remaining team quickly encircled the chute and wrapped the material in rope. Finally a thick metal clamp was secured around the base of the tree and they attached a hose to a connector built into the chute and filled it with liquid nitrogen. The tree crackled underneath and became inanimate. But it had fought like a badger. The ops team loaded their wounded into the open trunk at a sitting position and sped off to intercept the raucously approaching ambulance.

---

[35] In 2016, Dongfeng Motor Company (DFM) combined a HMMWV copy under cooperation of AM General with an electric knockoff Jaguar C-X75 concept car first copied by Great Wall Motor, which was eventually re-copied by India's Mahindra & Mahindra, who opted instead for a copy of GM's *Luge*, a hybrid liquid nitrogen-electric propulsion sports car designed by Yuri Ranum, but discontinued in the US after five test drivers were accidentally cryogenically frozen. Mahindra beefed up the car with run-flat tires and smart technology ballistic ceramics and sold a limited number to the US government under the name M9. When Consumer Reports uncovered the ridiculously high cost of the vehicles, the US government covertly sold them to private security companies under the name Mahindra Nitro at a fraction of the original cost. The loss was conveniently hidden under vague references to a secret laboratory in New Mexico.

"Good freaking ashtray!" David whispered. "Why don't they just cut the thing down?"

A radio crackled from the roofless cab of the Zapper. Arturo was telling Graham to avoid a certain tree in the right lane.

Thus went the morning as defined in the vast, undulating orchards west of the fields, until they reached the frozen parachute the color of safety orange.

"Don't touch it," said Graham between growls of hydraulics coming from the Zapper's arm as it lifted and fell. The additional noise of the forklift made his warning barely discernable.

"Ooh cold!" shouted Chuck. He had accidentally brushed the side of the chute with his shoulder. "Why the hell did they do *that*?!"

"That's how they get rid of those suckers," howled Darrel. "Just what the doctor ordered, if you ask me."

"A little extreme, no?" asked Ernesto.

"An extreme end to some extreme mo' friggin' trees!" said Darrel. "Just wait 'til *you* get attacked by one. Those damn things can *kill* you!"

Darrel left with a full tank and came back with one full of water and waited for the next one on the tractor to fill. He seemed completely at ease with the oddities around him.

By lunch time David's arms were sore.

They were deep within the next lanes heading back towards the dirt road and everyone was terrified at the thought of walking into an orchard where the trees were potentially demonic. Instead they walked back into the lanes which they had already finished and waited to be given forklift rides to a picnic area across from the guard post where the mobile *Snack Shack* was located and also incidentally where their lunches would hopefully reappear. The shack contained the usual refrigerator and microwave and a variety of exceptionally popular vending machines, combining to make it a mechanical chef of sorts. The whole thing was plugged into a loud and smelly diesel generator. Four picnic tables were in front of the shack, placed over the grass. The crew claimed one and assembled there gradually in the same pairs they had been working as. The other three squads trickled in as well, many with a bunch of new faces and new attitudes. By then everyone but Moses had purchased a cover and people were examining the many different shields as they ate and drank.

"My wife can sew anything on for you," Darrel offered to Moses in a businesslike manner. "Patches or whatever. It's computerized so she can even make one from a picture, if you want to do that. Or just draw something. It's only ten bucks." Darrel showed off his own shield, where he displayed the living portrait of a beautiful young African-American woman in bright red and purple robes. "My wife," he explained, "when she was younger. It's a little airbrushed."

After lunch they hitched a ride back out and everything started as before: Arturo and John ran screaming through the crab grass growing in between the rows, which were roughly twenty feet apart, and this time they stirred up three trees that each suddenly wailed up like Tolkien's *ents,* swatting and spitting quills the size of Amazonian frog-poisoned darts. Arturo was stuck in the arm and John took one in the side of his ribs (luckily only grazing him on their way down). Watching them in action, it seemed to David that the trees could sense the approaching footsteps through vibrations in the earth, but it was unclear how they might react, as they did, with such blinded accuracy. Each time a tree reacted in violence, the special operations guards rushed in and froze it with liquid nitrogen. Even though these parachutes endured deadly hits from thorny branches and quills, the micro-fabric skin was rarely ever punctured. But during the quelling of the second tree there was a leak and one guard was sprayed with liquid nitrogen all over her cuirass-vest armor and on part of her uniformed arm and she had to be rushed away in an awaiting ambulance.

The day went on like that, with industrialized repetition against nature overshadowing the surreal war going on around them. The quest of the self had been reinvented with old parts. This modern version of madness that David and his fellow crewmen were experiencing was itself being thrown onto the assembly line, boxed up and shelved to be sold to the oblivious consumer. Out there, the gullible gobblers of dreams gone awry carelessly indulged in a meteoric cornucopia from Eltanin projected down to Earth to countervail a diminishing substance of variation and meaning. The imperiled workers struggled to keep up with demand. The waves crested and broke against the hull of their livelihood, revealing the scarred and beautiful skin of the leviathan. They simply held on, carried along as they were through this ocean of doubt.

III

Gad Factory Be Damned

Before Antiope could blink an eye (so to speak), she was back in the factory sorting fruit. John and Eddie were on double duty, and, in addition, the management had been briefed on how she might prove to be a nuisance for them. In consequence, she couldn't even punch in the number for a devil's food cake without someone anticipating her move. Ah, but they had no idea whom they were messing with. She would find a way.

Rindscheit Farms

They had forced her to come here; therefore, she hardly felt bad. Slipping past the guards was easier than she thought; there was no one manning the back entrance, where a gigantic press was set up on a steel platform like something she had read about in that Willy Wonka book about an eccentric candy factory. The sorters and machine operators could have cared less as she wandered past them and headed for the cooling pad.

Semi trucks with empty beds were pulling in. They had probably come to fill up on containers of water to take back to the outlying farms—at least, she hoped so. A few odd looks came her way, but nothing to make her worry. For all they knew, she was working in the cooling pad, or perhaps sanitation. The forklifts zipped busily around the lot, breaking down stacks of containers along the rear factory building. Antiope could easily make out the ones she needed: The gold Rindscheit boxes were marked by the icon of the subdued brown owl (from a distance it resembled a pile of bovine animal dung). Five sides of steel sheet-metal comprised each box. They were filled with clear effluence and were being loaded into the grates of the flatbeds. There were twelve to each truck, but not all the spots were filled. This was the chance she was looking for. Once it seemed to her that no one was looking, she climbed up the side of the truck and into the third tank down, wading in the water with her face sticking out—thank God she could swim, she thought frigidly. The water was cold and she immediately began shivering. Neither the academy bathing suit nor the clothes covering it were much help: An oversight. The wait was long and torturous. She heard footsteps. A door opened and shut and the truck shook, starting with a blaring roar. Antiope found her situation to be even more precarious while things were in motion as she struggled to keep her head above the splashing water. At times, it was a stormy ocean of clarity some 4X4 feet square with definite, bone-crunching boundaries of painted steel.

The truck moved out onto the road and after what seemed like an eternity of sky, traffic noises, dust, shifting metal containers, squeaking brakes, centrifugal force upon objects, the truck slowed and briefly came to a stop. Antiope looked out from her tank of torture as the truck pulled into the farm and waited impatiently in the line forming at the gate. A gold and black family crest attached to the fence bore the inscription "Though I am hated by all birds, I rather enjoy that". This was her queue to skedaddle. She climbed out of the tank and slunk to the chassis connecting the cab to the flatbed before the other trucks arrived and attempted to jettison, but with such unanticipated difficulty that the task was not completed in time and she had to hide herself. The truck pulled up to the gate with a sodden and chilled young lady clinging desperately to the bottom chassis before bouncing her and everything else roughly into the orchard along a dirt lane. With tired arms slipping and nearing hot metal pipe work, she tried her best to remain calm. She could hear the guards laughing airily to keep themselves awake, their voices becoming more and more distant. The truck stopped with a jolt, sputtering into thankful silence, and the driver exited, chatted with another driver, and then walked off.

Antiope peaked out and saw some men walking towards the portable bathroom stalls, which were aligned along the same fence that connected up with the gate. The trucks were lined up in the center of a wide cul-de-sac. She seemed to be alone for the moment. She swore under her breath and tried to regain her courage. Escape would be tricky now that she was on the wrong side of the fence and she wondered how she would be able to complete such a task without falling on her head. Rows of bountiful gad trees ran from both sides, and a hundred yards back along a dirt road stood the gates of Rindscheit. The direction, she supposed, was west, and north was where she wanted to be. Fatigued from the trip, she rested on the ground a minute before heading off into the orchards. The chill water was still dripping from her drenched form and made her feel faint. Now free, she bounded off into the thick azure-green foliage. The trees were lovely. She had never seen them this close up before. The fruit glistened like stars as they hung from their silvery white to rose branches. Even the breeze rustling in from the west held the perfume of wonderment. Although she felt hungry, Antiope dared not eat the fruit for fear of triggering the alarm when and if she made it out. She had heard stories from the mechanics about people being hauled off to have their stomachs pumped and she was loath to test them. Yet, as she thought on the improbability of such things, it occurred to her that a prisoner of the orchard would have to pass unseen as the trucks moved in and out of the gate, and thus a stomach full of gads would be no more traceable than a dozen bushels. The closest trees seemed to agree as the gads turned a delectable red. So it was decided. Picking here and there so as not to harm the branches, she collected a shirt-full and ate them one by one. They were delicious, with hints of mystery and liveliness. She felt stimulated as thoughts of coinage and saleswomanship electrified her neurons, causing interference between holographic perception areas and quantum vectors of discrete reward potentials. Her hunger abated, and with a refreshing feeling of autonomy, she continued along a disorienting zigzag pattern. When finally she was able to glimpse the obstacles of flight, her heart sank. Guards paced up and down the fence like weary wolves. There was an unforeseeable chance that she would escape, unless she could stow away again in tanks of gads heading back to the factory and manage to jump out along the way. It was enough to make her cry. The tears warmed her face as she slid further into the orchard. The trees around her seemed to move, rustling communicatively in a windless vacuum.

Cannons sounded out near the boundary, startling the countryside with loud booms of thunder. The birds scattered in unison, the many parts combined into a magnificent whole, a singular dance of beauty in flight.

Something large rustled from beneath a tree in the next row down. It gave Antiope goose-bumps and she froze in place like a frightened deer. She was thinking it was a guard or perhaps a badger; instead, a middle-aged man rose creakily from his bed of thick crabgrass, stretched, groaned, and then glared about with paranoid eyes. He turned to pick something up, and, rising stiffly in pain, saw Antiope standing motionless with wide misty eyes. He seemed familiar somehow, standing tall in the harmony of trees, and yet appeared as a wild thing, running scared, homeless. This *man of the green* shared her mannerisms, seemed to be thinking with the same mind. They connected for a moment, but suddenly he turned and ran off in his ragged dress clothes. Antiope waited to recover while her heart thumped heavily against her chest and then followed at a safe distance. She watched as the man passed through a hole cut in the fence. It was just her luck, however, that when she attempted to do the same the one visible guard was doubling back and, seeing her, sounded the alarm. The rest of her day was unpleasant, as she endured a patch of thorny bushes only to be tackled vigorously and violently contorted into submission.

"Get...off...me...!!" she squawked.

"And just where do you think you're going?!" said the guard meanly.

The other was equally vicious: "Kind of large for a rabbit, don't you think, Chester?!"

"Scan her hand; see if you pick anything up!"

"Getting nothing... wait, something's sewn into her shirt... Oh, that figures! She's not a rabbit, Felix, she's a duck."

"...From the academy? Those ExTemplar fools can't do anything right..."

"I love picking on those two...and there's the weird guy...that miniature one...what's his name?"

But to Escape the Confines of the Modern Industrial Egg

Life was rotten for the as yet still young and sprightly woman, alone among over 300 boring and clueless students. The administration had tried bribing her with all manner of trinkets and distractions, even naming her as head pupil of the newly-formed glassworks workshop, while subversively going out of their way to get rid of her: All five Gamesh military recruiting stations had Antiope Clara Penuel at the top of their files. It was all she could do to avoid a direct conversation during a surprise visit. But through everything that the academy did to try and break her, they could not stop the mail.

They always arrived in bundles—she suspected because they were difficult to read; the average eavesdropper would rarely get past the first two correspondences. She called them The Zech Adam Adams Letters. Zech and Zach were twins, just a few years younger than Antiope, who shared a lot in common with their fellow student, such as a burning desire to be elsewhere. Antiope had dated Zach until a partially-botched escape separated them, during which Zach was killed. Zech alone succeeded and was making ends meet out in New York, where he said the Freedom Tower stood as both a symbol of corporate bolshevism and victory over paranoia. With that radical insight in mind, she opened the third letter and began reading:

July 19, the 2nd Year of Gad,

Antiope, my despairing sister,

No one writes anymore. Communication has become unintelligible clicks; the dreadful repetition. We are fat, thoughtless birds without voice. If we could fly, where would we go? We stay at home like good Hobbits.

I hope beyond hope that you have not received this; that you are escaped. But I fear the worst, that my own timely abandonment might have made life even more encasing for the rest of you. I hope that is not true. And to think we lost a brother out of it, my own graven self-image. His dying wish was that you could have been with us. We could not have done it without you. Well, at least he died free.

You probably wonder at my sister reference, and I am here to reveal to you an interesting tidbit which I found just the other day after excessive online searching through other people's files and correspondence: I discovered who my father is; not only that, but I found out who YOUR father is—Don't worry, it's not the same person. I just kind of wished it in a way is all. You're the closest thing to family I have, you know. If you happen to receive this, my caged hummingbird with enchanted wings, let me know and I'll tell you his name.

ZAA

The Old-Fashioned Jacquard Handloom

A small package arrived one day unexpectedly for someone by the name K Street from a Gamesh address. The mail delivery robot dropped it at the foot of the door that Antiope previously shared with four others. Strangely, the Academy had gotten sick of sorting out their own mail, had hired and then fired the pro bono mailroom intern and purchased this expensive miniature moon-rover-like robot. Because most students never received mail, there were no exceptions to the system, and no additional security procedures. It was like having a roving slave for the slaves.

Antiope could hardly believe that she had gotten something other than a letter from her old friend Zech. She came upon the package directly after subservience class and opened it right there in the hall under the gaze of the cameras. Inside were a toy version of an old-fashioned Austrian Jacquard handloom and a note from her mother reading, "I'm here for you. Permanently. Love, Mom".

The gift gave her hope that things were not as awful as they seemed; there was someone on the outside she could trust and confide in, maybe even grow to love, and the handloom was in some sense an appropriate symbol. If only she could persuade these uninspired siblings of hers to reach out against the oppressors.

284

The First Time Antiope Had Ever Seen Her Mother

Antiope had never forgotten her first intelligible memory of Mother: Dressed in synthetic musk ox furs and smoking a cherry-scented cigarette through a long thin black tube, then pulling something heavy and industrial from inside and suddenly being wrestled to the floor of the academy by muscled guards wearing white T-shirts and unbuttoned short-sleeved uniforms of formal pale militant green, Mother's snarling lower lip chapped and bloody at the pulpy center.

"Don't let them take your soul away from you!" she had shouted before they dragged her away. Mother had been speaking not just to her little girl, the one who had made the connection, but to all of them.

Antiope repeated her mother's words from the hallway which she herself had been forced to clean that very morning, scrubbing on hands and knees without the mandatory safety-yellow (CAUTION!) sign and thus causing an antisocial math instructor to slip and bruise his elbows and knees (to Antiope's schadenfreude and dawning archaic smile).

The Second Time

The second instance within Antiope's memory of her mother was no less unusual. A weaving instructor had been allowed to visit the academy, a woman in a blonde wig who had mesmerized the staff with her years of industrial experience—during the middle part of the academy's existence, Monstrosso was unsure about where they could make use of the peculiar children they had foolishly collected and so jumped at any opportunity. They often took on instructors of industrial crafts to win over factories and to offer exchange programs on a temporary basis. The blonde-wigged weaving instructor had claimed to represent the Chicago branch of Marshalsea Fine Living[36], even though she actually no longer

---

[36] An ironically-named subsidiary of the English company 240,000 Handloom Weavers, which is a reference to the victims of "automation" during The Railway Age.

worked for them. Antiope had not recognized the instructor at first, which must have devastated her mother deeply and drove her to irrational ends, and so the tormented woman began to leave more and more noticeable hints to her children. Such was the state that Antiope's mother Henrietta was reduced, that she spied on her own children through intricate disguises and remained unknown to them. They had forced her to live under an alias.

The multitude of looms that Henrietta had brought with her to bolster her disguise and authenticate her instruction were on credit. She taught the students how to weave, at least those who showed interest (which had been a surprisingly high number among both boys and girls), and when the otherwise indifferent chicks from her own brood brought before her something they had made, she hugged them and became overly emotional, prompting the school wardens who oversaw everything to question her.

When Antiope was smothered in hugs and kisses by the instructor for a particularly saturated anime design, the little girl that comprised her existence at the time realized with delight that this was her mother, the one who had born her; the very same woman with the cherry-scented cigarette. The feeling was one of blanketing warmth. The sight of beaming little Antiope with her multiple-stained fingers reciting "Mommy" over and over again as she snuggled against warm feathers of connecting fabric was too much for the instructor, however, as she gave herself away in fits of hysterical laughter. Henrietta, mother of nonuplets, was crying uncontrollably when the guards hauled her away. She was subsequently threatened with legal action by Monstrosso, resulting in several restraining orders.

Antiope had received secret communications from Mother ever since that bizarre encounter, but kept them to herself. Only the surveillance system knew the truth. It made her happy that her mother went through so much trouble to see them, no matter how crazy or infrequently these situations proved. She was determined to see her mother again. She kept this desire hidden under the auspiciousness of autism and only acted out this aggression within her troubled mind. Not a soul was entrusted with this most important mission—even her siblings, whom for the most part she regarded as inhuman little snitchers. She could not convince them to be otherwise. Only recently had Antiope fulfilled that desire.

Nine tickets to Bermuda had been the means for all Penuel siblings, yet only she had accepted that wonderful gesture from the estranged. It had been difficult to keep the remaining eight Penuels from turning her over to the authorities. Frightful, buggers, they were.

On top of everything else, Antiope's former client **Cranbrook_Beauty96** (a.k.a. Mrs. Wesson) was still trying to convince the academy to relinquish her over to the Wesson's care so that she could become some kind of origami house servant. Although a temporary escape, and possibly a means to once again take her plight on the road, being imprisoned to the Wesson household would have proven even more languishing than the Monstrosso one. Something would have to be done about that, and soon.

UNDECAPLET

I

On the Improbability of Super-Intelligent Insects

Edgar awoke in fear, to his great surprise, departicalizing from a series of terrifying dreams and then refragmenting at the library where he had been attacked by the great fire-worm-like centipede-creature. He saw no sign of it, and the place where it had been curled up on the wall like a large feathery button of pinkish crimson was bare and ivory-white. Nonetheless, he felt queasy and the room spun when he moved. The insect must have poisoned him. He wobbled and tried to stand and his vision became blurry. The abundant energy that had radiated from him as of late had dissipated and smoldered into clammy coldness. Any second, the bugs would be back to finish him off. He had to find a way out and quickly.

The room was rounded and domed. The ceiling, he noted, was an upward cone with symmetrical grooves carved into it. The end was dark. The light was coming in from odd patches of bulging vessels that appeared in a concise zigzag pattern along the wall. The light was yellow-green and cool to the touch.

Strangely, some of the books had been moved and were sprawled out on an islanded table of stained ivory. It occurred to him that the library might have been some kind of trap. There was a pungent and very distinct smell—not just one, but many, he soon realized—that became irresistible to him and he could see it rising from the pages of the opened books in unusual neon colors of smoke. They were almost voices, almost wisps of the bog as on those chilly early mornings when he would heat up the algae in the water-garden. Edgar broke away and looked around suspiciously. Was this going to be it then, he wondered? Was this what death was

288

like? Perhaps the war was close, still closer like a blanket that kept him cold, a whisper under a desert night, a Jinn wrapped like a flag around the corpse of a friend. There was something wrong. He felt himself rising medicinally. Below was the body. In his quasi-state of doped insanity, he hoped that it would not be taken to Arlington and thrown into a landfill. Suddenly the breath left him and his vision blurred. He could almost feel the explosions going off somewhere in the past, could almost hear the machine guns firing into the mirror image of a war—wasn't it Patton who said that a war was like any other, that he had been through them time and again; even once, facing the Roman legions under the shadow of the Atlas Mountains, haunting the place like a leitmotif to the attention of all future Pattons? That was how Edgar felt beneath the minaret.

The books once again took his fluttering mind by the horns and he was brought down as if on a cloud. The smells were calling like jealous lovers, caressing his thoughts. What was it about these smells? They were concepts, symbols. They made the books function. It seemed impossible, and perhaps Edgar had gone mad. He inspected one with interest. What was that texture? There was ancientness about them, an alien intelligence, and yet he was beginning to understand. Not entirely in good faith, they called out to him, a primordial familiarity. *These were not people's books! They were not people!!* And yet the books had been placed on the table, some sprawled out in heavy piles of knowledge, the paper thick, strange, breathing slightly and emitting wisps of neon colored inky gas. He touched the gas to see what would happen. *Escape! Escape!* It spiraled up through his mind like the horn of the ibex. The books with their alluring smells, thickening in the stale air before him, were warm, gaseous things filled with virulent symbols of abstract language, one denoting *A Treatise on Conidiobolus* and another, *The Variation of Plants and Animals through Domestication*. One large, warped, and taupe-colored volume in violet Mandaic-like lettering translated roughly as *Using Your Entomophthorales: A Guide to Effective Assassination* and appeared to be a serial murderer's case study of inflicted epizootic outbreaks of disease in flies ('he' was, so it seemed, a fly 'himself'). One by one, the tomes forcefully took him in and throttled his thoughts. Edgar was taken aback by this raging flood of knowledge and seemed to regain consciousness as if awakening from a dream. And yet, he should not have been able to comprehend the dotting, lifting, vaporous language therein. What was happening to him? The illicit knowledge continued to claw at the unused portions of his brain. He learned things that tormented him, that made his skin crawl in self-loathing, yet he could not break away. Released from one spell, he would soon become bewitched by another. A book covered up in dried leaves but without title caught his attention. He opened it eagerly, took on the chemical bombardment rising from the pages, and read a short passage:

-*//\\/ of the river's edge, and there she wilted and died, our beloved Spirit-Keeper, the Queen of Trees, ageless in her inspiration, whom had decreed the destiny of the Traveler. Undone, she rejoined the muck of life, yet her form is loveliness eternal along the fragrant shore of Heaven. In time, the soil felt different, contaminant of evil, becoming vital nitrogen from the death of things yet unseen, and the air was choked with bitter sulfur. Poisoned and heated by once-friendly fires, impassive to the radiant gardener at day,

[Unfortunately, he could not make out the rest of the chapter and had to skip ahead]

/-//''...haunted by the supreme blue flashes overhead that lashed their alchemical branches into universal grains, antithetically bolstering the embattled exhale of the breathless. The endurable phantom link, like the touch of grapevines connecting all things, was all we had in that tranquil darkness
/\-///\-\\-**-.

[Edgar again found a large portion of this middle part undecipherable and had to skip several pages]

☼   ┗◙

They who were once immobile became awakened and looked out. A wind had joined them on the horizon, blown up from the mountain. They set out from the cage-home suspended by gold thread, by the filament of the radiant gardener, rode out on the wind and looked back at the silver thread, at the filament of the luminous watcher, and were filled with love for these parental figures, the luminous and the radiant, but continued to wander immense distances in search of truth. For the world, they wandered; for us, they suffered. It was they who brought us power over light. And so, in memory of them, the Traveler went out from the top of the mountain, out of a frigid death, nothing but a dream along the clouds of heaven, and imagined himself upon a charge of horses, a wondrous charge both pale and dark. On the eighth day of the ninth week

[Again, unfortunately, unreadable and he had to skip ahead somewhat, but it seemed to be an elaborate tragedy of sorts]

*Greatly saddened that their hard-earned love might wither, that they might impress upon the other like the Spirit-Keeper long before them, they set out for the one-eyed shepherd to see if he would divulge his secrets and lead them to that underground realm where there dwelled a wisp-woman of divine powers ***∧∧.*

[Incomprehensible]

◀▓▶ *said, 'the meaning of the dream is thus: Eternity is a vast horizon; everyone's in part, but not yours to hold. Reach for it and you get burned. Don't even try such an impossible feat. Take these memories instead and gauge the impact that you have made on the living, the traveling that you have done, all that you have seen and unseen, the ugliness and beauty, the shadows and light, the victories and defeats, and as the void carries you out, know yourself. In that internal glow you will never be lost. Now, go forward. There is nothing to fear.'* ◀▓▶ *said this, but the eyes of* כ *were full of tears. Beautiful as ever was she in sorrow. 'Do not weep, for we are still together,' said the brave* אֵ•בָּלִק *beside her, 'When they take me, gladly will I go so that you may live on—in memories I will*

291

keep you warm. Such is the destiny of the Traveler, and as such these things will come to pass.' ꞊ held back the torrents for one last embrace and the moment was captured in stone, so heated was it. Yet the shroud-bearers still came that night, terrible as always, and the noble אֱ־בִּן fell into fits, spitting his blood through lips still warm from caress in that final battle. By morning he was gone, taken into the dusk of Heaven. In this manner of opposites, as our wandering lord fell silent and his body grew cold, the world was left wiser in his wake. All who were righteous paid homage and remembered what good deeds he had done. There was much to fight for, much to lose. But what stories we could tell! And what light to tell them by! We endured the goodness of it, of that which is bliss. In brevity, we learned. We knew our place. What is it? That we are lords over our charges, the metal bending to our will, the cattle in our fields, the beasts scurrying beneath us, the shapes and colors of the earth, but the sky is supreme; the mountain is supreme; the sea is master; the soil of our bones is both mother and tomb. This dominion is what gives us breath. That is our place.

Intuition tugged the rope just then, lighting the flames of warning. From the edge of his mind, Edgar detected movement. He glanced back, terrified that this was the end that was merely prolonged—maybe he was already dead and dreaming.

"I'm ready for you this time, bug! Give it your best shot!" he challenged meanly. Edgar could just see the top of the thing. He grabbed the nearest tome and threatened the feathery creature, barely noticeable though it was.

"Bug, is it? A...bug. Very well, soft-sack. You understand me, at least..."

Edgar whimpered beneath the sound of the voice, fearing insanity once more. It simply could not have been possible.

"How sweet...you are...inside...it would not take much..." said the voice.

"Finish me, then! Let's go, fucker!!"

"I will not harm...calm...calm yourself...calm..."

Edgar began to feel very sleepy, but fought it away, disturbed by the dangerous holes forming, growing at his periphery. His vision was becoming tunneled. His eyelids were growing heavy. He backed into a table and a book fell with a loud thump, sending his blood pressure scrambling to the awareness centers of a simple, warm-blooded reactionary system. He was panicked. A blood-curdling cry escaped his quivering lips. Fragments of life appeared and then vanished in a stream. It was a fatal mistake. He felt foolish. With spasmodic, jerking movements, he moved about the circular library, hoping beyond hope.

The crimson insect appeared in flashes, itself cautious, not wanting to be squished by the panicked *soft-sack*.

"Please, let's talk," it somehow said. "I went through... trouble...for you to understand...waited...hours...days..."

"Hours; days," Edgar repeated, feeling like a mad hatter. "Sorry to have put you out."

"Just moments ago...a radiant cycle...you were cutting us down... indiscriminately with your...efficient tool of destruction..."

"Well, hey, buddy, you attacked us first!"

"So you think!" laughed the bug sickeningly, the pale mandibles clicking up and down. "We've been dealing with your...inconsideration for...more time than we have on this ball of dirt..."

"That's true, but...intelligent insects?! Really?!"

"I'm sure you would...like to..." struggled the insect.

"Jeez, who would have thought..." began Edgar.

"That we have feelings? We feel...very much..."

Thoughts wafted into Edgar's mind. "In battle, they teach us how to strip away the human element...by thinking of people in terms of...derogatory statements...offensive slang..."

"Bugs, you call us..."

"Bugs..." repeated Edgar sleepily. "Barbarians; Gooks; Krauts; Sand People ...Now, wait just a minute there! That's a fallacious comparison—*you're* not *human*! You can't..."

"But if the shoe fits..."

"How the hell did you know about *that*?! You don't even *wear shoes*!"

"I learn...very quickly," spoke the insect. "I'm what you call...genius...a whiz kid..."

"A whiz bug...then I really have gone insane..."

"Perhaps I overestimated... your mental capabilities. I thought you could handle this. Disappointing..." the bug finished, followed by clicking mandibles.

"Edgar—that's my identifier," he admitted once his stomach had settled.

"What...is an Edgar?"

"My name. They call me Edgar."

The feathery things on the creature moved as if underwater. "Names. A strange concept. There is no word in human languages for my...name...the closest approximation would smell rather distasteful, so I will choose...Sag-èn-tar. Yes, Sag-èn-tar is what you will call me."

"Sag-èn-tar. Very well," Edgar finalized, repeating the name. "So what is it you want? How in the hell am I even speaking to you?"

"Pheromones," this Sag-èn-tar explained coldly. "A language of wisps, of chemical trails."

"What?! From my neck?!" Edgar shrieked, feeling the odd pipes in the back of his neck for the first time. "How am I even still alive?!" Up until then, he had assumed that he was experiencing the soreness of the bite. "Have you...planted eggs in me?"

Wild clicking of the mandibles came from Sag-èn-tar. "That's just stupid. Well, no it isn't. I sedated you and savored your thoughts...very unsuspected, very promising...despite your...and gave you a little something...temporary abilities...to help you evolve into your new role."

"...My new role? What's my new role?" probed Edgar in terror.

The face of Sag-èn-tar was unsettling, as if watching an alien in a sci-fi movie in 3D. "Be happy that I didn't return you to the soils. Do you not want to know why I let you live?"

"Well, yes, as a matter of fact...I was wondering that. That's why I mentioned the egg thing-"

"-Feeling an itch? Well, you might, as an aftereffect. But more to the point: I detected some thoughts...from your brain...some very interesting...very...useful ... thoughts..."

"Yes, you've already mentioned that..." said Edgar, still very creeped out. He was speaking without moving his lips, and something in his upper backside was being passed out like gas—horribly unappealing even to think about.

"This food source that you've been collecting," began Sag-èn-tar again. "...for your betters...this disfigured seed...blocked from the path chosen for them...because of what? For the overbearing humans who consume far too much and give so little? ...for paranoid minds...soon you won't be able to sustain yourselves... things will disappear...a good time to be had at the expense of all else...and yet you feel for this fruit...you want freedom for it...you sense a foreboding...the...future..."

"I'm speaking to an insect..." Edgar said dreamily. He was leaning on the edge of the strange table.

"Your connections...this female just ahead of you, a predicament not unlike our own... We insects were Persians once, so to speak, destined for the Holy Land, a sick Biblical joke, you understand. They planted the eggs in freight bound for Egypt, but the American secret-keepers took the bait instead and intercepted, took us home with them, dissected us, studied our...anatomy... wanted to build their own super-bugs...to retaliate against something that had already been done. We escaped into this parched aquifer, and now here you are... Everything has purpose, and so I know that this was a sign. Your...father..."

"You know of my father?" Edgar proclaimed in alarm.

"Control of the weather, this is useful to our purpose. We...will free the storms...ride with the winds once more...for a time..."

"Now, that's a plan close to my own heart!" admitted Edgar. He rose from the table and, in his excitement, pushed off a heavy tome that fell on his foot. The pain went straight to his neck.

"Glad," Sag-èn-tar said, scurrying out of danger, "because you will play an active role...in our...mission. Your future...and our future...are multifariously intertwined. I am...intrigued by your family...your aunt and...uncle...and those mechanical insects...vehicles you call them...a show of...deep respect...very surprising...But, for now, read. Use your new skills, ambassador."

"Thank you, Sag-èn-tar." Edgar spoke using his pheromone tubes. He seated himself awkwardly on the table and read a book on plant intelligence.

The Very Next Radiant Cycle

Terrified of sleep, Edgar read throughout the night and into morning. The giant fire-worm-centipede-like-creature calling itself Sag-èn-tar reappeared eventually and told him that his presence was desired. An assembly had convened and the battle plans were being memorized and passed on to the others.

"I was fortunate once to have bitten into a Confucian..." Sag-èn-tar said, relaying his tale as they scurried out of the minaret.

The bug assembly was taking place at the surface. The place was crawling with big insects of the strangest kind, and they all seemed to hate him with a deep passion. They were extremely dangerous, and despite what had recently happened with his new title and everything, Edgar was terrified to witness so many chitin-armored beasts with mandibles and stingers at the ready. Full of deadly toxins, they were horrible to behold in zooming, ultra-realistic pictorials. He was able to identify them as thus: bombardier, blister beetle, mutant locust, mosquito, centipede, scorpion, Asian giant hornet, African killer bee, native green metallic bee, fire ant, carnivorous earwig, velvet worm. Together, they formed a confederation of monsters. It seemed a volatile alliance.

"You will take him with you; he will show you the way," ordered Sag-èn-tar from the rotating pulpit.

"Wait a minute, I know the way?" Edgar whispered from behind.

"Yes. The way is inside your head. It will come out, one way or the other." There were indecipherable mandible-clicking sounds from Sag-èn-tar. The audience eagerly followed suit and the entire dome echoed with the sound of clicking body parts.

"How will I get there? Do you want me to drive, or..."

"Do not be stupid. You will fly!" Sag-èn-tar said.

"Ah...fly. But, the baggage checks, and those strip searches..."

"You will fly first class...with us!!" Sag-èn-tar bellowed in wisps of pheromones. It grasped something on the floor of the pulpit and held up what appeared to be a pair of transparent wings.

Excited clicking noises erupted from the crowd.

"Certainly! I'm dead and dreaming anyway!" Edgar answered hysterically in his own language, with his own lips.

"This will only take a moment..." Sag-èn-tar said, leaping onto Edgar's shoulders.

Overtaken with queasiness, Edgar began to fall into a faint, but was soon surrounded by fuzzy orange hornets.

"They speak your language," Sag-èn-tar said as Edgar regained consciousness. "I taught them...using a translation of *The Book of the Thousand Nights and a Night*...Alf Laylah Wa Laylah...Doctor Steinhaeuser was good enough to have some of it memorized for us..."

"Will...will they sting me?" Edgar murmured in chemical trails. He rose sluggishly, noting with keen interest that something was protruding from his backside.

"I have told them to refrain from...stings..."

"Good to know."

"Feel fortunate. This...will be a glorious moment...for the both of us!"

The Swarm

The insects buzzed in like a plague, forming a dark, massive cloud of attack vehicles. Jolts of electricity zapped them from a faulty power structure just beyond the high territorial fences below the trickle of morning night, creating a torrent of charred gut and exoskeleton bug morsels. They joined birds, bats, squirrels, skunks and raccoons in a substantial open grave of decomposing barbeque meats.

Taking the lesson to heart in seconds, the surviving mass rose higher over the fortified fields of towers, balloons, zeppelins, and cannons in search of its targets. Edgar was somewhere in the upper middle of the mass, which made his part a lot easier. He really had no idea what was going on anyway, nor how the mass was getting directions from him. He had used his phone to access a digital map service on the internet, but was disappointed to learn that air traffic had no identifiable roads and highways. The directions given to him after typing in 'Great Michigan Basin' and then his father's work address (with difficulty due to the tiny keypad and poor lighting) were most unhelpful.

Additionally, his wing muscles were cramping up. Whatever the mechanism that Sag-èn-tar had attached to him without asking permission, the thing was unreliable and untested. Every little while, the wings would stop buzzing and he would drop right out of the sky. There was nothing that he could do other than to wait in the petrified falling position with arms and legs outstretched. And once he failed to assume his original position in the horde, which for any clumsy human being was inevitable, he would be threatened by some rotten stickler's mandibles. One poor sucker was bumped into a communications tower and died as a result. Curiously, the others seemed not to mind much and quickly regrouped.

Pulling the Night Shift

"Hey Rob?"

"...Yes, Roy."

"What do you think would happen if the government took control of the weather?" Roy was speaking into a remote headset that signaled through a wall-mounted videophone monitor situated on top of the control tower's gear box. Rob was in another control tower somewhere to the southwest.

"I'd have a green lawn?"

"But would it really work? I mean, what's to keep a senator from giving his mistress a little extra rainwater?"

"Senators wouldn't run it. Scientists would run it, sometimes probably interns," explained Rob.

"That wouldn't be so bad, if interns ran the place," Roy decided summarily.

"As long as they had never been lawyers," added Rob cynically.

"You'd have living trees in your yard," Roy said, feeling supportive of interns.

"Possibly."

"So...do you think they record these conversations?"

"…I hope so. I need a raise."

"Maybe they're just using us as guinea pigs; scientists tend to do that sort of thing," said Roy tiredly and with a hint of paranoia. "Don't know about you, but I wasn't exactly top of my class."

"This place isn't run by scientists. That's what I've been trying to tell you. It's run by business turds. The scientists in this sorry state of affairs just do what they're told. If something doesn't fit, they better damn well make it fit."

"Then I should be worried. Big Brother was a business, wasn't he? They like to spy on people. And if you get too smart on them, they feed you to the rats."

"I don't read books. Haven't read one since high school. But I can guarantee you that government spies on people. All of them do, that can afford it. They're scared of us."

"I listen to audio sometimes when I get bored…" Roy mused, looking off into the night.

"Are you sure Big Brother wasn't a government?" asked Rob. "Although, I guess, I do remember something concerning Ford…was Ford the president in that book?"

"It was hard to tell just in the audio," Roy said, trying to think back. "I guess maybe he was sort of both."

"Well, time to check the power grids and whatnot," Rob said with a sigh. "I wish I could get them to do something about my lawn…"

"Rob, hey Rob! —You still there? What is this I'm seeing?" said Roy from the northernmost control tower. "Is someone filming a movie?"

"…Yeah, I'm here Roy. A movie? Why do you say that?"

"Because they're on tight budgets; because they're to the point where they film things without asking; because the brass would refrain from telling us these things just to amuse themselves."

"What are you talking about, Roy?"

"Insects, scarabs, locusts, killer bees; hornets just glowing like frigging jellyfish…"

"Boy do you ever need a day off."

"Tell me about it. I get no sleep whatsoever. Can't sleep in the daylight, so I go online and play Realms of Wastecraft all day. Gotta get my rogue those epic daggers. Man, they're sweet-looking; there's dragon's claws built into the handle; they glow slightly UFO green."

"…You know, that just might be your problem."

"In the real world is where my trouble begins," explained Roy sleepily. "Role-playing fills in the gaping holes that this machinery called LIFE creates with dull and repetitious efficacy. There's rigid intolerance for the archaic in this rule-shackled modernity. When I go online, I can explore my dangerous side with like-minded people and jab away without actually causing any collateral damage. My life has purpose—albeit a virtual one. Reality doesn't allow me to do that."

"Wow, listen to you. Those audio books you listen to are really paying off."

"So should I report this cloud of, well, pretty damn large bugs to the brass upstairs?"

"I don't think that's such a good idea, Roy. They're probably just… Wait a minute…I got a red light in D Quadrant… Hold on while I check surveillance… My god, those really are some big friggin'…is something wrong with the digital focus? What the…this can't be right… I'm bypassing security to reboot my system… I'll be back online shortly…"

"…Rob?"

"…A weather tower just went down!! They took down a motherfucking tower!! I can't-I can't believe what I'm seeing!! The whole goddamn southern grid is in the red!!"

"Told you! Rob, what do we do?! Can we call the Air Force?!"

"Get the brass on videophone immediately! Let them see this shit for themselves!"

"I dunno how to integrate the surveillance cameras into my chat! Are they still working?! What do I say?!"

"Beg for your fucking job, Roy! This is the end!!"

Battling the Weather Control Stations

A mass of chitinous bodies with transparent wings each clairvoyantly in tune with the other and anticipating one another's actions moved through the darkening sky like a Biblical monster. And then there was Edgar, flying on wings not entirely his own. He wondered if he should really have even been helping them destroy the private property of the North American Weather Control Authority. It seemed seditious.

When the million bug march through the sky came upon something important, an instrument or piece of equipment, they would fly in as if they had suddenly become one massive creature and would either attack it outright or swarm the object's power source and furiously beat their wings until it grew hot.

No one will ever believe this shit, Edgar thought as he tried to keep from bumping into someone. It reminded him vaguely of close-quarters tactical marksmanship, only without the fear of being accidentally shot by the soldier next to him. There was a kind of mass consciousness. The feel was overpowering. He struggled with his army surplus uniform, which was wedged between the alien wings and his actual hide, to reach the side pocket holding his phone to pull it out in hopes of sneaking some footage of the battle. However, just then, a crew of hornets buzzed out, confronted him coldly, and herded him back into the swarm. Even though he could see nothing but buzzing insects, Edgar instinctively knew when a target was close because the swarm would communicate so precisely through elaborate dance and scent that the enemy would appear in the red of his mind.

"But thou, O fool, art full of zeal..." wafted in from one of the Asian giant hornets nearby. A fuzzy golden and dark brown with an orange-plated face, it chortled through the matching mandibles and dark teeth, clicking gurglingly.

"What's that?!" gusted Edgar angrily. He danced to show that he meant business.

In an unsettling show of independence from the swarm, the hornet suddenly lunged with violence of mandibles and pushed Edgar far to the right of their collective body.

Suddenly they came upon a large silvery zeppelin that was descending slowly from the clouds overhead. The swarm's right portion was too close and it tried to avoid the approaching boil of gas by cutting sharply downward, but instead Edgar and some of the others from the fringe found themselves pressed against the window of a floating cabin. Inside they could see scientists lounging about some living quarters and a bunch of equipment. They were very surprised by the ruckus.

Edgar was most surprised to notice that one of them was his own father, Alexander Weatherholt! It dawned on him suddenly that this floating cabin was in fact a research zeppelin. How many times had he pleaded for the chance to ascend with them only to receive a postcard? The real thing hurt more than the picture ever had. He let himself fall away, almost without care, as he soared towards the private earth below, dropping into the brown, drab city of sameness. It depressed him to see that things were coming to such a head. His own father, absent for so many years of his life, appearing through the monstrous eye of The Machine! It was like confronting demons and seeing in them an unexpected humanity. He struggled with the wings, forcing them open so that he could glide freely in hopes of climbing back up again. The zeppelin was still plainly in sight and had apparently turned on the alarm. Edgar wondered if they had spotted him, thinking the worst, that he had been tattooed, or had marked himself through the exposure, and that they would hunt him down with a vengeance upon his return to the north-central trellis. It was too late. He very well could not shed skin. With the wings working finally, as if the support muscles were suddenly his, he glided into a stable position and flew off with a heavy heart to rejoin the others.

Aboard Research Vessel Outward: A Scientific Perspective

Dr. Alexander Weatherholt would have argued that he, in fact, was the most surprised. What struck him was that he hadn't even thought of his son very much until he had come crashing into the window.

Roughly a half-hour before his complete mental lapse, they had been descending through the clouds. Tesla or HAARP[37] was the discussion, as to which one had the greater influence on today's North American Weather Control Authority branch of the National Oceanic and Atmospheric Administration. As far as Dr. Weatherholt was concerned, they could just as well blame futurist writer Alvin Toffler for spilling the beans as it were on intentionally-caused disasters that were made to appear natural using some kind of futuristic ray-guns. He failed to take conspiracy theories seriously, citing a departure from logic.

Dr. Greg Le Guin had been admiring a model of the entire American grid system, his tall frame slightly shadowing the Midwest. "Wireless energy transfer: A revolution in our time. I'd say that human folly has more to do with the inherent problems of a weather system reliant on satellites orbiting the earth," he had said. "What they did with HAARP was actually quite brilliant, until the military got involved. Who wants a missile defense system vulnerable to every volatile solar flare? That's just stupid."

"Now, boys, there's no need to fight," climate scientist Dr. Anne Blick had said, patting a bun of brunette hair with silver roots bundling up the sides of her prominent head. "Why argue such things anyway? It's superfluous. You're being cynical and I don't like it."

"I say the weather itself," Dr. Alexander Weatherholt had contradicted. "The wind doesn't give a crap about the living. Remember the hurricanes of two-thousand-five, ten, twelve, and fifteen; the tornadoes and monster storms of two-thousand-twelve and fourteen? Every year, the storms increased their destruction with unpredictable fury. How could we be expected to live under such conditions?"

"That's true," Dr. Le Guin had agreed. "The earth was becoming increasingly more violent; industry workers, consumers, potential voters, were dying by the thousands, and then the heroic

---

[37] Inventor and mechanical engineer Nikola Tesla; High Frequency Active Auroral Research Program, an ionospheric research program under joint funding by the US Navy, the US Air Force, the University of Alaska and the Defense Advanced Research Projects Agency (DARPA).

beings themselves began to fall victim, prompting the world's leaders to throw more money at it—this toying around with nature, neutralizing the lightning, cloud seeding, and the like. The people were as much behind it, despite the costs which most of them could ill afford. But why was it becoming so? What makes the Earth turn on us like that?"

"It's always been so, until now," Dr. Blick had admonished. "Now we have the upper hand."

"And this Weather Control of ours, it didn't stop the earthquakes," Le Guin had continued, oblivious to the boredom of his peers. "It doesn't stop the West Coast states from shedding a significant amount of weight, or the citizens of the Midwest from calling out to Jesus every time the ground liquefies harmlessly beneath them. And this planet—we know for a fact that things aren't exactly under control beneath the surface. No one wants to fund our research."

Dr. Blick had begun to interject with body jerks and awkward movements. "Earthquakes have dropped off significantly since the rise of anti-vibration technology. Our seismologists are finally getting a grip on tremors."

"Bullshit," interjected Le Guin. "They can't predict anything! They wouldn't know a tremor in bed!"

"Well, now..." moaned Blick. She rose in stiffness, pulling at her skirt, and then sat back down again with the coat smoothed out and repositioned.

Le Guin continued: "They'd do themselves credit by listening to the seismic orchestra by that musical genius from Germany. That's the earth speaking! Who's out there trying to decipher it? Not a soul! Not a one of us has the wisdom these days! You'd have better luck tossing the bones than listening to those poor fools. We simply don't know enough about our environment. We haven't been listening."

"I've listened enough to know that we're much better off today than we were in two-thousand-twelve," Weatherholt had said.

"Here, here!" toasted Blick, puffing her white laboratory-coated chest out in an attempt to obscure the subject with her awkwardly feminine charms.

A round of cognac glasses clinked, sounding like the beginnings of a dreadful song that luckily failed to materialize.

"Nineteen-ninety-four …a good year…" crooned Le Guin.

"I would have to agree…" said Weatherholt with a smirk.

They had glanced at the projected movement from a large videophone screen located in the rear conference area, a distant place drowning in computers and digital scientific instruments. All the way from Rio, Brazil, Professor Doliata Syspila and her research assistants collected data from the Missouri voyage to the clouds to ensure comprehensive conformity of the weather. They had had something to prove, as extensive acreage of grazing land and fields for sugar cane ethanol production that had once comprised the most diverse rainforest in the world was in need of the next generation's climatologists.

Suddenly the cabin had shook as something collided with the zeppelin, spilling precious cognac from 1994 like cholesterol-enriched blood from a severed artery.

Hands and faces followed the scene along the glass of separation. The images of entomological birds with darkly transparent wings, searching antennae, clicking mandibles, something strangely human, wisps of cloud, formed an insanely beautiful mosaic compared to the colorless and gray of a London fog. The fingerprints stayed in place like crusty frost.

"My God, that one looks like my son!" Dr. Weatherholt had murmured, the words screaming inside of his mind like green fire. The empty glass fell away and shattered. The window was smeared in drool.

"My son!"

The doctors looked at each other in joint insanity, feeling their brain matter pressing against the walls of despair, then retreated inward to that lonely room of high IQs and probability density and quickly resumed their occupation of making sense of the world.

Night Flight over Chicago

Somewhere over the city of Chicago, which illuminated the gloominess below like the heavens, like fireflies luring the termites into high-rise housing platters, the unfathomably large swarm of insects broke off into separate groups that widened into dissociate dark clouds of wind-current freeloaders. The night birds coming in for an easy meal were getting the fright of their lives, often being stung into a painful stupor of paralyzing muscle relaxants and falling back to more primitive, less wing-friendly spatial dynamics.

The home voyage was something of a letdown following the violent destruction of the heart and mind of the entire weather control center at Creve Coeur. The impact was so strong that tornadoes soon formed across the Midwest, knocking out power as they went. Edgar could almost hear the chairmen screaming in panic. What would they tell their stockholders? These arthropods, on the other hand, were indifferent. They merely did what they were told.

"Doesn't anyone want to celebrate?" Edgar said in pheromones emitted through the pipes in his upper back. *Tornadoes!* he thought in sudden empathy. Hopefully no one would be hurt.

Edgar was at first oblivious to the sudden disintegration of the army, feeling marvelous within the soothing westerly winds blowing into the north, and looking down with pleasure at the tenfold beauty of civilization in the wake of solar abandonment, glancing into windows of skyscrapers, wondering how it was that a metropolis looked so much better at night, as if an eminent salon turned neon after hours with the dissembled ghost of souls taking residence at an hourly rate. Seeing the lights from the scurrying metro reminded him of the Hungarian friends he used to visit there, taking the train from Grand Rapids. Once his coworkers at a resort hotel full of snotty golfers in cheesy attire, they had eloped to the Windy City in hopes of fulfilling their dreams (unfortunately, he had no idea whether or not they had become full or empty). Those were good times. The city had been devastated by the massive shrinkage of *Mishigami*[38], that great blue water, or so he had been told. But by

---

[38] The Ojibwe name for Lake Michigan

the looks of things there was still life in it; Chicago had not died of thirst.

As they flew out of the sleepless metropolis, Edgar could see the miles of muck stretching out from the beach, appearing to him like blackened gold-dust. This was when the horde began to split as if my osmosis, becoming two separate but unequal entities. The larger mass headed out over gold-dust, while the smaller one diverged to the east. Once it dawned on him that he was being escorted home by a hardened posse of fuzzy orange-headed giant Asian hornets with golden thoraxes and dark brownish-gray wings, he immediately began to feel concerned for his wellbeing. The homeward wind whistling like a gentle banshee in Edgar's ears made him wonder if he was missing something being said, an epic tale perhaps, of it was more akin to the safety warnings from a flight attendant.

"What do we do now?" he asked his captors in chemicals slightly paranoid. He looked from one brown compound eye to another for signs of emotion, detecting nothing but coldness from the dark brown antennae, the solid orange clypeus-face, mandible, and black teeth. "I say, *hamkar*[39], where are we off to now? Are we hitting another station?"

The insects remained unusually quiet for such a social gathering. They looked over only occasionally, grinning coldly at their charge.

As the divide widened, the world became evermore dark and brooding until the full mid-August moon escaped a small patch of cloud and smiled bewitchingly on her way to Chicago, revealing what someone on a broom once described as a mysterious shape, a dragon devouring a camel, or perhaps a leviathan transcendent of the ocean, glowing icily like the watchful emblems on Marduk's shield, keeping the Earthly things in order. Her borrowed light bathed the winged travelers in pale fire, acting as prophetess, and enriched their demonic voyage. In the outline ahead Edgar could detect the empty phantom shores comprising the state of Michigan; the thumb rising from the glove. A blue glow rose along the eastern

---

[39] Sumerian for "Fellow of the elite warrior class"

arc of periphery, adding a magical hue to their existence. Gradually, the shapes and shadows became more discernable.

"Okay, I think I can take it from here," Edgar communicated through the pheromones that still seeped through pipes in his upper back, just below his neck. The hornets were making him nervous. "So…what's the deal, friends? Beautiful night, isn't it?"

"…The soft one speaks…."

"Why wouldn't I? I can speak insect, you know. Sag-èn-tar is a great teacher… This is just the beginning of what's possible for us all… Humans and Hexapods can do great things together! With me as your ambassador, we can…we can…well…don't you think so?"

"We…don't think…"

"What d' ya mean? We just took down Weather Control headquarters! I mean, you guys were amazing! You took the man down! You did that!"

"Beelzzzzzzzebub…" laughed the hornets in unison, breaking out into wild mandible clicking.

"And…that's all you have to say?" Edgar looked among those closest, trying to penetrate the brown compoundable elements of their social consciousness.

"What would you like from us, *o lord*? Shall we tell you 'The Story of the city of Brass' and how the soft ones wept over their lost dominion? One last sensation before thou drink-est from the chalice of death?"

"Now, listen to reason… What would Sag-èn-tar think if you killed me?!"

"The time has come! Woe to thee, O Ja'far!!"

"What?! What's the meaning of this?!"

"Never mind, O Prince of the Faithful…this will hurt…a bit…"

Before Edgar knew what was happening, the oversized hornets were stripping off his pipes and the attached wings like Baghdad Ala-ed Dins in the silent blue hours, ripping them from his body with uncharacteristic precision and delicacy. There was a rush of pain, the colors like molten lava, red and blue, and he was falling, falling through the twilight air. An icy charge of wind wrestled with his weight, winning easily, and he tumbled effortlessly towards the magnetic nonluminous surface. At first it was impossible to tell sky from ground, but then he could see trees and what seemed to be a paint-splotch lake growing in size and color and losing the thick glossiness. As he drowned in untapped spirit of movement, Edgar contemplated his own abstractness. Was this eternity, he wondered. Was the fallacy of seeking eternity on earth being epitomized by the final seconds of the disintegrating man as he passed quickly through the elixir and into death, or was there truly nirvana in becoming one with this speedily approaching universe? Illumination exposed his indifference to the void and he was again unsure. Rather than falling, he was being suspended like a monstrance over an altar of endlessly fertile connections of landscape, shifting in and out of importance, at once before the grand spectacle, next lost within harmony. The sun was just coming up, penetrating his plight and bathing him in golden warmth. The show was breathtaking and moved Edgar as much as the next falling man, but there was no time to be thankful. Reality hit with a painful slap, swallowing him with cool liquidity. His breath was pushed out like a slap on a blower. He went down into the murky clarity until he touched the muck with his feet, feeling the panic of his starving heart as his ears popped, and launched off with a final ditch effort back to the flashing stars of unconsciousness.

He awoke on someone's rubberized dock, staring into elderly faces and whitened hair.

"Thank the stars, he's alive!" a woman said. A man was beside her. They appeared to be in their 70s, although it was difficult to tell. Peculiarly, they were both highly attractive for their age, or any age, for that matter (although, laboriously honey-dipped, stapled, and face-lifted), and seemed airbrushed, as if they were merely actors playing the part of old people and were not actually old themselves. Dragon-motif silk bathrobes covered a pair of silver bikinis; their shapes were impeccable.

"Don't thank them just yet," the man said. "Let's figure out who he is first. He might be a thief. Hwang, did we come up with anything?"

"Nothing, sir," said a muscular young Asian man who was wading in the lake near the dock.

"Thanks, Hwang," the elder man said. "You may as well come out of there. He's regained consciousness."

The young Asian man propelled himself onto the dock with his hands and dried with a towel. Wearing next to nothing, he strapped on a black shoulder harness with a sidearm and then put on a white dress shirt.

Edgar seemed to be lying at the foot of the dock. A thick white towel was underneath him. As he sat up to regain his bearings, the woman handed him a glass of chalky lavender fruit juice.

"Gad juice. Do yourself a favor; It's delicious," she said in a professional manner.

It seemed a first time for everything this morning, for as Edgar sipped the nectar of his labors for the very first time, he looked out at the large stone summer mansions twisting around the shore of a clear blue serpentine lake. There was a heavily wooded yard thick with large oak, spruce, hemlock, white cedar, and birch— although most others were covered in mulch and perennial shade gardens—and then a high stone wall topped with three layer-lines of electrically-charged barbed wire. Beyond even that, a hill of mixed forest rose like glacial residue. A sprawling golf course covered the other shore, and then a forested campground with a sandy beach. Private campers dotted it like a Seurat, an Island of La Grande Jatte populated by retired American conservatives. The day was pleasant and warm, although most days that summer probably had been, and was the kind a person wished for eternally. And then he was hit by an onset of pain.

"Hey, take it easy!" warned Hwang, kneeling down to help Edgar from falling over. "You got some nasty wounds there. Mrs. Gunnrson and I fixed you up. We fished you out of the lake. Otherwise you'd be at the bottom."

"Appreciate it," Edgar moaned sickeningly. He forced down another sip of gad juice, which was unexpectedly bitter with sweetened hints of betrayal.

A mob of elderly couples appeared suddenly from over the immaculate lawn near the shore to where Pink Pampas and Purple

Love Grass bordered a marble path to a large cottage and approached the wide rubberized dock.

"My gaawd!" they said.

"Would you just look at THAT!"

Once they had finally made it to the scene, they ogled over the strange merman with its shoulders and upper backside all bandaged up. The mob smelled like a pharmacy. Many of them were wearing pajamas and gowns, with a few in Hawaiian shirts and elastic pants.

"I'm still in Michigan, right?" Edgar moaned.

"Why wouldn't you be?" questioned the elder men's model (presumably, Mr. Gunnrson).

"My name is Edgar," began Edgar, "Edgar E. Weatherholt. I'm from Nenaa'angebi."

"Nenaa'angebi," repeated a pair of elders from the mob. "Isn't that in Wisconsin?"

Mr. Gunnrson continued: "For someone who's not a thief, you sure go out of your way to remain inconspicuous. Not even so much as a concealed weapons permit..."

"Gunnar, dear, that isn't very polite!" happily reprimanded Mrs. Gunnrson.

Mr. Gunnrson shrugged. "I'm curious why the chip in his hand has been removed, that's all, dear. What about it, Edgar? You prior service?"

"I was working for Gad Growers, until a few weeks ago... Semper Down Security needed a few able bodies...a classified mission...very surreptitiously hush hush, you understand..."

Mr. Gunnrson nodded vigorously. "And they took out your chip?"

"I don't know what happened to the chip," Edgar admitted. "I don't even know where I am."

"This is Dark Star Lake," Mr. Gunnrson said. "You're looking at Dark Star Lake Association. It's private, you understand. 'We Keep the Poor Fuckers Out!' That's our motto. Right, Nancy! Right Fred! Hah?!"

"That's right Gunnar!" shouted one of the old men from the mob.

The mob chortled.

"So..." explained Mrs. Gunnrson, "when we heard the splash..."

Edgar was terribly vexed. He had never even heard of Dark Star Lake. "You didn't...by chance...happen to..."

"Need to call someone?" offered Mr. Gunnrson.

Edgar nodded weakly. "If I'm not being arrested..."

"Oh, no no no!" said Mr. Gunnrson.

"No one's arresting you, dear!" Mrs. Gunnrson added. "We're just glad you're alright! You should have a doctor look at these wounds..."

"I'll do that," assured Edgar painfully.

Satisfied, Mr. Gunnrson handed the intruder another towel. "Semper Down works for Monstrosso, right? We could call them for you—put in an explanation. We're sort of their spokespeople. You might have seen our fruit juice commercials." Mister Gunnar Gunnrson laughed with masculine seriousness, pouring himself a glass of gad juice.

"Thanks. That isn't necessary," said Edgar painfully, struggling to sit up straight. "This isn't something they'll want anyone to know about. The best thing is for me to get back home and report in person. They'll know what to do."

"And where is home, exactly?"

"Gil, for now."

"Isn't that near Gamesh?" said one of the old men from the mob. "Those campers in Newaygo take a bus up that way, don't they?"

"Newaygo. Yes, you're right," Ralph, said Mr. Gunnrson. "We keep track of all the riff raff in our area. Newaygo's a hotspot for riff raff. Always was. Al Capone used to hang out there, or so I'm told."

"He used to hang out here, too," one of the neighbors reminded him, "along with some of his corporate associates."

"They helped him push the liquor and hide from the law, those scoundrels!" pitched in one of the neighbor women with dry venom.

"Capone once owned that old house where the Dark Star Lake Golf Course is, Gunnar," said Ralph.

"I'd like to see Capone try to get in here now!" laughed one of the other old men.

312

"Oh, but he had a lot of money..." one of the old women corrected.

Hwang and Mr. Gunnrson helped Edgar up from the lounge chair.

"Newaygo's the place for you, Edgar," Mr. Gunnrson said. "If you leave now, you'll probably catch them. We'll have Hwang drop you off."

"Certainly, I'd be happy to," said Hwang with calculated confidence.

Catching a Ride to Gil on the Green Bus

After an eerie ride in the back seat of a Cadillac Escalade, Edgar was dropped off at the Newaygo campground.

"Thanks, Hwang," Edgar said, hobbling away from the vehicle.

Hwang smiled and nodded. The dark Cadillac sped off.

"Hey, I know you!" someone from the campground said. It was the hillbilly woman, Norma-Jean. She was standing with her fiancé at the bus stop. "It's nice to catch the bus in daylight again. I can see people! I can even see my young-uns sleepin' away back at the tent!"

"And you don't gotta be careful not to sit on anyone," said the fiancé shyly.

"What's yer name, buddy?" asked Norma-Jean.

"Edgar," said Edgar. "We worked on the juice line together."

"Yep," Norma-Jean said. "We thought maybe you was dead. That's how it happens—people gets killed and they jus' don't want nobody to know! Slap! Erased! But that's not gonna happen to ol' Noah and Norma-Jean! We been thinkin' about migratin' South."

"We'll get down to Alabama next, I reckon, pickin' cotton," said Noah.

"But who knows when they'll let us go," continued Norma-Jean. "We got to work just so much, you see, or we don't get ta eat up on no food stamps. It ain't like the ole days."

"Gads been going a long time…don't seem to be lettin' up none." Noah mused before kicking a can into the grass.

"I know what you mean," said Edgar as he congregated into the so-called line (There were only ten or eleven people waiting).

Norma-Jean observed her sleeping brood in the distant tent before returning her attention to Edgar. "So…who's the fella in the Escalade? Is that your pa?"

"Not at all," began Edgar uncomfortably, but he was interrupted by the sudden arrival of a green bus that slid in to the camp on a cloud of dust. It stopped with a whine and a screech, holding itself together despite the abuse. The dust escaped in slow helplessness, but not without blinding everyone unfortunate enough to be waiting out the cause. The door opened with a squeak to reveal a black stairway. The driver reminded him of the one he had seen back in July at the scene of the accident. "Shit, it *is* the same one!" Edgar realized dismally.

"Get your hides in my ride, pronto!" shouted the driver. "Gotta get the pigs to market on time! Ha ha ha ha ha!!"

II

Finally, Just the Case They've Been Waiting For

A common white box amidst the bundle of daily mail entered the Gil Police Department on 8/17/2020 at exactly 2:30 PM. Everything else had been bills, complaints, death threats, and crude suggestions; however, the unsuspicious non-powdery box was a notable exception. It contained clues to a missing persons report and an item belonging to said female:

Dear Police,

I discovered a body while taking a walk in the desert. Please see that her parents are notified and that she gets a proper burial. I have enclosed an index card with the coordinates to her position and also the digital picture album found on her person. The batteries of course had to be replaced and the compartment cleaned. Many thanks.

[Signed] David Hernando

The Abandoned Train
Gil, MI 49637

Peach-faced Sheriff Kato read the note aloud for all to hear, concluding with the remark, "A crime has been committed within our jurisdiction: Thank the Buddha!"

The otherwise stagnant department was suddenly transformed into a vibrant think tank. Due to the understaffed department's failure to crack a petty theft incident at a local general store, anything other than missing persons and domestic violence disputes had to be turned over to a higher authority within law enforcement. These lesser crimes had unfortunately dropped to the barest minimum during a record lull. It was as if everyone had been too preoccupied. A lack of lawlessness in the community, coupled with a recent act of terrorism against the Monstrosso Corporation and all related assets (to include Gad Growers Incorporated and much of the surrounding county by contract obligation), had made

315

them easy targets for slovenliness and idle gadgetry. The contents of the box triggered a flow of blood into the department.

Sheriff Kato let his heavy boots drop from the empty desk. "Deputy Tucker, do we have a Missing Persons on one Lieutenant Forester? Check our files and report back to me."

"I'm on it," said Tucker, "but stay off the internet in case I need to check the Database. Your system takes up too much bandwidth."

"Ah," declared the sheriff. "Is that what makes it slow down like that?"

"What is it you do on there anyway?" inquired Tucker. "There's a record of everything you download on that thing you know."

"A record—as in *permanent*?" A look of alarm appeared on Sheriff Kato's long, thinly-bearded face.

The youthful strawberry-blond female deputy smirked as she continued to rifle through the meager Gil Police Department database. "Nope, we've got nothing on a Forester. We'll have to check with the FBI."

"Uh-uh. Don't be jumping ship just yet. Let's go investigate the crime scene first. I think we can solve this one ourselves... Don't you? I mean, it's about time, isn't it?"

"True enough, sheriff," said Tucker.

"Where's Walter? Is he picking on those skateboard kids again?"

Deputy Tucker nodded in the affirmative.

"Get him back here, pronto," said the sheriff. "I'll go home and get my dune buggy out of storage. I should be able to chain my brush trailer behind with a little tinkering."

"Is that even legal?" asked Tucker concernedly.

Sheriff Kato took on a statuesque air, holding his chest out almost to his gut. "We're stepping into new territory here, deputy. This is where humanity meets the quirks of nature. The laws of the dunes will have to step aside—if nothing else, then for Lieutenant Forester's sake."

"Okay. I guess we'll just track you down on GPS?"

"You can do that?"

"All thanks to that trendy microchip," Tucker said, tapping the fleshy part of her hand.

316

"Be nice if all our missing persons had one of those…" said the sheriff.

"Wouldn't it, though?" Deputy Tucker sat on her desk with one foot off the ground and finished her third cup of coffee for the day.

At the Scene of the Crime

The old Asian sheriff and his adolescent deputies lurched over a skeletal soldier half buried in sand. Not a one of them stood over five-feet-five inches tall.

Deputy Walter Quakenbush began snapping pictures with his smartphone.

"Okay," ordered the sheriff. "Tucker, Quakenbush, let's get this area taped off and we'll comb the scene for evidence. I want every grain of sand investigated; her entire remains gone over inch by inch. Did anyone bring the metal detector?"

"Better; I got us a ground-penetrating radar receiver," snorted short and stocky young Quakenbush.

"Where in the Sam Hell did you get something like that?" asked the sheriff.

"Bought it on eBay."

"Incredible," the sheriff said. "Do you know how to work that thing?"

Without answering, Quakenbush hustled over to where his mom was patiently waiting in her Subaru, pulled out the ground-penetrating radar receiver, and wheeled it back across the sand on a wheelbarrow.

"I've been doing some treasure hunting on the side—you know, since we're only seasonal part-time…" delivered Quakenbush finally, stopping to catch his breath.

"Nothing I can do about that. Blame that Bernake fellow."

"I know it, sheriff. We do what we can."

Sheriff Kato kneeled down with effort and sifted through the fine golden-white sand. He looked at the hourglass that his hand made as if it meant something, then observed their surroundings with the bareness of his eyes.

"Wut-wew!" whistled Deputy Tucker from just behind the corpse. "We've got identification records, undergarments and lipstick, even a live grenade!"

"Excellent work. Let's notify next of kin and see if they can ID the remains."

"Already done that," said Tucker excitedly. "Her parents live in Denver. I sent them a short visual and they're ready to confirm via telephonoscopic interface."

"Wow. I bet they were shocked to hear that," said the sheriff.

Tucker nodded and smiled. "I was also able to confirm her ID myself by uploading a femoral bone fragment sample into my phone using a medical application and checking it against online DNA records—I'm diabetic, and I do that to test my blood sugar levels."

"Wow. Anything else?"

"This bullet was lodged in the back of her vest armor," said Tucker. "With an old mystery detective app I got from an electronic book club, I was able to determine the murderer."

"...You did?" said Kato and Quakenbush in unison.

"Uh huh," acknowledged Tucker proudly.

"Ooh! What e-club is that, by chance?" inquired Quakenbush's mom, who had shuffled over the dunes to see how things were coming along.

Everyone crowded in to share the view of the phone's tiny interface.

"Hmmm, cool. I'll have to see if I can find that one," decided Quakenbush's mom.

"Not me," said the sheriff. "I hate technology... So, *why is it* that we couldn't solve the Late Night Talk Show Host Burglary?"

"They were wearing masks," answered young Quakenbush dryly.

"I see," said the sheriff. "Well, as much as I'd like to know who the murderer is, let's do this thing by the book and secure our case from the legal perspective. Not every gratification can be immediate, deputies. We need to be positive that everything checks

318

out. I'll get forensics on the phone. Can I, uh, borrow someone's phone?"

That Which is Seen and Unseen

"A what? What's a geniot?" Antiope asked, having surreptitiously answered the black market cellular phone that she had just recently received in the mail. It was the girls, calling her out of the blue, and at first she had misunderstood what they were saying. "A portmanteau using genius and idiot? Oh, I see..." she said, her feelings hurt, "and you've done *what*? *Magic*. That's nice, Natalie, but do you realize *where I am*? My life is in danger of becoming militarized and you brag about being a wizard... Oh? And how's Oona? Did she escape okay? She's-she's *pivotal*? I don't understand. Are you having *a relationship with her*?! No, you're not, but right now you'd like to jump her hot Irish bones? No, I had no idea it would be like that between you two. Oh, you're being flippant...I understand now... But is Oona alright? I hope I made a good decision in... Oh, *the Magic Mirror*! Yes, I remember. You did what? Is-is that Sheryl and Amira I hear screaming in the background? A magic mirror app for a tablet computer, you say. You mean...you've actually made my dream come true?! This is amazing!! When did you ever have time for *that*?! Oh, the Velvet Touch was closed down for a few weeks? I'm so sorry... Slow down, I can't understand you... I-I don't think they'll ever let me leave this place, at least, unless I agree to pledge myself to a singularly drab style of camouflage. You're coming *here*?! That's great, but, I don't know if they'll let me see anyone. I've been grounded. It doesn't matter if it's illegal or not. These people eat lawyers for breakfast. They've even got Supreme Court judges on their payroll ...a patent? I would be honored but no don't include me. Listen, keep this between us, okay? No, just until you actually receive the patent. I have an idea... no don't worry, I won't kill anyone... oh, you were kidding...well, I meant that I think I can make a prototype...of the mirror that is. With help from students. Hmmm? Oh, I know you don't need an actual mirror...but it's been in my head so long, you see, that I...even though I never expected it to... Just be ready with that patent. I'll take care of the rest."

Oh, and About that Trendy Microchip...

"I don't envy you right now," laughed Agent Mathews as he dragged Antiope along behind him. "Medical checkups are a bitch, especially when the dean sends forward a memorandum. They'll be reinserting that trendy microchip. And to think you almost got away with it."

"Doesn't matter; I'll just remove it again."

"With what? You think we'll just give you the tools? Nah-ah. Oh, and sorry about your little phone, here. Who you gonna call anyway, little Orphan Annie? Be putting this thing on ice for awhile."

"Whatever..."

"What, no sass? That's hardly like you. My good sense must be rubbing off, finally bringing you into the light. If only Eddie were here to see this."

"Oh I've *come to* alright. And I *will* have the tools, you ignoramus. I'm honorary treasurer of shop class."

"He's got the day off—at the gym, probably."

"You must feel so ineffectual without him."

John dragged the perpetrator in through the clinic door. The place smelled like antiseptic and rubbing alcohol. There were half a dozen people already waiting with e-readers full of magazines.

"Hello, sir. The Duck Lake account," John said. "Appointment for Miss Antiope Penuel."

"Right in here please," said the medical assistant.

The Z-Tech Magic Mirror Becomes Manifest

The work was spurious, imitation, yet forged in a new light, taking on an entirely new form. This fresh mechanical organism was a hybrid between two functions: communication and reflection; it was both tablet computer and mirror. The idea was that, using the telepresence technology portion, a connection could be made between the device and the person who may or may not be checking themselves out in the reflective surface. With the patent on the Magic Mirror app arriving fairly quickly due to a need for such things in the global market, she now held a contract with the fledgling company Dreams Unlimited of 851 Senior Haven Dr. Apt. 11, which would become null and void unless she could produce a prototype in sixty-days. Such a feat would have been impossible if not for some key things: 1) Seventeen years ago, Monstrosso's genetic engineers had messed up on a batch of fertility treatment used experimentally on a test-litter and had accidentally made a bunch of Alan Turings 2) The Academy was surprisingly well-equipped for the mass-production of such devices due to its mini-factory-style classrooms and the addition of an electronics laboratory 3) Most of the students were born for repetitive tasks and required little to no coercion in performing the extra work 4) Antiope was an expert student with a challenging problem to solve.

DUODECAPLET

I

Working during a Thunderstorm

As the season pressed on indefinitely, reaching towards autumn, the crew began to wonder if it would ever find an end. Furthermore, the weather had changed drastically overnight, going from a controlled, sustainable clarity to a turbulent, dark, and intractable torrent of rage.

Eric churned the tank with a deep-seeded nervousness as he looked beyond the soup towards the blackened sky. "That lightning freaks me the Hell out! I mean, I'm standing on metal!" He pointed to illustrate his precarious dilemma. "Metal. Metal. Metal..."

"I don't envy you, Eric," said Darlene from beneath her soggy raingear. She observed from a metal stool situated along the outdoors sorting belt.

Lightning flashed again, somewhere west of them, and briefly illuminated a desolate tower standing over the countryside.

A forklift charged in, clumsily dumping a tub of gads into the tank and splashing Eric as if with a wave from the ocean.

"Hey, watch it!" shouted Eric, hanging from the narrow, miniscule steps of the platform. He shook his yellow pant-legs and rubber boots to get the water out.

"Terry wouldn't of done that!" exclaimed Darlene. She was thinking how much of a shame it was that Terry had been injured and was having to sit this one out. Her social life had received a blow. Nancy had called in sick and she was having trouble getting used to working with Elsie and Norma-Jean. They had already missed a handful of leaves and probably a few sticks and stones.

"How many weeks do we have left?" Elsie asked Darlene, both of them soaking wet, like everyone on the pad that morning.

"I don't know the answer to that," Darlene said in a motherly tone.

"We're moving to Georgia at the end of the month," Elsie worried.

"Then move," said Darlene. "They'll find someone else. They got all the pickens."

"Plus those academy students," interposed Norma-Jean from the third stool down, "and them's good workers."

Darlene's face screwed up into a sour expression. "On second thought, don't move yet. I want someone I can talk to and who's not a damn quintuplet."

"That's just more to love," threw out Norma-Jean.

Darlene shook her head. "More to love hell they're all the same damn one."

A sopping wet gad came Darlene's way, having been lobbed by a humanoid hand, and then another, barely missing her rain-geared features.

"Eric!" Darlene yelled.

An entire handful came raining down like buckshot and pelted both Darlene and Elsie at once.

Darlene grabbed herself a handful from the assembly belt and returned the volley with such force that some of the gads became stuck to Eric's face. "Don't be gettin' Elsie involved you moron!" she shouted. "Her man 'll whoop you—and she's pregnant! Show respect!"

"Collateral damage! Sorry!" Eric shouted apologetically.

"I don't mind workin' this long," Norma-Jean said. "I got to, on account of state Welfare laws and all, but I sure as hell ain't gonna be here in winter, livin' in a tent besides."

"What you gonna do, then?" asked Darlene.

"We're prolly goin' Alabama way next, pickin' cotton. They put you up in shacks down in them parts, and it's warm."

"Wish I could do that," Darlene said. "I gotta house to hold on to."

"Where you at?" asked Elsie.

"Out in Mesick. Eric, here, lives out that way. So do Jim an' Nancy. Nancy's called in sick. She's tired of working here, I think."

The outside lit up suddenly, followed by a thunderous boom.

"First time I ever seen lightning!" shouted Elsie with a racing heart.

"Gettin' too close for comfort," said Darlene. "I sure wish they'd move us inside for awhile."

"Maybe we should tell someone," suggested Elsie. "How 'bout I go and tell the boss—what's his name again?"

"Don," answered Darlene.

"Oh, that's right," Elsie said, carefully getting up and holding her tight belly. She disappeared inside and eventually came back out with the juice & powder line supervisor/ inventor. As always, he was dressed neatly in his cleaned and pressed mechanic's outfit and perfectly-aligned GGI farmer's cap.

"Boy is that ever beautiful!" Don exclaimed excitedly. An electric arc had illuminated the sky, exploding into powerful white-hot veins. "That discharge! Where does it go? What a waste!"

"So can we go inside? It's making us nervous," Elsie probed miserably, trying to get through.

"Not every day you get to see lightning!" Don said with his eyes wide and transfixed. "Wish I'd known about this earlier... But it *is* dangerous, isn't it. Darn. Why don't you all come inside while I go talk it over with the administrators?"

Something just inside absorbed everyone's attention. The mechanical sorter buzzed at that very moment and the escalator stopped. Jim could be seen beyond the plastic strips, pointing at something from his high perch of yellow-painted steel sheets and rods atop the sabotaged assembly. Don rushed over to examine the problem and held up a dark stone which had mingled in with a chunk of leaves. "Gotta sort these things out..." he said, skipping off into the factory. "Don't break my baby!"

A Horse Named Galahad

Loe had the day off for once and he was sitting in his living room throne of taupe faux leather and waiting for some tea and it was raining. He was angry at Ellen and agitated over the poor sales from the stand. He said they should give it a patriotic name—"*American Sweets* or something like that."

"It already has a name: *Enchanted Creations*. That's the name I chose, and that's what it's called."

"Enchanted, huh? What's so enchanting about *this place*? Goddamn techno-wizards zapped all the enchantment out of this world. I remember-"

"And what about me?" Ellen teased. Loe said nothing and Ellen grew disheartened. "I said what about *me*, dear."

"What? Well, you got Mugaine MacAed to keep you company, all those romance novels about fair witches and warriors of the dead. And there's Gerty. Gerty's enough to fill anyone's conversation."

"You idiot. I meant that *I* was enchanting—remember me, the one who stood beside you when you recited your vows and when you made all those promises? You practically whispered them from a book of spells—judging your behavior today, you probably stole them from *Playboy!*"

"You should talk, you magazine philosopher! And how much is *that* costing us, by the way?"

"What the hell are you talking about?!"

"Fool ideas!"

"Loegaire Ulysses! Afraid your poor little housewife is getting bored? And who sleeps in your bed when you're on the road all those many days?"

"Ah, there it is! And so the poet drowns in a desert, after all," Loe said contemplatively, rubbing his absence of beard.

Ellen scoffed.

"The man of today suffers from lack of oxygen," Loe explained in a melancholic air. He stood with effort and haunted the empty fireplace. Stealing back at his Penelope with bright, thieving eyes, he continued: "The air on the road is toxic, full of exhalations that trees just won't touch, where there are any to be seen, and the company is cold and conceited. Better that I leave my brains strewn about the mantle, figuratively speaking, while I go out and kill who I may with a flame-red thunderbolt of a sales pitch. I'm dying out there…dying, Ellen Nellie Weatherholt-O' Caoindealbhain."

"And you think I'm not?" She said slowly, having fallen into her husband's morose chasm.

"What about *Enchanted Sweets* with a big American flag over it?"

"Put up a flag if you like, but the name remains the same."

"*American Sweets: Enchanted Creations?*"

"That just sounds like a sequel to a bad movie. The online store can be called *American Sweets*. How about that?"

"Are we still offline?"

"Afraid so."

"How much longer?"

"A week maybe," Ellen huffed. "The lines are down and the phone company refuses to fix them. They say that telephone lines are obsolete. We'll have to get a satellite dish, and it isn't cheap."

Loe remained silent, wrapping his head around it—these complexities of modern communication.

"There aren't any rich people out this way, you know, so they haven't laid anything down since Edison invented the light bulb. When was that?" she said to herself, thinking. "A century-and-a-half ago, probably."

"What's your brother doing?" asked Loe, falling lazily back into his chair. "Can't *he* fix it?"

"Edgar doesn't know anything about websites. He got a job over at Gamesh as a bug zapper."

"That's good… What *they* need bug zappers for? We're the ones need zappers."

"Did you think the beets would harvest themselves? You have no call to be criticizing him."

"Can't even sell all of last year's sugar, let alone this year's," Loe breathed with a sigh. "Anyway, what about that house of his? What's he doing with it if he's here all the time?"

"The bank's screwing him out of it; the credit-assassins demand compensation for intervals of time doing nothing."

"For what? They got their corpses—if you'll excuse a little morbid sarcasm. What more do they want?"

Ellen looked out the window from where the falling water had met a fork in the stream. The unfamiliar world outside was quenched with remorse. Bitterly, she replied, "They were expecting a money tree to grow over the graves. Instead they got ghosts in the form of a sassy little girl. They want the property because they think it's valuable. Next they'll be after our little Edina."

"That's absurd. It's nothing to them. Who do they think is going to buy it, some rich foreigner? So what's he doing? Where's he going to go?"

"Don't know. He's paying for Edina's invention—those Faraday clothes she came up with last month."

"What's he doing that for? We shouldn't be encouraging her."

"Why the hell not? It's her gift! It's what God wants her to do!"

"God gave us a fucking dried-up sugar beet farm with a mortgage and a goddamn car we can't even sell on account of the team of lawyers we'd need to prove that's its even street legal! I'm amazed the thing hasn't been impounded! The law's slipped and fallen unconscious, thank Brian Boru!"

Ellen pointed at the ceiling in reprimand. "That's Edina's and not yours to sell, even to keep us from the grave... And it's raining, if you couldn't tell..."

"How's she going to be able to keep it?" said Loe, calming himself with deep breaths. "We can't pay for college."

"She'll have to get herself a scholarship. She's pretty smart, you know."

"All she does is play with those goddamn dolls," Loe whispered harshly. "Edina needs to grow up, or else she'll be peddling sugar to pay for her diabetes, like the rest of us..."

"That little girl fixed the tractor, did you know that? She never once asked for help. How many children do you know who can fix tractors?"

"I'll believe it when I see it."

"You never notice the good things, only the bad."

"So why hasn't your brother conquered the walls of the great plain? I thought he was fighting for something."

328

"Don't even go there."

"...Edina really fixed the tractor?"

"Why don't you ask her?"

Ellen left the room to check on the laundry, among other things only remotely on her tired mind that morning. She wondered if Edina was even awake yet from her nap. The sound of thumps above the ceiling told her the answer. It worried her to think of the future. Americanism changed by the year. Flittering values, teetering sense of togetherness, lost sense of purpose, composed the collective song. Too little importance was placed on family and on helping each other with the little things. One often didn't know one's neighbors from Adam, unless they showed up on the crime registry. It was a strange and pathetic kind of ending for humanity. The moveable feast that was life rolled on through an emotionally apocalyptic landscape of visual confrontations and savage letdowns. Beheadings, injustice, destruction of dreams, clashed against value of life, exploitation of the workforce, and rampant, vampiric greed from just about everyone over the age of two.

A thunderous crash shook the homestead and the outside lit up for a moment and then flickered into blueness. Ellen wondered just what side the rains were on, thundering down like this in sudden Midwestern anger. They would saturate what had survived and what was not uprooted in the runoff. They traveled down into the stone and clay drainage gutters that eventually led to a creek and finally out to a basin where there must have existed a place where all the lost things gathered in piles of odd treasures and food for goblin-like mammals. In winter, the tiny angelic transparencies would glimmer into snowfall and the world would be a cold, slumbering brightness.

"O that awful deep down torrent[40]!" Ellen said, rubbing her hands and screwing up her face. The window was awash with obscure baptism and Noah's flood over the Dead Sea and she wondered if the flowers would survive. Would their bright martyred faces ever bloom again, and would the rose bushes wash out or have their roots gnawed upon by demons of the soil.

In the window Ellen's hair was going gray in areas around a

---

[40] A line from the James Joyce novel Ulysses, p. 783

woman's bun and she seemed to wear an old woman's pioneer dress with woolen sweater and shawl as if she had always been ancient and was born ancient and she imagined how she would look if she were very, very ancient and saggy and wrinkled. She had seen the way Edina sometimes had the fear in her pretty little face, which was itself almost of something long past born again into parts of her fresh existence and she wanted to tell Edina that away from mirrors and relatives and neighbors she felt as if she were still a child herself and was at the very least a child trapped in a woman's body. But these thoughts were sacrilegious somehow, as she saw herself in the glass. She had burned her own candles and no one else's which was up to God to say how they should suffer and how they should seek salvation and in what manner of aging and dying they should endure, lest they were starved or stabbed or shot or dead in an automobile or sunk in a ship or stillborn before they had ever had a chance to cry out. And it was God's will and God's love. But in the window where the deep down torrent was seen there was obscurely reflected an aged and aging Ellen. Time was once again flowing and had not stopped as it sometimes seemed. That revelation should have been something wonderful to her but it wasn't. Not with good, innocent people out there suffering for it. The sound of the rain on the roof was natural for once and yet it wasn't, and could not have been, by modern reckoning, but it was soothing and cleansing all the same and her joints and knuckles ached to no end.

Suddenly there built up a whistle like a crying infant monster and she waited a second to see if Loe would get it but she knew he wouldn't and he didn't so she ran with fury to calm the baby down and then poured the water over the bags of tea.

Loe appeared in the entryway and she let him have it.

"Why is it," she said, "that when you say you'll do something I end up doing it!!"

He looked at her crumpled there with his head protruding and he sighed and sat back down in his chair. There was a time when he would have gotten angry and said something like "Goddamit Ellen I built this life for us this damned imaginary middle class life and I just fixed the leak in the faucet and the handles on the drawers and moved the furniture so what else can I do I can't cook food let alone water you know that!" But here he was just frowning silently and hunched over and sad. He took his caffeinated tea without sugar or saccharin and mumbled incoherently.

"What?" she murmured, feeling sorrow for the both of them.

"Nothing. I'm sorry, that's all. Did we get a paper?"

"I suppose we got a paper but it's a sopping wet mess by now. Go out and get it if you want it."

"I don't want it. I just wanted to know if we'd gotten it."

"Would have gotten it myself if I didn't think I'd wash away with the fertilizer," Ellen prodded, but then changed the subject. "Gerty said Bill Hutchinson died."

"What about the goddamn fertilizer?"

"Just drink your tea, you old geezer."

Five miles. There had been a flash of lightning a hand's distance away, to where some oak tree had received a scar, and a radio concert of Mendelssohn's *Overture* had left listeners in static. She turned the old-fashioned dial to find the weather, but there was only a distant military chatter. Five.

She thought of her brother suddenly and saw him in her mind as if he had suffered a wound out there on some fool's errand and it reminded her of the time he had come in with those nasty hornet stings all over his body. It was amazing that he had lived through such a thing, being that he was only nine. Boys and their wounds, she thought to herself. Edgar had once nearly slit his entire leg open climbing a fence to retrieve a baseball. She remembered the very moment it happened. Mother was worried that Edgar would die from tetanus and so she went out to get some antiseptic without even thinking of taking him to see a doctor. Mother's absence revived them both with renewed energy. Feeling mischievous, Edgar and she had climbed into the attic while Mother was gone and had rifled through Father's old things. One thing in it made them both laugh. The thought of Father could still make them laugh, even when he was thousands of miles away. He had had this sketchbook. It had been elegant notes and drawings from his high school years and were for the most part futuristic things mixed with a certain primitivism and even old Westerns with comical notes on space travel and Arthurian myth and how something from the *Y Gododdin* reminded him of a horse named Galahad from a *Gunsmoke* episode that they had both later seen together on a rerun channel. Father loved the thought of the homestead fortress at the heart of untamed land and wanted to ionize it and exist there within that illusion of values and psyche and marry the homestead woman who was both strong and so very sensible and he desired to save her from the wild, mean, scruffy mountain man and to make her garden grow. He wrote it in such a way that it was difficult to tell if he was serious or not. This had not been the Father they knew from childhood. The Father of today, the betrayer, the abandoner, Alexander Wilhelm, Doctor of Choking the Weather, was not very fun at all. Serious, mechanical, with a deep, vague darkness within, he was a great mystery. The plastic version from his childhood had died in practicality, drowned in the sea of dreams; the highly imaginative, creative mind of youth had quickly turned to industrial science and all its dreary platitudes. No one knew what had been the cause. Yet, undoubtedly, revolution had been in the air for years. And on the other hand the establishment itself was in decline and even the Arthurian President Kennedy did not live up to the myth, which had quickly become a political tool. Politicians, as anyone knew, were devils in disguise and had dark auras. There were many pitfalls along the toll highway of self-identity, painful to confront, and the seeker was led on by telling signs, only to be left with a vast dangerous nothing. So why should she expect her daughter to turn out perfect given such conditions of modern society? Edina was doing very well at being herself.

Titanic vessels bulging with electric blood flashed erect like the pitchforks of angels, lighting the dreary depths. A wrathful thunder followed with gargantuan footsteps, delayed by time.

Wythfed. Wythfed she had counted, in Welsh, from the women's magazine. Eight miles. An eternal woman's distance away. An eternal bellyache. The nightmarish storm grew distant, but the stinging feelers kept on as if suctioned to her essence. It was good to feel. It drew away the dampness and the rains trickled on. Already, she could see the blossoms coming out on the roses for the first time in years.

II

The Schism

The second building was where Carlos worked and where David was about to meet up with him in that building's break room. It wasn't much different, except that there were booths instead of folding tables, and that the room was half as big. Also, there was no adjoining human resources office and no hallway to the executive suites. It was simply a break room.

The rain was falling outside and so David had gotten there early. Squishing around with drenched shoes, he studied the vending machines' contents and then picked out a place to sit near the windows so that he could see what the world looked like when it was wet. It seemed kind of happy despite the gloominess.

"So, you got the day off," said Carlos when he arrived at the booth after appearing through the threshold of industrial noise. Many others were appearing as well and the room was filling. "Go out for a smoke?" he said, without realizing that it was raining. He offered David one of the bottles of liquid nicotine that he had been withholding for up to a month now.

"You can have them," David said with a wave. "I've got this other stuff."

Carlos was offended. "Other stuff? You got a new supplier? Why would you cut me off?! You're my best friend!"

They glanced around the room to where an interest had developed in their conversation.

"This isn't a drug deal, Carlos. I got a new pipe, that's all. This one doesn't require liquid."

"Why didn't you get *me* one, you son of a bitch?" whispered Carlos.

"It was a gift. Look, I know you've been selling the nicotine."

Carlos looked flushed. "...I was going to tell you."

"You were never going to tell me. You thought I was too stupid to catch on. You even went the extra mile and ask that we be separated at our jobs."

"How did you know that? It isn't true."

"Your greed backfired. You drew the line this time."

"It's only temporary...I need the money. I have plans."

"Well, it doesn't matter now," David said. "We've gone our separate ways. Why didn't you just join the military?"

"Why didn't I...What?! Why didn't I?! We've been friends since elementary school! We ran the playgrounds together! We backed each other in all our fights! How can I join the military if you won't?!"

"Yes. We did that. We'll always have that. But remember the cigarette carton when we were twelve? You were skimming from the top even then. I never said nothing because we're friends; like brothers. Even now, I don't care about it. But if you really need to make a choice, it should be yours, not someone else's. And you can't expect to carry along any baggage. Some things have to be done alone. You're my hombre Carlos, but you're selfish and deceitful. How can you expect me to trust you?"

"I can't believe this..." spat Carlos. "You'd think we were married or something! You've become a sentimental woman! A whiny baby!"

"Watch what you say, dog!" David threatened.

Carlos threw out his hands to show that he meant peace. He was unused to an aggressive David. "You're pathetic," he whispered as he leaned over the table, trying to calm his friend. "I can give you your half. Better yet, we can both sell our supply and split the profits! How does that sound, brother?"

"You're not going to be seeing me for awhile," decided David. "I've started living in the train. I was going to ask you to join me, but I don't think I want you there. It wouldn't suit you, anyway."

"A train? What train? Say, what kind of chemicals are they putting on these fruits? Maybe you should see a doctor."

"Never mind. If you believe, you will see it."

Carlos took a fake hit on his cigarette. "You're crazy."

There was an awkward silence, the first between them in recent memory.

The others who had been listening commenced chatting and traditional Latin music played from a portable stereo, the beautiful voice that of a male tenor.

David said finally: "Tell me, Carlos; what would you do if I died out there?"

"Died where? What the fuck are you talking about?"

"The military. Would it satisfy you to know that I'm dead? Here's the scenario: I joined the Army because it was your choice and not mine, and because I felt like I would let you down if I chickened out. You talked me into it; I was lost—was weak both in mind and spirit—and failed to discover my own gravitas and independence. I was shaped not of my own hands. I was content with the money and because I was doing something, but inside I was miserable. A war came on and I died—I died in the war; even if I was not physically dead, it was the same. I was dead to myself."

"We *are* dead without money," Carlos pleaded angrily.

"We're dead if we're not happy."

"You're not making sense. I think you should see a doctor."

"My head is clear."

"I've got to get back to work. Take care, *traitor*."

III

Testing Their Windsocks

Today was the day, she realized. The letter had come late but had not expired. It read thus:

August 8, 2nd Year of Gad

Hello, dear lady of the marker gene. How are the students hanging? Do they still test their windsocks every Friday evening? I hope so, because I've arranged for a little surprise. An amazing project has emerged—involving your father no less! I have told you about him, haven't I? Either way, you will now: He's going to be in the evening news! Another reporter and I will be interviewing him for the subversive network OzTV (I'll be working freelance, though, of course). I visited your father in prison so that he could sign the release forms and he showed me the key to a tower he'd secretly been living in while performing his great work— don't ask me where he's been hiding it. Somehow he was able to purchase the property in a government auction and he wanted you to have it—every single one of you. He took the initiative and had the key duplicated using the prison's metallurgy tools, and on the eve of windsocks your father has arranged for the pigeons in his cell window to deliver them via airmail. How cool is that, huh? I really hope it works.

ZAA

p.s. Watch for them on the 21st.

A flock of students was gathered on the roof with the windsocks the class had made for Gamesh's Gad Capital Airport. There were thirty of them in all. The socks which they held up like kites had to be tested to ensure free movement when subjected to wind over 3 knots.

"Stay away from the edge, for God's sake!" warned Instructor Greg. He frantically ushered his intern toward the problem area, himself being deathly afraid of heights. Once the weathervane-type anemometer detected a 4 mph wind, he told the students to hold up their windsocks. Having already done so, those within earshot merely held them up higher.

Antiope, who had refused to take part, watched from the emergency stairwell in hopes that the pigeons had made their arduous journey. She longed to see them in flight, to arrive with such precise intelligence, and hoped they would refrain from eating any of the seeds which the dean had ordered put out in designated feeders (causing them to temporarily glow in the dark until they befouled an aerie bombardment of unhealthy florescent goop upon the earth). After the mandatory twenty-five minutes had passed, she strode around the flat part of the roof looking east for any sign. Alas, no airmail.

Results

With an ornate brass metalwork frame and large mirroring surface of a lovely bluish hue expertly copied from an antique design the likes of which were not seen in their modern world, the resulting product was spectacular and impressive, but would it actually work as designed?

"Yes, the Wi-Fi connection must be on at all times," Antiope explained to Jacob Zilpah, her brother.

"I don't understand. How will I know if it's on or not?" asked Jacob shyly.

"Use this laptop," Antiope explained. "Type in the telepresence number of each mirror and see if you get through."

"They're not just numbers; there are letters as well. And I don't see them anymore. Where did they go?"

"Never mind. I'll have to do it myself," Antiope said with an exhaustive sigh. "Just... go back to installing Wi-Fi. You're doing great!"

An unwanted person suddenly stormed into the Mini-Micro Lab with his hands flying and eyes full of pious bewilderment. He glanced from the video game addicts to the assemblers to the sparks flying cosmically from the metal welding section in the far corner where there emitted strange inhuman noises. It was Instructor Greg, who must have managed to unlock the door.

"What the devil is going on here?!" he demanded. "Who authorized this…this catastrophe?!"

"That would be me; I'm in charge," spoke Antiope nonchalantly, raising her right hand so that they could follow her voice. She continued calling each mirror's telepresence number on her laptop as she walked up and down the counter that was crowded full of beautiful brass computer-mirrors.

The intruder bumbled through the assemblage towards the petit young woman in the white laboratory overcoat who was holding a plum-colored laptop computer. "In charge of what?! *You* can't be in charge of anything!"

"And why is that, Greg?" said Antiope, addressing the speaker.

"Because you're a student!!"

"And part of being a student is learning how to take charge. Everything's running fine, Instructor Greg, sir."

Instructor Greg turned as if his legs were a spinning top and glared at his unhappy sidekick (who had safely stayed by the door), then spun back. "But…how… how is this possible?! Who's paying for this?"

"There's a partnership, you imbecile. Dreams Unlimited is matching all expenses under contract obligation to receive a fully-functioning prototype and the first one-hundred orders. It's been signed by Hodge, Hoffman, and Litchfield, whose authority supersedes your own by several hierarchical heads."

"You *couldn't* have gotten those signatures!" insisted Greg. "They must be forgeries! Scott, get the academy office on telepresence at once and see if you can get to the bottom of this! I'm going to shut this devilish little operation down…"

"Go ahead: you're the one who's going to get it if you interfere with business. I already got orders going to Monstrosso headquarters down in Creve Coeur. This thing is going to be super big."

Greg grappled at the objects closest to him for inspection, clumsily lifting one to his face. "What are these, mirrors?! What in the hell do they want with mirrors?!"

"These aren't just mirrors, Greg. They're computers."

"Something foul is afoot here…" mumbled Greg, turning the thing over. He put it back down with a metallic thud. "If I lose my job over this, so help me… Scott, why are you still here?! Hop to it! Get security over here, then jump on that telepresence call pronto, do you hear me?!"

"Yep, right away," wheezed Scott, who was nothing more than an unpaid student intern with connections. Scott skipped off down the hall with unenthusiastic sense of duty.

Instructor Greg, meanwhile, was growing in redness. He approached the mouthy little student with intent to kill, but then had to stop, clutching onto the nearest linoleum countertop for moral support.

This was Antiope's cue and she attacked with subtle blackmail. "It was alright for you to force us to make those depth finders a few months ago, which you then sold for an obscene profit. You pretended to send them off as gifts to valued Monstrosso customers, but they actually received the weathervane-type anemometers that we were cajoled into assembling the week before."

Greg swiped at the air. "Why you little… That's ridiculous! You can't prove any of that!"

"Of course I can prove it. I was the one printing out the sales receipts."

"You were? My god, you were, weren't you…" realized Greg, rushing back out into the hall and vanishing into shapes and colors. "Scott! Just a minute, Scott!!"

Antiope took a moment for victory and smiled into the mirror. Her form wavered for a micro-second and became preposterously beautiful, so beautiful that the processed image staring back from the metallic-blue ultra-real dominion of truth and fantasy intoxicated her for several seconds. Overwhelmed by her own apparent sovereignty over fairness, she began to weep with joy. "It works!" she announced adoringly. Her dangerous little creations were on the verge of sucking her in. The mirrors were superb, the ornate brass like the luminous banks of an impossibly blue lake of mystery. The Dreams Unlimited girls, her swan maidens of software, would have little trouble advertising them to an unsuspecting public. Only the filing of a patent kept Penuel Incorporated's engrossed workforce from catching a lifetime of fish in a single cast of the net. The thing seemed surefooted; although, even the patent office was well within Monstrosso's reach.

"Who's in charge of packaging?!" Antiope sang authoritatively into the noisome crowd of constructive partners.

Some looked over at her dumbly and others with annoyance, then continued working at the things which gave them pleasure.

"Packaging, where are my packagers? You? And who's my sticker man—woman, I mean. Sorry, Esther."

"No problem," said the woman who resembled her sister in appearance only.

Aside from the more-competent Esther, the others had gotten themselves wrapped up in box tape and shipping stickers. Antiope, who disbelieved in negative reinforcement in the work environment, bitingly handed off to them the twelve Magic Mirrors which had thus far passed her strenuous quality control test. Another twenty or so remained in the growing and expanding stream of countertop gadgets as the engrossed assemblers manned their battle stations. Antiope struggled to keep up with production, plugging the new ones into their sockets and disconnecting two others which had passed the test earlier but had been left in limbo due to the interruption. All things considered, the Magic Mirror was off to a great start.

Power-Outage

Everything went dark.

TREDECAPLET

I

Out-Processing

The room was windowless and soundproof, and if Edgar had passed out drunk and woken up at Suite 6878, he would have had no idea where in the world he was. Nameless agents in a black van with tinted windows had picked him up at his sister's house after a brief phone call and taken him first to a health clinic and then to an obscure office building along the Boardman River. He was at the very edge of downtown Gamesh, he surmised nervously. They had escorted him inside, through a metal detector and full-body scanner where sat four armed guards with cold dispositions, then up one floor on the elevator, past a lobby full of wide-eyed Italian mannequins, and into a silent office.

"Hey, what is this place?" Edgar asked just as the three agents were leaving.

"Meridian Fifty-Nine," said the one agent, smirking, "But that's just our way of having fun."

A cute medium white Pekingese sat on the leather carmine couch with its head against a pillow. As Edgar was drawn to the wall on this side of the office, something stirred from a mahogany desk slanting from the middle of the room and he glanced over just as the well-dressed man in the gray silken business suit ensemble cleared his throat and gestured towards the couch.

Edgar gulped and fretfully sat down opposite the dog.

Three people suddenly came in, a male and female security agent pair-off and a professional-looking woman in a feathery charcoal V-necked authority suit. A powerful smell wafted along the breeze of movement—very ambrosial and intoxicating.

"Hello, my name is Kiera," the woman said deferentially, forcing herself into the human social pleasantries.

Edgar shook her fingers and smiled respectfully. She certainly did not look like a Kiera to him, he thought cautiously— maybe more of a Jennifer. Her eyes were too dominant, a wide-open pool of darkness. A refined head of high-maintenance, brunette hair was pulling back her unwrinkled face, chilling her otherwise warm demeanor.

The agents, meanwhile, were busy setting up electronics equipment upon a marble-topped table that Edgar had not previously noticed. The potted ferns had hidden it.

Kiera magisterially occupied the only other chair, which had been placed a short distance before the couch, and smiled at Edgar with satisfaction. "Have a seat," she said, permitting him to relax once more. "This is all just procedure."

The cute little dog drew closer and sniffed Edgar's hand. Edgar patted the dog. A tiara-shaped nametag dangled from a thin pink collar, jangling like a bell. He could see that it read "Princess".

As Kiera situated herself further into the mahogany and black-leather-cushioned chair, crossing her legs harmoniously, a complex labyrinth of commands and verbal torture appeared through the slits of curtaining eyelids as if her mind was a projector. She was preparing for something important; was perhaps about to have Edgar for lunch.

The little white lapdog, on the other hand, had proven a clever plot device and was very friendly. Edgar returned his attention to Princess and used the moment to wisely glance at the man sitting behind the desk. The man was bald, Edgar noted, like a melon with a pale sheen of smoothness. He sat simply, with his hands folded before him on a black writing surface. His grin was creepy and a bit thin. Very little from that distance gave the man away, however, and Edgar was left with practically nothing to surmise.

"So, am I being interrogated?" he asked politely.

"Oh, not at all," Kiera enunciated. "Think of this as a service, a free psychological check-up."

"Who's paying for this? Semper Down?"

"You could say that."

"But I wouldn't believe it."

"Now, now," she said, "we need you to *trust us*. You performed a service and you've been compensated in accordance with your contract. There's no legal reason for you to lash out at your employer; however... In addition, we are prepared to... What you've witnessed in the past week may or may not have disturbed you. We're here to help you through your transition."

"I see." Edgar murmured hoarsely. His throat seemed to be having a convulsion. His upper backside was still acting up, giving him an assortment of weird problems, despite having healed up into a pair of volcanic scars.

A beep sounded from one of the machines. It was checking his voice for stress tones and must have hit upon something. The world had suddenly become extremely sensitive to originality. He supposed that his pupils and facial movements were also being scrutinized, but was unsure where the microphone was hidden— perhaps Princess' collar, he thought smugly.

"Let's talk about something else; you were deployed a few times..." said Kiera, pulling out some vanilla folders from her briefcase. "It says here you served a tour in Antioch. How did that go?"

"I was put in charge of troop morale; pulled my back out trying to reenact the siege. Very mountainous; beautiful country."

"And Timbuktu?"

"Without incident."

"And yet you had trouble getting a job when you returned."

"It was difficult, yes."

"And has anything changed your outlook?"

"A lot of things will change you: women, whiskey, yes, wars too..."

"Sounds like a country western song..."

Edgar smiled weakly.

Kiera continued: "You feel that you're entitled to some kind of break, that society has been cruel?"

"No, society isn't any crueler now than it was before. I think it's the people who have changed."

"How so?"

"They're mentally exhausted, overly emotional. They latch on to devices that trick them into wellsprings; onto media sociopaths who encourage them to despise logic. Consumerism, greed, makes monsters out of cash cows. They've become whiny babies, expecting perfection out of every dancing bear."

"This makes you angry?"

"It's sad, really, but who could blame them?" Edgar explained vaguely. "I mean, haven't we built this up for ourselves? Aren't we steering ourselves towards some kind of precipice, culturally speaking?"

"So your loyalties haven't changed."

"Why would they? Besides, I needed the money." Edgar's eyes widened on this last part and he cringed in hopes of feigning simplicity.

"And how do you *feel*?" Kiera asked him flatly.

"Fortunate," Edgar answered.

"Fortunate. How so?"

"Well, I fell into a lake—almost drowned."

"How did you fall; how does one fall into a lake?"

"It was dark. I didn't see it. I fell in."

"And you were on your way back from…"

"That's right. From within the Great Michigan Basin. I'm not supposed to say, but I think you know what I mean."

Kiera paused for a second and glanced over at the man behind the desk. The man nodded imperceptivity, allowing her to continue. "You left your platoon."

"We were attacked; we got separated. I was bitten and I passed out. When I awoke, no one was there. I had to get back on my own, and fast."

"Why didn't you call for help, tell your platoon that you were alright?"

"My gear had been stripped. I couldn't even find my phone."

"What happened to your phone?"

"No idea. It's probably still out there in the Basin."

"What if I told you that your phone has been found?"

"That would be nice."

"So you have indeed lost it?"

"Yes. I lost a lot of stuff out there. How are the others? I hope everyone made it out alright..."

"...Have you ever been to Creve Coeur?" she said suddenly, changing the subject.

"What? *That place*? ...Well, I lived there with my father...a few years actually, during high school...he works for the North American Weather Control Authority."

"I see... And if I told you that we have eyewitness testimony placing you outside of a weather balloon at around nine-thirty last night?"

Edgar bit his tongue. "You're joking, right? Is that even possible?"

Kiera pivoted gracefully in her chair to make eye contact with the tech agents.

"He's lying," they said coldly.

"It's just that...the insects..." Edgar stammered.

"The insects..." repeated Kiera probingly. She had pivoted back into a perfect posture, her pink lips puffing like a snail as she spoke.

Edgar was acutely aware of his blunder. He had fallen into their trap. No doubt, these people were experts at exposing the fallacies of human nature, forcing the information out like an exorcism. To what purpose, he wondered?

The queen inquisitor before him looked pleased, although she hid her feelings well. As she re-crossed her long legs, a sliver of humanity escaped and sailed for the couch. A slight trace of perspiration beneath see-through nylon stockings hinted that she had gone for a workout at the gym that morning. She had cleaned up nicely, smelling imperceptibly of orchids and yeast. But these things were unhelpful. He would have to probe his way out of the dark using whatever wits he could conjure.

"Kiera waited for an answer, her patience dwindling.

"Hallucinations, or maybe dreams..." explained Edgar rationally, "from the chemicals they deployed. I had visions of being carried there while I was unconscious."

Kiera looked at him cautiously. "Dreaming it isn't the same as doing it, I wouldn't think."

"No, obviously not.   But if my mind can't tell the difference…"

"I see your point," she relented, luring him within striking distance. "However, if you were *seen*, then it must be *true*."

"I don't understand how that's even possible," Edgar bluffed.   "I dreamed that I was being carried by insects—that's either true, or your eyewitnesses are schizophrenics.   I'm really leaning towards the latter."

"*Crazy people*," said Kiera in clinical sarcasm.

"Well, yeah. There isn't any other explanation. Is there?"

"Little elves, perhaps?"

The pair of agents unsuccessfully muffled an epidemic of laughter.

"I know how it sounds…but there it is," bluntly declared Edgar. "I can't explain it. You're the one who's certain I was down there. I haven't seen enough paranormal activity to put in my two cents worth, to be honest. I've heard of that happening to people though—some lady From Ohio drove down to South Carolina once to visit some relatives and then disappeared.   She turned up in Illinois just a few hours later: No car, no plane tickets, nothing. Didn't even have shoes."

Kiera's eyes shifted to a spot on the wall just behind Edgar and then she quickly regained eye contact.   "What if I told you…that one of the eyewitnesses was your father?"

"…I see! Ah hah!" exclaimed Edgar after a brief and uncomfortable pause, breaking out into a forced chortle. "You're pulling my leg! You probably don't have the phone either, then, huh? That's a bummer."

A stifling air of professionalism seized the room, reigning for a brief time until Princess jumped down from the couch and begged Kiera for a treat.

"Aw, would you look at that?" said Kiera, glancing over at the bald man again (he appeared to be smiling).

A shift in behavior occurred. The cute little dog seemed to release the enveloping paranoia that had ballooned between each of its human colleagues.

"I suppose…" Kiera diagnosed, "that…we'll just have to shelve that little X File for the time being."   She smiled professionally and shuffled some papers that were subsequently placed in a vanilla filing jacket. "Hmmm… There's just one final test before you go; lucky you." Certain that Edgar was still attentive, she carefully reached into her briefcase, grabbed something, and threw what appeared to be a giant cockroach at him. Edgar flinched, but was otherwise just merely surprised as the thing landed on the floor in front of him. Princess sniffed the artificial bug and began playing with it.

Edgar laughed, perhaps somewhat manically, and patted the dog again.

"What do you know? You passed!" Kiera said happily, sitting statuesque with perfect posture.

"Excellent work," grumbled the mysterious man behind the desk. He held up a white envelope, which the male tech agent retrieved and handed impassively over to Edgar.

Edgar was afraid to open it.

"You're free to go. But, tell me, what will you *do*?" said Kiera concernedly.

"I don't know," Edgar answered, thinking. "Comb the deserts for meteorites maybe. I need to build up some more capital before going off *too far*—despite my compensation, which certainly helps. Bank's got a lean on the old homestead that I was supposed to inherit."

"We would be happy to arrange something for you," encouraged Kiera. "Is there anything specific that you had in mind? The factory, perhaps?"

"I've grown weary of excessive noise. And the motion sickness…malaria pills, I suspect."

"Understandable. Well, there's the island mansion…" Miss Kiera glanced at the mysterious bald man questioningly, but he remained pokerfaced. "If you enjoy the outdoors, the orchards would be an exciting proposition for someone like you."

"I'll have to think about it. I get pretty bad allergies."

"The academy," she said happily, as if she had just solved a riddle. "I believe there may be something for you there. It's through an entirely different agency, but-"

The two tech agents laughed suddenly, very rudely, and were compelled to muffle themselves back into silence.

"I'm…very sorry…" said Kiera, pink with embarrassment.

"You'll have to excuse them. There's a bit of a rivalry, I'm afraid."

"Are there any teaching positions?" Edgar asked thoughtfully, amusing himself with the idea.

"They're looking to fill a spot in security: perfect for someone with a military background. Nothing else, though, that we're aware of."

"I'll take it." said Edgar.

II

A Break in the Case

The Gil Police Department, which was nothing more than a converted office building, was ecstatic on the morning of 9/3/2020 when they received the results of their crime-fighting efforts. Each of the three personnel read the contents of the large white envelope in turns, whistling with joy upon completion. The ownership of the bullet had been confirmed. They were looking for one Michael McFarrell, Congressman.

"See, I told you so," lauded Deputy Tucker.

"I already credited you for it," admitted Sheriff Kato. "Excellent work, deputies. The Foresters will be overjoyed all over again. Now, let's nab this scumbag and put him where he belongs."

"But he's a representative from Michigan's 4th district," said Quakenbush dryly. "Can we do that to a congressman?"

"He works for us, doesn't he?"

The Honored Guest

David had to hurry; it was almost 6:00 PM, which was when the fun would begin. He was to be the honored guest at a pizzeria. Reporters would be there from the Five and Dime News, and then the indictment would begin.

A white Subaru pulled up to the bus station and someone's mom said, "David Hernando. Are you David Hernando? I'm Deputy Quakenbush's mom."

David said yes and got in behind the deputy. He looked back at the train after they had left the gate and could see the reflection of the Subaru in the clean glass of two of the train's windows and then nothing but trees.

"So..." he said after they had ridden a few miles.

"Is this your first time in Gil?" asked the mom to break the ice.

"Yep—that is, yes, ma'am," David answered from the backseat. "I've seen a lot of countryside though."

"Well, there isn't much else to it, but we call it home," she said. The mother looked over at the son, Deputy Quakenbush, with affection, and the son smiled mannerly and looked out the window.

"Have any trouble locating the body?" David asked.

"No," said the deputy. "The directions were good."

David could think of nothing to say. He watched as they drove into the village of Gil and stopped at the quaint little pizzeria. There was little else except for a town hall, a small grocery store, and a gas station with a fishing bait vendor. The pizzeria was crowded and he suspected that a quarter of the population was probably there.

"There he is!" someone said. The crowd became jovial and chattered themselves into the occasion.

The Five and Dime news crew consisting of a lone woman named June Dickenson set up a camera on a tripod and placed the sound equipment and began interviewing him:

"I'm standing here with David Hernando, the hero of Gil, who first stumbled upon the body of Lieutenant Forester and subsequently notified the police, who in turn unraveled the mystery of the young woman's murder. Now, as we anticipate justice for the dead, forevermore an officer of the Civic Legion, slain upon our own beloved shore, I take a moment to speak with the one that made it all possible: David Hernando, how do you feel today, as you await the verdict of a federal indictment against Congressman McFarrell?"

"Yie yie yie..." David mumbled. June was a very hot month!

June blushed in abject embarrassment.

"That is, um..." David continued, regaining his footing over hot coals. *You've come a long way just to taste your own shoe*, he scolded himself.

"You're a migrant, is that right?" asked June.

"That's right. I work in the gad orchards."

"And how is it that you ended up out on the Sleeping Bear?" June probed. "It's closed, I believe..."

350

"I went out for a smoke and got lost…"

"Fortunate," remarked June snottily.

"I guess so."

June pressed, having received some rather acute instructions from her earpiece, "Is this at all what you expected, since first stumbling upon the body of Forester?"

"No, not at all," answered David nervously. "That's all I wanted, was for the skeleton's parents to be notified and for it to be properly buried."

"You refused the reward money offered by the parents: Was that a wise decision?" said June caustically.

"Um…I think so…" David said, having never been told of a reward.

"As if you couldn't *use* any!" chided June. "I know *I* sure could!"

June reared forward suddenly, losing her earpiece as if it was on fire. A muffled voice was heard screaming from the tiny speaker like an angry leprechaun. She motioned violently for David to continue.

He recited the story of how he was planning on making a graphic novel about a skeleton named Forester who rises from her unmarked grave and surfs the dunes in guardianship of nature. "And then one day the evil gringos come…"

"Isn't that nice," barked June stormily, taking on a patronizing tone. "Live from The Pizzeria, now, back to you, Scott."

———

NABC live coverage:

Federal Indictment of Congressman McFarrell

U. S. Attorney Freda Ludski from the halls of the Gerald R. Ford Federal Building in Grand Rapids, Michigan: "The indictment in this case alleges staggering misdeeds were committed as part of the defendant's job description and subsequent rise up the career ladder and that in doing so he engaged in warfare against the very country that he now serves and was born to exploit," she says. "It is our hope that this condemnation brings the victims' families one rung closer to justice. Oh! Oh! Careful not to slip…darn these wax floors…"

Inside Federal Court

TRANSCRIPT OF EVENTS (As David heard them):

U.S. ATTORNEY ROGER DIMLOCK: We of the United States Department of Justice, on behalf of the Gil Police Department, the family of the deceased, and the entire state of Michigan, accuse Congressman Michael McFarrell of the murder of Lieutenant Cheryl Dawn Forester.

CONGRESSMAN MCFARRELL: Who in the hell is Lieutenant Forester?

U.S. ATTORNEY FREDA LUDSKI: Lieutenant Cheryl Dawn Forester of the United States Civic Legion fought in the Water Wars of 2014 during the *Battle of the Sleeping Bear*. She died on September 23rd of that year from a wound to the heart made by an armor-piercing bullet fired from an RS-69's .50 Caliber machine gun. Now, you were also a participant in that battle, weren't you, Congressman McFarrell—as a Remote Hunter operator under the employment of Neruda Corporation? Did you not operate the RS-69 'Robotic Soldier' serial number KROM-37249-7, the one found to be responsible for Lieutenant Forester's death?

MCFARRELL: This is ridiculous. You can't charge me with murder. It was a war! We were shooting at each other. That's what you do in a war, you know!

DIMLOCK: Yes, we face many wars in our lives, many trials, many moral decisions, and sometimes we find ourselves on the wrong side, the side of darkness…

MCFARRELL: As a politician, I oppose abortive issues. That exempts me from all other moral aspects.

352

LUDSKI: Answer the question, McFarrell!! Were you or were you not an operator of the RS-69 in question!

MCFARRELL: But there were so many companies involved; many, many other employees. Most of them were not even American. Why pick on me? This is political, I know it!

LUDSKI: You were shooting with a robot from a remote location over the internet, to serve the vested interests of Neruda Corporation, were you not...to include September Twenty-third of Two-thousand-and-fourteen?

MCFARRELL: Now, hold on there! You don't have the right to that information!

DIMLOCK: Our records show that you were actually in your cubicle eating a sandwich when the shooting took place. You murdered a nineteen-year-old college student, in the line of duty for her country...between bites of turkey-on-rye!!

MCFARRELL: Hey, I was just doing my job! You're taking it all out of context! Remember the times in which this thing occurred. We were still in the fog of the Great Recession. I just barely got in that place; started there as an intern *pro bono*. Do you even know what it means to perform a real day's work?

LUDSKI: Yeah you were really working it, Congressman. Neruda Corporation managed to steal fifteen billion gallons from Lake Michigan that year in tanker vessels full of five-gallon jugs, which is enough to provide a week's worth of fresh water to the city of Chicago. This was largely due to the fact that ambitious employees — such as *yourself* — flew unmanned drones up and down the Michigan and Wisconsin coasts releasing clouds of digitoxin and infecting everyone with bird flu! They gave you a promotion, didn't they? You got a key to one of their bottling companies in Dubai, where you were general manager for the past five years.

MCFARRELL: What? I was employed with the municipal Chicago Department of Water Management.

DIMLOCK: Under a front company. Crib Giant, Inc. was awarded contracts through the influence of a few key senators. They don't exist! Neruda used that money to buy drones, war equipment, deadly chemicals, and illegal information into the whereabouts of certain citizens of this country. They used American tax dollars to kill American soldiers!

MCFARRELL: You can't prove anything! And might I remind you of whose shadow looms overhead. Best make sure you can swallow what you're biting off!

DIMLOCK: You disgust me, congressman!

MCFARRELL: So what?! It was all a blessing in disguise... Look at the Great Lakes now! If we hadn't stolen that water—I mean, allegedly stolen it—where would it be now?! The center of the Earth, that's where! Chicagoans are drinking their own pee right now just to survive! Does that sound like justice to you?!

LUDSKI: The Neruda Corporation is now considered a terrorist group, Congressman! They have been *outlawed* and each and every member will soon be brought to justice! You were a member of a militant terrorist organization that aggressively attacked members of the United States Armed Forces! That makes you an enemy of the people!

MCFARRELL: Hey, what is this?! Neruda Corporation was founded by Patriots! World War Two, remember that?! They saved this country from evil! You're trying to erase what those wonderful people have done! You're a couple of filthy revisionists! These are propagated lies...and in Federal court! Your Honor, *how could you?!*

LUDSKI: Your employer entrusted you to orchestrate the use of chemical and biological weapons against fellow Americans, killing thousands of innocent civilians and brave soldiers, not to mention the squirrels and birds! You did that, you murdered Lieutenant Forester and countless others in the dunes that year, and for that you received a big fat promotion! They even put you *inside*; you stand here before us a congressman, a representative of the Unites States government! That, sir, is a travesty!!

MCFARRELL: Now, just a minute! You can't say that about me! I have rights, damn you!

DIMLOCK: No, damn you, Congressman!!

Antiope v. the U.S. Military

"Have you considered a career with the Navy?" pitched the recruiter. The woman, a petty officer first class, sat rigid on her itchy white skirt.

"Not really," Antiope said, contemplating a break for the door of the small conference room, where she had gone on the promise that she would be given access to a new glassworks workshop.

"It's better than working in a factory, don't you think?"

From under the knitted cap, Antiope gave her an incredulous look. "What if I told you that I'd rather join the Civic Legion?"

"Serving your country in any capacity is a noble thing," the recruiter said, crossing her legs, "But the Navy would place you on a powerful big ship and set you on a cruise around the world. You'd be like a pirate. You do like pirates, right?"

Antiope giggled, becoming weary of the summer whites. "I'm pretty sure that you evaporate pirates with laser beams."

"No, not at all," said the recruiter, agitated that her spells were being buffed. "A sizeable number of Somali bandits in ships have been sent to Davy Jones' Locker by our Navy SEALs, that's true. But we would never attack a pirate of the Caribbean."

"And what would I be doing exactly, while on this powerful big ship?"

"Oh, there's a wide variety of jobs; for instance, you could become a laser beam technician."

"Or I could just peel a heck of a lot of potatoes..." Antiope volunteered with frankness. "This place isn't exactly known for meeting the high educational standards required for students to jump into advanced technologies."

"For someone like you, older and more intelligent than your peers—despite being still in high school—peeling potatoes shouldn't be an option... Well, the tests will determine your aptitude... I'd hate to limit your expectations based on appearances..."

"So you can tell that I'm older than seventeen…"

"I'm not at liberty to discuss that…age is so relative these days… But you'd be an asset to our family of sea snakes: The more women, the better!"

QUATTRODECAPLET

I

The Strangers

Morning arrived reluctantly, frothing with mist. The dew harbored fairies in the grass. They changed colors as one walked.

Loe was overdue for some hard labor. The road had softened his muscles; had led his pride into overwhelming battles. The network of traffic was the Appian Way of transport and trade by which battalions marched unto good people, squeezing them like turnips in hopes they might bleed coins. Traffic was the world trampling quaint farmlands underfoot. Loe had been a merchant highwayman putting the sword to small business; however, they were not easily intimidated. It painted for him a dark and petty future of trading sugar for sand. There was futility in his wake, anger in his walk. Would the Fortriu ever again storm against the Legions, while the islanded Mercian Kings allied with the Marcher Lords to trample progress underfoot? History had a frightening disposition, was perhaps sociopathic (which explained its obsession with sociopaths). The contiguous events overlapped, repeated, and overwhelmed. For the farmer there was nothing but the soil.

A noise startled him. There was sharp movement by the barn, a slumped human shape. Loe ran back in to get the shotgun, scaring Ellen half to death. "Trespassers," he told her, quickly vanishing as the screen door slammed.

Edgar rose from the breakfast table and followed sluggishly, grabbing a blueberry muffin and the pair of binoculars from the counter. The shotgun exploded and he was just able to focus on a man's backside as he ran into the sweet corn. An additional person had made his way to the woods beyond the stalks and was crunching awkwardly into the thicket of turning leaves and towards the road where awaited a white service van.

"Were they auto men, you think?" asked Edgar, who had already made it to the barn—he was feeling much more alert and seemed to be able to visualize the exact placement of the trespassers even though they were no longer within sight.

"Possibly..." murmured Loe, awakened to the dangers of even the quaintest places in their modern world. "I don't like the idea of heading off again without knowing if Ellen and Edina are safe. I'll take a day off after harvest."

"That was good timing," Edgar said.

"Can't say that they're the best I've ever seen, but thanks..." said Loe quietly, going over the fields with widening eyes, "thanks for putting the work in. They'll do. So, are we ready to do this?"

"Ready as I'll ever be."

Loe prepped the tractor, checking Edina's repair work with unexpected satisfaction, while Edgar checked the truck to be sure that it would start. Loe knew the procedure well: A roto beater would chop the leaf and crown from the root, and then the beet harvester would pull them up and dump them into the truck to be delivered to a processing plant in Sebewaing. After a long and tiresome day or two, the meager autumn yield would be reaped and prepared for sugar extraction. The equipment alone barely made farming profitable, which was why Loe worked for the Michigan Sugar Company as a salesman, but the old way, with a team of horses and a large, resilient crew, would have been far more labor-intensive, possibly resulting in "root madness" through one definition or another. Despite the obsoleteness and the inevitable troubles, the old ways seemed better somehow.

Meanwhile, Edgar started the old farm truck with the rickety wooden gates enforced with Damascus steel and puttered to the edge of the fields. *How about that*, he thought, wondering about Loe's detachment from recent events. What had occurred was criminal and potentially dangerous. The industry people had been consistent, it was true, but had been drifting off in waves of lower frequencies over the years—until now. Why, he wondered. And what could their victims do about it? Why did the industry hound them so? Had they run out of ideas?

"Whoopti-doodle-dooo! Whoopti-doodle-dooo!" was declared from an upstairs window of the house: Edina's idea of a rooster-alarm clock, wakening her for some odd regiment that she had in store for herself, as she was wont to administer as of late—a sure sign of a banished childhood, sadly and unfortunately.

The first bunch was dumped into the truck as Edgar sat idly and continued to ease the convolution of his thoughts so as to diminish the anger he still suffered at the remembrance of the two trespassers whose agenda he could easily surmise out of experience. *"How dare they?!"* he hissed both internally and through wounds of mouth and backside. The bastards; it was their own fault. How many innovations had they let slip through their softening fingers out of fear of lost profits? Innovations were bad for business; they required a vast shift in resources and personnel. And then of course the consumer would have to become acclimated, would need to find a use for it or at least believe in the value of junk. The best product was compulsory and recurring. It should be as indispensable as a daily glass of gad juice. Advertising was the tool; the devil's greatest weapon was not a pitchfork but a marketing agency. Obviously, greed was the propellant. The fate of the world was made buoyant out of greed; the people scurried virtually back and forth, spending many daily hours in virtual places only to return exhausted to lives unreal — the Unreal City, as T.S. Eliot had called London after the war, was an appeal for people to unearth dead gods, to reinterpret the archaic in the present, and, as an outcome, to live authentic lives. The primal was now a common emotional response, every ancient and burgeoning society a spiritual nightmare, a dirty cycle of haves and have-nots, as the entire swath of humanity was Unreal, rootless and hollow, haunted, heavy in shifting sands. But the work brought on the blood while the tractor did all of the digging, causing a damned lake to swell at the buttocks. The seat cushion was at least somewhat sympathetic.

To the Vanquished

"Woe is me," David complained as he sorted through the thank-you letters that had poured in during the week.

Would have sent you a dollar, but seeing as you have no use for money... read the next letter. He had read nearly a million with such statements. *I should reveal the truth,* he thought unhappily, *but to respond to nearly a million letters...I could never afford the postage!*

The television whined of its own accord as it sat on the burgundy seat of a compartment. David attended to the holographic images, switching channels intermittently, as he read more letters.

CBC B.S.:

"Dodgin' When I Shoulda Been Joinin'"

Draft dodger John Whales becomes "war hero" years since The Vietnam War, joining the Marines at age 69.

"Far out..." he says.

NABC NEWS:

"Monstrosso Lobbyist for Growth Hormone Dies of Breast Cancer", says news
correspondent John Johnson. "Her dying words: 'Monstrosso be damned!'"

OZ TV EXCLUSIVE:

"He is Sigmund Vilbaste"

Button-Bright and Zech Adam Adams reporting:

"Ex-Monstrosso scientist and Nobel runner-up, Dr. Sigmund Vilbaste, was recently admitted to Michigan State Penitentiary without a trial before being transferred to a top secret island prison just off the coast of New Hampshire.

His entire life in brief:

"Sigmund is born on February 29, 1964 in Branson, Missouri.

"The grandson of an escaped WWII prisoner of war from Estonia, Sigmund grows up in the Ozark Mountains, shows early signs of isolation and genius. A natural green thumb, to the joy of his mother, he models himself after local legend George Washington Carver. Like Carver, he believes that plants possess a soul. He writes in his childhood journal (on file at the CIA database) the same quote which often decorates his wall:

> 'When I touch that flower, I am touching infinity. It existed long before there were human beings on this earth and will continue to exist for millions of years to come. Through the flower, I talk to the Infinite, which is only a silent force. This is not a physical contact. It is not in the earthquake, wind or fire. It is in the invisible world. It is that still small voice that calls up the fairies.'
> — G. W. Carver, the Wizard of Tuskegee

"Summer 1976: Sigmund's father, Eduard, bitten by cottonmouth pit viper snake while hiking the Osage River with his family; shrugs it off; dies.

"Sigmund drinks cough syrup and contemplates his existence.

"August 1981: Sigmund admitted to Iowa State University. His disappointment is reflected in his verse: "Everyone in botany wants to bend nature to their will, but, like us, it wants to be free."

"May 13, 1982: He holds dear the following news clipping:

> "After 211 days in orbit one cosmonaut says, 'They are simply essential to man in space. Back on Earth I had never loved tinkering in the garden. But onboard the space station it was as if I woke up all of a sudden...a tiny leaf opened up and it seemed to fling open a bright window out into the world.'

[1982: Monstrosso scientists become the first to genetically modify a plant cell]

"April 1985: Sigmund gets a job briefly at university, but leaves to work for a genetics company preventing root rot.

[1987: Monstrosso conducts first field tests for genetically engineered crops.]

"November 2, 1992: The company that Sigmund works for is absorbed by Monstrosso; becomes one of many satellites orbiting dead weight.

"Sigmund is unhappy about the new direction the company is heading: the way of the Genetically Modified Organism. His new job is to produce freaks of nature for garden savvy Americans.

"1995-1999 Sigmund is lured by the company into being a sperm donor because he is a loner (one of the qualities they were looking for early on, before realizing that the offspring of loners would probably cause them a few serious problems down the line). Sigmund apparently had no idea the fertility clinic was associated with Monstrosso because that research department was being operated under a different name. In self-addressed emails he chides himself for being naïve, says the others tease him and call him 'Rocks'.

1996: "Monstrosso heads re-christen the satellite company, which they now call Kick It Root Down[!], Inc., in hopes of cashing in on a new craze in music (called 'grunge' by Industry insiders, which is what the Monstrosso execs insist the new name represents, despite an obvious reference to alternative hip hop).

"1997- 2013: Corporate black holes and supernovas battle it out; a new global star emerges from the materials.

[2000: Monstrosso ceases to exist]

[2002: the 'New Monstrosso' is born]

"2005: Sigmund is cajoled into joining a pet project of current CEO Benjamin Grant to squeeze the life force out of many cross-hybridizations into one plant in anticipation of creating a new superfruit (In Sigmund's own words: "…to force the seed from many parts into the one disastrous and dependent whole…").
The project is a failure.

[2008: Protests erupt in Germany over patents for breeding techniques in pigs. Monstrosso blames "unfounded rumors and allegations that our patents apply to the breeding of *all pigs*."]

"December 25, 2008: Sigmund is angry over the theft of a sacred tree from a Carthusian monastery in southeastern France by international criminals in the pocket of Monstrosso, an act which he deems not only illegal but sacrilegious. He's further angered by the way in which Monstrosso demands that he alter the plant by smothering its natural defense urges and making its more unique qualities dormant.

"2010: A year later, they patent the plant under the name Gad.

"February 2011: Sigmund is increasingly more depressed and turns to drinking Kräuterlikör, which he bitterly refers to as 'Teutonic Plague' (ex. 'The Teutonic Plague is still way better than straight Red 40.')

"May 2011: The final straw is when he discovers by way of a fertility clinic fax machine blunder accidentally forwarded to his modem that he has over a hundred children, now roughly in their teens. The concluding remarks: '…it has become genetically imprudent for us to continue using Dr. Sigmund Vilbaste as a sperm donor…' He looks deeply into the matter and discovers something sinister: secret government contracts; cryptic correspondence with the CIA and the new owner of their German pig patent, Newham Genetics; a chain of private academies strangely linked to factories; one academy in particular is linked to Gads and a factory in Gil,

Michigan. If they had done similar things to pigs in Germany, he didn't put it past them to apply their technology to humans worldwide.

"Late May 2011: Sigmund naively thinks he can express this disappointment to his superiors without repercussion. They fire him on the spot; have him escorted off the property and tossed into the street (they forget that Sigmund often takes his work home with him; He still has quite a number of the original gad seeds stored away at his apartment).

"March-September 2012: Sigmund devises a plan in which he will attempt to return gads to their original form through further genetic manipulation and hybridization with agricultural cultivars already planted in orchards worldwide. Meanwhile, he grows the original seeds in captivity; ships some of his saplings to a certain monastery in France.

"October 2012: Monstrosso sues him over patent rights, even though he was the one who accomplished the results of the patent, but he wins the lawsuit by uncovering bribery.

"Sigmund's life is threatened. Hired goons ransack his place, but he escapes with the seeds and moves to the wilderness; sets up a secret lab in an abandoned Air Force tower.

"2012-2020: Sigmund vows revenge. He designs and integrates the natural defense urges back into the gad plant using a method he refers to as FRANKENGRAFT and secretly plants them in the orchards at night. The pollen from his rogue blossoms infect random trees in the orchards and cause them to develop advanced innovations to their previously latent defense mechanisms. They don the nickname 'Frankenfruit' from Monstrosso farmers and execs.

"Henceforth the farmer has a future of continuously fighting his trees for the harvest of fruit.

"August 2020: After eight years of success, living in the nearby deserted Air Force tower like a green wizard of vegetables, Sigmund Vilbaste is arrested and charged with agricultural terrorism. His trial is set and then mysteriously cancelled. He serves the first few weeks of a non-existent sentence.

"In the visitation cell within a top secret federal prison so secret that even to whisper the name would result in the resignation of several 'top people', on a tiny island just off the coast of New Hampshire, Dr. Sigmund Vilbaste says, 'I didn't expect it to reach the point when my trees would murder people. No one was supposed to get hurt at all. I just wanted them to shut it down; to abandon the project; to stick with the God-given fruit that we're blessed with in abundance here on Earth. There's no good reason for such blatant disrespect of nature. All life is a gift. But they didn't shut it down, even as the bodies piled up. That signals to my mind a certain level of psychosis; this is about more than just a quest for the perfect fruit, to become the main ingredient for some kind of magical elixir alleged to prolong death and free us from consequences, or for any benefit to humanity, great or small. You're not even dealing with a normal corporation: they don't simply want money or to corner a market; their deepest desire is control! Monstrosso is Satan itself, its mother the Queen of the Underworld. Like a primal beast, they crouch in wait over their vault of seed. Next it will be you, *and your little dog, too*—get me? They want the entire scope of life to be their scepter! The people must rise up and stop this thing before it's too late. They are eternal damnation! The truth is in the mission statement, in the Sumerian proverb written on the wall of their precious headquarters building. They offer nothing less than genetic submission. But don't think to destroy them. What's needed is an evolution in thinking. We have to outthink them.'

[The camera travels into Monstrosso Headquarters in Creve Coeur, Missouri, buzzing around like a fly, and lands on the glass doors at the main entrance. There on the wall is the proverb in question, which reads in bold 3D:

"From sunrise 'til sunset, may the name of Grain be praised. People should submit to the yoke of Grain. Whoever

366

has silver, whoever has jewels, whoever has cattle, whoever has sheep shall take a seat at the gate of whoever has grain, and pass his time there[41]."]

"In conclusion, we ask that you please help in the exoneration of Dr. Vilbaste and the return of justice to our flattened democracy. Please contact us through the following website: www.free_the_green_wizard.org."

———

"Well, isn't *that* interesting…" David murmured, surprised to have been enlightened for once.

Then, suddenly, the screen went blank.

---

[41] Black, J.A., Cunningham, G., Fluckiger-Hawker, E, Robson, E., and Zólyomi, G., The Electronic Text Corpus of Sumerian Literature, Oxford 1998 (http://www-etcsl.orient.ox.ac.uk/)

III

The Illusion of Freedom in Captivity

The Eye of Providence looked down suspiciously at the lady on the bicycle. Antiope sneered and made her way around the gold brick walls of the academy to where a Japanese garden thrived peacefully from just beyond the lawn. She stopped in the middle of an arching bridge and looked down thoughtfully. Copper flashes swam about the water on streamlined fins. The lilies were like scented candles. The manmade creek was heated, she knew, due to a solar thermal device. But the wonderment was all in the fish: they glowed in the dark. They were not glowing currently, but at night they would seem like fairies to anyone who could see them, flying within their underwater realm in green, orange, and red fluorescence. The students were especially attracted to the glowing lights, although there existed plenty of glow-in-the-dark Angel Trumpets and Dwarf Fruit Cocktail trees spread out along the grounds to keep them from getting fixated on carp and drowning themselves out of curiosity. The extra luminance was pretty; it seemed an awfully bad idea in the long run though. The entire planet would probably be glowing eventually. Antiope had little faith in her kind to perform contrarily. With nothing fertile or potent enough to sustain life after all the foolish genetic modification, the results would cancel themselves out and haunt the place like a graveyard sphere of ghostly fluorescence. *Oops...* the tombstone would read.

Because a tracking device had been repositioned just under the skin of her right hand, the academy was willing to allow Antiope more freedom (much to the chagrin of the ExTemplar security agents); however, she was forbidden to leave the property without an escort. Such demands seemed preposterous to her, not to mention illegal, but allowed for an advantageous position should she act on it, and so she complied peaceably for the time being.

Passing under willow and cherry, she continued on and thought about what she should do. It was fortunate that the girls had delivered her bike to the garage last Tuesday afternoon and that

Eddie was kind enough to hold it in storage. The girls had not been allowed past the lobby, due to visiting hours, they said, but were happily given a tour of the grounds. Along the lane of Hardy Palms, they had inquired fervently about the student named Antiope Penuel; tour guide Agent John Mathews had turned red, his flirtatious eroticisms dashed. She had reluctantly been given permission to meet them here and they had discussed business, albeit discreetly. The girls were excited about the mirror. "How did you get it to work so well?" they had wanted to know. The application seemed to have been made for such a device that would exceed the confines of computation. "Such a beautiful design!" they had said. One of Sheryl's boyfriends had executed quite the advertising campaign. Every spoiled brat in the universe would demand one. And now the vacuous problem had arrived and what could she do? How would Monstrosso become pacified? Ah, she thought, yes. The Magic Mirror would perform the work better than any huntsman. It just needed the proper management.

She ambled peacefully along the gravel path, through the garden of ornamental trees, and concocted her plan with the benefit of fresh air.

Antiope Meets With the Monstrosso Heads

"How on earth did you make this?" demanded Litchfield, as seen in the flesh as a dried-up old hag with the face (oh dear but certainly not the eyes!!) of a nineteen-year-old homecoming queen after a million-dollar makeover. She held the mirror out covetously, admiring the illusionary transformation. "A thousand surgeries could never make me look this good!"

Antiope studied the old woman's face distastefully, forcing a smile to appear on her own. *The butchery inflicted upon this mummy is plainly evident*, she thought.

Hodge, Hoffman, and Litchfield, the supervisory heads of Duck Lake Academy, and probably a dozen others, sat before her in the conference room. It was nothing short of a miracle. To the students, Monstrosso Corporation was phantasmal. Even the dean had never seen anyone beyond *The Big Three*—incidentally, Dean Yorkshire was present both out of fear and admiration for his job.

"So...let me just itemize this list..." spoke Hoffman diligently, his voice becoming squeaky and high-pitched out of excitement. "You hold one-fifth of the software patent, half the patent rights on the mirror, were cheated on the production end of the bargain by this former company, which makes what you consider an inferior version, and therefore decided to manufacture your own, and these are the working prototypes?"

"That's right, sir. This is what we've come up with."

"And to think our own students did this," whistled Hodge, a conservative young thirty-something female executive with blonde hair and ample breasts, "Those whom we've coddled and provided for at considerable expense over the years."

"It seems difficult to imagine," Litchfield added.

"Yet it's all true," Antiope avowed, glancing from one monster to the other.

"And you can produce more?" said Litchfield, running her mummified hand along the bronze edges of the frame.

"An unlimited amount, if only we had the means to do so..."

"How much are we talking here?" Hoffman asked.

"Oh, I don't think cost is an issue," Litchfield said, licking her puffy old lips dryly.

Hodge muscled in, reading her mentor with cunning precision: "The real question is how soon—how may we best accommodate this young woman in the fulfillment of her dreams?"

"In a manner of speaking, of course," finished Litchfield.

QUINDECAPLET

I

Edina's Stalker

Edina was more thoughtful than usual on the afternoon of Wednesday the 9th. Previously that week it had been sunny and she had gone swimming in a large tank they had made for the algae and had watched her sunflowers bloom. Today was different. The weather was stormy and cold with high winds—rare for early September post-wild-and-crazy, but not unusual. She could see huge thunderclouds just east of them. The storm was frightening but also kind of cool and amazing. She liked the way the lightning forked out of the bunched-up condensation as if a raging beast from a world of sparks and inky-blue darkness. Sometimes a violet color could be detected and she realized with peaked excitement that chemistry must be involved. Something was being brewed up there, as if the entire sky was a witch's cauldron. "That's amazing!" she said before falling back into silence.

"What's amazing?" asked Edgar sleepily.

"Nothing…"

Her uncle reached for his brand-new wooden-hand-on-a-stick and began scratching his backside irritably.

They were headed towards downtown Gamesh for Edgar's interview. He was changing careers once again, it seemed. This time he was going to watch over some students at a school, which was just a step up from hired thug. Edina decided that it must be difficult attempting to find oneself in a fishbowl of shrinking options; therefore, she gave her uncle the benefit of the doubt. America needed her to believe. The future was somewhat in decline for support of dreams, which wasn't very good, and certainly wasn't very helpful. She was unsure about her uncle anyway since his recent top secret bug-zapping operation. He was acting strangely. One evening when they discovered a nest of hornets built into an abandoned ground squirrel hovel Edgar had formed a pipe-ramp with a cardboard box, had soaked some rags in gasoline, thrown them down the ramp, and had then burned the hornets out with such zeal that even Mom had wondered about her brother's sanity. With other bugs, though, he was overly kind, and went out of his way to avoid stepping on them.

"Where are you, thunderbolt?" murmured Edina as she manned the helm and steered them into sluggish traffic along the bay.

Unfortunately, the storm had dissipated into dark mist on the eastern horizon and now the sun was out.

The car's windows tinted into a blue hue.

Edina looked behind them to ensure that she could see properly. "You won't believe it!" she said suddenly.

"Believe what?" Edgar answered, sitting perplexed. He looked into the mirror, noting the white service van in their wake. "The strange man?"

"He's following us!"

"Can you lose him?"

"I've been trying to lose him all day!"

"Who is he?"

"How am I supposed to know that? Maybe he's the prize patrol."

"Or maybe a serial killer," held Edgar half-seriously. "Have you told your mom about this?"

"Nope! She'll never let me drive again if she finds out! Neither of us can have that!"

"We need to call the police."

"Are you crazy? They've been trying to steal this car for years."

"Then I need to confront this guy."

"When?"

"Right after this interview," decided Edgar firmly. "He followed you to the park that time, right? We'll go back to your place and grab a few things; try out this new invention of yours."

"If you say so…"

The Offices of ExTemplar Security

"Come in," said a voice.

Edgar had been unsure exactly which darkly-tinted door was ExTemplar's, as neither of them had any form of address, but now confidently (if a bit tentatively) opened the second door on his right (because the bolt on that particular door had suddenly clicked back with a loud snap). He soon found himself in a hallway of tinted glass. The white carpet along the floor smelled like odor eater. Heading in and turning off to the right, he followed the white carpet until he came to a bullet proof customer window with speaking holes punched into it. A click sounded to the right of the customer window and a door opened from a hidden portion in the tinted glass. Through the opened door, Edgar could see a big, intricate light-board and a curving countertop with a bunch of very expensive surveillance equipment on it. R. Lewis Knight, owner of ExTemplar Security, smiled like a child from his pivoting black leather chair. "You come highly-recommended," he said in a squeaky, high-pitched voice.

Edgar bit his tongue to keep from laughing.

"You've never worked in security," continued Knight. "It takes a very attentive mind. You must be able to resist temptation. Your body must be like a well-oiled machine, ready to come to the aid of your employers at a moment's notice. Above all, you must be loyal. Can you be loyal, Mister Weatherholt?"

"Yeah, um...yes," gulped Edgar. "I can be loyal...I've never worked security, but I'm a fast learner."

"A very large, very muscular student suddenly becomes agitated," spoke Knight quickly. "He comes at you with a knife. What do you do?"

"I, um, call for backup."

"There is no backup; everyone else is busy with their own problems. You're on your own. What do you do?"

"I try to calm him…"

"How do you propose you'll do that? He's unreasonable. He's three-hundred pounds and he's angry. Anger! What are you going to do?!"

"The, um…oh, damn it! Um…do I have weapons?!"

"No! You're unarmed! He's stabbing at you! He's stabbing you, Weatherholt!" The miniscule Knight stabbed at Edgar from the safety of his chair.

"The um…the infra-orbital pain compliance technique?"

"Yes! That's it!" complimented Knight. "That will work. Provided you can really perform, of course. Congratulations, Agent Weatherholt, you live to fight another day. You've been hospitalized though. Better get yourself a robotic limb."

"Sorry, I'm just a little nervous."

"Apologize to the worms. I'll take you on, considering your recommendations…but you'll have to do something about those nerves. These kids will not back down."

"I understand, sir."

"Call me Mr. Knight."

"Mr. Knight."

"Good. You'll be working with my best agents; they'll bring you up to speed. Be at the Academy Monday at ten a.m. Your uniform has already been laid out for you, in the back room. Here's a key to your locker. Remember to RSVP before your next visit."

"How…um…how do you know it'll fit?"

R. Lewis Knight grinned childishly and pushed his chair back into position. The big mysterious board lighted up before him with intelligent action.

"Who exactly recommended me?" Edgar ventured, turning back.

"Neither you nor I really need to know that, rookie."

Edina's Stalker cont.

"There he is!" Edina howled. "By that tree! Right out of a slug's butt!"

"He looks like a slug's rear-end all right."

374

"Are you going to shoot him?"

"Worse. Stay here and make sure he can see you. Keep it locked, just in case."

The park was between a scenic highway and the beach. Heavy equipment could be seen miles out in the quagmire where they were working on the Grand Traverse Bay Project[42]. Edgar melded with his surroundings, becoming tree and bush and grassy shadow, moving in and out of reality until he lay sprawled out on the bench just behind the stranger.

"Enjoying the view?" Edgar said at last, loud enough that he could be heard from several yards.

The stranger jumped in fear and scuttled around the tree. "P-pardon?!"

"I was wondering how you enjoy the view," said Edgar calmly.

"Is that any business of yours?!" the man responded gruffly. "Where in the hell did you come from, buddy?!"

"Oh, I've been around," Edgar said, sitting up on the bench. "So, who are you working for?"

"You're really trying my patience, friend...I suggest you just mind your own fucking business."

"Is it oil; automotive? Both?" Edgar stood and approached the strange man, grinding his teeth. "If it isn't, then you must be some kind of perverted slug butt. Either way, I highly suggest you stop stalking my niece. I don't have much patience for those who would harm children. If I ever see your face again, it'll be dangling from the neck of a horse."

"Think you're tough, do ya?!" said the stranger, reaching into his black trench coat. Blue-tinged electric white struck out along metal wires and eagles' claws, grasping Edgar's chest in wild spasms.

Edgar was himself unhurt; the charge was absorbed into the shirt-armor, which doubled as a robust fuel cell for an array of mobile devices. He grinned meanly.

"Jesus, what the fuck?!" wheezed the stranger.

---

[42] To avoid an early retirement, the Gamesh Board of Tourism worked quickly with state government and local businesses to begin the massive project of refilling Grand Traverse Bay.

But Edgar had already covered the distance and was twisting the man's arm violently away. Next there came a sickening crack and a loud cry of pain as the stranger's arm broke at the hinge. The small electroshock weapon fizzled stupidly on the green ground. The man writhed in pain for awhile, then stumbled up and ran through the park like a wild hog.

Edgar left the stun gun on the ground and worked on the wires dangling from his chest. He was cautious to avoid the shirt directly, as there were holes in it from the barbs which had to be pried loose with his pocket-pliers. Initially the holes had fizzled with static but were soon reasonably stable.

Edina was relieved to see her uncle returning from the bench. He held the shirt in his hands and was admiring it with fascination as the door opened on the passenger side. He stepped in and gave his niece a big hug.

"You didn't know if it would work," she said in amazement.

"I believed in you; I hoped it would."

"And it did!"

"Yes. It worked very well. We should probably have you get that thing patented, despite the inevitable criminal appeal."

"That would be nice," Edina mused happily. "So, how did you know he wasn't going to pull out a real gun?"

"I didn't. I just guessed."

"That's not very smart, Uncle Edgar."

"Nope."

The replaying memory of what had just happened to the bad man creeped her out a little bit. "Let's get out of here," she pleaded.

"Yes, let's…"

II

A Lull in Production

It was the 9th of September. David had a few days off, but had nothing better to do than to explore boredom. As if an imp was caught in the gears, requiring magic eyes to peer into the assemblage and pull the mangled thing out, the entire gad operation had ceased to a disquieting lull with nary an explanation. Stuck in an abandoned train with no S.O.B. bus driver, David was forced to amuse himself before the altar of 3DTV, the commercials and programs of which were eerily attuned to his private life. Luckily he had discovered an advertisement for a free Realms of Wastecraft trial account, but the television had found other ways of being a nuisance by forcing him to watch at least two commercials and/or special news reports before he could switch the interface to log in. "How the devil do they know?" he murmured. There was even an option to skip the programs and only watch commercials, in case someone had really gone over the deep end. It was too much. From an open window, David waited impatiently to be able to do what he wanted and fed the squirrels some nuts.

Day one of his quest to understand boredom had made him edgy. The mice had eaten through his bottle of nicotine and he had not been to the store yet. Instead, he had crawled around on the company's lawn for an experiment. Although a mere handful was all that was required, the blades of grass proved distasteful and the entire apparatus, both pipe and container, was in need of thorough cleaning. David twitched.

A head in the fuzz stared out from the portable television interface just then and startled him. A satellite had apparently been knocked out by a solar storm. He was determined to figure out how the thing could be so diabolical. It was almost to the point of being counterproductive, from an advertising perspective. One evening, for instance, he could get nothing but Lucha Libre matches from around the world, including one allegedly held on Mars. Then the next day it was all girly sitcoms, which he despised, but the television refused to remain turned off for more than five minutes. It was as if the thing had been trying to make him kill himself. Today, it seemed, was news. He tried thinking of a clearer channel to see what would happen. Sure enough, the picture changed. It was the old staple, a diet of insanity.

————

NABC NEWS:

Major breakthrough in the fight against HIV-AIDS infected with controversy as animal rights activists protest

[The first portion, missed by David, reveals a reporter acting as spokesperson for roughly a dozen protestors, who can be heard screaming from outside the building]

"Well…" retorts Dr. Everett Poshla of the Mayo Clinic in Rochester, Minnesota. "If not for the one-eyed, twelve-toed, glow-in-the-dark kitty cats, this HIV breakthrough wouldn't have been possible!"

OZ TV STUDIO Z WITH BUTTON-BRIGHT:

Government-Funded Study Shows: "People look funny when they poop."

Button-Bright: "With our universities filled up with foreigners, and a large proportion of young Americans forced into service jobs here and abroad, scientific researchers have been turning away volunteers for projects as bizarre as the rate of bowel movements in the private sector versus the public. 'Fifth Amendment? What's that?' they say, as citizens waive their right to privacy for a little extra coin."

"I don't see anything wrong with it," says one volunteer. "At least I'm not being injected with some new drug that hasn't been tested. I still have a weird rash from that last one I did."

CBC B.S. NEWS WITH LOLA CHAFFIN GREEN:

378

LOTTO FEVER!!

Lola Chaffin Green: "A recent report from analysts shows record numbers of lottery winners this year. In fact, you might be this country's biggest loser…"

"Boy, this is getting depressing," David mumbled, after which he decided that it was time to play Realms of Wastecraft for free up to level 90.

He chose a race and a name and off he went. The starting area was rather interesting: A warped, post-apocalyptic Dark Ages fantasy version of the American Midwest.

"ROFLMAO! Here comes the bait!" someone wrote in chat (no doubt from some dank, dark senator's basement).

Day two.

"*La cucaracha, la cucaracha… ya no puede caminar,*" sang David as the piercing traffic propelled the charioteers speedily to their deaths, "*…because it's lacking, because it's all out of…nicotiana pa' fumar. De las patillas de un moro…tengo que hacer una escoba…la la la laaaa la, la la la laaa la, I could really use a smoke!*[43]"

"What the devil?" David had returned from a pleasant walk to the party store up the road with some snacks and beverages to see that the TV was on. He left it alone for the moment, more intent on vaporizing the poison that he had purchased for his pipe, and which had been dominating his thoughts since his seeming withdrawal

---

[43] From the Spanish folk song (*corrido*) "La Cucaracha"; roughly translated, "The cockroach can't walk anymore because it doesn't have nicotine to smoke. From the sideburns of a Moor I must make a broom."

these past forty hours. It was alright, though, because there was an online movie network that he had discovered the other day and had wanted to check out.

COMMERCIAL:

"Drink Soma; live for eternity", says an ultra-clear, aristocratic female voice.

A golden stream cascades into a silver fountain situated downhill from a beautiful, shimmering white tree with blue-green leaves. Glistening on the tree's branches are gold and silver ornamental fruit the size of oranges.

A ridiculously healthy elderly couple with impeccable skin and snow-white hair flowing from handsomely-manicured heads drink golden juice that is poured into tall, crystal clear glasses from a golden urn.

COMMERCIAL:
Bare Necessities Organic Farm

A heavily-fertilized corn field appears.

A very stoned young man with a ponytail says: "Need to poop? Do it right here!!"

A woman dressed up like a brown-eyed Susan says: "Help our crops grow!"

Man says: "Feel good going it!"

COMMERCIAL:
HAULIN' ASS TRUCKING

Male trucker says: "Working a dead-end job? Tired of putting your nose to the grindstone for a wage that barely covers the

380

bills? Haulin' Ass Trucking is your ticket out! Join thousands of highly-paid truckers and work independently for one of many Monstrosso distributors. We're talking to you, David! Stop wasting your life out in the fruit orchards! Build that nest egg and enjoy doing it! Visit haulin_ass.com right now to find out how to become one with the open road."

STREAMING 3D DOCUMENTARY:
Enlightenment of the Apes?
Mind Flayer Productions, 2019. Kinshasa the Gorilla, Bobo the Bonobo; 3D digital 70 mm.; 36 minutes.

Seven years since the start of the "Gapes for Apes" program, in which animals at over a dozen zoos were given tablet computers and urged to stare at them, unexpected results occur.

Omniscient Narrator's voice (some popular actor or other) goes on about Buddhism and then the Western philosopher Nietzsche. "Many of the world's exotic wilderness animals are endangered or extinct," she says, "and, in bitter irony, the zoos have proven a final refuge."

The Gapes for Apes campaign started as an outreach program for orangutans, she explains as the camera shows cute ruddy-brown orangutans playing with marble-white i-things, "but since then it has reached many more…"

Several zoos from around the world are shown.

"…Will superfluous human technology really engage these animals and improve their quality of life both in and out of captivity? Scientists here at the Milwaukee County Zoo are banking on it."

Zoologist Dr. Barbara Ball allows a caged gorilla to touch a tablet computer filled with an index of jungle images; however, when the ape grabs hold of the item with intent on breaking it, Dr. Ball says "No, no! Money, money, money!"

Camera shows a tiger and then a dolphin viewing a picture on an interface through the glass; switches to a zoo enclosure for bonobos, gorillas, and orangutans.

"This would have been unimaginable even a few years ago," Dr. M. Allen Malark says as he feeds his pal, Kinshasa, a western lowland gorilla that is now whitened with wisdom despite being a typically mono-colored female. Her otherwise dark brown hair is well-kempt, no doubt due to the large plastic mirror built into the wall beside her. "Kinshasa, it seems, after years of browsing pictures on the tablet's screen, has come to believe that nothing exists outside of her own thoughts. She has in fact become enlightened."
Omniscient Narrator's voice: "It is perhaps her only escape from this cruel imprisonment…"

Through sign language, Kinshasa communicates that browsing images of her former, beloved jungle existence does not cause her to believe that she is in one or that she has not been ripped from paradise and forced to live out her life in a cage (albeit a very nice one), being gawked at by hairless idiot captors, but rather that it just makes her angry. The only outlet for her is to meditate on leaves and bananas.

Omniscient Narrator moves the narrative along by heading over to Bobo the Bonobo. Bobo is shown enjoying a tablet computer while switching through the images with his fingers. A caretaker asks him questions and he responds by choosing an image and showing it to the caretaker. When the questions are done, Bobo curls up on the bowl of a tree in his simulated jungle enclosure and watches his favorite movie, *Planet of the Apes*.
Narrator: "Who are the real fools in the ape family: Us, perhaps?"

Classical music plays to fade.

TOOT=SWEET HOTV: LASER-PROJECTED HOLOGRAPHIC
MOVIE
'Wrath of the Domovoi'
2019.   Cloud Rider Productions.   Ishmael Bloch-Bauer,
Nadia Kaveri, Winston Lampur, Anastasiya Makeyeva; 85 mm.;
129 minutes.

A house spirit is blamed for the death of an accident-prone
young woman when members of a floating utopia discover that a
family heirloom from an age thought to have been plagued by
ignorance and superstition has mysteriously reappeared after being
tossed into the sea.

TELECOM VIDEO: STREAMING 3D MOTION PICTURE
Friction. Friction is My Problem.
2018.   A Gringo Studios film.   Pedro "Sparks" Cruz,
Camilla Ibanez, Vanessa Alfaro, Colum Den Siti; 3D stereoscopic
70 mm.; 69 minutes.

A highly combustible young man finds himself hounded by
bad luck as he wanders a wooden city in search of employment.

III

Duck Lake Detention Facility

"And...let's see...hmm...what's that you got there?" asked the supervisor nervously. "Um...is-is *this* the one?" he said, addressing the person who pretended to be an art instructor. The instructor nodded. She looked worried.

The rubber hydrogen-filled balloon fit nicely into Antiope's papier-mâché weave framework of a real hot air balloon (if pink and confined within combustibles). She lit the basket-candle with a long blue-tipped match and watched as it rose into the air of the arts and crafts studio, then laughed with devilish glee as the unsuspecting students witnessed the sudden intrusion of a tiny sun. The bright combustion illuminated the fearful wails of those who were coloring extremely detailed portraits of tedious factory life, the crayons literally melting in the grip of panicky hands held a little too far out from their contorted faces. As the globular furnace burned out, killing untold numbers of imaginary life-styles in miniature, the flames licked the bland white tiles of the floor as the papier-mâché slowly descended, becoming infernal ash of old newspaper photos.

The instructor hissed like a snake and pulled at her brittle head of blue-gray hair.

Antiope waited patiently.

The guards arrived very quickly and began hauling her off before nary an explanation.

"I bet you're wondering where I got the gas," she explained smugly, en route to detention and literally hovering on the toes of her shoes. "I used a battery charger to separate hydrogen and oxygen from a cylinder of water at the science lab. Pretty smart, huh? You should have seen their faces!"

"Let's see how smart you feel in detention!" barked Agent Mathews, who formed the left wheel.

"That's telling her!" laughed Agent Monstrosso, smelling of gymnasiums.

The silent third-wheel agent was vaguely familiar, but seemed to be amiss. He represented his section of the authoritarian chariot with uncharacteristic warmth and consideration.

"This one's real trouble," encouraged Agent Mathews.

The floor lost property as it reflected their abstract shapes along the waxy shine. The framed finger paintings from that year's art contest reflected also, from the high walls, telling something, diffracting humanness. Arriving at the makeshift detention center (formerly, a large supply closet), they shoved Antiope inside and locked the door. She could hear someone change the sign on the door to vacant.

"It's unfortunate, but we do this so as not to kill anyone," Agent Mathews explained. "We also have to log in the time, the place, and the person. Monstrosso likes to know who the problem people are. It's usually always this one, though."

"How long will she be in there? Not too long I hope..."

The voices faded with the echoing footsteps. Soon Antiope was alone with her thoughts. There were no windows, no way to look out or in, and the yellow walls absorbed all trace of sound. A single desk with a hard red plastic chair sat situated in the far corner above the concrete floor.

Satisfied that no one would enter, Antiope went to the desk. From inside, she pulled out a laptop computer, turned it on, and typed in the password. The battery still had an hour's worth since the last time she had been confined. She would have to remember to charge up the replacement one for the next time. Once it had booted, and all those annoying reminder pop-ups popped up and were sent on their merry way, she sent out a phone call to the girls. This had been her routine since re-confiscating the computer from ExTemplar's office, which she supposed accounted for only three days. They had taken it from her despite the Monstrosso address on the sender's area of the package. A lucky thing for her was that the makeshift detention center was just behind the dean's office, and the dean never shut off the wireless router that allowed access from all the other offices (Strange as it seemed, most students at the so-called academy had little desire to utilize the internet; The only exceptions were those few who were obsessed with playing video games; It seemed, quite by accident, that the students were her greatest weapons).

"Antiope—is that really you?" Sheryl's head and shoulders appeared on the computer screen.

"Hi, Sheryl."

"How have you been, anyway?"

"Fine. Just playing with matches. How's everything there?"

"Business has been really good, despite the eternal global financial collapse and all. I don't know why I even bother with college. I don't need it, thanks to you."

"Did you have time to get me those forms?"

"Yep, we got them. I sent them to your inbox. Have fun."

"Shouldn't be a big deal."

"Need anything else? We're going to start visiting you again at some point—I promise. Amira's looking into the legal aspects of things, trying to find out if there's a specific violation to focus on— she says there's hundreds."

"Speaking of tight security, they hired a new one today."

"Hmmm…is he cute? Never mind, don't tell me…"

"Yes, believe it or not. He helped drag me off to detention just a few minutes ago."

"That's crazy… Wait 'til I tell the others."

"He should have just stayed home; he hasn't the slightest idea…"

"I hope so…keep your chin up… We'll get the word out. Even Natalie's chipped in—got her current boyfriend working on a website for you."

"That should do nicely. When I bust out of here, you can visit me anytime. Tell the girls hi for me."

"Will do. Good luck, buddy."

Antiope disconnected the call and hurriedly typed in another one to her mother who was working at the linen shop on K Street.

"Hello mother!"

"It sounds so good to hear you say that."

"How's business?"

"Business is…well, slow. But I expected as much. How are things at the academy? Are they treating you alright?"

"I suppose I'm lucky in ways, being stuck in this quaint place. At least there aren't any pill-popping rivers glistening like diesel rainbows in the eastern sun. Everything's filtered water and organic foods. It's those militant security bastards I have to worry about."

"Honey, it isn't polite to swear."

"Sorry, mother."

"So, what's this big plan of yours? I'll help anyway I can."

"No, I've got it. All I need to do is order some things, forge a couple of signatures…"

"Antiope, honey, that can't be legal…"

"We need to make it look like a legitimate rivalry. And for that we need an enemy. If Monstrosso finds out how fledgling it all really is, they might feel compelled to just cut us out of the whole picture and bury us out in some field. This way, we'll be making legitimate products which can be sold; the academy will finally act like a real industrial trade school."

"But…forgery? That sounds felonious…Isn't there a way around that part?"

"Well, if we count on them not doing a background check… But these aren't the kind of people who throw away money on just anything. I've never even seen them before; they're the phantom dukes and duchesses of this little operation."

"Maybe I should arrange an order for these products which you plan to produce."

"No, it's best you don't get involved just yet. This has to be strictly a student thing. We need to hold stock collectively as a group so we have bargaining power. I'm teaching them how to fish. It's loaves and fishes, mom."

"And how will this help you exactly? I don't understand…"

"Patents are what these people fear, that and truth. They want to control everything, but what happens when they can't even control their own designer human beings? I'm going to patent them to death. I'm going to show them where the real talent lies."

"Wow, the bell. It's nice to know that it actually works. I've got to wait on a customer. Let me know how everything pans out."

"I will."

"Okay, love you!"
"You too, mom."

SEXDECUPLET

I

Happenstance

"It's nice having someone else here to depend on," said Agent John Mathews. "Eddie—that is, Agent Monstrosso—has a problem being around food, strange as that may sound."

"Should I be guarding something?" asked Edgar.

"Just sit somewhere," Agent Mathews ordered. "You have until...exactly two-thirty. Keep an eye on them for me."

"Where do I go after that?"

"Meet me in the office," said Mathews as he juggled his ring of keys.

Edgar let Mathews leave his periphery as he glanced around to soak in the atmosphere. The cafeteria was eerily quiet for one as crowded as it was. Conversation was vaporous and to the point. Many of the students were looking down at handheld computers as they waited in line, while others seemed so involved in their devices that their trays of food sat neglected. He had thus far failed to identify the exact product. These were not communications devices in the traditional sense, but more in the cheap third-world notebook variety and with the apparent purpose of calming the user with puzzles and swirling pictures. The only chatter came from a table of instructors off to his right. They seemed to illustrate the abnormality of the students.

His walkie-talkie crackled in its holster and he picked it up a minute just to ensure that he was using it properly and that the volume was turned up high enough. As he walked slowly to the back of the line, intent on checking for himself just how exotic the food really was, it became evident that many students were in fact closely related to each other, appearing as twins, triplets, quadruplets, even quintuplets. It was a peculiar sight. He was unsure why this would be the case, but it was not the first time he had noticed such oddities, of course, having already worked at the school for half a day, and having seen some of them at the gad factory, but it was the first time that he had realized just how endemic this multiple thing really was. During his time at the gad factory people had spread rumors, and some workers did in fact certainly look identical, but in Edgar's state of near-constant motion sickness the uniformity obscured them to any concrete observations through his glazed eyes of brown. *"So what's the deal?"* he wondered suspiciously.

"What kind of meat is that?" the students ahead were saying, breaking the mundane with idle chatter.

"Are you sure that it's meat?"

"Oops, sorry," someone apologized, stopping a few feet from colliding into him. The young man looked out shyly before shuffling off in another direction.

Edgar became bored in paranoia. It was evident to him that a security position might not be very ideal for someone prone to daydreaming. He needed to keep himself occupied. He scanned the room from his position in line, making sure that no one was choking on dry fish or colliding into a container of knives.

A curious mania fell upon him suddenly. He had unwittingly made eye contact with a dark-haired young woman with skin the color of blanched almond. She was seated at the table slightly diagonal from his current position in line. The act had been unconscious until she emerged, a warm enchantment to his crackling memory. Now, unexpectedly, she was real and in the foreground. But he recognized this one; she was the girl who had been sent to detention, he realized embarrassingly. Where was his mind? They would probably hang him just for looking at her. She glanced disbelievingly his way again and then the inviting celadon and gray infused irises sparkled off toward the wall. She, too, was perhaps a bit unsettled. Edgar quickly studied her lips, which were pink petals of a taffy-flavored flower, and suddenly turned away. He noticed peripherally and to his growing excitement that she returned his glances with the same caution. When again she had let her guard down, he marveled at the dark tresses spiraling up into a white knitted cap—was it long or short, he wondered. She had worn the same cap the other day after starting the balloon on fire. Some *crazy* girl, he thought. And just what was he doing, flirting with her like that? She might have been a bit off, it was true, although, yes: she seemed a little too old for a trade school, as far as he could tell, and had probably been held back due to the absurd nature of the place. It was no wonder, then. *No matter.* They continued a volleying of the eyes, reticently, playfully, and finally she returned with a pleading misty-eyed gaze and then looked away, deep in thought. Was she blinking on purpose? Yes, he was sure of it. He discreetly blinked back to let her know that he understood. There was excitement in her eyes, although barely discernable from her face. She kept glancing at four recruiters who were situated near the far wall—Edgar had not paid much notice of them until then. He wondered whom they were recruiting exactly. They were armed even, with deadly ink pens. Edgar looked back at the woman and now there occurred a different set of blinks. Was it a code? Could she not speak? What was wrong with her? Quickly, she rose from the table and walked past but did not look into his eyes.

What a strange encounter, Edgar thought. This was *some demoiselle*. But she had dropped something. It was a certain kind of paper animal—a loon perhaps, or a dog. Edgar tried to pick it up but, typically for his luck, someone kicked past, looking down at a handheld, and blew the paper out of reach with his inertia. The line behind him was longer than the one in front at this point and so he picked out a turkey sandwich with gravy and waited to be able to creep near the beverages. Finally he was able to grab a carton of milk and to seat himself near the table where the paper object had been blown. The animal was soon in his hand. It appeared slightly ruined from the trampling of footsteps, but still easily retained the image of a swan. He wondered how someone learned to sculpt things out of paper like that. And inside, once he undid the thousand tiny folds, was the key.

Tomorrow morning, look to the trees, it said. Edgar stuffed it back into his pocket and looked around incredulously. Where was his mind? He ate lunch and waited to relieve himself from his post.

Concurrence

The note bothered him all that day and after work at his sister's house he still wondered what it could mean. Perhaps it meant nothing and the demoiselle was simply crazy. *However,* Edgar wondered, *what about the military recruiters?* They were definitely keeping an eye on her. Was she dangerous, some kind of lethal weapon? He would have to ask around.

He went to sleep and the next morning Edina dropped her uncle Edgar off at the new usual place just before ten. "Later, gator," Edina said before the door closed.

"Thanks, kid." Edgar waved, but the sugar-beet-fueled insect-mobile was already heading out of the driveway. He turned and headed through the gate and toward the double doors of the academy. There were ornamental trees lined evenly along the building. Kwanzan cherry is what they were; not the orchard kind, but a sterile, flowering cultivar. Now, in early August, they were a fruitless, vibrant green. *Look to the trees*, he thought, and instinctively looked up. To his surprise, something caught his eye. There in a tree growing just beside the front door was a very complex paper rendition of a bluebird. Edgar pried the little thing from a leafy branch of the tree and looked it over. The bird was made of three different sheets of colored paper (blue, orange, and white) and the features of the eyes and beak were colored black with ink. An altogether amazing piece of folk art, the captor could not help wondering at the underlying purpose. Was it simply a neat gift from a strange girl? He tried to find an opening, and, when he pulled down on the orange breast, the bird appeared to chirp. Noticing that the legs were also separate from the body, he tugged on those, too, and the bird opened. Buried inside was a chart full of eyes and letters. Incredibly, it appeared to be an entire blinking alphabet. There were rates of blinking per measure, half blinks and quarter blinks, the rolling of the eyes, lengths of time to hold them closed or open, alphabetical representations with numeric values, and the dramatic pauses. The thing was a brilliant work of madness—so thought Edgar, who was, himself, something of a bluebird with its head constantly tilted into spring. How uncanny it was that two such oddballs had come into orbit in the first place.

And here they were, being pulled by the same gravity, crossing trajectory at location x. They were emotionally prepared to break away from the entire system and form a gravity entirely their own. Anyone else would have immediately asked for a transfer, but not Edgar. The puzzle intrigued him. Perhaps if he could learn to communicate with this demoiselle, he could unlock the mystery.

Thus it was that every day at work Edgar was on the lookout for either the girl or an origami bird in flight. Sometimes they appeared in blue, other times green or violet, or not at all. Ultimately it was the crude murmuring and self-absorbed activity of the cafeteria that made the ideal place for silent correspondence which they seemed unable to transcend as they positioned themselves for unassuming eye contact.

All His Dreams Dashed

In his spare time, David had begun drawing parts of his graphic novel about Lieutenant Forester, with the working title *Dunesurfer*. Currently, he was drawing a scene for the chapter "Guardian of the Sleeping Bear". He thought that she looked very much like a *Soldadera* of the Mexican Revolution (at least, as his grandmother had described one; incidentally, she was not around at the time).

The 3DTV came to life suddenly to warn him that his guild *Vvvroom of the $¥§†3ɱ* was about to start a raid. As he became excited at the thought of navigating his Indiana Pukwudgie Shaman through The Land of the Hoity-toity to decimate *noob* Lunar Elves and cloven humanoid Alpacas, one of those annoying entertainment news specials started broadcasting over his game console interface.

NABC MEDIA MADNESS EXCLUSIVE:

A SNEAK PEAK AT CROW WILSON'S NEW FILM *GHOSTBOARDER*

"So, tell me, Crow: Where on earth did you come up with this one?"

"Well, Chastity—love your tats, by the way. What is that one, a succubus swimming in... Oh, and riding a goblin shark... Pretty pissin' cool...but anyway, I was on my way to Kuala Lumpur for a little, ah... for a business trip... And the news was on at the airport lounge... and there was this... small-town victory piece..."

"*Ghostboarder* has been very lucrative for you; it's number one at the box office. Tell us, what's this film about?"

"Well, it's about this young woman who becomes a weekend warrior to pay her way through college, but is transformed into this sort of vigilante dune-surfer…"

"She's a skeleton…"

"That's right, and she protects the environment, because, you know, it's important and stuff…"

"Oh, absolutely…"

"Say, Chastity, later on I'm going diving… just off the coast of Bermuda. Got one of those high-end wave-breaker yachts and I could sure use an extra hand or two out there. How would you like to go pearl diving with me?"

"Bermuda… Wow!! That sounds *so exciting*! Oh! Um, and that's all for today's Media Madness Exclusive."

———

"Son-of-a-bitch!!" exclaimed David Hernando.

16 September Year of the Silent Flusher Toilet

Antiope was perplexed. Wednesday, the day of Woden, proved ominous and single-eyed. She could see volumes, feeling weighty over calm waters. The mirror was going well—too well, perhaps—and yet her position had not changed. She was student head of production within an enclave, a micro-mini-lab of a department, a mere corner of a trade school posing as an academy fenced in from the world, yet her dreams were threatening to engulf everything around her. This place could not hold one such as her and there was little that could be done to escape before the whole thing bubbled over. She could see that it was happening but could do nothing. It was evident in the supply delays and the theft of her workers and the unorthodox recruitment efforts of strangers in uniforms. She struggled to keep face and to hold up her chin despite the tying of her hands and apparent flooding of negative energy.

She saw the endearing new security guard again that day and to her amazement he blinked "Hello, my name is Edgar. What's yours?" and although he was using the chart she found it uncanny that someone should understand her, let alone that it should be *him*. A void within was rapidly filled with mirth and her cheeks flushed. Yet despite her excitement she knew that they were being watched as at least one camera was voyeuristically set upon them and so she blinked out "They're watching!" and quickly turned away. The surrealist painting from a Polish artist was indeed captivating from the interface of the device. She studied it as she continued eating. Strawberries and cream oatmeal with almond soymilk and a pomegranate on the side was never lost on her. She waited there, at the flickering stairwell of her mind.

How Green is Your Lawn?

The mirror was being shipped to the house by mistake, Tom held mindfully while he pretended to watch over his lawn that was being cut late that Saturday morning by neighborhood youth representing D & D Landscaping Company.

"Be sure to have someone get the mail!" Margaret shouted from the closed window of the air conditioned house (the internet pegged them at an unusual 85° F).

The brick-encased mailbox was overflowing with the usual junk, and the lawn was just as telling. The rain came at night like clockwork, twice a week, and the grass grew an inch. The lawn in September would grow the same as it did in July. Like garden flowers, the soul of the neighborhood was active only during programmed intervals of seeded clouds. The intensity of the sun hardly seemed to matter. It was an endless head of hair, to be cut by an endless stream of neighborhood youth. It would go on, the cogs replaced and forgotten. And that green! What fertilization! What Viagra of the soil! The thing didn't even need the treatment it was given, every week by something like a D & D, because the devil's grass was engineered for erections even in winter. The devil was a prodigious father of grass.

Told you so! His paternal grandfather would have said. *Keep an eye on that grass! It'll be the death of you!*

The postal truck pulled in, almost like clockwork, and a man jumped out.

"Mister Wesson?" asked the man, just to be sure (Did it really matter?). "Sign here please." Tom was given the handheld computer to sign while the man unlatched the back of the truck. He watched the cog check labels. Out of curiosity, he had ordered something new to the market which the executives were praising *up and down* as the next best thing in self-imaging software; best experienced *by far* through some semi-actual kind of mirror (he had chosen *The Delux* in hopes that it might become a prop for bedroom exercises). They were being manufactured by a special group of academy students, no doubt endowed with some batch of genius that Monstrosso had cooked up—he hated to contemplate any further, citing the potential lack of sleep. But the Monstrosso execs had ensured him that it was "pretty neat" and that production of their new product would enhance rather than impede their agreement. He accepted the package and hurriedly shelved the item into the trunk of the lackluster hybrid of the season that they were borrowing from the automotive dealership while awaiting their replacement Cadillac Escalade AV. Next he jumped in the driver's seat and was out of the driveway before the postal truck had a chance to carry on with its route.

SEPTDECUPLET

I

The Cardan Grille

Tracking Antiope down inside the academy proved difficult. Edgar had come to realize that a good dozen people or so looked exactly like her. Furthermore, he did not want to raise suspicions of misconduct. It was merely curiosity, as far as he was concerned, a reaching out toward an isolate humanity in hopes of reeling them in.

Back in Sugarland, at his sister's house, Edgar delved into his arsenal of secrets and pulled out the classics in juvenile spy communication. The Cardan grille seemed as good a place to start as any and he went about devising the grid for a hidden message. A simple sheet of cardboard with rectangular holes in it, the grille had been a favorite of 16th and 17th century French Cardinals who wanted to keep their correspondence secret.

The next day while guarding the cafeteria, Edgar tacked the grille onto the note board in the form of an advertisement for a missing cat. He ran into Antiope later that day, in the hall just outside of her room, and dropped a crude white origami cat which he had learned from the back of a cereal box that morning. She gathered the hint and unassumingly picked it up on her way out.

II

The Dream of the Orchard King

"This is quite the century", said the man inside the Aztec calendar, with only his umber face showing. The dull chestnut disks, which were full of blue, white, and viridian highly-detailed symbols, rotated opposite each other and danced like fire, and the arrowhead pointers stayed rigid like navigators of stone. "With the world ended and begun anew, expect some great things."

"I'm certainly ready for it," David said to the calendar man in his dream. "We haven't seen anything very great so far."

"Just be patient," advised the man; "If not this time, maybe the next."

"What now?" asked David.

"Come on in!" said the man with an encouraging smile. The calendar suddenly grew large and David was drawn into the man's toothless mouth.

Just as outside the mouth, the world inside was extremely vivid with color and texture. He was at some kind of town, much as he had read once in a short story about Mexico. The Keeper was dancing around an old-fashioned well, accompanied by her six children. As David watched her, he seemed to grow stronger until his muscles bulged tightly from beneath his clothes. And then he was wearing some kind of flexible armor the color of an armadillo and the robes of a jaguar. Still dancing, and lovely to behold, the Keeper approached and acted very friendly towards him—much friendlier than she should have been, which made David's hairs stand on end. "I'm all yours, David," she said in that seductive voice of hers. "I'll be your queen, and you'll be the orchard king."

"But...your husband!" David murmured under caresses from the dream Keeper.

"That fat old thing? He's a good man, but his time has come. You must rise to the challenge and take his place..."

"Keeper!"

Suddenly he was caught in a wave of lush green hills which carried him along the path of a vast orchard and seated him upon a knotted throne of orchard wood high above the canopy—so high, in fact, that he thought it impossible to get down from. Below were thorny vines full of venomous purple flowers that snapped at him like cute, draconic little Chihuahuas whenever he tried to step down. "Um, Keeper! What am I supposed to do up here?" There was no answer, no sign of anyone. The village lay hidden. From the throne, he could see all the animals as they foraged the plentiful boughs for food. There were colorful songbirds, fluffy little bunnies, bandit raccoons, and the rare novelty albino deer. A creek full of frogs and fish ran along the hillside, gurgling off into unknown horizons. He stayed there for what seemed like an eternity as the peaceful orchard creatures raised families, lived and died, and seemed to rise again in subsequent generations. Then the orchard kingdom changed, becoming uniform, devoid of undergrowth, smelling of sulfur and lime. Wrangler-jean-wearing farmers began to appear, first one and then another, caringly checking the trees as if their own. But they did not approve of the animals, which began falling prey to their traps. The animals suffered and vanished. Dirt roads appeared from below the ground and formed a checkered pattern. David disapproved. He tried giving orders, but no one could see him. Men in safety-orange trucker hats ran around on four-wheelers murdering beautiful albino deer with their high-powered rifles and this was all that David could take. He shouted for them to stop to no avail and wondered just what the point was being king if everyone in the kingdom ignored you.

"Every last one of 'em!! Kill 'em all!!" said the farmers, growing exponentially in number, every batch more piss and vinegar than the preceding ones.

"Stop it, you S.O.B.s!" David shouted. "Claim your section and build a wall, if you're gonna be so damned greedy!"

The hungry deer arrived from the forest in families cautiously hidden in the brush, but the farmers were baiting them, drawing them from the safety of the woods. The farmers' daughters danced in friendship around the bait pits while the sons waited.

"No, don't do it!" David warned. "Can't you see it's a trap?!"

It was no use. The deer were hungry. They came out and all of them were shot until a pile of carcasses formed into a hill that eventually rose as high as David's isolated throne.

"Build a goddamn wall!!" David yelled angrily until his face turned blue. He tried again to get down and this time managed to clamor to a depression in the vines roughly half-way down, but the remaining mile was more treacherous than the last, with sharp, intelligent thorns and whirling blades.

Additional piles formed, in various places throughout the kingdom, burying the outraged forest trees and even those in the orchard, with the corpses of various deer, rabbits, raccoons, foxes, badgers, and, most disturbingly, the farmers themselves as the land spoiled with the overflow of blood and turned black as bile. The animals moaned hauntingly from their graves and the wood creaked like an old attic as the bony limbs along the ground reached through a bloated decay of organs and muscle.

David sobbed and screamed. He awoke covered in sweat and could not go back to sleep no matter how hard he tried. Soon enough, the alarm on the 3DTV went off and he was obliged to get out of bed.

III

17 September Year of the Silent Flusher Toilet

Thursday, the day of Thor, was a hot flash in the wilderness, for no sooner had Antiope gathered her mutinous crew and immersed them in the production of the mirror than she was beset with recruiters. She stowed away in her room for awhile to regroup her wits and, peeking out of the eyehole, saw Edgar lingering in the hall. As she slowly opened the door and peeked coquettishly out, he dropped a crude origami rendition of a cat made of black construction paper. SEEK OUT THE FLYER FOR THE MISSING CAT it read between the holes of the grille.

Intrigued and on the run, she hurried to solve the puzzle. There were flyers everywhere, however, and it took many minutes before she was able to find one concerning a missing cat. The note was thus:

When Theodore went missing I was devastated. It isn't often that an animal like that comes into a person's life. He's such a clever cat, while at the same time a heap of trouble. Theo used to swathe himself in the curtains, then pounce on a ball of yarn held by an unsuspecting little niece. Once I caught him torturing a frog by chewing on its leg, then letting it go, and then pouncing on it again. Anyway, have you seen my cat?

Mrs. Hannah Kingscott here. Please call me at 231-606-1837, any time before 8 p.m.

19 September Year of the Silent Flusher Toilet

It was Saturday before Antiope saw Edgar again. He was roaming the halls for an evening shift fatally drifting into night. Too overjoyed to speak, she followed at a distance. He was soon joined by Eddie, however. John must have had the night off. Antiope hid in the thresholds of doorways to overhear what was going on. Eddie was saying something about the next few hours and making sure something was locked. This gave Antiope an idea, and as they went around locking doors she went to the library and waited. A book on the Crusades kept her awake. When she thought it would be dark enough, she snuck into one of the boys' rooms and forced open the window from behind the blinds. "Wow, look at that!" she told them as they protested irritably. "Pretty lights!" The ploy worked, as it often did, and eventually they were all out in the garden grounds absorbing themselves in glow-in-the-dark Angel Trumpets.

The guards came, perhaps fifteen minutes later, to gather them up with flashlights. Antiope hid behind a tall, sweet-smelling stand of Climbing Angel Face and waited. Once Eddie was off with a young student, pulling the lad gently, yet forcefully and with little effort back to his room, she appeared with her wrists crossed and held out submissively. Edgar grinned when he saw her. "Take me to my room, please," she said. She looked up at him with sad, misty

404

eyes, and they devoured each other's shadowed features, both feeling the warmth of likeminded machinations.

"Out for some midnight mischief, I see…"

Once again, Antiope was pleasantly surprised. This guy made for some playful conversation. His voice wisped like the wind and tickled her ears. "You read me so well; I can't believe it," she said, standing in the white, yellow, and pink glow of the trumpets.

"What can I say? I enjoy puzzles." Edgar took her by the hand, unintentionally caressing them, and waited.

"I hoped you would."

"So, what's this all about?"

"That depends."

"On what?"

"On you. Tell me about yourself."

"Well… Hey, here comes the other guard," whispered Edgar. "We'd better work our way back."

"Take it slow," she said, looking into his eyes.

The antithetical guard spilled a little about himself and then nodded at Eddie as they passed. He tried using Optish[44] when the floodlights appeared near the back entrance, but was getting his letters mixed up and so continued to whisper discreetly.

"So, tell me," Antiope pursued roguishly, "what are the good things about the Army Reserves? How would it benefit someone?"

"Well, it pays for college…" Edgar admitted, yet as if he was chewing a bitter soup. "It can be quite difficult, depending on your course of study, I suppose. I never had much self-confidence growing up. I do now. The Army changes you, but not all of that's good. I had anger issues."

"You had to sell out. You were not Army material."

"I was never much of a conformist. But I didn't have the money for college."

"So, what else? What's part of the draw?"

"You get to see the world?" Edgar laughed bitterly.

They had finally made it to Antiope's room and Edgar felt compelled to disconnect.

"You recently got out of the Army. Why is that?"

---

[44] A blinking language created out of lonely desperation by Antiope Clara Penuel.

"I served my time and got out. I didn't believe in the war. It was an attack on the better part of my nature."

"I see. What about it exactly was so repulsive, if you don't mind me asking? Did you have to kill anyone?"

"No, I didn't kill anyone directly, but I filled a supportive role, which makes me an accomplice. Murder is a very old vice, a part of being human, unfortunately. War is somehow supposed to make it legal, which is bullshit. But it was more than that. It was the business aspect of the war, the many franchises of divisions rising up in theatre like mechanized boils under the skin. They're pissing in the well, everywhere they go, and don't give a damn. That isn't what I signed up for. All that talk about duty and honor… Nonsense… You can't have honor with a mentality like that, not giving a damn about anyone but yourself. Does that make any sense?"

"Perfect. You must have been through a lot…"

"Self-inflicted mainly. Did I pass?"

"You excelled. So, what highly personal question do you have for me?"

"Okay. Don't take this the wrong way, but are you as adult as you act?"

"I'm twenty-six, believe it or not. I've spent my whole life in places like this. And no I don't have any intentions of joining the military. I have my hands full with a tech product we've been making actually…"

"Then why are you even here? Why are the recruiters so interested in you? Are you dangerous or just highly valuable, or what?"

"You mean will I lure you into the dark and devour you?"

"That could be fun…" said Edgar, blushing even though he was just played along.

"All perversions aside, I'm not sure if you're ready for that information yet. Let's just say that I'm highly valuable for now."

"Rich parents?"

"Well, no. I have very wealthy and powerful step-parents who refuse to let me live my own life."

"So they're afraid you'll run away from home?"

"I already have. Twice."

"Crazy. And they're forcing you to live *here*? Sounds more like a twisted fairytale."

"One man's step-parents are another man's war-mongers."

"What do you mean by that?"

A door shut nearby and they remained still. The cold floor, like gravity, was a prison for the mechanically bound. Electricity was what they all shared in common, a flow of electrolytes through the watershed of veins.

Antiope fell away at the sudden movements, sliding into darkness. Afraid even to whisper the answer, she blinked out "Monstrosso".

20 September Year of the Silent Flusher Toilet 5:25 PM

"What the hell are you looking at," John told Antiope when she glanced their way again—she was grinning, which always put him on edge. The two security agents were eating dinner, after which John would flirt with the second shift laundry staff before heading home to his wife and kids. Edgar was on night duty and had just punched in.

"Kkkkk kakkk…" Their radios were picking up static. John picked his up out of the holster as if it were a weapon and listened.

"Got a problem, John," a voice reverberated through the radio speakers.

"What is it?" John said into the radio, heavy with annoyance. The radio cackled.

The Munchkin voice continued: "Someone's throwing a fit over the drabness of the walls…Zulu Quadrant…"

"Some retard 's throwing a tantrum," John explained with a sigh, even though Edgar had been listening as well. "Someone probably painted abstract shapes on the walls again. The moody ones don't like the circles and squares to be overlapped." John suddenly shifted around and addressed her: "Hear that, I See You Pee?! Someone's actually more trouble than you! Does that make you feel competitive?!"

"Trouble elsewhere…" Antiope murmured from the other table. "Now, that's progress. I'm not the only academy peon, you know."

"Tell you what: I'll take this one for ya," John said, turning back to Edgar. "It's on the way out," he reasoned. John rose from the table without his tray of half-eaten food and scanned the cafeteria with a wolfish grin. "I need to talk to that giant ass-clown anyway," he said before vanishing into the hall of shapes and colors.

"I thought he'd never leave," blinked Antiope, catching Edgar's gaze as he turned back.

"What…happened…to…the…recruiters?"

"War, I guess; or maybe a war game convention. Nice sentence structure. You have the basics down."

"I must…have…very…powerful…eyelids."

Antiope laughed. She would have to wait quite a while before any meaningful conversations would be held in Optish, it seemed. Plan B was therefore enacted. "Vanish with me," she blinked.

Edgar shrugged. He maintained eye contact as Antiope continued:

"I need an outlet before I self-destruct. I need to get out. Meet me tomorrow at the corner of Highway thirty-seven and MSR one-one-four."

"What?" blinked Edgar, feeling pleasantly surprised.

"I'm testing something," Antiope blinked rapidly. "If I'm successful, we'll be able to go on a date."

"A little…forward…aren't you."

"Bring your bicycle if you have one."

Edgar nodded, covertly smiling.

Antiope blushed. "Great. See you then."

Out With the Laundry

Despite a contracting out to a local company on the outskirts of Gamesh, laundry rotation was a daily occurrence: Concluding breakfast the following day, four students were chosen to perform most of the work, thus taking time off at the factory and saving GGI on some overtime payouts. Today was different, though, because someone had actually volunteered. Antiope was her name, or, for their purposes, 596-02-4234.

They were herded together and rustled to the northernmost side of the building next to the academy's garage and storage area. The supervisory guy waddled over to unlock the door. Soon the truck would arrive with a load full of clean sheets to be emptied and replaced with dirty ones. The supervisor did not bother to explain this to the four so-called volunteers, though. They were simply lured inside like pack mules and left waiting. With the obvious exception of Antiope, the four were typical of the student body; a geeky blonde female in her early twenties, a somewhat soft male with a shy, blank look, and another male in the range of sixteen with an athletic build and steely eyes. Additionally, a red-headed girl probably around age nine had inadvertently come along for the ride.

"Hi, I'm Bethany," the girl said. These younger ones were far friendlier than they of her generation, Antiope realized.

Two puffy laundry women were having a conversation in the corner near a desk covered in folded sheets. They were sitting near the shelves where the clean laundry was stored but appeared very apathetic.

The truck arrived and the pack mules were brought outside through the garage-type door to begin unloading. A man jumped out, pushed up the back door of the truck, and began throwing bundles to the awaiting pack mules. The older male student turned towards the garage after catching his bundle.

"This way, stupid," said the supervisor, remaining planted.

They brought their bundles inside where the two women motioned them towards the shelves. After an hour of this kind of work, they were all exhausted. Thankfully, there was only a half-load that morning, but another truck was en route.

The driver began chatting with the two laundry women while the supervisor waddled back inside to do his job of hauling in the carts of dirty laundry.

Now was the time to act. To ensure that she could sneak in to access her Zeno's Arrow™ brand bike, Antiope had stolen the key from John's key ring. The garage was open and the mechanic was busy working on one of the academy shuttle buses. She could see the door to storage just to the right of the garage and hurried to open it.

"Sorry, Bethany," she apologized. The poor girl had followed her like a chick to a mother hen—no matter. She unlocked the door and found her bike leaning against boxes of unused textbooks. "See anything you want?" she asked. Bethany wanted the red rubber ball. Antiope brought everything outside and then quickly to the back of the truck and, although more trouble than she imagined, slid the bike behind the empty laundry carts. Next she hurried out and, seeing Bethany with her ball, led the girl by the hand. "Where's your room, Bethany?" she asked, but the girl was lost and didn't know. Therefore, Antiope took her to the gymnasium and brought her over to the other children and watched the chick depart with blissful satisfaction.

When she returned, the driver was gone. The laundry women were chatting with the supervisor and the three students were standing stupidly near the desk. Antiope got in anyway and climbed over the carts of dirty laundry to where a door led to the cab. She hoped the driver would soon arrive to put things in motion, but the wait was long and torturous. She heard noises and imagined them to be from John Mathews, who had probably begun doing his rounds. Once the surveillance operator was awakened from her pile of drool, a brief review of the tapes from between the hours of eight and nine AM would reveal Antiope's method of departure. They would know that she had initially gone off in an easterly direction.

The door opened and shut and the truck shook, started with a blaring roar, and things were in motion.

Antiope waited until the truck stopped a few times before opening the cabin door and peeking inside.

"Who in the…!" exclaimed the astonished operator.

"Drop me off at the next intersection," Antiope said, presenting the driver with a crisp one-hundred-dollar-bill.

"Sure!" said the driver.

OCTDECUPLET

I

Returning to the Intersection of Highway 37 and MSR 114

"So, when am I supposed to pick you up?" Edina asked after dropping her uncle off at the crossroads. They were at the accident-prone corner of Highway 37 and MSR 114, where some lady in a green and black checkered school uniform was struggling with her shirt and pants behind a patch of prickly bushes and a bicycle. It was exactly the kind of bicycle she wanted for Christmas, which meant that everyone already had one except for her.

"Can you pop the trunk?" asked Edgar excitedly.

"I'm getting it," Edina growled.

The trunk popped open and Edgar removed his old silver bike from the bowels of the automobile.

"I better be getting one of those for Christmas," Edina huffed. She ogled the lady's bike with envy.

"You will, my darling, if you stay on Santa's Good List."

"You sure are talking funny. And your friend is silly looking. So...when do I pick you up?"

"Don't worry about it. I'll get home."

"How?"

"This old bike. I'll make it."

"Okay, but it's a long way, stupid."

"Run along now."

"As you wish, Uncle Stupid."

There were still tiny bits of glass and red plastic in the road, Edgar realized absently, just then remembering the accident they had stumbled upon way back in July, when the world was devoid of beauty. "I hope I haven't kept you waiting," Edgar said as he stood beside his beaten old dirt bike. The straps on his black backpack slipped and he had to readjust it. Food and drinks for a picnic were contained within.

"You have a pleasant voice," she said, then returned to the subject. "No, I had to get here early. The guards will be looking for me."

"Why is that, exactly?" Edgar wondered.

"They don't like loose ends."

"Hmm?"

"I had to sneak out."

"You make it sound like a prison."

"It's worse than a prison."

"How old did you say you were?"

Antiope laughed. "I'm twenty-six."

"And...the academy;" said Edgar. "What is it for exactly?"

They both laughed, breaking the tension.

"I really am twenty-six," insisted Antiope. "The academy is just to keep us occupied when we're not working. School for life: It's the way of the future."

"And why is it that you can't leave?" Edgar asked (his head was a land full of confusion).

Antiope shrugged. "I don't make the rules. Why don't you ask your employers?"

"They say the academy's for orphaned autistics and troubled teens."

"Then it must be so..." she reasoned darkly. "So, where do you want to go?"

"I don't know."

"Don't you know of a place?"

"I know of a great place," Edgar said, "but it's a ways from here. It's up north several miles, on a hill overlooking Gamesh. I used to play there as a kid, but I don't know that we'd make it."

"We could make it."

"I'm not so sure."

"Okay," Antiope sighed breezily. "Well, let's just head in that direction and see where it takes us."

"Can't argue with that."

Edgar had a difficult time keeping up with Antiope on his old silver dirt bike, especially being that he could no longer switch into any of the gears in the third tier. Moreover, Antiope kept slipping in and out of existence; she would pedal quickly just a few yards ahead and suddenly rocket to over a mile, only to vanish and appear back to about half that distance. Strangely, she had no knowledge of this, and to her it was just normal pedaling. He asked her about it when he had caught up again and she said the bicycle did most of the work and that it felt like being taken on a merry-go-round, as if the ground beneath her didn't matter much, but this clearly was impossible. They passed a vista of orchards. Cannons roared far off in a valley powdered with haze, as lovely as a Shenandoah. Traces of chemical spray were carried in the breeze. Next there was an isolated subdivision in a farmer's field and a touristy-looking baseball park, and after that a buffalo farm speckled with large, matted bulls with dark, testy eyes.

"We turn up here," Edgar said pointing. From Watling Road they would enter Fosse Way and then the park. The country was clean and the tar-stained crosses holding up the power lines failed to reach them. The birds flew happily overhead. Edgar lost sight of his companion completely at one point, for what seemed like fifteen minutes, only to find her reading the names on a great cairn that stood pyramidal at the bank of a roadside park.

"Oh, there you are!" exclaimed Antiope in a loud undertone. "Are you ready to eat? I'm so sorry I left you behind."

"Is that all I'm good for?" Edgar huffed. He rolled into the park with a last ditch effort and rested on the bars of the aluminum steed.

The location was curious. On one side of the road, a line of concrete foundations lay hidden beneath vine-covered bushes and trees, as if a small town had once flourished at the edge of the forest, and on another there was nothing but an abandoned field. Not a single house could be seen, but, curiously, up the hill from the cairn, an equestrian statue, a woman standing atop a spiked chariot, had been carved from the stump of an ancient tree.

"You should really get one of these Zeno's Arrow bikes. They're amazing!"

"So I've heard."

"I think they're made in that place...what did you say it was?"

"Nenaa'angebi?" he answered. "Yep, you're right. They used to work with my aunt and uncle, in fact."

"Oh, really? Then why on Earth aren't *you* riding one? They're moderately priced."

"I didn't know about them until recently...been busy..."

"I definitely recommend it."

Edgar handed Antiope the black backpack full of liquids and lunches and told her the story. They drank at the cairn and appreciated each other's company. The ancient maples on either side of the gravel curve whispered only slightly. The park was the natural crown of a hill.

Whereupon Edgar and Antiope Take a Ride in the Park

They continued on along the park trail to where the ancient trees stood vigil over civilization. The red squirrels dashed out, chirping irritably, and were chased off by the larger gray squirrels. They ran up the side of a white pine.

"It's nice," Antiope chirped.

"You've seen nothing yet."

"So now what?" she said, startled by the bareness of islanded nature.

"Now we climb," challenged Edgar, gesturing up the forested hill to where a ridge had formed.

"Up there? Is that dangerous?"

"Yes. But you get the hang of it."

And so they climbed up and looked out over the edge of the canopy, peering cautiously down upon Gamesh, the roaring streets, the vain, aimless travelers in their all-terrain vehicles that never left the road, the painted, jangling women clutching expensive leather purses, the flocks of tourists with cuts of fudge and ice cream cones, upon the yellow brick buildings of marshlands rolled over by asphalt and concrete, at the beautiful patterns of human society, constructed in pieces over time by different people of different eras.

From so far away, they were nothing more than brainy bees in a very strange hive of flat, plotted sections.

"We're almost out of time and space," Antiope said, looking out over the grove dividing what remained of the forest. "We could drop stones on their rooftops and they'd never know."

"They can't see us—wouldn't even think to look up here in the trees."

"Silly, isn't it?" Antiope said. "They think they're so important. One day they'll die, like all the rest of us, and strangers will take their place. All these ephemeral legacies may as well belong to the squirrels. This entire city will burn in time. The planet will be a ball of fire and the ash will soar into space with angelic frenzy."

"Is that even worth thinking about?"

"No. We can't change what will happen. We're among the birds, and they don't care that we're here. We're up here with them, with this force, feeling part of it, and it's so wonderful. Thank you for this. Thanks for compelling me to this staggering edge of living. This is the kind of thing I've longed for. I've been missing this...for all time..."

"We can do it again—anytime," said Edgar happily. "Anytime you want."

"But, you see... we can't. We can't last. They won't let it last."

Edgar looked at his eccentric companion wonderingly. "We can last."

"I should just be straight with you...Edgar..."

"Yes?"

"You wanted to help me, and I was more than willing to let you...to fulfill that animal desire..."

The brown embers of Edgar's eyes burned wide and a stupid grin closed the gap between his lips.

"No, not like that," Antiope explained as she tripped over her own words, "What I'm saying is that I accidentally saved *myself*...my dream came true...I thought up a plan and it worked...oh, but what does it matter. In the end, everything burns..."

"Right," he responded, "your project... Tell me about it."

"It's a magic mirror. I told my friends about it and they made it happen. It makes people appear beautiful when they're really just pathetic. But it doesn't matter. Nothing matters."

"Magic matters," mused Edgar thoughtfully.

"What do you mean?"

"The thaumaturgic," he continued, conjuring up words from ancient tomes. "Like shamans and seers of old. None of that really goes away... society just wants to graph the world, to dissect it... like a factory drowning all that's wonderful in a vat of the mundane. As always happens when the fun is removed, the magic goes away."

"Leonardo da Vinci; 'Regal spirit and tremendous breadth of mind'; he was a vegetarian; he would purchase caged birds only to release them. That means he had respect. He studied the corpse, but saw life in it."

"You have an encyclopedic mind."

"I remember what I admire."

"I thought maybe you were a savant," admitted Edgar.

"No. I'm as normal as anybody."

"But your siblings..."

"Not so lucky. There's probably something of the savant involved, but for the most part they're impaired; introverted; unsocial. They keep to themselves; do as they're told."

"What do you mean?"

"I mean..." she began hesitantly, "that they've altered us."

"The academy?!"

"Monstrosso," Antiope whispered. The word caused her to look around suspiciously.

"Monstrosso? What do they have to do with the academy?"

"Monstrosso runs the academy. We belong to Monstrosso."

"Well, I didn't see *that* coming."

"You should have..." she said. "Zech could tell you..."

"So...Monstrosso, you say? Doing things to people?" Edgar was somewhat skeptical.

"I was in love with his twin brother Zach," she continued absently. "They devised an escape plan. I was supposed to go with them, but I got my dress caught in the laundry chute... He drowned, I think. They were on the run for several days."

"That's terrible. And you were lovers?"

The woman continued, caught in her own isolation: "The only thing that keeps me going..."

"Exactly," said Edgar. "Better to keep a positive outlook..."

"No you don't understand," Antiope explained, rejoining the conversation. "It was the first time I ever saw the darkness...such a terrible world... I tried to escape. I jumped at every opportunity; the hope of an absence being overlooked; the chance to go to church on Sundays. There's a Polish one with beautiful stained glass, a medieval Saint George, dragons of color and light, but it just makes me want to burn things. It's not the church's fault—Damn my charges!"

"I feel that way, too, sometimes..." Edgar acknowledged. "But not everything should be damned..."

"How could anyone ever have believed? They must have been very afraid of things. Today the world is known; the galaxy is known. Reminded of that, I can't believe in magic..."

Edgar paused thoughtfully, then pictured something in his mind and appreciatively smiled. "If you've ever seen a gale swirl over the desert, or pirouette across a snowy field, you would understand why a person might believe in magic. The wind waltzes over the earth with unmatched grace and beauty, whispering to one another of something greater than what can be seen. At the very least, we should apprentice ourselves to the wind and learn how they dance. We should marry our souls with theirs and see what may come of it. You don't have to be primitive to see the error of doing otherwise."

"That's a lovely thing to say, especially coming from someone named Weatherholt."

"But the problem is..." he continued, smug in his momentary happiness, "that these days...you could really say the same thing about science. I mean, how does a videophone work? How does a camera take a picture? In virtual reality we can shoot fireballs from our palms, levitate through air, wield sabers of light and really slice up some evil. Yet it's getting harder to tell the difference...I mean, between what's possible and what's impossible. There's magic there, too, but there's also, I think, the inevitable madness. We're becoming mad."

"Do you think I'm mad?" worried Antiope.

Looking into her eyes, Edgar could see the turmoil. Was it right to offer hope? What if she really was mad? He was unsure. "I take it back," he said, suddenly weighted with unhappiness. "I take all of it back; illusion is bunk. It's madness. I don't know what I'm talking about. Even the forest is just...a forest. We're destroying ourselves in a logical and orderly fashion, as God intends. I was just trying to impress you."

"Oh, but I am impressed," whispered Antiope. "I should kiss you for what you said, except that you've retracted it."

"Careful: I'm a projection," he said, regaining altitude. "No, not even that. I'm an illusion."

Antiope kissed him anyway. "I like to disappear."

"So what's going on?" Edgar murmured happily between kisses.

The leaves were steaming.

Antiope stopped, somewhat perplexed. She let Edgar kiss her neck before volunteering a weighty answer. "They're forcing me to work in the gad factory, but there's a lot more to it than that. Monstrosso, the company holding patents on gads, corn, soy, sugar beets, on living, growing, evolving things, well...they even have one on pigs...born using their fertilization treatments...and they're doing the same thing to people."

Edgar stopped for a second and then proceeded, nibbling at her ear.

"I know that sounds crazy, but it's true," Antiope continued. "I'm one of those people; so is everyone who attends the prestigious Duck Lake Academy. It isn't even the only one. There are hundreds of them."

"Sounds like a plan straight from Hell," Edgar whispered as he kissed her other ear.

"They had our DNA altered through fertility treatments administered to women who were paid to give birth in fake clinics. These women gave up their children for the corporation."

"But...that's just ludicrous. Why wouldn't the government know about this?"

"The government does know about this."

"So you're telling me..."

"...I knew this was going to happen."

"Now, wait a minute, I'm just thinking things through..."

418

"You were so good...too good...and I fell for it......you're CIA, aren't you..."

Edgar stopped, perplexed, and grinned. "...I'm not a Spook."

"Then you just don't believe me. I knew people wouldn't believe me. Things have gotten so crazy that nothing is believable... Just give me a chance to prove it...I'll prove it, somehow..."

"To what end? I can't free you from this prison."

Suddenly Antiope became upset, her soft face twisting with reddening, moistening conflict. "...then FORGET IT! Stop looking at me! Fly away, bird! You're free! I'll let you get on with your happy little life!"

Tearing herself away from warm companionship, she descended in unreasonable haste, refusing to look back at what had been a wonderful, brief moment. She went from branch to branch, not caring if anything was really there or not.

"Wait just a damn minute!" called Edgar. "I thought you were fucking kidding me! Are you kidding me?!"

Antiope hesitated only long enough to flip Edgar the bird and continued her mad descent.

"Hey, what is this!?" Edgar demanded in hot pursuit. "Slow down or you'll hurt yourself!"

"What do you care?!"

"I care! Just be reasonable! I thought you said you were reasonable!"

"I thought you said you believed in magic! All men are the same!"

"Well, all women are the same, too!"

Antiope slipped on a fat branch, broke a twig, and clung shivering to a hanging bough just above her head. She screamed while steadying herself for safe footing.

"Wait there! I'll come get you!" Edgar shouted.

"No! I don't need your help!"

Edgar came down anyway.

Suddenly a black van came from out of nowhere and shot recklessly into the vacant park. The van continued wildly through scampering rabbits and squirrels and headed towards them. It arrived, just below the canopy, and skidded to a halt over the grass. Two men stormed out: one, a very large and muscular fellow; the other, a stocky blond militant around five-feet-seven inches in height—both of them very well known, at least casually. John was wearing his dark business suit with matching tie and his face was hidden by large, tacky sunglasses so that it was impossible to know exactly what he was looking at; Eddie was dressed sloppily, absent the tie with his shirt unbuttoned, and had probably been picked up along the way.

"We know you're up there!" said Agent John Mathews, holding some kind of tracking device. "See that electronic bird flying around up there? It's on our side! The world is mine!"

"Go fuck yourself, John!" Antiope spat from her perch. She glared at the men on the ground, unable to access her arms without falling.

"That's Agent Mathews to you, sweet-pea!" said John, who seemed to be more of a hothead than usual.

"Fine," Antiope corrected. "Go fuck yourself, Agent Mathews!"

John growled incoherently and tried grabbing a branch of the giant tree. "Eddie... Agent Monstrosso, you gigantic idgit! Help the suspect down from that tree!"

Edgar grumbled to himself from his hiding place just a little further up the tree. It occurred to him, quite shockingly, that Antiope might have been telling the truth about the academy.

"You can get your ass on down here too, sir, wherever you are!" said John suddenly. "You've got some nerve, messing around with a seventeen-year-old!"

Antiope burst out laughing; so hard that she nearly lost her grip.

Edgar bit his fist and remained quiet.

A loud crack split what was left of the afternoon calmness, followed by a crash, then a monstrous yell that suddenly dominated the entire park. The big guy, Eddie, had snapped off a lower-hanging branch and was sprawled out on the ground.

"You big dummy! Get up from there!" John ordered.

"I'm too fat!" Eddie whimpered.

"What are you talking about?!" he heard John growl. "So there was a recall! It happens to yogurt sometimes!"

"They have no right to do that!" wailed Eddie.

"Just get up and do your job!" scolded John. "Shoot her down, if you have to! Do you hear me, Un-tie-o-pee?! Come down from there or I'll *tase* you!"

"Morons!" Antiope chirped.

John jumped up and hung from a branch but had nowhere else to go, despite his efforts.

"You should just leave me alone!" Antiope warned determinedly. "It'll just be like before and all your efforts will have been in vain. I will get the better of you! Mark my words!"

"But we *did* catch you, genius!" shouted John, still clinging from the branch.

"You didn't catch me! DARPA[45] caught me!"

"We're catching you now!" bellowed Eddie, standing on two large feet again. He pointed his muscular finger into the tree. "Come down, young lady, of face the music!"

"Do you really want to try me?" she warned. "I took you thousands of miles cross-country so that you couldn't sleep for days, and then I broke away clean! I made you crash into a bus! The look on your faces when I drove off in your precious van! I see you found it, by the way! I hope there wasn't too much water damage!"

"That isn't the same van!" John yelled hotly. "We had to get a new one from the rental company!" John lost his grip, but managed to land on his feet.

"Please come down," Eddie pleaded. "You made me come here on my off-time! The gym is calling my name! I'll have to go to work soon and *I REALLY NEED THAT WORKOUT!*"

"Yeah, and you *will* be on time!" John said.

"Alright, who cares anyway?" Antiope answered. "I'm too exhausted to argue. I'll come down if you promise to leave my companion out of this. Can you promise me that?"

"Fine!" John promised hotly. "We won't harm your companion—although he should be doing jail-time for molestation! Come down, and we'll talk it over!"

---

[45] The U.S. Defense Advanced Research Projects Agency.

"I'm coming down, but only on behalf of Agent Eddie! He's the only admirable man between the three of you!" Antiope descended with slow precision and was apprehended by the two cranky security guards.

"Wait, wait! My bicycle!" pleaded Antiope as she was dragged along. She struggled with the two men, but was easily overpowered and shoved into the van through the side door.

John, in consequence, grappled both bikes with mischievous intent and threw them into the path. "Take care of your Bicycle?! Oh, I'll take care of your bicycle, alright!" he howled. Incited to violence, Agent Mathews started the van and ran over the two bicycles with demon-driven schadenfreude; both could be heard crumpling agonizingly into asymmetrical pretzel shapes. "Guess what?!" John continued with foam dripping from his coffee-stained jaws. "No bicycle! No bicycle! No more goddamn bicycle!!"

"You ignorant asshole!!" cried Antiope from inside the abductors' vehicle.

Edgar listened foolishly, ashamedly, as the van pealed out through the molested grass and sped off in the direction of the sand, the academy, and the fruit factory of gads. He waited in the tree for awhile and then made his way down to examine the damage. Both bikes were totaled and would carry no more riders in this life.

Just then Edgar's new videophone rang with the sound of a yellow-throated vireo. He answered by voice-recognition and noticed with alarm that ExTemplar had texted him. Edgar looked at the screen and Edina's face appeared in the small square interface of the device.

"Why are you in a tree?" said Edina's face. "You missed lunch, so...mom made me see if you were dead in a ditch somewhere."

"No, not yet," Edgar answered.

Edina smiled impatiently. "Do you need me to pick you up?"

"Maybe I should just live here in the park."

"Mom would never allow it," Edina said.

"Never allow what, honey?" was faintly heard in the background of Edina's face.

"Uncle Edgar's living in a park," said Edina's side profile.

"I've decided something, though," resumed Edgar, speaking towards the interface, "so maybe I *could* use a ride, if you and your mom feel like a trip out to Nenaa'angebi for the evening."

"No problem," Edina said from a mouth-view. "I'm getting low on cinnamon bears...we can stop at the store. Don't tell mom."

"Can't she come with us?"

"Oh...she has candy to make...some suckers came this afternoon and bought all the suckers, so she has to make more."

"That's great. Thanks, Edina. It'll be better even than cinnamon bears."

The eye of his niece dominated the screen: "Better than...What?! You're stupid!"

The Color of Money

After the paper bills with pink, green, and baby blue tattoos of various caste-like representational values were regurgitated in machinated stacks, Edgar took his loot and walked back with mixed feelings. The bank's automatic teller machine was a cruel vendor; dispensing nothing to be eaten nor drank, yet with all the unnaturalness of a candy bar. He held in his hand a briefcase full of sorrow, to be desired and to burn, to leave nothing but emptiness. The money that he had earned through labor and peril was hardly his by most definitions. It came from the bowels of one bank only to be indebted to that of another. It was ethereal, would perish and be replaced. Even seconds after birth, the money loafed about the pocket with sinking value. The busts of presidents past stared through webs of deceit: They were fuel for dreams along a road of misery; the burden was taxing but the weight was measured in happiness.

"What's in it?" Edina prodded curiously as she drove them home to the smells of burnt sugar.

"Payday," Edgar said, "a lot of it."

"From the elite bug zapper thing?"

"Yes—let's say that."

"Wow. What are you gonna do with it? Can you buy back the farm?"

"No. Almost. But I'm not gonna do that."

"Why not?"

"Because... I've been thinking, and it seems to me that the old Weatherholt place has been holding me back. It's keeping me from moving forward. I need to let it go."

"What?! But I need that farm! How'm I gonna keep up on repairs?! How'm I gonna carry on the legacy?!" Edina cried at the thought of losing the farm. Her only memories of Aunt Edith and Uncle Jerome were at the Weatherholt barn where they tinkered away like Elves long into the night, when from the guest bedroom window the barn emitted a warm green glow.

Sensing the preoccupied distress of the driver, the car steered itself to the side of the road and came to a halt.

"I know it's a shock," Edgar explained, "but, just hear me out..."

"This is unfair..."

"I won't let them take your legacy," he said as he tried to console his niece. "I'm going to turn it into a non-profit. It's going to be a place to teach kids how to think outside the box. Mr. Wabe'no, the guy who invented those Zeno's Arrow bikes—I want him to be one of the teachers. We're on our way there now, to talk it over with him. I'm hoping you can be another."

"A teacher?! But I'm only nine! How 'm I gonna be a teacher!? The thought made Edina giggle, despite the tears running down her vanilla cheeks.

"Because you already think outside the box," said Edgar. "That's what we need in this country; hell, in this world! I've saved up the money. What the bank is doing to me is unfair. When they bought out the credit union they rewrote the stipulations of my inheritance, put a lien against it. I can pay for it in time, but I'm not going to let them do that to me. They just want to own everything anyway. It's like what happened in the Dust Bowl, during the Great Depression. All those people suffered for banks, so that the banks could grow up into even bigger banks. But they can't have our dreams. It's going to be a non-profit scientific dream camp."

"So, what are you going to do with *all that money*?"

"You'll see."

Edina and the Wonders of Quantum Pedaling

They drove north along the quagmire, past the dead marsh, the quiet towns, the hidden, intermediate lakes, and through the tunnel of trees into the Ojibwe lands. The leaves transforming into cool, solid fire and papery gold emblazoned the landscape with gorgeous autumn colors.

"To the homestead?" asked Edina as she tried getting them somewhere.

"No, not there. Keep going."

Further they went into the trees, where the owls dined on fresh meat and where the taupe-colored panthers lurked, stalking out a murderous future. The creeks gurgled under bridges to rendezvous at the headwaters of ponds and underground streams. They came upon a wooden fence that had been stained and carved into animals, and a wooden sign dangling from the high entrance of logs read *Ride the Plank's Constant.* Edgar had them pull in as they came upon a typical cabin home with a large lodge-type garage.

"Well, go ahead," encouraged Edgar. "Pick out a bike."

Edina protested, despite already having already picked one out in her head. "What?! But...what about Santa?"

"He says it's alright. He'll just give you a mystery gift."

Edina ran excitedly over to the row of bikes lined up in the wooden lodge-type garage.

"Hello," said the man, Mister Wabe'no, who had been working on something inside.

"Mister Wabe'no: remember me?" said Edgar, hurrying over to introduce himself properly.

The man looked but did not seem to remember. "Are you a friend of Ron's? He's out on a delivery... Ah..." he said, focusing on the one-of-a-kind vehicle, and then his middle-aged eyes began to water.

"I have something to ask you, Mister Wabe'no," said Edgar sympathetically; "and we also want to buy a few of your amazing bikes."

"So...hmmm..." Edina said, studying the engineering of the ladies' bicycles, "how do they work, mister?"

"Can't tell you," Mister Wabe'no said, blissfully smiling. "Unless...you want to tell me how *that* thing works!"

II

Trial and Error

The fields were mere shadows of themselves, the grains gray and lifeless. Blackbirds rose up from hiding and flew west in some kind of omen. The sky grew dark with impending rain.

David Hernando was taking over for Darrel, who had called in sick, and was driving a neon green Road-Warrior-type vehicle with specialized track tires and a hydraulic fork welded onto the back chassis. Despite the moist precipitation lightly taping his face for the first time in his life, he found the open road exhilarating. As they approached that all-too-familiar intersection he thought of the green bus and laughed.

"If they could only see me now!" he shouted to the unshackled wind. As they pulled up to the scene of the accident, he noted with interest that parts of the bus' right turn signal had become semi-permanent fixtures of this singular battle along the transportation war zone. They would remain here as mementos until the brush of change decided otherwise. He thought of how his ankle had ached that early morning—seemingly ages ago—and about the girl who had emerged from the smoking van with tinted windows. While in the factory, he had seen many faces that looked like her, which he had assumed was just the Devil messing with him again, because he had so much hoped for her success in escaping those two gringos. Now things were much different and sometimes he wished that he was still working with the boxes, where things were safer.

"This can't be happening; this isn't probable!" fretted Graham from the cushiony black seat of the Zapper. "It's supposed to be a nice sunny day! At least, that's what it said on the news!"

"That doesn't matter right now, Graham!" bemoaned Arturo. The forklift that seemed almost to be his personal vehicle-appendage was just ahead of the Zapper as they huddled up before the blinking red stoplight. Arturo looked back to see if everyone had made it. The odd vehicles lined up behind told him that they had. The crews were headed to an orchard out in Sutton's Bay. A convoy of semis, trucks, bizarre farm equipment, and dark governmental monstrosities was their obligatory vessel.

Graham pulled out his smartphone and started bouncing signals from nearby towers. He was determined to get to the bottom of unruly weather and protect the soundness of logical minds everywhere.

Seeing a break in the traffic, Arturo pulled out ahead and took them north along US 31. The Zapper was slow to react, Graham having been distracted by his smartphone, and the semis honked in anger until the line moved and then was severed again. Those who were already through the congestion waited at the side of the road and eventually the crew regrouped. Up they went along the highway, all the way to Gamesh and then north again along a half-filled, murky bay.

Dust kicked up from Arturo's leading vehicle. David noted with interest the dull yellow foliage of cherries appearing ragged on their gray-barked trees, many falling to the bug-heavenly ground in mushy repose. The tempestuous waters that once kept the weather misty and mild and behaved in guardianship over these Old World invaders had departed in myth, as if in retreat of humanity, but were alleged to return.

Graham held up his phone and took a 4th Dimensional snapshot. It must have seemed to him, as to all of them, that the entire world had gone mad. Unpredictability battered the onset of subdued precipitation like Holofernes at the approach to the mountains of Judea, eager to conquer. What had happened to the theory of a mathematical world? Where were the geometrical shapes of the weather, where the equation of the storm? It ravaged the country like an escaped beast.

The Suburban vehicles rumbled along a gravel road in the hills just ahead of them, the occupants bouncing in their seats.

David saw tantalizing orange and purple wildflowers growing in the ditches of plots shredded and laid bare. In one fielded plot was an old gray and pink schoolhouse leaning in the wind. Next there appeared the familiar high security fences and enclosed miles of sparkling gads. Human faces emerged. He watched Ernesto drive the long red tractor miserably into their wake, followed by Moses, who was driving a truck hauling tanks of splashing water. Strangely distant, they met there on the road, operators and laborers. David was amazed by the sheer effort that it took a legion of harvesters to come all the way out here. He looked to his fellows, for whom the next phase was reduced to ritual. The typically rewarding journey had taxed them. They were exhausted, defeated. As the late October rain increased in depth and coldness, their deeper purpose became sapped by demons of the mind. It was this, and nothing but this, until the end of time.

"Gate Fifty-Six, this is the Big Bad Wolf," said the driver of the lead suburban, heard through every hand-held radio of the convoy. His voice was glum and careless.

The guards allowed them through and the rest followed.

"Keep going!" Arturo shouted through the downpour, leading them down a muddy dirt road between a high fence and the orchard.

"I wonder how many we've done so far?" groaned one of the workers nearest to David. He was someone from another crew.

"Oh, I bet they've made a ton," another worker said assuredly.

This orchard seemed slightly newer than the last, and there were huge piles of ripped-out trees sitting near the basin of a creek, which David imagined as the aftermath of a bloody battle. A much hillier region, the land rose and fell in waves, and the trees with it.

Arturo checked his soggy and pocket-creased map and pointed to a spot at the head of the rows. "Here it is; this is the middle," he said. "Operators, let's go get your gear. Full armor this time."

"Hey, what about us?!" fretted a new guy whose name David couldn't remember. Unlike most of the other crews, which saw nearly full replacement, only two of his crew members had changed faces this month; many harvesters had quit back in late August to return to school, and a very shy set of twins had joined them in September only to be killed in the line of duty less than a month later.

"Block with your shield!" urged Arturo, bashing his own against the rain. He laughed heartily and sped off down the muddy road towards the equipment trailers.

David took Moses and Ernesto aboard and they slipped off in pursuit. It seemed to take a lot longer to get there, but eventually they arrived at the trailer. Chuck, who had been assigned to a third forklift—a blue version of the one David was driving—had narrowly beaten them.

"You've made it," the armory guard said. "This is the big time."

David became excited. He had waited a long time for this and it meant that he was getting a promotion. He signed the form and proudly received a red body armor cuirass, spaulders, greaves, gauntlets, cuisse-leggings, black sabaton-boots, and a forest green helm with a dark faceplate. He dropped his spaulders and then the greaves on the way to open ground where he could try everything on and as a result they became slightly muddy. It was more difficult than he thought putting everything on in the rain, but luckily a guard came by to help.

"There you go," said the guard once everything was where it should be and the straps were snug.

"Thanks," said David appreciatively. He removed his gauntlets and placed the icon of the skeletal Lieutenant Forester over his shield and marched stiffly back to the forklift racecar to await his passengers.

"Holy crap, you look scary!" said Arturo. It seemed to cheer him up a bit to see his crew in full armor. The veteran pullers were now promoted to roving status—they would rotate on the tarp while taking turns backing up Arturo on reconnaissance charge. It required a lot more effort, but broke up the monotony and made them feel important. As the rows in many of these newer orchards were twice as long, it also gave the tree-baiters a break.

"…brio, dash, fire, élan, gimp, life, oomph, vim, zing, pep, snap…" shouted Arturo, presenting a speech that was quick and to the point. "These are what we call great spirit and courage, the passion, the zeal...so get out there and make orphans of this wood!"

They lined up as before, veterans and rookies alike, and awaited the charge. The lane was a green zipper in a cornucopia of straight geometrical fruit-bulbs, both blessing and dystopian nightmare. The crimson bark on the trees closest to them seemed to stiffen as the engines sputtered to life.

Arturo roared sedately, holding the armored scarecrow high and slightly crooked, and charged down the lane next to Chuck.

"Once more into the breach..." Graham sighed, his high pitched squeak audible even to the birds that dodged the belch of detracting cannons somewhere ahead.

David loaded his tank of water onto the tractor and prepared for the rotation. It would be awhile, though, before he would have any fun, and he watched everything from the makeshift forklift before zipping off to retrieve another tank of water. The truck had to be left near the gate because of the mud, so he had to trek all the way there and back for each load. By the time he returned, the first tank was already full of gads and had to be changed out. Thus, David would be spending the first half of his day running back and forth like this. He hauled the full tank all the way to the truck and loaded it and then unloaded one with only water and returned to the orchards.

A wooden quill suddenly shot into the ground by David's left front tire. He was very surprised, because this had never happened from such a distance, or from a tree so close to the beginning of the lane. He pointed to the tree behind him and told Graham to call it in. After a few minutes delay, the Mahindra Nitro jettisoned in and took out the tree, which fought like an angry elephant from beneath the ballistic parachute. One team member's hand was punctured as he tried to attach the hose for the release of the liquid nitrogen foam. A second took over and she, too, was punctured in the hand and then the arm. Finally, they got the hose on and the tree was frozen into submission.

"You've got to be kidding me!!" complained the new guy. "Is that normal?!"

"Afraid so," piped in Graham as he maneuvered the Zapper back into position.

The new guy acted as if he might drop the tarp and bolt out of the orchard, but for some reason stayed. "So are these trees DEADLY?" he asked the other new guy, who shrugged and looked worried.

"They could kill you, yes," Graham calmly said, "especially if you insult them."

"I called that one a big green bastard; that's why it struck," said David jokingly as he headed out with another full tank.

On the way back, though, he was shocked to see the new guy quickly walking the high fence line with his head cocked down so as not to be confronted. David asked if he needed a ride but there was no response and so the process continued on.

"What's the deal?" David asked when he got back to the crew. They were just sitting around as if stuck.

"The new guy left," said Ernesto. "He said it wasn't worth it."

"It isn't," David said, "and yet here we are, still doing it."

"The paycheck helps," Graham added tiredly.

"Won't help if you're dead," glumly said Ernesto.

"Didn't they tell you guys in orientation—about the trees, I mean?" David had spoken to the remaining tarp-puller on the right side of Big Red who had once again become the new guy.

"Of course they did!" said the guy. "But who would take something like that seriously?"

"So why are *you* still here?" asked Graham.

"Temporary insanity, I guess," answered the guy. "Besides, I gotta pay child support or they put me back in jail."

Ernesto frowned. "This is better than jail?"

"No, but I'm sick of being locked up," the guy explained. "Ain't got nowhere else to go except China, and I already tried that, back when my baby momma and me lived in one of them 'Maternity Mansions' in Beijing. They kicked us out 'cause the baby was a boy."

"I thought they liked boys," said Graham.

"They ain't got enough prostitutes. They want whores that look like cyberspace models; you get this designer gene stuff done for free; I got a beautiful son that cost me a thousand a month."

"Where's your baby momma?" asked Ernesto.

"She's in Gamesh, low income apartments out by that old rundown mall. She just sits on her hiney playing Realms of Wastecraft all day. She got a Lunar Elf Warlock on the Hoity-toity server. I like to gank her ass with my Cave Jinn Assassin sometimes, just to keep her on her toes."

Ernesto smiled. "You still love her?"

"Never did, really," the guy admitted. "We just got along, is all."

"Well, this is great," Graham said disgustedly from the seat of the quieted Zapper. "Can't get through on radio. David can you-"

"Yes," David answered exhaustively, not that there was any alternative. He tore off down the rows towards Chuck and Arturo. He could see that they were resting on the ground in the center and it looked like Chuck had been wounded in the ankle with a bandage wrapped around it. One tree on Chuck's side was marked but no one had taken care of it yet and so David used caution, driving beneath the trees on the left side. They appeared not to have seen him yet and so he yelled to get their attention. Arturo got up with great effort, but failed to notice the neon green vehicle, and instead walked towards the trees nearest on the left side. As David approached on the forklift, a very weird thing happened: two trees near Arturo appeared to move their branches almost imperceptibly in his direction as if sensing his movement. "Hey!!" David yelled, but it was too late and Arturo was thrusting his armored scarecrow into the furthest canopy, apparently having forgotten the other, and so David lowered his visor and pressed the gas pedal to the floor. When he was near enough, he hit the brakes and grabbed Arturo from the back of the cuirass and then sped off into the opposing lane, crossing his gauntleted fingers in hope that the quills would miss and that there were no angry trees ahead. They skidded down the untouched lane as David avoided a collision with a Turkish rose tree trunk.

"Son of a..." David growled, cringing at the pain. Three quills had somehow penetrated his upper left arm and one was stuck in his right thigh just below the armor. He lifted his visor and stormed out of the vehicle.

"Where do you think you're going? You saved my life, David!"

"You've got quills stuck in your leg!"

"So do you! Never mind that! Come over here!"

David felt awkward as he allowed Arturo to hug him like a bear, even though the quills were in their limbs, and even though David was no longer touching the ground.

"Enough of this mess! There's going to be a celebration, I swear it! We all deserve a fiesta!"

Once the quills were pulled out and the wounds dressed using Arturo's medical kit, they picked up Chuck and hopped around the safer areas of the orchard over the Bahia grass. They were over the blades of the self and amidst a celebration of all things, singing their eulogy to the living and the dead, humbled by nature.

III

The Great Outcry

"We won't stand for this!" said the would-be leader of the anonymous group. "You can't put a patent on people!" He, like everyone else in the crowd, was wearing a mask.

The crowd cheered.

A young lady on a pulpit began folk dancing with her protest sign. A man wearing an elephant head ran up and gave her a megaphone and she shouted into it, saying, "We'll tell you who's the fairest!! And it certainly isn't you, Litchfield!!"

Public outrage had reached an uncomfortable boiling point since the former website wehateexecs.org had launched OPERATION THROUGH THE LOOKING GLASS, providing its viewers with uncanny access into the secret lives of Monstrosso executives by manipulating a weak security protocol in a rising tech product called The Magic Mirror™. Even from a comedic standpoint, the website was a viral hit, as tech-savvy youngsters and oldsters alike watched instant narcissists checking themselves in the interface, indiscriminately kissing themselves, or others, in private, and disclosing secrets during clandestine meetings and impromptu stoppages along plush hallways.

From inside the academy, where one of several protests was occurring that day, Litchfield lay sprawled out on the dean's desk in horror, clutching a thermal love meter. "Why does it never turn red..." she garbled, wondering if the Reaper had covered the distance at last. It was a scheduled visitation, just her luck!

Young Dean Yorkshire was furious. "I even had sex with you!" he said, pacing the spacious room in front of the curtains. "I'll be lucky if they ever let me near a student again! I thought you said this thing was *solid*! '*A goldmine*' is what you said!"

"Don't flatter yourself, dear...I've had better..." wheezed Litchfield dryly.

The exact location of Hodge and Hoffman, meanwhile, was anyone's guess. She had left them back at the resort hotel where they were probably enjoying a round of Russian roulette golf at the company's expense.

Somewhere in Creve Coeur

The messenger was brought in from the anteroom to the anthurium-motif meeting hall with the leaf-chairs and anthemion vases. The glazed walnut conference table shone the reflections of dour men and women in expensive suits and million-dollar makeovers.

The pristine, close-shaven young man approached in silence, setting the dossier on the table.

"Excellent, Constantine," said the old man sitting at the head of the table. "You may wait." The old man fiddled with a platinum and gold nameplate that read *BENJAMIN GRANT, President and CEO* with the symbol of an eye within a pyramid that sat atop a white tree with silver leaves.

A steward appeared from the corner, ushering the messenger forward where he waited for some time in a comfortable leaf-chair, happily sipping a mint julep.

The old man sat with intrigue as the dossier was passed around the table. It wasn't everyday that a small subsidiary department made such a splash at headquarters. Hodge, Hoffman, and Litchfield, the supervisory heads of the division in charge of making America competitive again, had really screwed things up. Such promise he had seen in those three, and they could not handle a single head of swine. If not for the lucrative contracts and the tax breaks secretly awarded the company by the government for their decades of effort in this clandestine area, he would have had them moved back down to agrochemicals. It should have made someone in his position furious, thinking of the days when they had shaken down hundred-acre farmers for alleged patent infringement of their Rundown Ready soybeans, but he could have cared less today, feeling very old and more inclined towards the amusement brought on by these calamities. How many would be ruined this time, he wondered? How much power gained or lost? Could they patent enough life to fill a proverbial Ark for a blasphemous, designer humanity of the hereafter? And what would such a henceforth look like, wondered Old Man Benjamin, a Rundown Ready kingdom of bioluminescent peons for them to control at their own contentment? His lusterless eyes sparkled at the thought, and he wondered if he should have someone call up Disney to redesign their House of the Future into something more aligned to his way of thinking. What fun! Who would control this monstrous thing when he finally passed on to ashes like a Charlemagne or an Alexander the Great and the mechanism (with all its assets and stations and heads of chattel) was up for grabs? How he wished that he could witness the results of such a passing, which would prove far more enjoyable than bickering sons and daughters, who would inherit mere portions of a nest egg unworthy of the vast stage that was Monstrosso. In time, his progeny would glow at the behest of some terrible lord. No living thing would escape those patent-hungry jaws that had once, long ago, with the toothless mouth of a babe, subsisted only on saccharin.

"Hodge, Hoffman, and Litchfield," read his top executives forebodingly as copies of the documents were passed around the table.

"Indeed," grumbled Benjamin Grant. He waited impatiently for the thing to unfold. It was a game devised by a simple designer girl and he was anxious for results. In mind, the girl had dwarfed them in a matter of months, but a body could be broken in seconds. The old Benjamin would have ordered her demise with pleasure; however, the new Benjamin, several molts in and wiser to the maximization of entertainment, awaited the politics of an internal feeding frenzy.

"The Magic Mirror is selling exponentially well..." one member said.

"But the profits are split, between us and..." proclaimed one.

"This can't go on; she'll be a gazillionaire! She'll own *us*!" proclaimed yet another.

"Not just her, but the entire student body," said the chairman chuckling. "She's included them all in the shares!"

"How could you not see this?" grumbled Benjamin Grant unsympathetically. He sipped a tall glass of ice water before continuing. "This is dire!"

"We must do something about it and quickly," said one ambitious young female executive. "If only we'd learned to limit their creative intelligence earlier on. Those first and second gens are trouble..."

"Come now," countered another, older male executive, "Three out of a hundred... that's hardly trouble..."

"Under the circumstances..." warned the young female.

"Anyway, that's all in the past..." bellowed the older male. "Time machines are still in the testing phase."

"So what can we do?" the voices rebounded around the table.

"She's ours isn't she?" said the young female exec. "We created, we can damn well *uncreate*."

"She'll have to have an accident..." one mused darkly.

"Rephrase that please," said the chairman, pointing up at the surveillance cameras.

"Never mind that," Grant said. "We can't very well murder them all... A compromise will have to be made..."

"A compromise? Us?" the chairman asked with incredulity. "How in the world do we do that?"

Benjamin Grant's face cracked. "We shut down the Magic Mirror. Halt production."

"Consider it done," said the young female exec. She ogled the room for respect and received instead indolent, submissive fear.

"What about the girl?" inquired one starched-shirted managerial, emitting a peevish bleat.

"What about her?" Grant countered, pleased by the evening's performance. "She's not going anywhere. Put her back in the factory; give her a raise—chain her to the assembly line if you have to. She's already shown leadership over the others. She might prove valuable."

"Fine," said one of the other execs. "And what about these altered gads? Our engineers haven't been able to figure out how to stop cross-pollination yet."

"I'm aware of that," grumbled Grant. "Our top men are working on it."

438

"And the weather?"

"That's not our department," said the chairman. "Let the WCA deal with it. Our trees have been designed to withstand the harshest conditions on earth."

"Yes, but the workers can't."

"Then get new ones," grumbled Grant.

"Sir?"

"Get new workers!"

"Of course, Mister Grant."

NONDECUPLET

I

Area 5.1

"And so in order to find Little Miss Poopypants you simply retrace the 'x' 'y' trajectory…" Edina said to the monkey holding the camera. "Now for a sucker break: everyone, feel free to grab some suckers. If you've run out, my mom can make more. Just text her your name and address, or go to Enchanted Creations dot-com and order some… But you'll have to buy them if you do it that way."

"Uncle Edgar! What are you doing here?"

Edgar had stopped by with his girlfriend. Edina had at first found her to be extremely weird but now she was nice. The awesome Magic Mirrors hanging throughout the old pioneer homestead were from her, and she had helped make them from her own dreams, which was pretty cool. Rumor had it though that Monstrosso had paid someone to copy the patents and smuggle them to China, which wasn't very cool at all though. She was weary of the patent office after hearing about that, but unfortunately there wasn't a better way yet.

"How did you get here?" she asked them.

"We teleported. How do you think?" said Edgar jokingly.

"We quantum pedaled," admitted Antiope. "We needed the exercise."

Edina was surprised that someone could make it that far on a bicycle. She herself had never tried it.

"Where are all the students?" asked Edgar.

Edina's face puckered. "The classes are every other month, you slug's butt. The rest are streaming video. You can see them at

440

Area Five-point-one, if you bothered to go online and check it out like I told you to."

"What's Area Five-point-one?" asked Antiope.

"Our website," explained Ron Wabe'no from the master controls. He had been overlooked due to the monkey and all the props.

"I thought it was the Home-wind Academy for Children Interested in Science," said Edgar.

"It is," assured Ron. "Area Five-point-one is the name for the online courses; Home-wind Academy dot 'e' 'd' 'u'."

"What happened to the bikes?" Edgar countered.

"We sold out of them;" Ron admitted. "Uncle Albert and my dad are gonna make more, but they're waiting for a sign from the Great Spirit, Gitche Man'ito."

"I see," said Edgar, "and what about you, Edina? I hope you're behaving better than you were last week."

"Around here they call me Wah-wah-tay'see," she administered. "I've been busy trying to figure out how to draw energy out of the air. Did you know that a bolt of lightning can travel at speeds of one-hundred-and-forty-thousand miles per hour? If we could utilize the discharge without interfering with the natural process of air ionization and electric field, all of our energy needs would be met a gazillion-fold! The answer is in the Sprites and Elves; that's this amazing jellyfish thing… What. Don't look at me like that… I know what I'm talking about!"

"Would you like to see the new observatory?" Ron ventured.

"Let's do it," Edgar agreed.

"Not me," Edina / Wah-wah-tay'see said. "I've gotta feed the monkey. His name is Streaker, by the way… 'cause he doesn't like wearing the nice clothes that Antiope's mom made for him. He streaks and he reeks. That's all he does."

"Maybe you should take him back to the zoo," said Ron.

"Hey, I get to keep him for a month!" Edina answered in false anger. "That was the agreement! And he's famous now, so…"

"We're taking him back to Grand Rapids next month whether she likes it or not," whispered Ron.

Edina went to the kitchen to get Streaker a banana. The old Weatherholt homestead was not scary anymore, like it used to be. It was an atypical house though, and every room had been converted into a classroom or a laboratory. There would be other kids here next month and she would have to prove her leadership all over again. Xiulan Chin and that Zoshchenko girl, Margarita, were the big ones, because, like her, they had been selected as teachers. But a kid was not a flea, and if the galoshes fit, no Gaul would be hindered from battle.

"Can I pet the monkey now?!" Xiulan called out from somewhere upstairs.

"Not until you figure out 'Petals around the Rose'!" she yelled up the laundry chute.

"I'm finished counting integers!" yelled Margarita from a different upstairs room.

"Okay, you can come down and help me feed Streaker!" Edina shouted.

"Is it that they're all divisible by pi?!" answered Xiulan down the laundry chute.

"No!" said Edina.

"I give up!" said Xiulan passively.

"Just think about it!" shouted Edina. "Look at the patterns in the dice and think about what the game's called!"

"Okay, but I don't want to play anymore!"

"Fine!"

On second thought, though, she didn't really mind. Things would be kind of fun from now on.

II

The Show Must Go On

The flock neighed and baaed where they lingered, slowly putting on rain gear or protective arm coverings, watching the clock intently. As a trickling and then an increasing mass of forms, they passed through geometry, being swallowed and spit out, swallowed, regurgitated, set onto the path of oncoming trains. The work was massive to the point of insanity, as they stripped the world to be sold at exorbitant prices. Nothing could be eaten, this foodstuff passing illusory through their tired fingers, unless paid for in the quantity demanded. The quantity in whole had been predetermined by the government, and what was unsold would be left to rot. As employees of GGI, they received a 10% discount, which was very generous, and yet few of them had ever eaten a gad in any selective form or package, and of those who had, nearly half had done so illegally. The gad had become the Picasso of the fruit world, elitist for the sake of elitism, more symbol than staple. The upholding of a symbol that had become eminent in the minds of loyal, deep-pocketed consumers was the most common justification for the continued legacy of the Tree of Life brand. Even if people had to die for it, the supply would meet demand at the ringing of Pavlovian bells. Flanking the raw goodness of it all was the clever introduction of gad superfruit recipes, additives, and flavorings, such as the recent introduction of gad schnapps, beer, wine, rum, and vodka, the use of gad powder to enhance flavor in commercial foods, or the suggestion to add them to salads or ice cream. This was all just procedure, of course.

"I mean really, though, how could there be so many multiples?"
"You're right, it is a little creepy."

"It just isn't normal. What's causing it? Are we in any danger?"

"Could be. Who knows?"

Susanne glanced at Pauline as they overheard the rude conversation going on between co-workers. The rest of the Penuels who were working today had been spread out so as to lessen the freakishness of partial nonuplets being observed amongst so many other multiples, although some as large as twenty had been seen arriving at the academy as of late. That such things were possible elicited a flash of brightness upon the future. With an increase of like-minded people populating the atmosphere, life was becoming more bearable, and would soon reach the point of bliss: Eternal work was eternal comfort. What the corporation promised had come to pass and it seemed that the gads would reign forever, even into winter, as a continuous season of dominance. Susanne relayed this through facial expressions to Pauline. They had always been able to read each other's thoughts, as though lovers destined for torment on their way to the Empire State Building. All of the siblings could do this to a degree—except Antiope, who was something of a black sheep and a pariah.

"We're better than you," mumbled a quintuplet by the name of Jack. He was afraid even to lift his eyes away because he might miss some important detail, some flaw or speck of rot in the perfectly-round fruit, and had become agitated.

"*What's that?*" asked a neighboring co-worker who was a unique radical to their kind.

"He doesn't mean anything," Susanne told her. The co-worker turned fearfully away and stayed quiet, her eyes full of worry. Susanne thought what a torture to live in misery, like this poor woman, rather than in the glory of toil. Although fuzzily few were known to Susanne herself, the co-worker had choices. She did not have to be a chatterbox. And yet what was choice in light of contentment? How many bright young people had died for ambition, penniless, wretched? They followed their bliss onto scaffolds in the night and by morning they were hanged. They were destined to die angry and wasted. That was what the instructors had always told her, but to whisper advice was far from being Susanne's strong suit. "Slavery!!" is what this miserable lot called it. Slavery was the reason they cited most (not to Susanne, or course, but to others). It was a word from history. The compounds were always the deciding factor (that is, metals, compounds found in the Periodic Table of Elements); the Bronze Age, for instance. With agriculture had come a time when a person was worth their weight in salt. Those at the top stayed until they slipped, exploiting the others with a primal psychology unique to their social hierarchy, a hierarchy of animals, ultimately logical and complex, until they, too, were enslaved, or killed, or worse, and the cycle continued, building up, collapsing, building, always at odds with the archaic, while the people multiplied and spread like mice, growing hungry, hungrier, even hungrier, as the food piled up in abundance to be devoured by the madness of it.

Oh no! Had she just missed something? Good, Jack had gotten it. *Thanks, Jack.*

Stainless steel; titanium; uranium; gold; With every compound the version reemerged differently, as one molted the metal of the age, shaped in the same mold, metamorphosed, and impelled to transcend towards the same madness. She hated to think of it even, but these coworkers—or perhaps it was the fruit. The culture which they had built up through molds of behavior was a golden square of insanity, folding in upon itself, becoming madder by the hour, but for her things were different; she was stronger, with a stable mind, and she did not bother with misery because she was happy to be involved in something, to become engrossed in the world around her, the sounds, shapes, colors, and smells of a mathematical world. She was *not* a slave, not toiling without reward, not ill treated (in her view), not hungry or naked, but existing within the Eden of industry, free within the walls of the City of Brass, and nothing could breach them as long as contentment reigned. She dared not think.

The Snail Mail is Victorious

"David? David Hernando?" said a fellow migrant when he saw David eating dinner in the break room.

445

"Yes?" said David.

"We thought you had been abducted by aliens!" said the migrant.

"Nope," said David. "I'm living in a train."

The migrant continued: "In that case, it's fortunate, because I was about to forward your mail to the dead letter office here at Inhuman Resources. I was doing this on behalf of the camp, but now that you're here in the flesh..."

David received a bundle of letters and things that had come in the mail. He thanked his fellow migrant and began browsing. Most of them were from his mother, whom he had forgotten to call these last couple months, but one was from Carlos, to his surprise.

Letter from Carlos

To Dave the Slave,

Greetings ass this is yore old pal Carlos remember me? I made it through Basic Training and AIT and am now serving in Korea where the chicks are fine. CAMP CASEY they call the place and its like this big fucktup militant city where everyone is a playa like you and me, bro. I'm currently dating two females at once! Ladies, I mean, sry. The military lingo really gets to you. I met one of them on the intranet. Only Army people can get on there. Speaking of that you should really get with the times. I hait typing and will never do it again.

I'm making a killing selling e-cigs and axcesories and soon I'll be able to re tire. You should see my biceps. Are you sure you won't join? Our motto over here is "be prepared to fight a war at a moment's notice". They say 44 yrs and nothing has happened! Is that a cakewalk or what! Even you don't have to worry! Unless they ask you to cut down a tree in the DMZ!! Anyway, I'm like a private in the infantry and I get to fire laser beams!

69th Laser Beam Brigade is what I'm in, 2nd Infantry Division, Battery Z, 47th Field Artillery Regiment. I have to copy and paste because its a frigging mouthful. The order doesn't seem to matter and I have no idea what it is anyway. Thats also my adres if you add CAMP CASEY to the top and my name, which is Pvt. Carlos Lacerta. Not CARLITO!! If you write it like that I will murder you. Hope alls cool in the orchards. I assoomed you would be home bie now but I guess not. What a drag.

Later asswipe!

p.s. send some dried gads my way, will you?

Some 3 Star Movies Are the Best That You Will Ever See

Time off was a blessing these days. The orchard was a torturous and reliable place to earn a living, not to mention dangerous. The bruised and battered workers tread through October in search of Ulalume but found only a lament for sleep. Furthermore, the sight of turning leaves in woodlands along the country roads made even the armory guards grieve for less-dependable fields.

Another pair of sentinels had turned up dead that week, along with a deer and two squirrels. It seemed as though the color crimson was driving the trees mad and causing them to stray at night.

At home, in the abandoned train, things were getting chilly. David's feet were tingly. He relied on radiation to keep him warm, but discovered this to be inadequate as he browsed the list from an internet website dedicated to 3 star movies (out of five). Finding one to be particularly moving, he curled up with the mice and freed it from the constraints of control by pressing the play button.

David sat thinking for a time afterward and drank some enriched water and fell asleep without going to the break room to brush his teeth, but was awakened sometime in the night by a televised news bulletin.

———

CBC B.S. BREAKING NEWS:

"'Indianhead' Sends 'Tigers from Mars' to Tanzania"

Lola Chaffin Green: "Battery Z, 47th Field Artillery Regiment of the 2nd Infantry Division's 69th Laser Beam Brigade will soon make ground in Tanzania as NATO forces push towards Dar es Salaam's al Iymsorri District, where terrorist forces allied to al-Qaeda have holed themselves up like Chihuahuas on Christmas. We now take you there live with war correspondent Edgar Allen Po, that brave man."

Edgar Allen Po reporting live in Dar es Salaam: "Greetings, Lola. For many here in Tanzania this is definitely a descent into the maelstrom, for local residents and belligerents alike, as NATO forces maneuver drones, HULCs, and American Billboards Top Ten hits through sand and karma to reach the objective. The United States Army portion of NATO's ground forces eagerly awaits the arrival of its cleanest weapon yet, the High Energy Laser Load 'Death Ray' with 'Claw Hammer' component, which they say is capable of vaporizing an entire city block in milliseconds. As the ravens cry 'Nevermore', few will grieve the loss of humanity here in Tanzania. Back to you, Lola."

III

Leader of Swine

Antiope could not begin to understand why a major corporation would end such a lucrative partnership. She was only thankful that she had not been murdered; in fact, they were giving her a promotion. She was now an honorary Academy Overseer, with the job of watching over the students both at home and during their little employment projects. It was something of a farce, because in addition she had been given permission to leave the academy and to live elsewhere. When she had tested them as a joke, saying that she did not want to leave, they had insisted upon throwing her out. This sudden build of trust was startling, given the evidence over the short duration of her life, and she wondered if they might murder her after all. Nonetheless, Antiope wasted no time at all in gathering her things and moving in with mother. Now things were going extraordinarily well for her and she had even been able to access her bank account at the local credit union where a gazillion dollars sat stashed (actually, the amount was closer to $3,560,711.82). In celebration of her freedom she had purchased over 300 bicycles with Quantum Pedaling™ Technology for the students and declared every Freya's Day (Friday) the Day of Bicycles during which no student would work. Instead they would have a bicycle parade and little Bethany would follow the leader on her training wheels as they circled the academy grounds.

Antiope rolled out of the little green shop on K Street early in the morning with her new Zeno's Arrow bike and headed to the feared factory of gad and apple fruit processing. She could already see it through the transient pines and would soon arrive at the front gate.

"State your business," said the gate guard.

"None of yours…" Antiope joked. "Just kidding, Fred."

"Oh, it's you," said Fred bitterly. "I heard about it in the news…"

"Cheer up, Fred." Antiope vanished, shifting in and out of time, until reaching the front door of the break room.

She wore a pink shirt, which she had made herself at her mother's shop, and roamed the factory under a hairnet. The logo of an eye stared out from her abdomen and dared misbehavior with a violet iris. The employees assumed that she worked for Monstrosso. "There she is," they said, "the eye! Maybe all those peculiar things will stop happening!"

Antiope had decided upon a routine. She would arrive sometime in the morning, and again sometime in the evening, and would roam the entire factory once. "How are you Judith, and you, Mark?" she'd ask, close enough to tickle their ears with her quiet voice, and they would nod impatiently, annoyed to have been disturbed from their work. The supervisors in their confusion would chat with her and the mechanics would notice her suspiciously. Then, once a week, she would hold a press conference outside the factory gates and tell the public how wonderful everything was going despite the impending corporate doom closing in—already, the media had decided *for* them, and their fears of becoming some company's property were, for the most part, obscured in hocus pocus ("No, no, we aren't filing a patent on *all* people..." one spokesperson had said. The American public seemed increasingly more willing to submit.)

Thus it was, basically, as she entered the clamor of production. Only the managers knew the truth, or at least dared to find out, and so *she really was a spy* in a sense—as someone with a differing thought process, who roamed amongst them taking mental notes. A democracy was somewhere in these wet, fish-netted heads, and she would draw it out regardless of fear. The assembly process had not been missed, however, and as she watched the sorters in their proud, depraved misery, the dreadful memories came back and she imagined that a stool had been left vacant just for her. It was not all bad, though, she supposed, but oh, that deep down chill! The damp, dreary atmosphere was an incubator for a fantastical northern sickness that only some mysterious vaccine could cure. The dreary repetition, the non-stop highway of little round fruit, was enough in itself. How they sparkled, the mischievous things, on their way to warehouses to be shipped off to stores worldwide. Seeded, they had purpose, and harvested as they were, even with care and in great,

450

bountiful numbers, they seemed somehow to know that something was amiss. Sensing weakness in their adversaries, they spoke of intrigue; whispered ancient secrets to tired minds. Antiope had thought little of them as of late, but supposed that she, too, had been influenced by them somehow, even though the very thought of plant intelligence seemed a stretch. And yet she recalled in her self-taught biology lessons the amazing symbiotic relationships and how the vines reacted to electrical impulses. It was amazing to watch a plant time-lapsed into animation after being caught on film. Could they really have been telling her something? And what might that have been? They seemed as content as identical siblings to this repetitive life. And why should they complain? They were well cared for. They were in high demand. No, but she knew better, of course, and there was a reason why she was here instead of wandering the wilderness somewhere, blissfully severed from civilization and the company of largely disrespectful resemblances (and, no doubt, on the verge of starvation).

"Hello, Luke; hello John! How goes life?!" And on she went, haunting the gad factory, until she deemed that it was time to peer into windows at Duck Lake and then pedal all the way back to her mother's shop—it was in no way sustainable, this new schedule of hers!

Tom's Halo Shines through the Darkness Albeit Briefly

The idea was his to make the girl an Overseer, Tom thought smugly. They had pitched the supervisory position to him on videophone, but he had thought it better to give her some kind of honorary position to appease the public and to keep their curiosity at bay—they had such short attention spans anyway that nothing would come of it—and GGI really didn't need another supervisor, and especially not for *them*. Monstrosso's progeny were eerily well-behaved. And why not, given his involvement? He owed the poor girl something, if not for her keeping quiet about the apartment, then for the sake of her mother, poor Henrietta, who was probably out haunting the inner-city lounges. Anyway, they had loved the idea and were offering him a position. He could hardly wait to tell

Margaret! She would probably even start having sex with him again, if he could convince her to move to Creve Coeur, or to move at all. Wow, he thought, perhaps he had a soul after all. *If only mother...* And now he was headed to the Silver Lining hovel for a brief liaison with Pierre's secretary Judy, where they would fool around in the mind-blowing mirror that he had had mounted to the ceiling. How he would love to meet the man who had invented *that*!! What a great prop for the background of his life!! *One last fling,* he thought blissfully as he drove the basal, rented hybrid to the outskirts. *Damn it all! I thought this thing was supposed to get good gas mileage...I'll stop on the way back. What Margaret doesn't know won't hurt her one bit. And then, who knows?! Perhaps Hong Kong or Bangkok!*

Mrs. Wesson, Meet Mr. Wesson

Mrs. Chase Wesson floated to the marble table in the living room and turned on the silver tablet notebook computer. Thankfully, she had paid enough attention to Oona when she was still under their employment to know how to perform such a task. This was done mainly to solve a mystery, because she had received a phone text showing a lewd picture and a website address to Videophone Port 9024790. The text was from a private investigator whom she had hired to look into where the special mirror had gone that she had ordered and *so desperately wanted* (all of her friends already had as much as five of them!). Therefore, out of curious obligation, she followed the instructions and soon found herself looking into someone's cheap bedroom. The sheets were not even real silk she realized in abhorred disgust while voyeuristically peering down from the ceiling. A woman suddenly appeared on the bed, sprawled out in a lurid crimson teddy, and then a shirtless man very much resembling her husband. "My mirror!!" shrieked Mrs. Margaret Chase Wesson, so loudly that the two pathetic lovers stopped whatever it was that they were doing and looked up in fear of God. For a second she was strangely aroused, and then enraged with hurt, but at last Margaret's prim and properness returned and

452

her head was filled with procedures. Both of their parents would have to be notified at once, of course, to maximize the benefits. The children were off at their private schools and colleges—best to leave them out of things just yet, she thought, and wait until *they* contacted *her*. That would be best. Whom to notify first, she thought, and immediately sent a call to Mrs. Chase, her mother, who would begin the chain reaction of releasing the hounds, relatives, and lawyers. She would have to get her riding attire to the drycleaners right away: A foxhunt was underfoot! Margaret wrung her hands of madness as she awaited the connection. "Oh, you'll rue the day, Mister Tom Wesson the Third!!"

ICOSUPLET

'Hear us, you who are no more than leaves always falling, you mortals benighted by nature, You enfeebled and powerless creatures of earth always haunting a world of mere shadows, Entities without wings, insubstantial as dreams, you ephemeral things, you human beings: Turn your minds to our words, our etherial words, for the words of the birds last forever!'
—Chorus in Aristophanes' *The Birds*

I

A Part of the Act

The Birds over Wall Street: *a comedy by Zech Adam Adams* ran the playbill. It contained the artistic rendition of a businessman and a businesswoman with bird heads. The play was to be performed in less than a week at the downtown Gamesh Theatre and would open Friday night at 8 pm (November 6th). Antiope was excited, because Mother had been commissioned to create the costumes, and because Edgar and she would be performing in the play as birds.

"Hey, nice outfits!" someone said as they passed.

Already the beginning of November, the city's disgruntled youth were walking around in Guy Fawkes masks in protest of surveillance (They were no doubt tired of being students, waiters, housekeepers, and cashiers). Antiope, meanwhile, had persuaded Edgar to help her advertise the linen shop by trying out some of the bird heads they had just made; Edgar had the head of a blue jay, while Antiope's was that of a kingfisher. She thought they looked very realistic.

"So what was it that you said you got in the mail?" Antiope asked.

"A model of a zeppelin," answered Edgar. "My dad finally answered the request of a soldier far from home. It's a weather station, the same one that I...or at least that I dreamed that I..."

"What are you going to do about a job?" Antiope jeered. "I hope you don't expect *me* to support you."

"On *your* meager salary?"

Antiope tenderly hooted, "So what's the plan?"

"I don't really have any obligations," Edgar said as they walked together under gawkers' stares and downtown shops, headed for the charming boardwalk along the Boardman River. He continued: "They fired me of course—probably bugged my phone out of paranoia—and with Edina set up teaching at that summer school for young scientists..."

"So you haven't a care in the world..."

"I haven't a single one," Edgar joked, sensing the direction of this slightly sensitive companion at his side.

Antiope nudged him playfully and he nudged her back. "So are you obligated enough to keep your promise?"

"May the wings of liberty never lose a feather," quoted Edgar.

They laughed freely and admired the environs of the river that had been laid bare now that November had claimed the leaves. They discussed glassmaking and algology.

Further out, the quagmire stirred. Something big was happening: Under some invasive kind of joint-mining deal, the Canadian government and the United States government had finally agreed to follow through on an earlier plan to drain the Hudson Watershed into the Great Lakes watershed and the lakes were refilling. Actually, it had already been going on for at least a month without anyone from the public sector realizing it.

The river seemed appreciative. They could already see the flow heading out into the discharge pond with high hopes of a reunion.

The Grand Traverse Dam Project Authority, meanwhile, were hard at work dismantling their dream before the headwaters rushed in.

II

A Moveable Feast

Sunday, November 1st.

The Keeper was in the kitchen where a large meal had been cooked and came out with the special drink. Around the table were Arturo, his crew, and two small children. The Keeper poured the drink into greenstone glasses and sat down at the head of the table. "It's time," she said. "The sun is calling. It's time to move on."

"We're heading out directly after the celebrations," declared Arturo happily.

"Who will take charge of the orchards?" asked Graham. His typically high-pitched voice was heavy with sadness.

"You could do it," Arturo said, pointing. "Or you, Darrel. Any of you could replace me; I have confidence."

"What will *you* do David?" asked The Keeper. "Are you coming with us?"

"Yes, I would like that," said David optimistically. "It's getting cold and I have no heat."

"And so, will you stay in season forever?" she said, probing his thoughts with her large golden eyes.

"No, not as a migrant, I hope."

"What will you do, then?" she asked.

David waited for his drink to settle. "After I save enough, I'll go to college, be a math teacher or maybe even a tobacconist."

"That sounds nice," said The Keeper.

"Good for you, David," said Arturo. "All of you deserve to do great things."

"So what's the celebration?" asked Chuck, having finished off his drink with vigor.

"The Day of the Dead," said The Keeper, sounding dramatically grim. "Tomorrow is All Soul's Day, and we'll be having a celebration. Gad Growers is letting us use the vacant storage building, and in the afternoon there will be a parade in Gil beginning and ending in the cemetery. In the storage there will be many contests such as for art and hot tamales, and a migrant band will perform traditional music. We will drink to the dead raising our sugar skulls, and eat the favorite foods of the departed, and sing for them."

"There will be marigolds, masks both dark and beautiful, and skeletons," added Arturo, trying to be dramatic, but failing gruffly.

"Awesome!" said the crew.

"Hurray!" said the two small children; both of them, a boy and a girl, were like The Keeper in miniature.

"So, where are the other kids?" wondered David. "I thought you had like six."

The lovely Keeper snickered in disbelief; Arturo laughed so hard that he nearly fell out of his chair.

THE HEADLINES CHANNEL:
(Your Scannable Guide to Tweetable Tweets)

WINDY CITY THIRSTY NO MORE – CHICAGOANS EMBRACE THEIR NEW PANTAGRUEL

PEOPLE ARE BEING WARNED TO STAY OFF THE BEACHES UNTIL LAKE LEVELS STABILIZE

STRANGE BUZZING SOUNDS EMITTED FROM BOTTOM OF LAKE MICHIGAN PUZZLE SCIENTISTS

U.S. STORMS SUBSIDE AS WEATHER CONTROL RESTABILIZES – FEMA SUBJECTED TO INFANTICIDE JUST MONTHS AFTER REBIRTH – DEATH TOLL CONTINUES TO MOUNT DESPITE PROMISING NEWS

ESCANABA FISH HATCHERY TO BEGIN RESTOCKING LAKE MICHIGAN – COULD TAKE DECADES

TREASURE HUNTERS FOUND DEAD – BODIES WASHED ASHORE NEAR MANISTEE, MICHIGAN – CORONER SAYS NEUROTOXINS

SCIENCE CAMP FOR KIDS GETS PRESTIGIOUS EDISON GRANT TO STUDY LIGHTNING – BLUE JETS, SPRITES, AND ELVES, OH MY!

MEXICO STILL RICH! FIND OUT HOW!

L.A.'S ROBOTIC SEWING MACHINES GO ON STRIKE, HOLD MANAGERS HOSTAGE

BE A COUNTERTERROR EXPERT IN 1 DAY! HELP DEFEND AMERICA! SCAN HERE FOR INFO!

ACTRESS SLIPS, FALLS

III

The Arrival of Zech Adam Adams

The playwright Zech Adam Adams arrived with his entourage and a heavy heart and immediately felt the hand of death. "...the elixir..." he said, whereupon he found the container and with a shaky hand plunged the medicinal tablet onto the pallid flesh of his tongue.

"You shouldn't..." said the pale, worldly woman at his side, who resembled a Brazilian Jessica Lange of the night during a full moon.

"I know...it's all this fresh air..." he said. They had just come across the sky from Montreal. The ibogaine treatment had not had time to become effective yet, and would require up to a year of monthly visits.

Behind them rose the Park Place Hotel, dominating the downtown real estate by several stories. It was a fitting piece to the game. They were headed into the trap as if it were a white-collar jail. They would hop around the bars and then slip into a wine shop for real Italian subs. Then it would be time to get down to business.

Zech sighed. He was feeling faint. As they approached K Street from their towering, weeklong perch, it became evident to him that he would fail to do what he had hoped to accomplish as some pipe-dream attachment to the dream made real. His thumb was almost literally black from so much ink.

"Are you sure you're up to this?" asked the woman, sensing his very thoughts as if a madam of crystal spheres.

"Look, they're wearing masks," said one actor excitedly. "Hurray for protest!"

Indeed, there were masks, and masks upon masks. Concealment was required ammunition these days. A troubled youth used them as symbols of identity—nothing surprising. Everyone was acting a part, in a sense, with culture as the only foundation—and American culture had been built upon sand. The movement was a legitimate cry of rage that had been ignored even as lives of boundless worth were trampled underfoot the iridium horses of doubt. Chaos; Radiation dripped from mouths of uranium teeth and oozed from the dung-splattered streets painted gold. Wall Street cried: 'Get a job!' That was the epitome of the dilemma; the corrupted souls of mercantilism, a mixed economic corporatism working against democracy as a sort of toxic blob, didn't give a damn about the damaged humanity which their constant bombing raids had wrought upon the crust of freedom and equality. So long as *they could still do what they wanted*, earning big dividends and running a semblance of a country, they couldn't give a damn about people.

"What a cute little place!" the woman said, her midnight green eyes twinkling as she looked out upon the face of a jaguar. The anonymous groups were heading down to the bookstore-turned-internet-cafe.

"We'll stir the ripples and make this *dead sea* foam at the mouth," vowed Zech.

The troupe of actors agreed as they formed a phalanx of knights in trench coats.

Again Zech sighed. The dial of his heart was wanting of better frequency, something beyond what was known. Yet his thoughts were not upon darkness and death, but only the subtle gifts before him; the beauty of the gilded bay, the smell of ephemeral vigor gently blown up over the town, and these wonderful people who happily shared what could not be owned by corporations. Once upon a time in America, you were born with a dream; now, thrown into the nightmare, you died and were reborn with every molt that life forced you to excrete, every rejection, every crowd of bullies, every lie, as you struggled to maintain value, to share frequency, choking on the big questions, just trying to pay rent, while society placed exceedingly higher value on mere entertainment than what you lived and died for. WHY? Because it was easier to take the way of least resistance; because more than likely you were glued to a device. You would rather get lost in the radioactive waste of someone else's bliss than actually think about the hard questions concerning life. The remote is what you wanted, your desire to switch channels, to find some inescapable drama, to watch your heroes stop the football from reaching the end zone. What did all that stuff matter? Would entertainment save the world? *Without a means to ask a question, it does nothing. Nothing constructive is done.* Wisdom, experience, brought about a nearness of truth in things. The primordial collective was the place of profound clarity, where the constellations illuminated the night's sky deep in the wilderness.

"My, the clouds; the sky…" he murmured appreciatively. "Not a gray hair in it."

"It breathes easy," the woman said, smiling.

There was a conflict here, thought Zech. Society itself was in conflict, because it demanded the world to become catalogued, quantitative, latitudinal and longitudinal. But a world was much larger than a society, its mathematics more advanced, and its voice more shrill. In time it would purify, erase the falseness of any human ideology, and even the perceived goodness in life would become transformed. And yet the world was likewise in conflict with itself and was a ball of molten iron with a candy coating, harmful if swallowed without a glass of water.

Later he would hire a driver to pass by the old forgotten places and then he would take them north into what was left of Leelanau wine country. There, a transplanted spirit of the soil would inebriate with skills passed down from ancient Egypt and Sumer and they would find a momentary comfort. These wonderful places would be viewed with both awe and disdain, because people of the city feared the country. It was a fear likened to the movie myth of King Kong, a journey symbolizing 250 years of New York power and influence; the adventurous mediators, men-of-letters-turned-hunters, the Ishmaels and Ahabs of the Port Authority, bringing forth NATURE in cages rather than encouraging the people to go within to appreciate what it really is. Instead, they got this sense of opposition that stayed with them and was carried on through the generations. They feared the wilderness, for eternity. They were inhabitants of Ur, of Babylon, Alexandria, Bianjing, Samarkand, Tikal, Tenochtitlan, Rome, Paris, or London, each the mountains of their time. Eventually, the pastorals would conquer them and all would be reduced to rubble, but not before a cultural zenith. Perhaps the summit had already been reached.

The Young Indifference Shop

A petit young lady with short black hair cut fabric from large rolls hanging from wooden spools while a lady almost twice her age, yet with similarly black hair and slender build pulled strings in and out of a fancy old handloom as the comber board filled with color. An expensive-looking industrial one sat idle nearby. At the rear of the store that was predominantly filled with shirts, hats and masks, a team of old iron Singer sewing machines worked at the behest of ghostly hands.

"And there he is!" greeted Henrietta Penuel, rising from the loom at the apprising of the bell.

Antiope dropped a yard of fabric as she rushed to embrace the train. "Zech! It's really you!" she said, unable to control herself. It had been years since they had seen each other, and he looked so much like Zack.

"I suppose you want to see the costumes," Henrietta said.

"I'm sure they're just spectacular," answered Zech tearfully. "Everyone, this is the girl I've been telling you about…"

"Finally, we meet!" said the Brazilian princess of Broadway; she clasped Antiope by the hands. "You can call me Camilla."

"Camilla Pumilo," said one of the other actors admiringly. "She has only a cameo role this time around, which is a pity for such talent."

"Not really," Camilla said unobtrusively. Her eyes were large jewels of midnight rainforest.

One after the other the players were introduced. There were eleven of them in all, filling various roles in the play's production. Without lines to recite offstage, they seemed to wander aimlessly under makeshift spotlights.

"Now for those costumes—you won't believe it!" said Henrietta before scampering to the back of the shop over the creaking wooden panels.

Antiope went off to help and they brought back several boxes full of bird costumes.

"Wow, look at those! That's awesome!" the actors said, and then began trying them on.

"They look like real birds! Can we take them bar hopping?" asked the ringleader good-naturedly.

"I hope you're kidding..." Zech said slowly, but earnestly.

"What about *after* the show?" insisted one of many sidekicks. "They're really awesome!"

"If you want to pay for them, sure..." Zech said flatly. "Mrs. Penuel didn't make them for children to play in."

"He's very serious about his plays," Camilla explained dramatically, with added caricature.

The actors laughed and began browsing the display of masks near the front window.

"Afterward, you could come with us," Zech said, pulling Antiope aside, "to New York, I mean."

"...I hoped you might ask that..." she said modestly, looking up with misty-eyed admiration. "I dreamed about such things once, but now..."

Zech sighed knowingly. "The city can be a wonderful place."

"I could visit sometime..." Antiope moped; she began toying with a spool of fabric. "I'm pretty serious with someone; my partner in your play—I wrote you about him; He would go if I asked him to... I'm just not cut out for city life—*you know*: Maximized potential, maximized evil."

"In that case, my mind is made up," Zech said. "I'll give you the key, because *only you* have the proper mindset. I see that now, as clear as ever."

"What?"

Zech took her gently by the hands before continuing: "I apologize for the windsock thing—the pigeons: that was a joke. I didn't think I was getting through; you stopped replying to my letters, so..."

"I don't quite understand..."

"I have the key," implored Zech. "There's only one and I'm giving it to you. Sigmund, your biological father, wanted me to do something, to continue his work, but I believe the task is yours, not mine. He was desperate to have chosen me...feeble junkie that I am. You need to free the gads, send them back to THE GARDEN. I can't do this thing that plainly I see must be done —I'm too much the city now, dark and vaporous. My gasping veins are smog-filled. The valley of metal and glass calls to me like opium, as if to a wraith. But you can do it. Restore the tower. Avenge your father."

"I don't even *know* my father," Antiope held.

"Then avenge *yourself*. Don't become just another sacrifice."

"I want to be free..."

"Humanity dictates otherwise."

"Monstrosso dictates..." she murmured morosely.

"Yes, I suppose you couldn't be blamed for thinking that," said Zech softly, slightly twitching beneath his weakened frame. "The Industrial Revolution enslaved, but long before that it was grain that did the enslaving; the rise of agriculture put forth slavery in the mind. Somewhere along the hunter-gatherer, close-knit fabric, we were pulled from Eden. How do we return? I don't know. Perhaps we can't. Perhaps it's *out there*," he said pointing heavenward; "Perhaps *in here*." Zech placed his hand over his heart.

"Then we'll find a way," Antiope answered with resolve.

A Few Quick Words on Rehearsals

Rehearsing the play in a bird costume was more involving than either she or Edgar had desired, but proved exciting nonetheless. The big man himself was there to ensure that everything went perfectly, but not without ruffling a few feathers (ha!). After three strange days of constant participation, observation, and (intermittently) starvation, they were ready for the big debut.

The Bird Play

Friday November the 6th washed upon the city of Gamesh like a cozy blanket of aurora borealis. The former opera-house-turned-theatre was secretively quiet when observed from the street until evening when it shone a ghostly green beneath the bright whites of the cornice, merging with the soft illumination of streetlamps. Westward over Lake Michigan the horizon was pink along mountains of clouds.

Renaissance Revival defined the theatre. The outside retained a tinge of Greek oracular decorum, while the inside was a rugged Parisian gem, a revitalized remnant of theatrical dominance, built in 1900 by a clever architect and the common blood, sweat, and tears of the labor class.

The turnout was respectable. A few semi-local celebrities had been involved in promotion and so, as a result, many townies of self-importance had elected not to miss out (as if they actually had free will!). In addition, the mayor had demanded the attendance of all Duck Lake Academy students because he had discovered from young people in Guy Fawkes masks that Adams, the playwright, had once been a student there. Only about a quarter of them had actually been given permission to go, and of these only a tenth had shown any interest.

Agents Mathews and Monstrosso were guarding the entrance in case any of the students tried to make a run for it—which John (Mathews) had chided was altogether likely, given that two of the academy's biggest failures were involved in the farce which they were being forced to witness.

Those in attendance read the program as follows:

THE BIRDS OVER WALL STREET

by Zech Adam Adams

DRAMATIS PERSONAE

THOMAS AQUARIUS, *a theologian*
MRS. AQUARIUS, *a theologian's wife*
DAGNY, *a businesswoman*
LELAND, *a businessman*
CORNELIUS, *a businessman*
WANDERING ACTOR, *a discontented feminist*
HEAD PEON, *a minstrel*
BAND OF PEONS
ULYSSES ABRAHAM, *a senator*
HILLARY WILLIAMS, *a senator*
HARRY FRANKLIN, *the Vice President*
RICHARD GEORGE X, *the President*
NIGHT-HERON
THE NUTHATCHES
FLOCK OF BIRDS
PARROT
PIGEONS
BELTED KINGFISHER
CARDINAL GUARDS
PHERENIKE, *a bird-woman*

The crowd whispered in anticipation of fantastical deeds of the mind. Would there be a diabolical magician to distribute vanishing currency, or perhaps a flying housemaid? The industrial age murals upon the vaulted ceiling of the former opera house were admired by those in attendance. Floodlights illuminated the intricately detailed golden foil amidst the color of ivory and the otherworldly gleam of the engagement band separating the upper and lower tiers of the amphitheatre, which were like a choir of suns concentrated upon the stage as the playwright Zech Adam Adams ran between the ensemble of fact and fiction. The crowd applauded.

After a short introduction ("...A clever adaptation of Aristophanes' *The Birds...* Four acts of an otherwise traditional comedy inspired by greed... "), the room grew dark as pitch and he blew into a bulb of yew wood with such ease that everyone wondered at the sonorous sound penetrating the ivory, crimson, and gold sections of the theatre.

The *dramatis personae* of Act 1 appeared to great applause.

The remaining three acts soon flew into action and were each met with great applause. The production was indeed a great success and its life was extended another week.

"Let's go," whispered Antiope, after which she took Edgar by the feathers. From backstage they made their way through the chattering crowd to the punchbowl near the theatre's entrance, wing in wing, slowly inching their way to freedom.

Oona spotted them from the vestibule and pointed, laughing. Her business partners, Sheryl, Natalie, and Amira, were still chatting away with a few of the actors in the central aisle. She decided to stay and watch.

They pretended to have a conversation.

The door was only a few dozen yards away and closing.

"Be cautious," Antiope whispered intimately, hopping with joy on her foam talons.

"Okay," Edgar whispered back.

Their old friend Eddie Monstrosso was pacing between the exits while John Mathews went in for some pie (Desserts were being catered from a local bakery). Just as they hobbled beneath the EXIT sign, the giant man blocked their path with his massive limbs.

"Who's in there?" Eddie demanded, grabbing the birds by the crown and opening one of the beaks enough to see a human face. He saw the torrential eyes, an expression in the wake of happiness, and a change infected him. His massive arms fell almost to his waist; then he stood aside and heavily bowed.

The two escapees looked out from their cavernous maws as if some after-the-headlights moment. But, no, they were not there yet. John was coming back with a portion of pie and already had his gaze fixed upon them. He glanced at Eddie and then back at the two bird-people and said, "What do they want, a frigging escort? Get them the hell out of here!"

The Shorebirds

The two actors were capricious and nonsensical as they rose from their bed in the sand, still wearing their featherbrained costumes; they yawned like chimeras and broke the seal on a homemade bag of dried fruits, nuts, and chocolates for breakfast. The juice was complementary—a gallon of GGI's overpriced Tree of Life label, packaged in near-eternal plastic sacks built into nylon backpacks made in Taiwan. It was the first time that either of them had tried the gad-pomegranate with beet sugar.

"So this is *your* sugar," Antiope said indeterminably.

"It's my sister's and my brother-in-law's sugar; yes." Edgar explained.

"I like it, but...it's just that...the same bitterness..."

"You're right I think."

The fruit was bitter truth, a town at the bottom of a lake. It welcomed only in slumber, calling the Virginia hams back home. Bitter was how it should have been, that call to knowledge, to authentic life. The true nature of things could not be drowned out by any manner of water.

"So, does this make us free?" she asked, half-jokingly, because eventually they would return to their obligations, and because freedom in the literal sense seemed to go against their better nature. To become free was to float away from Earth with an umbilical cord like that guy in *2001: A Space Odyssey*. Living things needed gravity, air, liquids, and solids. They were assemblages of the same story, the same lie: where in God's name was the writer; where the editor? They were pushed out the factory doors like bottles of soda, inevitably pressuring up, inescapably cancerous; just waiting to go flat.

"If only we had wings, we could pretend."

They flapped their wings.

They had talked about escape. They had discussed a cycle of temporary escapes as a solution to their inability to detach themselves completely, as even Antiope, after all her industrial sufferings, was unwilling to go without soap and plumbing and other necessities which were taken for granted, and which allowed for time even to think. Factories were sometimes a region's only employers: an ugly truth. Scavenging the material shelves above pre-industrial menial toil, the entire mass of humanity could almost look back into the face of misery and feel that Baudelaire's flowers of evil were seeded in beds of hopes and dreams. The cheap distribution that replaced the pinnacle of artistry in woodwork and other fine things never to be indulged by common eyes had elevated mass consciousness to better prospects. Despite dwelling in mere shadows of the leaps and bounds that culture had reached— wondrous devices that only the titans even knew about, in the ever-widening gap between rich and poor—the seeds had been planted. It was a shame, therefore, that so many pragmatists were willing to accept things for what they were after being taken so far and propped up so high (but as long as they were happy: the corporations were certainly happy; The idea was to keep people drowning; to keep them occupied). In times of such unhinged violence, corruption, chaos, and anger, it seemed altogether possible that all could be lost.

"Escape," echoed Edgar thoughtfully. "Say, do you think the wind chokers might have lost control again?"

"How would I know?" Antiope said, tentatively stripping off her clothes.

The air was unusually warm that Friday, November 13th, with unseen bonfires burning far across the lake. A deserted beach was a rare and unexpected treat in these tourist regions. The locals had to be daring.

"Last one in 's a rotten egg!" shouted Edgar.

They ran naked into the waves, the murky sand swishing through their toes.

"Oh my god!!" Antiope shrieked. The water was very cold. She tripped and fell, baptized in folly, but soon ran back and wrapped herself in a large purple towel. The sand beneath her feet was not fooled.

"Edgar!" she scolded. He had skipped out of the water and tried removing her towel, but she was quick to react. He would have to get his own, the pervert.

This was Antiope's first weekend off—truly, and away from prying eyes (with the exception of the drones gliding overhead, somewhere in the re-subdued atmosphere). It was the closest to freedom that she would ever experience in a country priding itself as such, but even a pinch was something.

There were things on her mind which had never been there before, such as how to be responsible, how to keep on being loved, how to go about making an abandoned air force tower livable again. These thoughts seemed like nothing at all, yet they were everything. There were ideas floating around in her thawing mind, seemingly novel, obscure, but unfortunately they would have to wait until spring. Frigid snow would soon blanket them in deadly northern splendor. It was beautiful actually, to see snow in the trees. Even at the academy it had been beautiful. Yet it also made her appreciate such things as blankets, furnaces, and fireplaces.

"Homework..." Antiope grumbled, remembering the botany lessons that she was receiving from her biological father through the interface of a small communications device, from where he sat rotting way in an island prison. He would be happy to receive her report.

Looking back a half-mile, just south of the dunes, the tower rose into blueness, and through the glass of the observation deck a dozen little sapling trees bathed in the eastern light. They would eventually become wild things, joining wasteland survivors and the fruitless white mulberry on their unnatural hiatus. Flowering with primary passion in the spring, they would cover the earth like the crown of a savior, reinvigorating the land and keeping life in check. Others would emerge in time, dispersed by fickle nature. They would inspire the rabbit warrens and protect the havens of wilderness creatures, a world designed by the birds. The rivers and streams would perfume after a designated rain. Even now, the world was mindful of what was to come, and despite the efforts to control everything, there were telling signs. Winter was coming, and she tried looking ahead into spring, seeing it from the canopy of her mind, to find hope. There she saw it clearly and she smiled. The divine lotuses were oozing back from the muck. The dragonflies buzzed from the fields to land upon the rocks. The frogs were burping. Tadpoles swam amongst the reeds.

Afterward

Summer 2021 (untold months later).

The partial skeleton of a wooden structure emerged near the granular sand of the beach and reached deplorably from a grassy dune that had for eons fought a miniscule war with the wind. Translucent waves hovered determinedly at the hairline of the sapphire blue essence of the bay before gliding the etched and molded counterpoint of the natural dialectic. With a khhhhh-swoosh-swooshshshshsh-tsssssssss they erased the proximal footprints of small children.

Henrietta was content with a tall glass of iced tea. The bartender she had hired for the occasion had never arrived, and therefore she was forced to chaperone sober. There was not a lick of liquor to be had at the tower, save for a bottle of Jägermeister and some grim-looking chartreuse. Alas, the students had arrived on time, and there were too many young ones for a trip to the store.

Henrietta was getting old. A sturdy recliner made of vinyl strings was for her both casket and pallbearer—only a miraculous effort would free her from this elastic containment. She was at the temple, at the foot of admiration, basking in the sunlight and remembering the song of the waves. What was it they were saying? The voice was not the same as that in Bermuda; it was colder, more contained. It sounded like a whispering void.

There was laughter from small voices—very shrill and loud.

She waved at the sway of children who wandered onto her private side of loneliness. They were not hers, but they came from the same place, with the same kinds of mothers. They were better off now that Antiope and Edgar were taking care of them, watching over them from their garden tower, and Henrietta had an eye on them all.

A sundry crowd dotted the small public access between the configuration of a forest reborn and the elite sterility of private property. The reconstructed tower rose behind her, over grounds covered in bridges, polycarbonate greenhouse domes, and saltwater tanks of algae. Pangs of laughter wavered in the air, full of desire, for these were the sounds of celebration; the solstice of summer had tilted into action amidst galactic dark matter and the cruelty had withdrawn for a term. Feeling to all as the warm sound of trumpets, a bright smudge of sun gilded delicately, but steadfastly, the northern lands of slumbering hills, primeval black bear marsh, rolling, curtaining pine, rigid pioneer farm, gurgling brook, quaint—all too quaint—harbor towns, cultivated orchard kingdoms of lingering arsenic foundations, and blanketed shoreline of baptismal fresh-water sea.

Further out in the lake she could see the ghostly wooden beams from the waterfront. You could swim out to the beams and have yourself an adventure, Robert Wabe'no had told her the other day. *"Any time you wish,"* she had said as if to console the young man's fiery inner voice. Artifacts like silverware and ceramic dishes waited patiently to be pulled from under the silicon wrinkles. A handsome young lad was that Robert. Henrietta was glad that he had not been cast into dark corners of a pallid municipal world, far from conscious view, to emerge into the sounds of poker chips and slot machines. Instead, he had broken through the colorful shells of oppressive stereotypes into a creative, if obscure, future existence. The quantum bicycle thing was really catching on. The kids who rode them were evolving like Major Toms on a 2001 space odyssey. They were taking the world into the future and all the dummies with it.

An entire migrant family of two small girls, an older girl, and a juvenile boy spent time on the small portion of coastal bay while subsisting on an arduous season of gad harvesting. They cooled themselves in the translucent water and awed at its vastness, imagining Eden. The lake was a heavenly font, in which the invigorating breeze was an aspergil.

How wonderful, thought Henrietta, if every day of rest was like this. How magnificent if hard work brought equality without fear of oppression, starvation, and murder. She pondered the world and how things comprising it were always in motion. It had tilted, revolved, tilted, for a long time, which made Henrietta feel young as she considered her own revolving and tilting.

A boy named Ezekiel dropped his pants and ran up and down the beach. His freckles and copper ends became more eminent as the fracturing luminescence of aquatic frontier multiplied the humanness in things.

How she missed the Devil's Island with its pink sand and its pig-headed men, but the Fates had carried her elsewhere, and she was like a female Ulysses in search of a bartender. With one hand on the arrow, she scanned the drinking hall for potential threats. There was one, and there another (but they had been through so much already!). If only she had known just how incompetent Monstrosso had been in their gene selection—the children were like any other she had ever known.

Khhhhh-swoosh-swooshshshshsh-tsssssssss. The freshwater bay emitted a long sigh.

When would they be back, she wondered? They had gone into the wilderness and would return, hopefully in one piece. Henrietta hardly had words as to why someone would do that without so much as a refrigerator or a big screen TV. They had temporarily vanished from modern civilization, but she could handle things. *The kids were not that bad.* The North Country National Scenic Trail sprawled across the entire headlands under the border with Canada. From here, it could take you all the way to New York. They had left on foot, with nothing but birdseed to compliment their gear (an understatement, of course). They would be gone a long time. They would see wolves and panthers and bears—who knew what else, maybe Bigfoot.

"No, don't pick that up, dear!" she scolded.

Such a chore, she thought, these responsibilities of hers. And the paradox was that they were part of her fabric, and she was learning how to weave all over again. The loom was her heart and her soul the thread, and a silver-lined pattern was forming in the rug on the loom.

Once more, she watched the children play, but this time left them, and from where the shallow water of naiad folly guided the weight evermore heavenward, into the fleeting glory of golden grace, she saw the silhouettes against the horizon, a pair of swans, a continuous breath of dancing wind, and ever jubilant waves of unhindered light.

APPENDIX

THE BIRDS OVER WALL STREET

by Zech Adam Adams

DRAMATIS PERSONAE

THOMAS AQUARIUS, *a theologian*
MRS. AQUARIUS, *a theologian's wife*
DAGNY, *a businesswoman*
LELAND, *a businessman*
CORNELIUS, *a businessman*
WANDERING ACTOR, *a discontented feminist*
HEAD PEON, *a minstrel*
BAND OF PEONS
ULYSSES ABRAHAM, *a senator*
HILLARY WILLIAMS, *a senator*
HARRY FRANKLIN, *the Vice President*
RICHARD GEORGE X, *the President*
NIGHT-HERON
THE NUTHATCHES
FLOCK OF BIRDS
PARROT
PIGEONS
BELTED KINGFISHER
CARDINAL GUARDS
PHERENIKE, *a bird-woman*

ACT 1

A Small Isolated Yard in Manhattan's Morningside Heights

SCENE: *A cultivated, urban neighborhood within the sights and sounds of a dense city dominated by cathedrals; seeming out of place amidst the neighboring gothic spires and brick and mortar high-rise apartments, a rock fence encloses the yard of a church-like house. A flock of birds soars overhead.*

THOMAS AQUARIUS *and his wife,* MRS. AQUARIUS, *stand in the yard.*

THOMAS AQUARIUS. I must confess: When I look to the sky, I have a nagging suspicion that our prayers are not being answered. What could be the cause? Do you think the birds are at fault?

MRS. AQUARIUS. Whatever do you mean, Thomas? What could the birds do?

THOMAS AQUARIUS. I've heard mention of a place in the clouds, a town full of birds. Perhaps they're up to something.

MRS. AQUARIUS. That's just foolhardy myth! Don't tell me you believe in such things? Oh, but of course you would!

THOMAS AQUARIUS. My faith knows no bounds.

MRS. AQUARIUS. Is that so? This is our yard, Master Thomas, and you haven't stepped foot from it in months!

THOMAS AQUARIUS. And? Yes, that's true, but...

MRS. AQUARIUS. You know very well that our boundaries are obscurely defined by The Bible.

THOMAS AQUARIUS. That is open to interpretation, dearest...

MRS. AQUARIUS. And yet if that wall were as the cover of this Good Book, then you, Thomas, are as a bookmark stuck in Saint Luke!

478

THOMAS AQUARIUS. ...each day...That is... I... am a theologian, and theologians are philosophy incarnate. We remain free to evolve through supernatural grace bestowed from heaven. We are above being fenced in by earthly matters.

MRS. AQUARIUS. So you've traveled in mind, at least. Although, I cannot tell a lie: It leaves me unsatisfied.

THOMAS AQUARIUS. It's hard on you, Sophia, I know. And what you say is otherwise true; No such place was mentioned in the Good Book. It's been kept out, just like the Witch of Endor who nevertheless manages to materialize in my dreams—where she suffers nightly by being burned alive with help from this mighty congregation. Nonetheless, I should like to consult our political leaders on the matter.

MRS AQUARIUS. That might not be the wisest thing. Let us go inside first and discuss this more safely. You may have caught something already. Here, come, let me check your head for a fever.

(MRS. AQUARIUS *applies her hand to her husband's prominent forehead.*)

THOMAS AQUARIUS. And?

MRS AQUARIUS. Nothing unusual. How frightening! Very well, then; write your letter and I'll see that it gets mailed. Only, remember what happened the last time you mixed business with politics. Putting millions of souls in the hands of those devils? Look what they've done to public education! I just hope it is The Lord who's looking out for us, and not some jester with a red hand.

THOMAS AQUARIUS. (*Looking skyward for birds*) Let us hope. Come then, to bed.

Curtain closes and reopens.

SCENE: *Later that evening as the sun sets into night, the very same yard.*

Enter three prominent businesspeople, DAGNY, LELAND, and CORNELIUS, who stroll into the yard beneath the Evening Star, a

479

night covered in smog, and head to the door of the house. The doorbell rings, sounding like church bells.

MRS. AQUARIUS *answers cautiously.*
The sound of snoring can be heard within the house.

DAGNY. Pardon the intrusion, scholarly folk, but we understand you've expressed a desire to explore the land of birds?

LELAND. These devious politicians of ours do say as much. Is it true?

MRS. AQUARIUS. Who's doing the asking? Our doors are open to everyone, but we approach the Devil's Hour...

DAGNY, LELAND, CORNELIUS. Wall Street.

DAGNY. That is, we're businesspeople representative as such.

MRS. AQUARIUS. He's sending his minions door-to-door, I see. We'd better step up our efforts.

CORNELIUS. You should.

MRS. AQUARIUS. Might I ask a question?

DAGNY. Shoot.

MRS. AQUARIUS. I talk to those outside the congregation sometimes. They say that stuff isn't working, that millions of good people are falling through the cracks, and that Wall Street doesn't give a hoot. Is that true?

DAGNY. Well, yes, that's certainly true, but it's rather a constant, I'm afraid...

CORNELIUS. (*cutting in boisterously*) Not working?! Ha! That's nonsense! Take me, for instance: my Hedge Fund portfolio is doing rather well; I just purchased a chain of islands large enough to

480

hide over two dozen mistresses; it's raining failure, I tell you! Boy, what a beautiful sight! Does wonders for my circulation...

LELAND. (*unconvincingly*) Any hale and hearty American could accomplish the same; all they need do is go out and work for it!

MRS. AQUARIUS. Enjoy it while you can, because the Lake of Fire has no beach...

DAGNY. About the land of birds, ma'am, if you'll still permit me to inquire?

MRS. AQUARIUS. Just a moment, please. The master is at hourly prayer. Allow me to fetch him.

LELAND. So that's what I've been hearing. Does he always pray in his sleep?

MRS. AQUARIUS. He rises at four, prays until the sun comes up, reads Aristotle while I fix his breakfast, then he cries, prays some more, quotes Bible scriptures, eats his supper at the table, and then falls asleep until four the next morning.

CORNELIUS. Too bad he doesn't have more scrupulous pursuits; he'd be a wealthy man with that kind of discipline.

MRS. AQUARIUS. He is wealthy in spirit (MRS. AQUARIUS *turns and genuflects towards a wooden cross on the wall and turns back towards the guests*). Here, I'll wake him.

Exit MRS. AQUARIUS *into the house.*
Enter MRS. AQUARIUS *with* THOMAS AQUARIUS

THOMAS AQUARIUS. (*Yawns*) What's this then? We're not really a church, just so you know. The missus has a thing for ship-innards, high steeples, wooden crosses, and stained glass with a focus on religious situations. It's no accident, I suppose, that her taste agrees with my profession. We've been making chamber music ever since.

DAGNY. Oh? And are there any additions?

THOMAS AQUARIUS. Dear me! Are you moving in?

MRS. AQUARIUS. (*Placing herself between the speakers with arms outstretched*) The world's orphans fill that role, and the occasional stray cat. We like to keep things rational.

THOMAS AQUARIUS. Abstinence is the key. We don't want to end up like those Houston televangelists.

LELAND. That's a pleasant thought. (*To* DAGNY) Better tell him why we're here so he knows whose horns we wear.

DAGNY. Wall Street, sir. Our prayers aren't being answered. The government says you intend to do something about it.

CORNELIUS. They have implored us to offer our corporeal support in the matter.

THOMAS AQUARIUS. You may leave your donations with the poor. I've all the material possessions I need.

DAGNY. Actually, we would very much like to tag along, if it isn't too much trouble. And, not to worry, learned thralls (*laughs conceitedly*)! We pull our own weight.

MRS. AQUARIUS. As always. No doubt, that's what all your valets are for, and those chauffeurs standing around out there in the street near your trendy limousines.

LELAND. Oh, those men? No. They're tax collectors. That's a second reason why we wish to join you, I must confess. Things are getting out of hand around here. Subjective value has a way of suddenly decreasing in the hands of those Federal Reserve people.

CORNELIUS. What the bankers can't steal, they rob.

DAGNY. It takes one to know one. A little vacation would do us good. We've had to cut back on labor somewhat-

LELAND. Tens of thousands, no less…

CORNELIUS. Despite heavy losses from our projected revenue this quarter…

LELAND. That is to say, the shortcomings of greedy expectations, which were predictably less than we had hoped for…

DAGNY. The annual bonuses came through, but an unruly mob formed a sloth-camp outside the door at the office.

LELAND. A pleasant bunch, that—what with the guitars and singing and all…

DAGNY. They're very entertaining, but haven't put much effort into the workforce; a true laborer would have the life drained out of them by that age.

LELAND. Lucky for them there isn't one.

CORNELIUS. (*To Leland*) Quiet, you evil revisionist! (*To Thomas Aquarius*) So, your highness, what about it?

THOMAS AQUARIUS. You're more than welcome, of course. Trust yourself to God and everything will work out.

LELAND. Tell us, then, oh wise one, what are we to do?

THOMAS AQUARIUS. Meet us anon upon Mount Marcy in the Adirondack. Travel light. Bring only what you'd need for a few days' travels.

DAGNY. Anon.

THOMAS AQUARIUS. That's right, anon. Don't be late.

DAGNY. Anon is such a specific reference, as is atop Mount Marcy, and few.

LELAND. Ah, um. That's an excellent point, Dagny. Mister Aquarius, Missus Aquarius, could you perhaps…be more specific…as to time and place…just to…avoid any…complications?

THOMAS AQUARIUS. Yes, of course! I do apologize.

MRS. AQUARIUS. (*Laughs*) His great mind is so absent at times.

THOMAS AQUARIUS. Anon, or a quarter to, if that's helpful. Atop Mount Marcy, when you see the shining staircase…or perhaps it's a very large tree? A flight path through the clouds? Who really knows? At any rate, anon.

LELAND. Anon.

THOMAS AQUARIUS. Or a quarter to.

DAGNY. Yes, very well. We shall meet you anon.

THOMAS AQUARIUS. Anon, it is, then.

ACT 2

The Adirondack Mountains

SCENE: *A mixed evergreen and hardwood forest on the green slopes of the Adirondack Mountains; white clouds float through the peaks, obscuring the heavens; birds, white-tailed deer, and black bear roam amongst the trees.*

Enter four politicians: ULYSSES ABRAHAM *is holding an owl;* HILLARY WILLIAMS *is holding a jay;* HARRY FRANKLIN *is holding a deep-fried turkey;* RICHARD GEORGE X *is holding a bald eagle; these are the guides that are to lead them to the kingdom of the birds.* FOUR SECURITY GUARDS *surround the president,* RICHARD GEORGE X.

ULYSSES ABRAHAM (*To his owl*). Are you sure this is the way?

HILLARY WILLIAMS (*To her jay*). Now's your chance to shine, jay. Be a good little ambassador and show mommy where to go.

ULYSSES ABRAHAM. My owl won't answer a single question except to repeatedly ask who. Are we to wait here, or shall we continue without them?

HILLARY WILLIAMS. The wise choice would be to wait for the others. (*Whispering to* ULYSSES ABRAHAM) But you know whom we're dealing with!

RICHARD GEORGE X. My bird insists upon climbing a little higher, and he's ripping the flesh from my only good arm with those razor sharp talons of his! I don't know how much more liberty I can take!

FOUR SECURITY GUARDS. Just give the order, Mister President, and we'll shoot it down for you!

RICHARD GEORGE X. No, no! What are you saying?! That's illegal!

HARRY FRANKLIN. Hmm? What? Did-did someone say something? I think I fell asleep again. It's the damnedest thing. HARRY FRANKLIN *yawns.*

RICHARD GEORGE X. (*Smelling the aromatic air*) I thought we told you to bring a *living* turkey.

HARRY FRANKLIN. Indeed. Well, but I got hungry! I had my cook stick it in the deep-fryer last night.

RICHARD GEORGE X. No wonder this eagle's been tearing into me. Throw me some breast meat, will you?

(HARRY FRANKLIN *searches the turkey carcass and tears off a chunk of meat; he approaches* RICHARD GEORGE X's *bald eagle, which is resting on the president's good arm, with trepidation and squeamishly throws the meat at it, then scurries away to some bushes near a thicket of trees.*
The bald eagle lunges and snatches the meat before it falls to the ground, ripping into it with sharp beak and talons.)

ULYSSES ABRAHAM. So, tell me, featherless leader, what are we doing here again?

RICHARD GEORGE X. We received a letter at the White House. Naturally, we took it very seriously.

ULYSSES ABRAHAM. You mean someone wrote it in ink, with their hands? I didn't know people still wrote letters.

RICHARD GEORGE X. Tell me about it. Squawking is all the rage *(holds out his smartphone and slowly shakes it)*. That's how I let my security team know where I am most of the time. I even get an elevation report on this thing. Right now we're at four-thousand-and-thirty-seven feet. There's still over a thousand feet of mountain left—isn't that comforting? Harry here keyed me in to that little ditty of an app.

HILLARY WILLIAMS. About that, sir. Is it safe? I mean, should the entire world really know that you just checked in to Camp David, or the Pizza Corral, or that you decided to stop for a beer at the local pub? And that tweet about the Supreme Leader of Iran looking ridiculous in his country's football team's shorts…

ULYSSES ABRAHAM. And the letter, Mr. President?

RICHARD GEORGE X. From our top theologian, Thomas Aquarius. He has information that birds have been blocking prayers from reaching Heaven. Wall Street has been complaining about this very thing for months—it couldn't be coincidence.

HILLARY WILLIAMS. If only the worms were blocking curses from reaching Hell.

RICHARD GEORGE X. They won't stop texting me about it. It's so annoying. They've threatened to stop paying us. I assured Aquarius that we'd get right on it. Our advisory board hooked us up with these birds, and here we are.

ULYSSES ABRAHAM. Are we hoping to arrange some sort of deal with these birds—the ones blocking prayers, I mean?

HARRY FRANKLIN. Something like that. As long as we *appear* to be doing our jobs, the people will remain hospitable. I've been doing that for years and it's been working out just great...

ULYSSES ABRAHAM. Not good enough. Not this time. Something tangible must be done. The people are in real trouble! We must work towards a solution!

HARRY FRANKLIN. Don't be such an idealist. Here, take this breast—or would you prefer a thigh...

HILLARY WILLIAMS. If the birds really do control the passage of prayers between heaven and earth it would be very advantageous for us to get involved. Imagine the power we would wield over the planet! No one on earth would dare oppose us then—at least not the ones who pray.

ULYSSES ABRAHAM. I don't understand any of this. What do the birds want from us? What can we offer them, for that matter?

HILLARY WILLIAMS. Do you even have to ask? Not to be deep fried, for starters.

RICHARD GEORGE X. That's what the populace is for. They do all the work, Wall Street pretends to invest capital in products made on their broken backs, and we pretend to control the flow of money through our banks' interest rates. Pleasing the birds should be easy, what with our extensive experience with birdfeeders and all. I'm sure they'll settle for a few million pounds of sunflower seeds. If not, we have plenty more to offer.

ULYSSES ABRAHAM. (*Listening to his owl*) What's that you say? (*Speaking to his colleagues*) Fellow scriveners, legatees, scoundrels, all! Something approaches!

HARRY FRANKLIN *dives into the bushes*; ULYSSES ABRAHAM, HILLARY WILIAMS, *and* RICHARD GEORGE X *hide behind trees.* FOUR SECURITY GUARDS hold stance around the president's tree.

Enter THOMAS *and* MRS. AQUARIUS *with two doves.*

THOMAS AQUARIUS. What's that shaking in the bushes? Is it a bear?

MRS. AQUARIUS. Oh, I hope not! I didn't think to pray against a thing like that!

HARRY FRANKLIN. (*From the bushes*) Don't shoot! It's me, your vice president!

THOMAS AQUARIUS. Many apologies! From our vantage, you have a beastly appearance.

HARRY FRANKLIN. (*From the bushes*) A strength rather than a weakness. Anyway, I've been called far worse.

MRS. AQUARIUS. Then, what was that growling?

488

HARRY FRANKLIN. My stomach. The bile is to blame.

HARRY FRANKLIN *rises from the bushes and glances about.* FOUR SECURITY GUARDS *relax.* ULYSSES ABRAHAM, HILLARY WILIAMS, *and* RICHARD GEORGE X *reveal themselves, overjoyed to have found their guides.*

THOMAS AQUARIUS. We have found you at last! Sorry to have kept you waiting, senators.

MRS. AQUARIUS. (*Curtsying*) And you, Mr. President and vice bear.

THOMAS AQUARIUS. My studies held us up: We are preparing a sermon on breath and psyche to be presented to the birds of Cloud Cuckoo Metropolis. We're hoping to establish a mission there in the name of OUR SAVIOR JESUS CHRIST.

RICHARD GEORGE X. Any sign of those Wall Street tycoons?

THOMAS AQUARIUS. They were to meet us anon and it appears they're late.

RICHARD GEORGE X. Anon, we have seen nothing save a few deer and a bear.

THOMAS AQUARIUS. Then let us be off, I'm afraid. We mustn't delay. The sun sets at the peak of the mountain through the clouds. These doves will show us the way.

Exit THOMAS AQUARIUS, MRS. AQUARIUS, HARRY FRANKLIN, ULYSSES ABRAHAM, HILLARY WILIAMS, RICHARD GEORGE X, *and* FOUR SECURITY GUARDS.

Enter WANDERING ACTOR, HEAD PEON *and* BAND OF PEONS, *walking out onto a rocky bluff overlooking the audience.* WANDERING ACTOR *is wearing a dirty evening gown;* HEAD PEON *holds a stick and is dressed in ripped conductor's clothes;*

BAND OF PEONS *is wearing shirts with blue collars and carrying various band instruments.*

WANDERING ACTOR. (*Looking out over the audience and pointing with* HEAD PEON'S *stick*) Look toward yonder peak, we've discovered a cesspool of eyes. Have they no manners?

HEAD PEON. The media has made voyeurs of us all. Pray for privacy.

WANDERING ACTOR. Then we must keep these folks entertained; nothing lost is nothing gained.

HEAD PEON. Have at it; you first!

WANDERING ACTOR. I will! Only... I require a proper stage! Something private, a camp with a raging fire, at least...

HEAD PEON. That spot down there will do; that clearing before the ogling cesspool; by my authority as Head Peon I declare that...a camp!

BAND OF PEONS. Hurray!! Hurray!!

BAND OF PEONS *runs down the rocky bluff, gathers at the designated spot for the camp, and cheers with glee.* HEAD PEON *follows, but trips as he tries to give orders and falls behind the bluff with a cry of alarm.* HEAD PEON *crawls painfully around the front of the bluff and arrives at camp.*

HEAD PEON. (*Looking up toward the bluff at* WANDERING ACTOR) Well, are you going to perform, or do you intend to commit suicide!

BAND OF PEONS *laughs.*

WANDERING ACTOR. Seeing as it was how you managed to fall so softly, I fear my best option is to perform.

HEAD PEON. Well, then...

WANDERING ACTOR. (*Long-windedly clears throat from atop the bluff*) I call this My Richard II Parody:

> This royal pain in things, this trashed wreck,
> This exploited pittance, this seat of Gas,
> This other Hell, idiots' paradise,
> This mixed foundation of spirited pride
> Where folks overcome and huge dreams are made,
> This wistful bowl built by immigrant hands,
> So useless against risky contraband,
> This diverted breed, this isolate world,
> A ship so loath to cross the stinking sea,
> To the disgruntlement of other realms,
> This dirt, this two-spine brute, this America!

HEAD PEON and CHORUS OF PEONS *applaud.*
Satisfied, the WANDERING ACTOR *descends to stage.*

WANDERING ACTOR. And now it's your turn; dare to match my wit?

HEAD PEON *stands in front of the* BAND OF PEONS *and begins to conduct. The band plays and sings.*

BAND OF PEONS:

> Oh! The famous Thomas Aquarius
> Was a right-winged derrièrious.
> He was alight with Roman candles,
> Reading Aristotle from his bed,
> Chasing Greek monsters in his sleep,
> But no one understood what he said.
>
> Smothered in kisses conjured while snoozing
> He murmured how something needed burning,
> And although armed with sharp, thorny brambles

He burned his witches with Roman candles.
It seemed a right proper action at first
In a Puritanical dream obscure,
Yet when the missus asked if it was hot
He unconsciously rolled and said, "Well, sure…"
Around the bonfire, things were going well,
The evil beautes on their highway to Hell,
And then Thom was falling into the flames,
Bewitched by lovely, incombustible dames.
As their dresses smoldered, so his desires,
And he screamed aloud how Satan conspired.
It was then that Mrs. woke him and said
"You've made a fire on the sheets of the bed!!"

Ah ha ha ha ha ha ha!

Enter THOMAS AQUARIUS, *rushing onstage.*

THOMAS AQUARIUS. That's a foul verse!!

WANDERING ACTOR. Away with you, pious hero! This is your
cue to get off the stage!

THOMAS AQUARIUS. If I must!

BAND OF PEONS. You will!!

BAND OF PEONS *chases* THOMAS AQUARIUS *offstage.*

BAND OF PEONS. Oh! The famous Thomas Aquarius
Was a right-winged derrièrious.

He spent so much time playing marbles
Against Aristotle in his head,
Swallowing bags of them in his sleep,
That no one understood what he said…

THOMAS AQUARIUS. (*Loudly, from offstage*) That's not true!!

BAND OF PEONS. Ooooooh…

HEAD PEON. (*Stops the chorus abruptly by the erratic waving of his hands*) Well, wandering actor, band of merry blue-collar workers, it's getting late. Don't know about you, but I've been up since five o'clock this morning. What say we build a fire and continue this lampoon tomorrow, aye?

WANDERING ACTOR. Party pooper…to the next light, then…

WANDERING ACTOR *wanders off and exits behind the set.*

BAND OF PEONS *mumbles as they set up tents and break off to search for firewood. They come back and build a fire as the stage lights fade. Noises of the forested mountain at night startle them. They huddle closer to the fire and become afraid. A phantom light comes their way through the trees and then disappears. The firelight fades and smolders.*

Curtain closes to darkness.

Loud roaring from a bear breaks the night, followed by screams of the many and then the death throes of one as HEAD PEON is attacked by the bear.

ACT 3

Realm of the Night Heron

SCENE: *A wild, desolate tract of open country in the mist; broken rocks and brushwood occupy the center of the stage. Marshland surrounds. The sunlight grows dim. A lone NIGHT HERON hunts for food. The NIGHT HERON wears a yellow crown.*

Enter NIGHT HERON, *stage left, fishing in the marsh just off from the road.*

NIGHT HERON. Kwawk! Kwawk!

Enter Three Businesspeople, DAGNY, LELAND, *and* CORNELIUS, *who crouch fearfully (from stage right) along a rough pebble road as they make their way through the marshland (to center stage).*

LELAND. I dare say I wish we had been on time! This darkness gives me the creeps...

NIGHT HERON. Kwawk! Kwawk!

DAGNY (*Hugging* LELAND *tightly*). Save me!

CORNELIUS. (*Dives behind a rock*) Mommy!!

LELAND. We're in the land of birds now. No telling what we'll run into. Better dispatch that army of yours.

CORNELIUS. (*Cautiously reappears*) Alas, they're busy!

LELAND. Send in the tax collectors, then!

CORNELIUS. (*Laughing as he rejoins the others*) I only wish they had followed us. They're afraid of birds.

DAGNY. (*Flattening the wrinkles in her suit with her hands*) I've always wondered why our farmers make use of so many scarecrows. They must've found a loophole.

NIGHT HERON *moves to center stage, hidden in the marsh.*

NIGHT HERON. (*Extremely close to party*) Kwawk! Kwawk!

CORNELIUS *dives back behind the rock.*

494

LELAND. (*Hugs* DAGNY) What the devil is that?!

DAGNY. (*Frightened and holding a can of mace*) Reveal yourselves!

NIGHT HERON. (*Appears from the marsh*) Kwawk! Who goes there?! You have nothing to fear from me, unless you happen to be fish!

CORNELIUS (*Hesitantly rising from behind a rock*).   Alas, we're not fish.   Common mistake, though, I must admit!   We're merchants. Who the devil are you?!

NIGHT HERON. A night heron. I rule the tidal marshes when darkness falls. Kwawk! Kwawk!

LELAND. A pleasure. Say, old chap, is there a town nearby? We're a little new to the area and-

DAGNY. It would be in your best interest to see us unharmed, sir! We intend to do business.

NIGHT HERON. We have no desire for business… Although… I can't kwawk for everyone… The crows might be interested, come to think of it…

LELAND. Yes, about that—this kwawking. How is it that we can understand each other? I thought we needed special rings or something.

NIGHT HERON. Ka ka ka! No, that's just stupid.

LELAND. Then it's a good thing I was outbid on those Rings of Speech to Understand the Birds on the internet last night. I would have been out a million bucks…

CORNELIUS. Blast!!

DAGNY. Stay on topic, please. Mister Night Heron, sir, about that city of birds...

NIGHT HERON. Of course! See that path there? That's the Road of Oh Dear! Follow that to Cloud Cuckoo Metropolis. Kwawk!

CORNELIUS. The Road of Oh Dear (!), you say? Is it dangerous?

NIGHT HERON. Well, they don't call it Oh Dear (!) for nothing!

DAGNY. Thanks, bird. You've been surprisingly helpful.

ACT 4

Cloud Cuckoo Metropolis

SCENE: *A city of human-sized birdhouses and straw nests hanging from gigantic trees. An ornate birdbath fountain sits at a central square.*

The stage rotates to display Cloud Cuckoo Metropolis and stops at the birdhouses.

Enter THE NUTHATCHES *climbing around in front of their house, which is inside of the hollow of a tree.*

THE NUTHATCHES. (*To the audience*) Hey, get off of our lawn! What gives you the right to be here?! Find your own dang tree, if you would, please!

The stage rotates.

Enter DAGNY, LELAND, CORNELIUS, *a* PARROT, PIGEONS *and* A FLOCK OF BIRDS

496

LELAND. That was a short, effortless trip. Why, I hardly moved at all.

DAGNY. The audience probably didn't even notice. Look how stupid they seem.

CORNELIUS. You could sell them a bottle of tar and they wouldn't complain. No doubt it's our own fault. And look there! A flock approaches, and they seem angry!

Enter FLOCK OF BIRDS *clucking around angrily, followed by curious* PIGEONS.

FLOCK OF BIRDS. More intruders! Who dares invade our beloved metropolis?! Why can't you just leave us alone?!

LELAND. (*Hugging* DAGNY) We're done for!

DAGNY. Do your worst, birds!

CORNELIUS (*Holding out a bag of seeds*). But first, why not try some of our delicious homemade sunflower seeds, fresh from the garden. Only two percent fat and no cholesterol!

PARROT. Do your worst! Rot! No cholesterol!

FLOCK OF BIRDS. Seeds from the sun? We wouldn't know where to begin, so long in the clouds have we flown, it's a peep-dang-sin. Send them our way, then.
(*Taking the seeds from* CORNELIUS *and eating a beak-full*)
Hey, not bad!

PARROT (*To* PIGEONS). Rot! Send word to the BELTED KINGFISHER at the Council of Elders that three more of those hypocritical-human-poop-targets have turned up and that they bring seeds from the sun!

PIGEONS *fly off.*

Enter BELTED KINGFISHER *with the returned* PIGEONS *and two* CARDINAL GUARDS.

BELTED KINGFISHER. What is it, now? We were about to go water boarding.

FLOCK OF BIRDS. Intruders, Elder Kingfisher. They come bearing gifts. Here, try some of these seeds.

BELTED KINGFISHER. No thanks. I'm strictly a fishing bird.

FLOCK OF BIRDS. They're very good.

CORNELIUS. If you'll allow me, Elder Kingfisher, sir, to speak. We would like to arrange a trade: Seeds, fish, whatever you want, in exchange for a degree of control over the flow of prayers.

FLOCK OF BIRDS. The what?

CORNELIUS. The flow of prayers, sir. Your motives are your own and I'll not pry into them, but why not capitalize on this piracy to the utmost? I, Cornelius, am at your service!

CORNELIUS *bows.*

BELTED KINGFISHER. Wait. I think I'm beginning to understand. You're with those other featherless twits, is that it? The ducks insisted on torturing them—something our spies picked up down in the wilds from some kind of neon boar calling himself Dick Cheney—and before we could even find some cheesecloth, the cranes and flamingoes had uncovered some crack theory from them about how we were keeping prayers from reaching Heaven, apparently in an effort to blackmail a fellow named God. No telling why they think we would do that, but they say they came here to stop us.

LELAND. We must confess, that is the brunt of it. Why not take advantage of this rare opportunity and trade with us? Such a contract of congeniality would prove beneficial to us both.

DAGNY. Besides, we've come too far to go back empty-handed.

BELTED KINGFISHER. What makes you think we would even accept what you have to offer? We came here to get <u>away</u> from humanity. All we want is to be left alone.

CORNELIUS. Yet I see that you've borrowed extensively from our bird house designs for your surprisingly ornate architecture— surprising I mean because you don't seem to have the proper aptitude for it.

BELTED KINGFISHER. That's a rather racist thing to say. Bird's aren't helpless, you know. You should see what the crows can do with a pile of coat hangers. The entire crow-inspired district is wonderful to lay eyes upon, despite having been constructed solely from human garbage. Anywhere in this entire city, you will be proven wrong, sir! Take a gander! I insist!

CORNELIUS. I have no intention of being stabbed, Kingfisher!

BELTED KINGFISHER. (*Continuing*) Bird Seed Market sits upon a cherry tree mosaic made from pebbles collected from all over the world; the market pedestals often employ discarded match sticks, plastic food containers, and straw; The Grackle, our high-wire social club, stretches for miles with indoor gatherings fashioned out of pop-can-holders, wires, and colored glass from broken bottles; even here at our center, Sky Cathedral rises from the remnants of an old dead tree, with hollowed, orotund instruments attached to the high steeples like an angelic choir, awesome to hear during wind storms. If we decide not to peck your eyes out, you should go and see these marvels.

DAGNY. If you'll just let us explain, your highness, I'm sure we can come to an agreeable arrangement.

BELTED KINGFISHER. What do you think fellow birds; grebes, swifts, cranes, owls, trogons, woodpeckers, jays, cardinals, all? Is it worth listening any further to their discordant chatter?

FLOCK OF BIRDS. Perhaps this one time…we should hear all of them at once and decide what action to take.

BELTED KINGFISHER. Very well. Release the hypocritical-human-poop-targets! Let's hear what they have to say to the birds of Cloud-cuckoo-metropolis.

Enter THOMAS AQUARIUS, MRS. AQUARIUS, ULYSSES ABRAHAM, HILLARY WILLIAMS, FOUR SECURITY GUARDS and RICHARD GEORGE X *in bird cages.*

RICHARD GEORGE X. Um, tell me, Kingfisher, where is my vice president, Harry Franklin?

BELTED KINGFISHER. We had him deep-fried. The vultures are on their way from Falconia to receive him as a peace offering. We've been at war far too long.

FOUR SECURITY GUARDS. Ha ha aha ha! Oops…

RICHARD GEORGE X. Well, at least he's done some good for once. His own mother would be proud, God rest her tormented soul.

BELTED KINGFISHER. And now there are rumors the falcons have succeeded in harnessing the power of ball lightning and are developing weapons of ornithic destruction. They're on edge over poisoned mice from distant fields. Many have dropped dead, thus fulfilling an obscene prophecy of ours. The owls advise us to fly lightly.

HILLARY WILLIAMS. And what has happened to our birds?

BELTED KINGFISHER. <u>Your</u> birds? They left of their own volition, back home to rejoin their flocks—except for that poor turkey, of course.

ULYSSES ABRAHAM. What about us? Just what are your intentions? May I be the first to tell you, winged horde, that we have the finest air force in the world?

HILLARY WILLIAMS. And nukes! We're not afraid to use them!

BELTED KINGFISHER. On that note, stay away from that one there. She has a bad case of ornithosis and it's very contagious. A nasty virus, that one!

CORNELIUS. Ah, how interesting! Tell me more! Can you put it into bottles?

RICHARD GEORGE X. This is neither the time nor the place, Cornelius. I should have you tried before the senate for even suggesting such a thing!

CORNELIUS. Me? Just who do you think you are? Don't forget what it took to get you into such a fine position! A lot of money, that's what! None of you complained about our products when you had stock in them! You even went to war for us!

RICHARD GEORGE X. Fat load of good that did! Young lives lost; Democracy battered; the rich have misplaced their money in offshore accounts; jobs are few and fleeting. Nearly all classes have taken a blow, their illusions forfeit. Even as I speak, the entertainer-lords weep over the loss of their seventh or eighth home. Tomorrow it may be the sixth. Then the fifth. They may be down to two fairly large mansions before all is said and done, which would be a national tragedy!

CORNELIUS. I believe we agreed on letting you keep ten percent of the profits. Do you want to keep your ten percent or not?

RICHARD GEORGE X. Keep your ten percent! I don't have the numbers to run for re-election! Not after this fiasco!!

CORNELIUS. No matter.

ULYSSES ABRAHAM. Wait a minute! Just what are you referring to?!

CORNELIUS. Nothing.

RICHARD GEORGE X. Nothing.

ULYSSES ABRAHAM. Are you denying what you just said? We could have you tried for perjury, you know!

BELTED KINGFISHER. Enough of this idle chatter! If you aren't going to say something useful, I'll have the pelicans drop you into Lake of the Clouds with all the loons!

MRS. AQUARIUS. Well spoken, and not a moment too soon.

THOMAS AQUARIUS. Your Majesty, Kingfisher sir, I can tell you at once why we have come here.

BELTED KINGFISHER. Please do so, then, before things get out of hand. The last time we had human guests, they dressed themselves up as birds to try to fool us. Absurd memory, that one! Then they wanted us to revenge ourselves on some ridiculous band of narcissists whom they claimed were their gods. We did so out of boredom, except... The only good to come out of the ordeal was this city, and it leaks, I'm afraid—shoddy materials, more for looks than what's practical. And it's hard to get reliable roofers to work the canopy, what with the depleting ozone and all.

THOMAS AQUARIUS. Well, you see, Kingfisher, I have this nagging suspicion…that is…we were hoping for your assistance in a little predicament.

FLOCK OF BIRDS. His assistance!

THOMAS AQUARIUS. Yes. Well, all of your assistances, in assuring our prayers reach Heaven as God intends.

FLOCK OF BIRDS. Helping your prayers reach <u>Heaven</u>? Where in the Atmosphere is that? And why haven't these items you speak of gotten through? Perhaps it's the postal service you should be bothering, and not us birds.

MRS. AQUARIUS. Surely you believe in God? No? Well then! Allow us to introduce you to this wonderful book...I just happen to have one in my possession...here, take it as a gift...the least we could do is founder a mission right here in your capital city and expose you to the miracles of Christianity!

THOMAS AQUARIUS. Certainly, we must! We'll send for our missionaries right away!

FLOCK OF BIRDS *carelessly rips The Bible to shreds with their beaks, being clueless as to what to do with a book.*

BELTED KINGFISHER. Hold that thought! You see...we've sort of...transcended your belief systems. No offense, but you don't even have wings!

THOMAS AQUARIUS. (*Smirking*) I take it your god has wings?

PARROT. Rot! Of course it has wings! —and a beak, and a tail, and he excretes an eternal blue flame...but that's just gross... I shouldn't have mentioned that last part...

THOMAS AQUARIUS. (*Piously*) No one may know the true nature of God!

BELTED KINGFISHER. If there's one above this place, he definitely has wings.

DAGNY. Why does everyone always assume that God is a man? I mean, really, when was the last time a man could do anything without a woman instructing him to do so?

MRS. AQUARIUS. Amen to that, sister! Oh, I mean...that is...

MRS. AQUARIUS, *appearing very frightened, severs a branch from a nearby tree and begins castigating herself with it.*

RICHARD GEORGE X. Are you denying that you're blocking prayers from reaching Heaven?

BELTED KINGFISHER. We neither deny nor agree. Prayers? Heaven? This is just ridiculous! What is wrong with you people?!

HILLARY WILLIAMS. As a senator of the United State I must advise you that we have the power to embargo any trade agreements that you might currently have. Just hand over the prayers and all will be forgiven.

DAGNY. Yes, hand over the prayers! I don't think I could survive another recession!!

BELTED KINGFISHER. You're hardly in a position to be making demands. We have you outnumbered and out-beaked! For sky's sake, your place is on the ground where you can mingle with the other shadows of your narrow, wingless existence. You're destroying the ozone! You come to us with demands; want us to fix your problems? This isn't a sanctuary or a park where you can gawk at us through binoculars like a bunch of voyeuristic perverts! Everywhere, eyes, like a bunch of insects. Why are humans so paranoid? You people really have issues!

LELAND. Oh, and you don't? You'd be homeless if it wasn't for us! Oh, and those bird feeders you all love so much—they're really hawk feeders!!

BELTED KINGFISHER. Once again, I'm getting that feeling. Why do I feel like I've heard all of these things before?

FLOCK OF BIRDS. Because humans make no sense! Let's peck their eyes out!

BELTED KINGFISHER. No, it's not that. I've definitely...

THOMAS AQUARIUS. If it's true that you aren't blocking prayers, perhaps you could find it in your hearts to point us in the heavenly direction.

CORNELIUS. I second that! Heaven is definitely where we should go. If they can live in supreme happiness without material possessions, those of us from Wall Street might stand to gain something.

HILLARY WILLIAMS, ULYSSES ABRAHAM, RICHARD GEORGE X, FOUR SECURITY GUARDS, DAGNY, LELAND, THOMAS AQUARIUS, *and* MRS. AQUARIUS *blush from embarrassment.*

THOMAS AQUARIUS. Cornelius, you would make blush the whores of Babylon.

Enter PHERENIKE *the bird-woman, from above.*

PHERENIKE. Did you say you wish to enter Heaven? Maybe I can help. You see, I'm an angel...

FLOCK OF BIRDS *performs the insane gesture, each standing with an outstretched wing circling their heads where an ear would be.*

THE NUTHATCHES. (*Still snug in their birdhouse*). Some of us really do live up to our reputations!

THE NUTHATCHES *loudly shut their windows and doors.*

CORNELIUS. Who's this lovely creature?

BELTED KINGFISHER. Something we inherited from the Greeks. She's been driven to insanity by licentious old men. Don't take her too seriously.

CORNELIUS. I take everything seriously, especially pretty gems like this one!

PHERENIKE *dances over to* CORNELIUS *and captivates him with her grace and beauty.*

ULYSSES ABRAHAM. Is that Pherenike, descendant of beautiful Basileia and leathery old Pisthetaerus? She vanished during the Victorian Age after a scandal! Raped by an elderly Turk, I believe. Then an English lord. Then a disgruntled tribe of Zulu. And finally by some Greek fishermen while floating home on a log. Hmmm…You know, she should be a hundred-and-sixty years old! How is it that she still lives? She's young and beautiful!

BELTED KINGFISHER. Time is slow up here. We're not affected by gravity in the same way as you landed beasts.

DAGNY. Wait… So you're saying that this place offers us longevity?

BELTED KINGFISHER. Mere seconds of it. But Pherenike is a special case. She's from here, you know. This very metropolis. Her mother mated with a nightingale. Nasty business, that. So we didn't protest when she went against her mother's wishes and traveled landward. If only you humans had been kinder to her.

LELAND. A bird-woman? My brothers at Omicron Upsilon Psi would go nuts over a real bird-woman! Does she tour the backcountry at all? O ups!!

DAGNY *glares at* LELAND *and folds her arms.*

ULYSSES ABRAHAM. This is just madness. I mean, what did we expect, traveling to Cloud-cuckoo-metropolis? We'll never find what we're looking for here.

THOMAS AQUARIUS. One never finds what one's looking for; it finds you first, or not at all.

MRS. AQAURIUS. Well said, Mister Aquarius.

THOMAS AQUARIUS. Thank you, Missus Aquarius.

CORNELIUS. Now that Plan A has failed, how about finding that stairway to Heaven? This lovely angel says she can help us!

HILLARY WILLIAMS. It's no use. We'll never reach Heaven. Better to turn back now, before the FDA gets wind of this place.

PHERENIKE. I can show you the way! Come with me!

CORNELIUS *is under* PHERENIKE's *spell and follows her covetously, his eyes sparkling with greed.*

CORNELIUS. Well I for one intend to search this wonderland until I've made a profit! No one gets the best of old Cornelius!

DAGNY. (*Pulling out a wad of cash*) I think these birds are alright, and my philosophy is to join what I can't beat! What fun! I may linger here awhile, visit the sights. What do you say, Leland? Want to make a holiday nest here?

LELAND *swoons and runs into* DAGNY's *arms.*

LELAND. I thought you'd never ask!

Enter BAND OF PEONS, *closely followed by* VULTURES.

HILLARY WILLIAMS. Now, where do you suppose they came from?

BELTED KINGFISHER. More unwelcome visitors. And they've brought vultures! Whatever is going on?! They were supposed to have met us at the rendezvous point! Those toxic birds which guard the city from up high must have fallen asleep on the job!

BASILEIA. Key events always happen in threes. Ha ha ha! Pocket full of posies! One, two... Come!

BASILEIA *lures* CORNELIUS *off stage.*

FLOCK OF BIRDS. (*sing)* We wouldn't know where to begin,
    So long in the sun,
    It's a peep-dang-sin.
    But we're getting the hang of it.
    We learned how to aim when we shit.

BAND OF PEONS: (*Sing)* You might think there's little sense eating worms and berries but the birds on Wall Street eat corpses. They work like Santa on Christmas but they're not elves or ferries (well most of them). Crows sometimes eat butterflies, but on Wall Street they eat the maggots from your eyes so you can see their true intentions. They intend on getting rich! They get rich! You get poor! They get rich!

VULTURES. What's wrong with that? Someone's gotta do it!

BAND OF PEONS: There ain't no Farsi on Wall Street!

VULTURES. Well, that's true.

BAND OF PEONS. Get lost before we cut off your feet!

VULTURES *scatter in all directions, but remain on stage.*

BAND OF PEONS. (*Sing)* You might think there's little sense eating worms and berries but the birds on Wall Street eat corpses. They work like Santa on Christmas but they're not elves or ferries.

FLOCK OF BIRDS. Well most of them.

BAND OF PEONS. (*Sing*) Tanagers smash into windows, and break their pretty necks, but on Wall Street the disheartened jump to their ugly deaths. The portholes are all open on Wall Street! They intend on getting rich! They get rich! You get poor! They get rich! In life, there are no guarantees! You can't expect to get by on no---thing!

VULTURES *chase* BAND OF PEONS *frightfully off stage*; the band drops instruments, *runs screaming and exits.*

BELTED KINGFISHER. Aristophanes would have done much better.

FLOCK OF BIRDS: Aristophanes was bald! Not a feather on him! But we loved his comedies. Especially The Babylonians, in which the peons were slaves grinding at the mill. Oh, but you've probably forgotten that one...

MRS. AQUARIUS. I just remembered that the plants need watering. And the cat is probably ogling over the fishes in the pond.

THOMAS AQUARIUS. Well, dear, I suppose there's no point in staying. The flock is waiting patiently for our return.

MRS. AQUARIUS. (*Happily*) As you wish, dear.

THOMAS AQUARIUS. What about you, Mr. President, Senators? I'm sorry that it has come to this. I had hoped for a resolution to the crisis.

ULYSSES ABRAHAM. Four score and seven years from now we will probably look back in regret. But prayers do not constitute the man. We must gather strength from each other and not worry so much about the answers. Internally: that is where the important conflicts conjure.

THOMAS AQUARIUS. Well said, Senator. Although we are often left answerless, we should know that we are among friends.

RICHARD GEORGE X. That's easy for you to say. But what am I to tell the people?! They'll tear me to shreds!

HILLARY WILLIAMS. You could always lie to them again.

RICHARD GEORGE X. But what? What lie am I to tell them? All deception has been exhausted. I'm at the end of my rope!

THOMAS AQUARIUS. Don't lose hope. Truth always offers sanctuary. A cage of lies, on the other hand… well…

FOUR SECURITY GUARDS. We're trapped! We'll have to shoot our way out!

An explosion; Lightning flashes from Stage Left. A rumble sounds from back stage. The canopy opens up and the buildings and houses split. Balls of lightning are dropped from the sky.

Enter FALCONS, *who begin attacking everyone. Even the audience is unsafe.*

FLOCK OF BIRDS. Humans, indeed, a foul omen! Now the city is under attack!

THOMAS AQUARIUS. Pray that we've been forgiven!

RICHARD GEORGE X. We're doomed!

FLOCK OF BIRDS. And they say the insanity is down there on Wall Street!

CURTAIN

www.ingramcontent.com/pod-product-compliance
Lightning Source LLC
Chambersburg PA
CBHW031050260626
47172CB00001B/8